Suddenly the tunnel shook as a monster roared overhead. Graystripe and Fireheart, already tense, jumped, but the WindClan cats didn't react. They simply huddled with half-closed eyes, numb to their surroundings.

The noise died away. Fireheart took a deep breath and stepped around the corner, out into the thin light.

A gray WindClan tom spun around, his fur standing on end as he yowled an alarm to the rest of the Clan. In one smooth movement, the WindClan warriors formed a line across the tunnel in front of the queens and elders, their backs arched, hissing fiercely.

With a feeling of dread, Fireheart saw the glint of unsheathed claws and thorn-sharp fangs. These half-starved cats were about to attack.

WARRIORS

THE PROPHECIES BEGIN

Book One: *Into the Wild*

Book Two: *Fire and Ice*

Book Three: *Forest of Secrets*

Book Four: *Rising Storm*

Book Five: *A Dangerous Path*

Book Six: *The Darkest Hour*

THE NEW PROPHECY

Book One: *Midnight*

Book Two: *Moonrise*

Book Three: *Dawn*

Book Four: *Starlight*

Book Five: *Twilight*

Book Six: *Sunset*

POWER OF THREE

Book One: *The Sight*

Book Two: *Dark River*

Book Three: *Outcast*

Book Four: *Eclipse*

Book Five: *Long Shadows*

Book Six: *Sunrise*

OMEN OF THE STARS

Book One: *The Fourth Apprentice*

Book Two: *Fading Echoes*

Book Three: *Night Whispers*

Book Four: *Sign of the Moon*

Book Five: *The Forgotten Warrior*

Book Six: *The Last Hope*

Tigerstar and Sasha #1: *Into the Woods*
Tigerstar and Sasha #2: *Escape from the Forest*
Tigerstar and Sasha #3: *Return to the Clans*
Ravenpaw's Path #1: *Shattered Peace*
Ravenpaw's Path #2: *A Clan in Need*
Ravenpaw's Path #3: *The Heart of a Warrior*
SkyClan and the Stranger #1: *The Rescue*
SkyClan and the Stranger #2: *Beyond the Code*
SkyClan and the Stranger #3: *After the Flood*

NOVELLAS

Hollyleaf's Story
Mistystar's Omen
Cloudstar's Journey
Tigerclaw's Fury
Leafpool's Wish
Dovewing's Silence
Mapleshade's Vengeance

Also by Erin Hunter

SEEKERS

Book One: *The Quest Begins*
Book Two: *Great Bear Lake*
Book Three: *Smoke Mountain*
Book Four: *The Last Wilderness*
Book Five: *Fire in the Sky*
Book Six: *Spirits in the Stars*

WARRIORS

FIRE AND ICE

ERIN HUNTER

HARPER

An Imprint of HarperCollinsPublishers

Special thanks to Kate Cary

Fire and Ice

Copyright © 2003 by Working Partners Limited

Series created by Working Partners Limited

Map art © 2015 by Dave Stevenson

Interior art © 2015 by Owen Richardson

Library of Congress Cataloging-in-Publication Data

Hunter, Erin W.

  Fire and ice / Erin Hunter.

    p.   cm. — (Warriors ; bk. 2)

    Summary: Fireheart, a full-fledged warrior cat, must confront questions of loyalty and identity as he faces the possibility of betrayal from within his own forest Clan.

    ISBN 978-0-06-236697-9 (pbk.)

    [1. Cats—Fiction. 2. Fantasy.] I. Title. II. Series: Hunter, Erin W. Warriors ; bk. 2.

PZ7.H91665Fi 2003   2002014415

[Fic]—dc21   CIP

                                                                              AC

Typography by Ellice M. Lee

21   CG/BRR   30

❖

Revised paperback edition, 2015

For my son, Joshua, whose smiles kept me happy as I wrote,
and Vicky, my editor, without whom Fireheart
would never have become a warrior.

ALLEGIANCES

THUNDERCLAN

LEADER

BLUESTAR—blue-gray she-cat, tinged with silver around her muzzle

DEPUTY

TIGERCLAW—big dark brown tabby tom with unusually long front claws

MEDICINE CAT

YELLOWFANG—old dark gray she-cat with a broad, flattened face, formerly of ShadowClan

WARRIORS

(toms and she-cats without kits)

WHITESTORM—big white tom
APPRENTICE, SANDPAW

DARKSTRIPE—sleek black-and-gray tabby tom
APPRENTICE, DUSTPAW

LONGTAIL—pale tabby tom with dark black stripes
APPRENTICE, SWIFTPAW

RUNNINGWIND—swift tabby tom

WILLOWPELT—very pale gray she-cat with unusual blue eyes

MOUSEFUR—small dusky brown she-cat

FIREHEART—handsome ginger tom
APPRENTICE, CINDERPAW

GRAYSTRIPE—long-haired solid gray tom
APPRENTICE, BRACKENPAW

APPRENTICES

(more than six moons old, in training to become warriors)

SANDPAW—pale ginger she-cat

DUSTPAW—dark brown tabby tom

SWIFTPAW—black-and-white tom

CINDERPAW—dark gray she-cat

BRACKENPAW—golden brown tabby tom

QUEENS

(she-cats expecting or nursing kits)

FROSTFUR—beautiful white coat and blue eyes

BRINDLEFACE—pretty tabby

GOLDENFLOWER—pale ginger coat

SPECKLETAIL—pale tabby, and the oldest nursery queen

ELDERS

(former warriors and queens, now retired)

HALFTAIL—big dark brown tabby tom with part of his tail missing

SMALLEAR—gray tom with very small ears. The oldest tom in ThunderClan

PATCHPELT—small black-and-white tom.

ONE-EYE—pale gray she-cat, the oldest cat in ThunderClan. Virtually blind and deaf

DAPPLETAIL—once-pretty tortoiseshell she-cat with a lovely dappled coat

SHADOWCLAN

LEADER

NIGHTPELT—old black tom

DEPUTY

CINDERFUR—thin gray tom

MEDICINE CAT

RUNNINGNOSE—small gray-and-white tom

WARRIORS

STUMPYTAIL—brown tabby tom

APPRENTICE, BROWNPAW

WETFOOT—gray tabby tom
APPRENTICE, OAKPAW

LITTLECLOUD—very small tabby tom

QUEENS
DAWNCLOUD—small tabby

DARKFLOWER—black she-cat

TALLPOPPY—long-legged light brown tabby she-cat

ELDERS
ASHFUR—thin gray tom

WINDCLAN

LEADER
TALLSTAR—black-and-white tom with a very long tail

DEPUTY
DEADFOOT—black tom with a twisted paw

MEDICINE CAT
BARKFACE—short-tailed brown tom

WARRIORS
MUDCLAW—mottled dark brown tom
APPRENTICE, WEBPAW

TORNEAR—tabby tom
APPRENTICE, RUNNINGPAW

ONEWHISKER—young brown tabby tom
APPRENTICE, WHITEPAW

QUEENS
ASHFOOT—gray queen

MORNINGFLOWER—tortoiseshell queen

RIVERCLAN

LEADER
CROOKEDSTAR—huge light-colored tabby with a twisted jaw

DEPUTY
LEOPARDFUR—unusually spotted golden tabby she-cat

MEDICINE CAT MUDFUR—long-haired light brown tom

WARRIORS BLACKCLAW—smoky black tom
APPRENTICE, HEAVYPAW

STONEFUR—gray tom with battle-scarred ears
APPRENTICE, SHADEPAW

LOUDBELLY—dark brown tom
APPRENTICE, SILVERPAW

SILVERSTREAM—pretty slender silver tabby

WHITECLAW—dark warrior

CATS OUTSIDE CLANS

SMUDGE—plump, friendly black-and-white kitten who lives in a house at the edge of the forest

BARLEY—black-and-white tom who lives on a farm close to the forest

BROKENSTAR—long-haired dark brown tabby, formerly ShadowClan leader

BLACKFOOT—large white tom with huge jet-black paws, formerly ShadowClan deputy

CLAWFACE—battle-scarred brown tom

BOULDER—silver tabby tom

RAVENPAW—sleek black cat with a white-tipped tail

PRINCESS—light brown tabby with a distinctive white chest and paws—a kittypet

CLOUDKIT—Princess's firstborn kit; a long-haired white tom

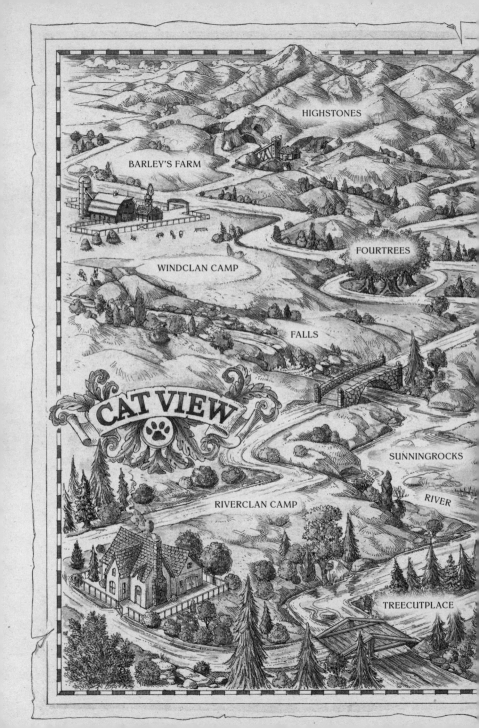

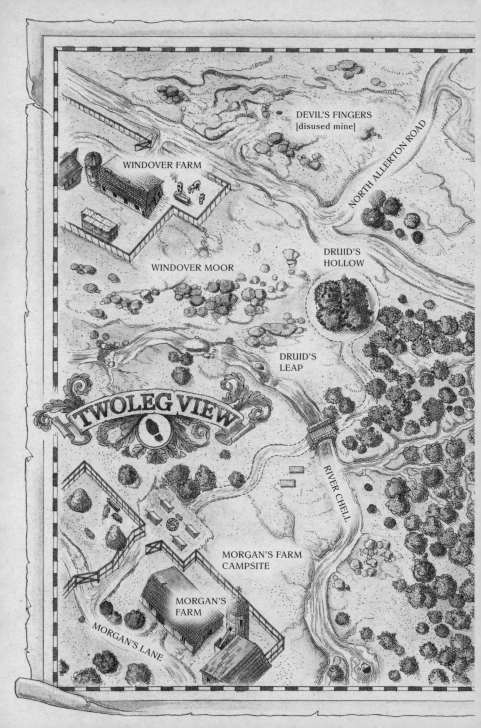

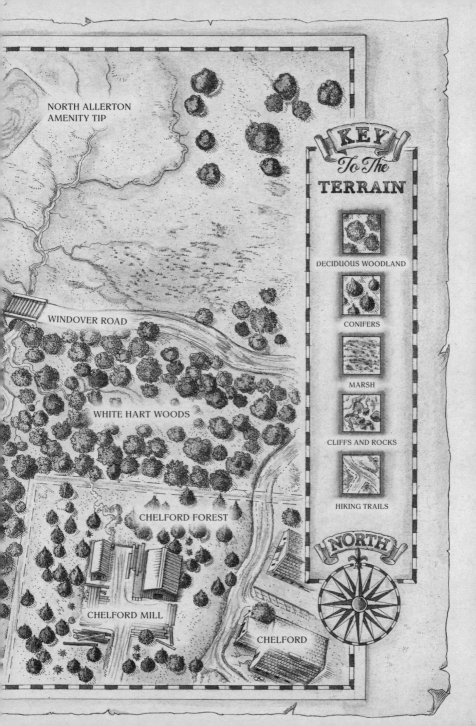

PROLOGUE

❧

Orange flames lapped at the cold air, throwing sparks up into the night sky. The firelight flickered across a wasteland of ragged grass, making silhouettes of the Twolegs huddled there.

A pair of white lights appeared in the distance, heralding the approach of a monster. It roared past on a Thunderpath that rose high into the sky, filling the air with sour fumes.

At the edge of the wasteland, a cat moved, its eyes glinting in the shadows. Pointed ears twitched, then flattened against the noise. More cats followed one by one, onto the filthy grass. They carried their tails low and sniffed the bitter air with their lips curled.

"What if the Twolegs see us?" hissed one of the cats.

A large tom answered, his eyes like amber disks reflecting the firelight. "They won't. Their night sight is weak." As he padded forward the flames lit up the black-and-white fur on his powerful shoulders. He held his long tail straight up, sending a message of courage to his Clan.

But the other cats crouched low against the grass, trembling. This was a strange place. The noise of the monsters battered their sensitive ear fur, and the acrid stench stung their nostrils.

"Tallstar?" A gray queen flicked her tail uneasily. "Why have we come *here*?"

The black-and-white tom turned to the she-cat. "We've been driven from every place we've tried to settle, Ashfoot. Perhaps we can find some peace here," he meowed.

"Peace? Here?" Ashfoot echoed in disbelief. She pulled her kit toward her and sheltered it beneath her belly. "With fire and monsters? My kits won't be safe!"

"But we weren't safe at home," meowed another voice. A black tom pushed his way forward, limping heavily on a twisted paw. He held Tallstar's amber gaze. "We couldn't protect them from ShadowClan," he spat. "Not even in our own camp!"

Anxious yowls rose from some of the cats as they remembered the terrible battle that had driven them from their home in the uplands, at the edge of the forest. A young apprentice wailed, "Brokenstar and his warriors may still be hunting us!"

The cry alerted one of the Twolegs around the fire. It stood unsteadily and stared toward the shadows. At once the cats fell silent, crouching lower; even Tallstar lowered his tail. The Twoleg shouted into the darkness and flung something toward them. The missile flew over their heads and exploded in a burst of thorn-sharp pieces on the Thunderpath behind.

Ashfoot flinched as a shard grazed her shoulder, but she stayed silent, curling her body around her terrified kit.

"Keep down," hissed Tallstar.

The Twoleg at the fire spat on the ground, then sat back down.

The cats waited for a few moments before Tallstar stood once more.

Ashfoot stood too, wincing at the new pain in her shoulder. "Tallstar, I fear for our safety here. And what will we eat? I can't smell any prey."

Tallstar stretched his neck and rested his muzzle gently on the queen's head. "I know you're hungry," he meowed. "But we'll be safer here than back in our old territory, or in the Twoleg fields and woods. Look at this place! Even Shadow-Clan wouldn't follow us here. There's no scent of dogs, and these Twolegs can hardly stand." He turned to the black tom with the twisted paw. "Deadfoot," he ordered, "take One-whisker and see if you can find anything to eat. If there are Twolegs, there must be rats."

"Rats?" spat Ashfoot, as Deadfoot and a smaller brown tabby bounded away. "That's no better than crow-food!"

"Hush!" hissed a tortoiseshell beside her. "Rat meat is better than starving to death!"

Ashfoot scowled and dipped her head to lick her kit behind its matted ears.

"We must find a new place to settle, Ashfoot." The tortoiseshell went on more gently: "Morningflower needs to rest and eat. Her kits will be born soon. She needs to be strong."

The lean shapes of Deadfoot and Onewhisker emerged from the shadows.

"You were right, Tallstar," called Deadfoot. "There are rat

scents everywhere, and I think I've found somewhere we can shelter."

"Show us," Tallstar ordered, gathering the rest of his Clan with a flick of his tail.

Cautiously, the cats padded across the wasteland after Deadfoot. He led them toward the raised Thunderpath, the firelight making their shadows loom against its huge stone legs. A monster roared overhead and the ground shook. But even the tiniest kit sensed the need for silence and trembled without crying out.

"Here," meowed Deadfoot, stopping beside a round hole, two cats high. A black tunnel sloped down into the ground. A constant stream of water trickled into it.

"The water's fresh," Deadfoot added. "We'll be able to drink it."

"We'll have wet paws day and night!" Ashfoot complained.

"I've been inside," the black tom told her. "There's some space away from the stream. At least we'll be safe from Twolegs and monsters."

Tallstar stepped forward and lifted his chin. "WindClan has traveled for long enough," he declared. "It's nearly a moon since ShadowClan drove us from our home. The weather is turning colder, and leaf-bare will be here soon. We have no choice but to stay."

Ashfoot narrowed her eyes but said nothing. Silently she joined her Clan as, one by one, they filed into the shadowy tunnel.

CHAPTER 1

Fireheart shivered. His flame-colored fur was still greenleaf-light; it would be a few moons before it was thick enough to keep out cold like this. He shuffled his forepaws on the hard earth. The sky was finally growing light as dawn crept slowly in. But even though his paws were cold, Fireheart could not suppress a glow of pride. After many moons as an apprentice, he was a warrior at last.

In his mind, he replayed yesterday's victory at the Shadow-Clan camp: Brokenstar's glittering eyes as the ShadowClan leader backed away, hissing threats, before fleeing into the trees after his traitorous companions. The remaining ShadowClan cats had been grateful to ThunderClan for helping them to get rid of their cruel leader, and for the peace ThunderClan had promised them while they recovered. Brokenstar had not just brought chaos to his own Clan—he had driven the whole of WindClan from their camp, right out of Clan territory. He had been a dark shadow in the forest since before Fireheart had left his kittypet life to join ThunderClan.

But for Fireheart, there was another shadow troubling his mind: Tigerclaw, ThunderClan's deputy. Fireheart shivered again as he thought of the great ThunderClan warrior who had terrorized his apprentice, Ravenpaw. In the end, Fireheart and his best friend, Graystripe, had helped the frightened apprentice to escape into the Twoleg territory beyond the uplands. Afterward, Fireheart had told the Clan that Ravenpaw had been killed by ShadowClan.

If what Ravenpaw said about Tigerclaw was true, it was best if the ThunderClan deputy believed his apprentice had died, for he knew a secret Tigerclaw would do anything to conceal. Ravenpaw had told Fireheart that the mighty tabby warrior had murdered Redtail, the old ThunderClan deputy, in the hope that he would become the new deputy . . . which, eventually, he had.

Fireheart shook his head to clear it of these dark thoughts and turned to glance at Graystripe sitting beside him. Graystripe's thick gray fur was ruffled up against the cold. Fireheart guessed he was looking forward to the first rays of sunshine too, but he didn't say this out loud. Clan tradition demanded silence on this night. This was their vigil—the night when a new warrior guarded the Clan and reflected on his new name and status. Until last night, Fireheart had been known by his apprentice name of Firepaw.

Halftail was one of the first cats to wake. Fireheart could see the old cat moving among the shadows in the elders' den. He glanced toward the warriors' den at the other side of the clearing. Through the branches that sheltered the den, he recognized the broad shoulders of Tigerclaw as he slept.

At the foot of Highrock, the lichen that draped the entrance to Bluestar's den twitched, and Fireheart saw his Clan leader push her way out. She stopped and lifted her head to sniff the air. Then she padded silently out of Highrock's shadow, her long fur glowing blue-gray in the dawn light. *I must warn her about Tigerclaw*, thought Fireheart. Bluestar had mourned Redtail's death with the rest of the Clan, believing him to have been killed in battle by Oakheart, the deputy of RiverClan. Fireheart had hesitated before, knowing how important Tigerclaw was to her, but the danger was too great. Bluestar needed to know that her Clan was harboring a cold-blooded murderer.

Tigerclaw emerged from the warriors' den and met Bluestar at the edge of the clearing. He murmured something to her, his tail flicking urgently.

Fireheart stifled his instinctive meow of greeting. The sky was growing light, but until he knew for sure that the sun was above the horizon, he dared not break his silence. Impatience fluttered in his chest like a trapped bird. He must speak with Bluestar as soon as he could. But for now, all he could do was nod respectfully at the two cats as they passed him.

Beside him, Graystripe nudged Fireheart and pointed upward with his nose. An orange glow was just visible on the horizon.

"Glad to see the dawn, you two?" Whitestorm's deep meow took Fireheart by surprise. He had not noticed the white warrior approaching. Fireheart and Graystripe nodded together.

"It's all right; you may speak now. Your vigil is over." Whitestorm's voice was kind. Yesterday he had fought side by side with Fireheart and Graystripe in the battle with ShadowClan.

There was a new respect in his eyes as he looked at them.

"Thank you, Whitestorm," Fireheart meowed gratefully. He stood and stretched his stiff legs one at a time.

Graystripe pushed himself up too. "Brrrrr!" he meowed, shaking the chill from his fur. "I thought the sun would never come up!"

A scornful voice mewed from outside the apprentices' den. "The great warrior speaks!"

It was Sandpaw, her pale orange coat fluffed up with hostility. Dustpaw was sitting beside her. With his dark tabby pelt, he looked like Sandpaw's shadow. He puffed out his chest importantly and mocked, "I'm surprised such heroes even feel the cold!" Sandpaw purred with amusement.

Whitestorm shot them a stern look. "Go and find something to eat; then rest," he ordered Fireheart and Graystripe. The older warrior turned away and padded toward the apprentices' den. "Come on, you two," he meowed to Sandpaw and Dustpaw. "It's time for your training."

"I hope he has them chasing blue squirrels all day!" Graystripe hissed to Fireheart as they headed toward the corner where a few pieces of fresh-kill remained from last night.

"But there aren't any blue squirrels," Fireheart mewed in confusion.

"Precisely!" Graystripe's amber eyes gleamed.

"You can't exactly blame them. They did begin their training before us," Fireheart pointed out mildly. "If they'd fought in the battle yesterday, they'd probably have been made warriors too."

"I suppose." Graystripe shrugged. "Hey, look!" They'd reached the fresh-kill pile. "One mouse each and a chaffinch to share!"

The two friends picked up their meal and looked at each other. Graystripe's eyes suddenly sparkled with delight. "I suppose we take it to the *warriors'* side of the camp now," he meowed.

"I suppose we do," Fireheart purred, padding after his friend to the patch of nettles where they had often watched Whitestorm, Tigerclaw, and the other warriors share fresh-kill.

"Now what?" asked Graystripe, gulping down his last mouthful. "I don't know about you, but I think I could sleep for half a moon."

"Me too," Fireheart agreed.

The two friends got to their paws and made their way toward the warriors' den. Fireheart stuck his head through the low-hanging branches. Mousefur and Longtail were still asleep on the other side of the den.

He pushed his way inside and found a patch of moss at the edge. The smell told him it wasn't a sleeping place already used by another warrior. Graystripe settled down beside him.

Fireheart listened as Graystripe's steady breaths relaxed into long, muffled snores. Fireheart felt equally exhausted, but he was still desperate to talk to Bluestar. From where he lay, his head flat to the earth, he could just see the camp entrance. He stared at it, waiting for his leader's return, but gradually his eyes began to close, and he gave in to his longing for sleep.

Fireheart could hear a roaring around him, like wind in tall trees. The acrid stench of the Thunderpath stung his nostrils, together with a new smell, sharper and more terrifying. Fire! Flames lapped at the black sky, throwing glowing cinders up into a starless night. To Fireheart's amazement, silhouettes of cats flitted in front of the fire. Why hadn't they run away?

One of them stopped and looked straight at Fireheart. The tom's night-eyes glinted in the darkness and he lifted his long, straight tail, as if in greeting.

Fireheart trembled as a memory burst into his mind of the words that Spottedleaf, the former ThunderClan medicine cat, had said to him before her untimely death: "Fire will save the Clan!" Could it be something to do with the strange cats that showed no fear of fire?

"Wake up, Fireheart!"

Fireheart flicked up his head, startled out of his dream by Tigerclaw's growl.

"You were mewing in your sleep!"

Still dazed, Fireheart sat up and shook his head. "Y-yes, Tigerclaw!" With a pang of alarm, he wondered if he had repeated Spottedleaf's words out loud. He had dreamed like this before—dreams so vivid that he could taste them, and which had later come true. Fireheart certainly did not want Tigerclaw to suspect him of having powers that usually StarClan gave only to a medicine cat.

Moonlight shone through the leafy den wall. Fireheart realized he must have slept through the whole day.

"You and Graystripe will join the evening patrol," Tigerclaw told him. "Hurry up!" The dark tabby turned and stalked out of the den.

Fireheart let the fur relax on his shoulders. Clearly Tigerclaw didn't suspect anything unusual about his dream. But while Fireheart's secret was safe, he was equally determined to expose the murderous truth about Tigerclaw's role in Redtail's death.

Fireheart licked his lips. Graystripe lay beside him washing his flank. They had just finished sharing a meal beside the camp clearing. The sun had set and Fireheart could see the moon, almost full now, gleaming in a cold, clear sky. The past few days had been busy. It seemed that every time they lay down for a rest, Tigerclaw sent them out on patrol or a hunting mission. Fireheart had stayed alert, looking for a chance to talk with Bluestar alone, but when he wasn't on one of Tigerclaw's missions, the ThunderClan leader always seemed to have her deputy at her side.

Fireheart began to wash his paw, his eyes flicking around the camp, searching hopefully for Bluestar.

"What are you looking for?" meowed Graystripe through a tongueful of fur.

"Bluestar," Fireheart answered, lowering his paw.

"Why?" Graystripe stopped washing and looked up at his friend. "You've had one eye on her ever since our vigil. What are you planning to do?"

"I have to tell her where Ravenpaw is, and warn her about Tigerclaw," Fireheart meowed.

"You promised Ravenpaw you'd tell them he was dead!" Graystripe sounded amazed.

"I only promised to tell *Tigerclaw* he was dead. Bluestar should know the whole story. She needs to know what her deputy is capable of."

Graystripe lowered his voice to an urgent hiss. "But we only have Ravenpaw's word that Tigerclaw killed Redtail."

"Don't you believe him?" Fireheart couldn't help feeling shocked by his friend's doubts.

"Look, if Tigerclaw lied about killing Oakheart in revenge for Redtail's death, that means Redtail must have killed Oakheart himself. And I can't believe that Redtail would have deliberately killed another Clan deputy in battle. It goes against the warrior code—we fight to prove our strength and defend our territory, not to kill each other."

"But I'm not trying to make accusations against Redtail!" Fireheart protested. "It's Tigerclaw who is the problem." Redtail had been the ThunderClan deputy before Tigerclaw. Fireheart had never met him, but he knew Redtail had been deeply respected by all the Clan.

Graystripe didn't meet Fireheart's gaze. "What you are saying has implications for Redtail's honor. And none of the other cats have a problem with Tigerclaw. It was only Ravenpaw who was scared of him."

An uneasy shiver ran down Fireheart's spine. "So you think Ravenpaw made the story up because he didn't get along with his mentor?" he meowed scornfully.

"No," mumbled Graystripe. "I just think we should be careful."

Fireheart looked into his friend's worried eyes and began to wonder. He supposed Graystripe did have a point—they had been warriors for only a few days, so they were in no position to start hurling accusations at the Clan's most senior warrior.

"It's okay," Fireheart meowed at last. "You can stay out of it." A twinge of regret flickered in his belly as Graystripe nodded and returned to washing. Fireheart believed that Graystripe was wrong to think it was only Ravenpaw who had a problem with Tigerclaw. Fireheart's own instincts told him that the ThunderClan deputy should not be trusted. He had to share his suspicions with Bluestar, for her safety and the safety of the Clan.

A glimpse of gray fur on the other side of the clearing told Fireheart that Bluestar had emerged from her den—alone. He scrambled to his paws, but the ThunderClan leader leaped straight up onto the Highrock and called to the Clan. Fireheart lashed his tail impatiently.

Graystripe's ears flicked excitedly as he heard Bluestar's call. "A naming ceremony?" he meowed. "It must be Longtail getting his first apprentice. He's been dropping hints for days." He bounded over to join the cats gathering at the edge of the clearing, and, still itching with frustration, Fireheart followed.

A small black-and-white kit padded into the clearing. His soft paws made no sound on the hard earth. He walked toward the Highrock with his pale eyes lowered and Fireheart almost expected to see him tremble—there was something in the slope of this kit's shoulders that made him seem too young and timid to be an apprentice. *Longtail won't be impressed!* Fireheart thought, remembering Longtail's scorn when Fireheart had arrived at the camp for the first time. The warrior had taunted him viciously on his first day with the Clan, mocking his kittypet origins. Fireheart had disliked him ever since.

"From this day forward," Bluestar meowed, staring down at the kit, "until he has earned his warrior name, this apprentice will be called Swiftpaw."

There was no flash of determination in the eyes of the black-and-white kit as he looked up at his leader. Instead his amber eyes were wide with anxiety.

Fireheart turned his head as Longtail padded toward his new apprentice.

Bluestar spoke again. "Longtail, you were Darkstripe's apprentice. He taught you well, and you have become a fierce and loyal warrior. I hope you will pass some of these qualities on to Swiftpaw."

Fireheart searched Longtail's face for an expression of disdain as he looked down at Swiftpaw. But the warrior's eyes softened as he met his new apprentice's gaze, and gently the two Clan cats touched noses. "It's okay, you're doing fine," Longtail murmured encouragingly. *Yeah, right,* Fireheart thought bitterly. *Just because he's Clanborn. Longtail sure didn't welcome me like that.* He glanced around the rest of the Clan and felt a pang of resentment as the cats began to murmur congratulations to the new apprentice.

"What's up with you?" whispered Graystripe. "That'll be us one day."

Fireheart nodded, suddenly cheered by the thought of getting his own apprentice, and pushed away his resentment. He was a part of ThunderClan now, and surely that was all that mattered?

The next night brought the full moon. Fireheart knew he should be looking forward to his first Gathering as a warrior, but he was still determined to find a chance to tell Bluestar everything he knew about Tigerclaw, and the thought of it lay like a cold stone in his stomach.

"Have you got maggot-gut or something?" meowed Graystripe beside him. "You're pulling some very weird faces!"

Fireheart looked at his friend, wishing he could confide in him, but he'd promised to leave Graystripe out of it. "I'm fine," he meowed. "Come on. I hear Bluestar calling."

The two cats trotted over to the group assembling in the clearing. Bluestar dipped her head to acknowledge their arrival. Then she turned and led the cats out of the camp.

Fireheart paused while the other cats scrambled past him up the steep trail that led to the forest above. This journey might give him just enough time to speak to Bluestar, and he wanted to gather his thoughts.

"Are you coming?" Graystripe's voice called down.

"Yep!" Firepaw flexed his powerful hind legs and began to leap from boulder to boulder, leaving the camp behind.

At the top, he paused to catch his breath, his sides heaving. The forest stretched away before him. Beneath his paws he could feel the crisp crackle of newly fallen leaves. Silverpelt glittered in the sky like morning dew scattered on black fur.

Fireheart thought of his first journey to Fourtrees with Tigerclaw and Lionheart. He felt a pang of sadness as he remembered Lionheart. Graystripe's mentor, and Thunder-Clan's deputy between Redtail and Tigerclaw, had been a warmhearted, golden warrior. He'd been killed in battle, and Tigerclaw had taken his place. On Fireheart's first visit to Fourtrees, Lionheart had taken the apprentices on a round-about route, through Tallpines, past Sunningrocks, and along the RiverClan border. Tonight Bluestar would lead them straight through the heart of ThunderClan territory. Fireheart could see her already disappearing into the under-growth, and he charged after the party of cats.

Bluestar was at the front, next to Tigerclaw. Fireheart ignored Graystripe's surprised meow and caught up with the Clan leader. "Bluestar," he called, panting, as he drew up beside her. "May I talk to you?"

Bluestar glanced at him and nodded. "Take the lead, Tigerclaw," she meowed. She let her pace slow, and Tigerclaw bounded past her. The other cats followed the dark tabby without question as he raced on through the undergrowth.

Bluestar and Fireheart dropped into a steady trot. Within a moment they were alone.

The path emerged from the thick ferns into a small clear-ing. Bluestar leaped onto a fallen tree and sat down, curling her tail over her front paws. "What is it, Fireheart?" she asked.

Fireheart hesitated, suddenly struck by doubt. Bluestar was the cat who had encouraged him to leave his kittypet life and join the Clan. Since then she had trusted him time and time again when other cats had questioned his loyalty to a Clan whose blood he didn't share. What would she say when Fireheart told her that he had lied about Ravenpaw?

"Speak," Bluestar ordered as the pawsteps of the other ThunderClan cats faded into the distance.

Fireheart took a deep breath. "Ravenpaw's not dead." Bluestar's tail twitched in surprise, but she listened silently as Fireheart continued. "Graystripe and I took him to Wind-Clan's hunting grounds. I . . . I think he may have joined Barley." Barley was a loner, not a forest cat but not a kitty-pet either. He lived on a Twoleg farm that lay on the route to Highstones, a sacred place for all the cats in the forest.

The ThunderClan leader stared past Fireheart into the depths of the forest. Fireheart searched her face anxiously, trying to read her expression. Was she angry? But he could see no anger in her wide, blue eyes.

After several long moments, Bluestar spoke. "I am glad to hear that Ravenpaw is still alive. I hope he is happier living with Barley than he was in the forest."

"B-but he was born into ThunderClan!" Fireheart stammered, taken aback by his leader's calm acceptance of Ravenpaw's departure.

"That doesn't necessarily mean he was suited to Clan life," Bluestar pointed out. "After all, you aren't Clanborn, yet you've become a fine warrior. Ravenpaw may find his true path elsewhere."

"But he didn't leave ThunderClan because he wanted to," Fireheart protested. "It was impossible for him to stay!"

"Impossible?" Bluestar rested her blue gaze on him. "What do you mean?"

Fireheart looked down at the ground.

"Well?" Bluestar prompted.

Fireheart's mouth was dry. "Ravenpaw knew a secret about Tigerclaw," he croaked. "I . . . I think Tigerclaw was planning to kill him. Or else turn the Clan against him."

Bluestar's tail flicked from side to side, and Fireheart saw her shoulders stiffen. "Why would you think that? What was this secret that Ravenpaw knew?"

Fireheart answered reluctantly, meeting her stern expression as boldly as he dared. "That Tigerclaw killed Redtail in the battle with RiverClan." Redtail had been the Thunder-Clan deputy before Lionheart. Fireheart had never met him, but he knew Redtail had been deeply respected by all the Clan.

Bluestar's eyes narrowed. "A warrior would never kill another of his Clan! Even you should know that—you've lived with us long enough." Fireheart recoiled at her words, flattening his ears. It was the second time tonight she'd referred to his kittypet roots.

Bluestar went on. "Tigerclaw reported that it was River-Clan's deputy, Oakheart, who killed Redtail," she meowed. "Ravenpaw must be mistaken. Did he actually *see* Tigerclaw kill Redtail?"

Fireheart nervously flicked his tail, stirring the leaves behind him. "He said he did."

"And you know that by saying this, you are questioning Redtail's honor, because he must have been the cat that was responsible for Oakheart's death? One deputy would never kill another in battle, not if it could possibly be avoided. And Redtail was the most honorable warrior I have ever known." Bluestar's eyes clouded with pain, and Fireheart felt a pang of dismay that he should have hurt her memory of her former deputy, even if unintentionally.

"I cannot account for Redtail's actions," he murmured. "I only know that Ravenpaw truly believes Tigerclaw was responsible for Redtail's death."

Bluestar sighed and relaxed her shoulders. "We all know that Ravenpaw has a vivid imagination," she meowed gently, her eyes sympathetic. "He was badly injured in the battle, and he left before the fighting was over. Can you be sure he didn't fill in the parts he'd missed?"

Before Fireheart could reply, a yowl echoed through the forest, and Tigerclaw bounded out of the undergrowth. His eyes flickered suspiciously over Fireheart for a moment before he addressed Bluestar. "We're waiting for you at the border."

Bluestar nodded. "Tell them we'll be there in a moment." Tigerclaw dipped his head, turned, and raced back through the ferns.

As Fireheart watched him disappear, Bluestar's words echoed in his mind. She was right; Ravenpaw did have a strong imagination. Fireheart remembered his first Gathering, when apprentices from every Clan had hung on Ravenpaw's words as he described the battle with RiverClan. And he hadn't mentioned Tigerclaw then.

Fireheart jumped up as Bluestar stood. "Are you going to bring Ravenpaw back to the Clan?" he asked, suddenly afraid he had caused even more trouble for his friend.

Bluestar gazed deep into Fireheart's eyes. "He is probably happier where he is," she meowed quietly. "For now, we will let the Clan carry on believing he is dead."

Fireheart stared back at her, his eyes wide with shock. Bluestar was going to lie to the Clan!

"Tigerclaw is a great warrior, but he is very proud," Bluestar went on. "It'll be easier for him to accept that his apprentice died in battle rather than ran away. And it would be better for Ravenpaw, too."

"Because Tigerclaw might go looking for him?" Fireheart dared to ask. Was it possible that Bluestar believed him, even just a little bit?

Bluestar shook her head with a flash of impatience. "No. Tigerclaw might be ambitious, but he is not a murderer. Ravenpaw will be better remembered as a dead hero than a live coward."

Tigerclaw's call sounded again, and Bluestar jumped down from the log and disappeared into the ferns. Fireheart cleared the tree trunk in one leap and raced after his leader.

He caught up with her at the edge of a stream. He watched while she crossed, jumping from stone to stone to the other side. Fireheart followed carefully, his mind whirling. The knowledge about Redtail's death had been resting heavily on his shoulders for days. Now he had finally told Bluestar, but nothing had changed. The Clan leader clearly didn't think Tigerclaw was capable of cold-blooded murder. And worst of all, Fireheart himself had begun to doubt whether Ravenpaw had been telling the truth. He leaped onto the far bank and charged on through the undergrowth.

Fireheart skidded to a halt behind Bluestar as they reached the other ThunderClan cats. The group had paused at the top of the slope that led down to Fourtrees, the giant oaks where cats from the four Clans of the forest met in peace at each full moon.

Fireheart's fur prickled as he felt Tigerclaw watching him. Did the dark warrior suspect what had passed between him and Bluestar? Fireheart shook his head to clear his mind and tried to think like Bluestar. Of course Tigerclaw would be interested in what Fireheart had said to Bluestar: he was the Clan deputy, so he would want to know anything that might affect the Clan. Fireheart looked again at Tigerclaw; the dark tabby was staring down the slope, his ears pricked and alert. The cats around him shuffled their paws in anticipation. Tigerclaw glanced at each of them, silently rallying them with his steady amber gaze.

Bluestar lifted her nose and sniffed the air. Fireheart sensed a tightening of muscles and prickling of fur around him. Then Bluestar signaled with a flick of her tail, and the Thunder-Clan cats plunged down the slope toward the Gathering.

CHAPTER 2

❦

Bluestar halted on the edge of the clearing with her Clan lined up beside her. Some of the cats from RiverClan and ShadowClan turned and acknowledged their arrival.

"Where'd you disappear to?" Graystripe appeared at Fireheart's shoulder.

Fireheart shook his head. "Doesn't matter." He was still troubled and confused by his conversation with Bluestar, and felt glad when Graystripe didn't press him, turning his head instead to peer around the clearing.

"Hey, look," he meowed. "The ShadowClan cats are looking stronger than I thought they would. After all, Brokenstar left them half-starved."

Fireheart followed his gaze to a sleek ShadowClan warrior. "You're right," he agreed, surprised.

"Mind you, we did do most of their fighting for them!" scoffed Graystripe.

Fireheart's amused purr was interrupted by Whitestorm. "The ShadowClan cats fought as hard as we did to chase out Brokenstar. We should honor their determination to recover," he meowed sternly, before padding over to a group of warriors gathered beneath one of the great oaks.

"Oops!" mewed Graystripe with a guilty glance at Fireheart.

The young warriors stayed on the edge of the clearing. Fireheart could easily pick out the apprentices from the other Clans—their fur looked kit-soft, their faces round, and their paws plump and clumsy.

Two warriors approached Graystripe and Fireheart. A small brown apprentice tagged after them. Fireheart recognized the gray tabby tom from ShadowClan, but not the smoky black tom who walked with him.

"Hi!" meowed the gray tom.

"Hello, Wetfoot," replied Fireheart. He glanced at the dark brown cat.

Wetfoot meowed, "This is Blackclaw of RiverClan."

Graystripe and Fireheart nodded their greeting. The apprentice stepped timidly forward.

"And this is my apprentice, Oakpaw," added Wetfoot.

Oakpaw looked up at Fireheart with wide, anxious eyes. "H-hi, Fireheart," he mewed. Fireheart nodded his head in greeting.

"I hear Bluestar made you warriors after the battle," meowed Wetfoot. "Congratulations! It must've been a cold vigil."

"It was!" Graystripe agreed.

"Who's that?" Fireheart broke in. A sleek she-cat with a

mottled brown pelt had caught his attention. She was sharing words with Tigerclaw beside the Great Rock that stood in the center of the clearing.

"That's Leopardfur, our deputy," growled the RiverClan warrior.

Fireheart's fur stiffened as he thought about the previous RiverClan deputy, Oakheart, and how he had died in battle with ThunderClan. He was saved from having to say anything by Bluestar's bounding onto the top of the rock to start the meeting. Two other cats joined her, and one of them, an elderly black tom, sounded the call for all cats to gather beneath the rock. Fireheart recognized the black tom, and couldn't help feeling surprised. Had old Nightpelt become ShadowClan's leader since Brokenstar had fled?

When the cats had settled in front of the Great Rock, Bluestar spoke. "ThunderClan brings to this Gathering its new medicine cat, Yellowfang," she announced formally. She paused while all eyes turned to the old she-cat with the thick fur and flattened muzzle. Fireheart noticed her shuffle her haunches on the hard ground. Early in his apprenticeship he had spent almost a whole moon nursing the she-cat back to health after she had come to the ThunderClan camp. Now he could tell by the way her right ear twisted slightly that she was uncomfortable under the gaze of the other Clans. Yellowfang had been medicine cat to ShadowClan, and cats hardly ever left one Clan to join another. She looked around the crowd slowly until she met the gaze of Runningnose, Shadow-Clan's new medicine cat. There was a brief pause; then they exchanged a respectful nod. Yellowfang's ear straightened and Fireheart relaxed.

Bluestar spoke again. "We also bring two newly named warriors—Fireheart and Graystripe."

Fireheart held his head high, but as he felt all eyes turn to look at him, a surge of self-consciousness made his tail flick nervously.

Nightpelt stepped forward, brushing past Bluestar to stand on the highest part of the rock. "I, Nightpelt, have taken over the leadership of ShadowClan," he announced. "Our former leader, Brokenstar, broke the warrior code and we were forced to chase him out."

"No mention of the fact we helped them to do it," Graystripe whispered to Fireheart.

Nightpelt continued, "The spirits of our ancestors have spoken to Runningnose and chosen me as leader. I have not yet traveled to Mothermouth to receive StarClan's gift of nine lives, but I will make this journey tomorrow night while the moon is still full. After my vigil at the Moonstone, I shall be known as Nightstar."

"Where is Brokenstar now?" called a voice from the crowd. It was Frostfur, the white ThunderClan queen.

"I think we can assume that he has left the forest, with the other banished warriors. He knows it would be dangerous for him to try to return," answered Nightpelt.

"I hope so," Fireheart heard Frostfur murmur to her neighbor, a plump brown queen.

RiverClan's leader, Crookedstar, stepped forward. "Let's

hope Brokenstar has had the sense to leave the forest for good. His greed for territory threatened us all."

Crookedstar waited for the yowls of agreement to die down before he went on. "While Brokenstar was ShadowClan's leader, I allowed him to hunt in our river. But now Shadow-Clan has a new leader, and this agreement can no longer stand. The prey in our river belongs to RiverClan alone."

Mews of triumph rose from the other RiverClan cats, but Fireheart saw with a feeling of alarm that Nightpelt was bristling.

Nightpelt raised his voice. "ShadowClan has the same needs as it did under Brokenstar. We have many mouths to feed, Crookedstar. You made an agreement with the whole of ShadowClan!"

Crookedstar leaped to his paws and turned on Nightpelt. He flattened his ears and hissed, and the cats below fell silent.

Quickly Bluestar stepped between the two leaders. "ShadowClan has suffered many losses recently," she mewed softly. "With fewer mouths to feed, Nightpelt, do you really need RiverClan's fish?"

Crookedstar hissed again, but Nightpelt held his gaze without flinching.

Bluestar spoke again, this time more forcefully. "You have just driven out your leader and several of your strongest warriors! And Brokenstar went against the warrior code when he forced Crookedstar to agree to share the river."

Fireheart swallowed uneasily as he noticed Nightpelt

unsheathe his claws, but Bluestar didn't blink. Her icy blue gaze glinted in the moonlight as she growled, "Remember you have not even received your nine lives from StarClan. Are you so confident you can make these demands?" Fireheart tensed as he felt the bristling of fur around him. The whole crowd was waiting for Nightpelt's response.

Nightpelt looked away angrily. His tail flicked from side to side but he said nothing.

Bluestar had won. Her voice softened. "We all know ShadowClan has suffered much these past few moons," she meowed. "ThunderClan has agreed to leave you in peace until you have had time to recover." She turned her gaze on Crookedstar. "I'm sure that Crookedstar will agree to show you the same respect."

Crookedstar narrowed his eyes and nodded. "But only as long as ShadowClan is not scented in our territory," he growled.

Fireheart relaxed, letting the fur lie flat on his shoulders. Now that he knew what it was like to fight in a real battle, he admired his leader's courage even more in challenging these two great warriors. Muffled mews of relief and agreement sounded in the crowd as the tension on the Great Rock suddenly eased.

"You won't scent us, Crookedstar," meowed Nightpelt. "Bluestar was right—we don't need your fish. After all, we have the uplands to hunt in, now that WindClan has left its territory."

Crookedstar looked at Nightpelt, his eyes brightening. "That's true," he agreed. "This will mean extra prey for all of us."

Bluestar drew up her head sharply. "No! WindClan must return!"

Crookedstar and Nightpelt looked at the ThunderClan leader. "Why?" asked Crookedstar.

"If we share WindClan's hunting grounds, it will mean more food for all our kits!" Nightpelt pointed out.

"The forest needs four Clans," Bluestar insisted. "Just as we have Fourtrees, and four seasons, StarClan has given us four Clans. We must find WindClan as soon as possible and bring them home."

The ThunderClan cats raised their voices in support of their leader, but Crookedstar's impatient yowl rose above them. "Your argument is weak, Bluestar. Do we really need four seasons? Wouldn't you rather go without leaf-bare, and the cold and hunger it brings?"

Bluestar looked calmly at the warriors beside her. "StarClan gave us leaf-bare to let the earth recover and prepare for new-leaf. This forest, and the uplands, have supported four Clans for generations. It is not up to us to challenge StarClan."

Leopardfur, the RiverClan deputy, spoke up. "Why should we go hungry for the sake of a Clan that cannot even defend its territory?" she yowled.

"Bluestar is right! WindClan must return!" Tigerclaw spat back, drawing himself up so that he towered above the cats around him.

Bluestar spoke again. "Crookedstar," she meowed, turning to the RiverClan leader, "RiverClan's hunting grounds are known for their richness. You have the river and all the fish it contains. Why do you need extra prey?" Crookedstar looked away and didn't answer. Fireheart noticed how RiverClan murmured anxiously among themselves. He wondered why Bluestar's question had ruffled their fur.

"And, Nightpelt," Bluestar went on, "it was Brokenstar who drove WindClan from its home." The broad-shouldered she-cat paused. "That is why ThunderClan helped you to chase him out."

Fireheart narrowed his eyes. He knew that Bluestar was gently reminding Nightpelt of the debt he owed to Thunder-Clan.

The ShadowClan leader half closed his eyes. After a silence that felt like an age, Nightpelt opened his eyes wide and meowed, "Very well, Bluestar. We will allow WindClan to return." Fireheart saw Crookedstar turn his head away in anger, his eyes black slits.

Bluestar nodded. "Two of us have agreed, Crookedstar," she meowed. "WindClan must be found and brought home. Until then, no Clan should hunt in their territory."

The Gathering began to break up as the cats prepared to travel back to their camps. Fireheart stayed where he was for a moment, watching the leaders on the Great Rock. Bluestar touched noses with Crookedstar and jumped down to the forest floor. On the rock, Crookedstar turned to Nightpelt. There was something about the look that passed between them that made Fireheart's fur prickle. Could it be that Blue-star did not really have Nightpelt's support after all? Fireheart looked quickly around. He could tell from the anger in Tiger-claw's eyes that ThunderClan's deputy had not missed this exchange either.

For once, Fireheart shared Tigerclaw's concern. This was a shift in Clan alliances he had not expected. After the risk ThunderClan had taken by helping ShadowClan to drive out Brokenstar, how could it side with RiverClan now?

CHAPTER 3

Bluestar led the way swiftly back to camp. The noise of their return awoke the cats who had remained behind. As the group streamed through the gorse entrance, sleepy figures began emerging from the dens.

"What's the news?" called Halftail.

"Was ShadowClan there?" asked Willowpelt.

"Yes, it was," Bluestar replied gravely. She strode past Willowpelt and leaped up onto Highrock. There was no need for her customary call for a Clan meeting—the cats were already gathering below the rock. Tigerclaw jumped up beside her.

"There was much tension between the Clans tonight," Bluestar began. "And I became aware of a possible new allegiance between Crookedstar and Nightpelt."

Graystripe squeezed into the small space next to Fireheart. "What are they talking about?" he asked. "I thought Nightpelt agreed with Bluestar."

"Nightpelt?" croaked One-eye's ancient voice from the back of the crowd.

"He has been named as ShadowClan's new leader," Bluestar explained.

"But his name—hasn't he been accepted by StarClan yet?" asked One-eye.

"He plans to travel to the Moonstone tomorrow night," Tigerclaw told him.

"No leader can speak for their Clan at a Gathering without receiving StarClan's approval first," muttered One-eye, loudly enough for all the cats to hear.

"He has the support of ShadowClan, One-eye," answered Bluestar, nodding at the old she-cat. "We cannot ignore what he said tonight." One-eye gave a disgruntled sniff, and Bluestar lifted her head to address the whole Clan. "At the Gathering, I suggested we find WindClan and bring it home. But Crookedstar and Nightpelt don't want them to return."

"They're hardly likely to join forces, though, are they?" called Graystripe. "They almost had a scrap over hunting rights in the river."

Fireheart turned to his friend. "Didn't you see the looks they were swapping by the end of the meeting? They're both desperate to get their paws on WindClan's territory."

"But why?" asked Sandpaw, who was sitting beside her mentor, Whitestorm.

Whitestorm answered her. "I suspect ShadowClan is not as weak as we thought it would be. And Nightpelt seems to have more ambition than any cat expected."

"But why does *RiverClan* want to hunt WindClan's grounds? They have always grown fat on the fish from their precious river!" yowled Willowpelt. "The uplands are a long way to go for a few windblown rabbits!"

The once-beautiful queen, Dappletail, spoke up in a voice cracked with age. "At the Gathering, some of the RiverClan elders spoke of Twolegs taking over part of their river."

"That's right," added Frostfur. "They say Twolegs have been living in shelters beside the river, disturbing the fish. The RiverClan cats have had to hide in the bushes and watch them with empty stomachs!"

Bluestar looked thoughtful. "For now, we must be careful to do nothing that may bring ShadowClan and RiverClan closer together. Go and rest now. Runningwind and Dustpaw, you will take the dawn patrol."

A cold breeze rattled the dying leaves in the trees overhead. The cats, still murmuring amongst themselves, went to their dens.

For the second night in a row, Fireheart dreamed. He was standing in the dark. The roar and the stench of a Thunderpath was very close by. Fireheart felt himself buffeted and blinded by the monsters that roared up and down with glaring eyes. Suddenly, through the din, Fireheart heard the pitiful cry of a young cat. The desperate wail sliced through the thundering of the monsters.

Fireheart awoke with a start. For a moment he thought that the cry had woken him. But the only noise was the muffled snores of warriors sleeping beside him. A growl came from somewhere near the middle of the den. It sounded like Tigerclaw. Fireheart felt too unsettled to go back to sleep, so he crept silently out of the den.

It was dark outside, and the stars dotting the black sky told him dawn was still far off. With the wail of the young cat echoing in his mind, Fireheart padded over to the nursery, his ears pricked. He could hear pawsteps beyond the camp wall. He sniffed the air. It was just Darkstripe and Longtail. Fireheart picked up their scents as they guarded ThunderClan's territory.

The calm of the sleeping camp soothed Fireheart. *Every cat must have nightmares about the Thunderpath*, he told himself. He crept back into the den and circled comfortably back into his nest. Graystripe purred briefly in his sleep as Fireheart settled beside him and closed his eyes.

Graystripe's nose woke him, prodding his side. "Leave me alone," Fireheart grumbled.

"Wake up!" Graystripe hissed.

"Why? We're not on patrol!" Fireheart complained.

"Bluestar wants to see us in her den, now."

Fuzzy-headed, Fireheart scrambled to his paws and followed Graystripe out of the den. The sun was beginning to turn the sky pink, and there was frost on the trees around the camp.

The two cats bounded across the clearing to Bluestar's den and announced their arrival with hushed mews.

"Enter!" It was Tigerclaw's voice that answered from behind the draped lichen. Alarm swept through Fireheart as he remembered his conversation with Bluestar on the way to the Gathering. Had she told Tigerclaw about his accusations? Graystripe pushed his way into Bluestar's den. Fireheart followed him uneasily.

Bluestar was sitting in her nest, her head up and her eyes bright. Tigerclaw stood in the middle of the smooth sandstone floor. Fireheart tried to read his expression, but the great tabby's eyes were as cold and steady as always.

Bluestar began at once. "Fireheart, Graystripe, I have an important mission for you."

"A mission?" Fireheart echoed. Relief and excitement swept away his anxiety.

"I want you to find WindClan and bring it back to its territory," announced Bluestar.

"Before you get too excited, bear in mind this could be very dangerous," Tigerclaw growled. "We don't know where WindClan has gone, so you will have to follow what is left of their scent—probably into hostile territory."

"But you've been through WindClan territory, when you traveled with me to the Moonstone," Bluestar pointed out. "Their scent will be familiar, as will the Twoleg territory beyond the uplands."

"Will it just be us?" asked Fireheart.

"Our other warriors are needed here," meowed Tigerclaw. "Leaf-bare is coming, and we need to gather as much fresh-kill as possible. Many prey-poor moons lie ahead."

Bluestar nodded. "Tigerclaw will help you prepare for the journey." Fireheart's paws prickled with unease. Bluestar had as much faith in her deputy as ever. Why was Fireheart the only cat in ThunderClan who didn't trust Tigerclaw?

"You must leave as soon as possible," Bluestar continued. "Good luck."

"We'll find them," Graystripe promised.

Dragging his thoughts back to the journey ahead, Fireheart nodded.

Tigerclaw followed them out of Bluestar's den. "Do you remember how to get to WindClan territory?"

"Oh, yes, Tigerclaw, we were there only—"

Fireheart interrupted Graystripe's eager reply, "Only a few *moons* ago," he meowed quickly. He flashed a warning glare at his friend. Graystripe had almost given away their journey several nights earlier with Ravenpaw.

Tigerclaw hesitated. Fireheart held his breath. Had he noticed Graystripe's mistake?

"And can you recall WindClan's scent?" the deputy meowed.

Fireheart sent silent thanks to StarClan.

The young warriors nodded, and Fireheart began to picture himself charging through the prickly gorse of the uplands in search of the lost Clan.

"You will need herbs for strength and to keep your hunger away. Fetch them from Yellowfang before you leave." Tigerclaw paused. "And don't forget that Nightpelt is planning to travel to the Moonstone tonight. Keep well out of his way."

"Yes, Tigerclaw," replied Fireheart.

"He'll never know we're out there," Graystripe assured him.

"As I would expect," meowed Tigerclaw. "Now, go!" Without

another word, he turned and bounded away.

"He might have wished us good luck," Graystripe complained.

"He probably thinks we don't need it," joked Fireheart as they crossed the clearing toward Yellowfang's den. But at the same time, he reflected, Tigerclaw seemed to be treating them with as much respect as he would any warrior—was it possible that he wasn't the traitor that Ravenpaw thought? It was still cold, despite the rising sun, but neither cat shivered—Fireheart could feel his fur beginning to thicken as the days grew shorter.

Yellowfang's den lay at the end of a tunnel under ferns. A large split rock stood in a corner of a small shaded glade. Spottedleaf had lived here before Yellowfang. The memory of the gentle tortoiseshell medicine cat tugged at Fireheart's heart. Spottedleaf had been killed by a ShadowClan warrior. He missed her desperately.

"Yellowfang!" Graystripe called. "We've come for traveling herbs!"

The two cats heard a hoarse mew from the shadow in the center of the rock, and Yellowfang squeezed out of the crack. "Where are you going?" she asked.

"We've got to find WindClan and bring it home," Fireheart told her, unable to hide the pride in his voice.

"Your first warrior mission!" rasped Yellowfang. "Congratulations! I'll fetch the herbs you will need." She returned a few moments later carrying a small bundle of dried leaves in her mouth. "Enjoy!" she purred, laying them on the ground.

Fireheart and Graystripe chewed obediently on the unap-petizing leaves. "Yuck!" spat Graystripe. "Just as bad as last time." Fireheart nodded, screwing up his face. Spottedleaf had given them the same herbs when they'd journeyed with Bluestar to the Moonstone.

Graystripe swallowed the last mouthful and nudged Fire-heart's shoulder with his nose. "Come on, slow slug! Let's get going! 'Bye," he called to Yellowfang over his shoulder, as he sprinted out of the glade.

"Wait for me," meowed Fireheart, chasing after his friend.

"Good-bye! Good luck, youngsters!" Yellowfang meowed after them.

As he raced through the tunnel, Fireheart heard the ferns rustling in the morning breeze. They seemed to be whisper-ing, "Good luck! Travel safely!"

CHAPTER 4

As they headed out of the camp, the two young warriors nearly crashed into Whitestorm, who was leading Sandpaw and Runningwind into the forest for the dawn patrol.

"Sorry!" panted Fireheart. He stopped, and Graystripe skidded to a halt beside him.

Whitestorm dipped his head. "I hear you two are going on a mission," he meowed.

"Yes," Fireheart replied.

"Then may you have StarClan's protection," meowed Whitestorm gravely.

"What for?" Sandpaw sneered. "You off to catch voles?"

Runningwind, a lean tabby, turned and whispered something into Sandpaw's ear. Her expression changed and the contempt in her green eyes switched to guarded curiosity.

The patrol stepped aside to let Fireheart and Graystripe pass. The pair raced on and scrambled up the side of the ravine.

Fireheart and Graystripe shared few words as they followed the route through the forest to Fourtrees, saving their breath for the long journey ahead. They paused at the top of the steep slope on the far side of the oak-shaded clearing, their sides heaving from the climb.

"Is it *always* windy up here?" grumbled Graystripe, fluffing out his thick fur against the blast of cold air that swept across the uplands.

"I suppose there aren't any trees to block it," Fireheart pointed out, screwing up his eyes. This was WindClan's territory. As Fireheart sniffed the air, he detected a scent that all of his senses told him should not be there. "Do you smell RiverClan warriors?" he murmured uneasily.

Graystripe lifted his nose. "No. Do you think there might be some here?"

"Maybe. They might want to make the most of WindClan's absence, especially since they know WindClan will be back soon," Fireheart warned.

"Well, I can't smell anything now," whispered Graystripe.

The two friends padded watchfully along a frozen turf trail sheltered by heather.

A fresh scent stopped Fireheart in his tracks. "Can you smell that?" he hissed to Graystripe.

"Yes," whispered Graystripe, flattening himself against the ground. "RiverClan!"

Fireheart dropped into a crouch, keeping his ears below the heather. Beside him, Graystripe lifted his dark gray head to peer over the bushes. "I can see them," he murmured. "They're hunting."

Fireheart stretched up cautiously to look.

Four RiverClan warriors were chasing a rabbit through

a patch of gorse. Fireheart recognized Blackclaw from the Gathering. The smoky-black warrior pounced, his claws unsheathed, but sat up again with nothing to show for the chase. The rabbit must have made it to the safety of her warren.

Fireheart and Graystripe dropped down again and pressed their bellies against the cold turf.

"They're not good rabbit hunters," Graystripe hissed scornfully.

"I guess RiverClan is more used to catching fish," Fireheart whispered back. His nose twitched as he smelled the scent of a terrified rabbit coming nearer. With a pang of dread, Fireheart heard the pawsteps of the RiverClan warriors fast approaching after it. "They're coming this way! We'll have to hide!"

"Follow me," whispered Graystripe. "I smell badgers this way."

"Badgers?" Fireheart echoed. "Is that safe?" He'd heard the story of how Halftail had lost his tail in a fight with a bad-tempered old badger.

"Don't worry. The scent is strong but stale," Graystripe reassured him. "There must be an old set near here."

Fireheart sniffed. His scent glands picked up a strong, almost foxlike scent. "Are you sure it's abandoned?"

"We'll know soon enough. Come on; we've got to get out of here," replied Graystripe. He led the way quickly through the low bushes. The rustle of heather told Fireheart the RiverClan warriors were closing in.

"Here!" Graystripe shouldered aside a tuft of heather to

reveal a sandy hole in the ground. "Get inside! The badger's scent will disguise ours. We can wait till they're gone."

Fireheart slipped speedily into the dark hole, and Graystripe followed him. The stench of badger was overwhelming.

Pawsteps thudded on the ground overhead. Both cats held their breath as the steps halted and one of the RiverClan warriors yowled, "Badger set!" From the rasping mew, Fireheart knew it was Blackclaw.

A second voice answered: "Is it abandoned? The rabbit may be hiding inside."

Fireheart felt Graystripe's fur bristling beside him in the dark. He unsheathed his claws and stared at the entrance to the hole, ready to fight if the warriors came inside.

"Wait; the scent leads this way," meowed Blackclaw. There was a scrabble of paws overhead as the RiverClan warriors charged away.

Graystripe slowly let out his breath. "D'you think they're gone?"

"Perhaps we should wait a bit longer, make sure none of them stayed behind," Fireheart suggested.

No more noises came from outside. Graystripe nudged Fireheart. "Come on," he meowed.

Fireheart followed Graystripe cautiously out into the daylight. There was no sign of the RiverClan patrol. The fresh breeze cleared Fireheart's scent glands of the badger stench. "We should look for the WindClan camp," he meowed to Graystripe. "It'll be the best place to pick up their scent."

"Okay," answered Graystripe.

They moved slowly through the heather, keeping their mouths slightly open to pick up the scent of any more RiverClan warriors. They stopped at the foot of a large flat rock that sloped up steeply, past the tops of the gorse bushes.

"I'll climb up and have a look around," offered Graystripe. "My pelt will blend better with the stone."

"Okay," Fireheart agreed. "But keep your head down."

He watched his friend creep up the rock. Graystripe crouched at the top and gazed around the plateau, then skidded back down to Fireheart. "There's a hollow over there, I think," Graystripe puffed, signaling with his tail. "I can see a gap in the heather."

"Let's check it out," meowed Fireheart. "It could be the camp."

"That's what I thought." Graystripe nodded. "It's probably the only place up here that's sheltered from the wind."

As they neared the hollow, Fireheart raced past Graystripe and gazed over the edge. It looked as if a StarClan warrior had reached down from the sky, scooped a pawful of peat from the plateau, and replaced it with a thick tangle of gorse that grew almost to the level of the ground on either side.

Fireheart sniffed. He could smell many scents, all WindClan, old and young, male and female, and, in the background, the faint odor of fresh-kill that had long since become crowfood. This had to be the abandoned camp.

Fireheart bounded down the slope and plunged into the bushes. The gorse tugged at his fur and scratched his nose, making his eyes water. He could hear Graystripe behind him, cursing as thorns snagged his ears. They pushed through into a sheltered clearing. The sandy ground had been trodden hard by generations of paws. At one end of the clearing stood a rock, worn smooth by many windblown moons.

"This is their camp, all right," Fireheart murmured.

"I can't believe Brokenstar managed to drive WindClan out of such a well-protected place!" meowed Graystripe, rubbing his sore nose with one paw.

"It looks like they put up a good fight," Fireheart pointed out, realizing with a jolt how badly ravaged the camp was. Clumps of fur littered the ground, and dried blood stained the sand. Mossy nests had been dragged out of dens and torn apart. And everywhere, stale ShadowClan scents mingled with the smell of terrified WindClan cats.

Fireheart shuddered. "Let's find the scent trail out of here," he meowed. He began to sniff the air carefully and moved forward, following the strongest scent. Graystripe padded after him to a narrow gap in the gorse.

"WindClan cats must be even smaller than I remember!" grumbled Graystripe as he squeezed through after Fireheart.

Fireheart glanced at his friend, amused for a moment. The scent trail was quite clear now—definitely WindClan, but mixed and pungent, as if made by many frightened cats. Fireheart looked down. Drops of dried blood dotted the ground. "We're heading the right way," he meowed darkly. Two moons of rain and wind had failed to wash away the signs of suffering. Fireheart could clearly picture the defeated and injured

Clan fleeing from its home. With a surge of anger he bounded after his friend.

The trail led them to the far edge of the uplands, where they stopped to catch their breath. In front of them the ground sloped away to the Twoleg farmland. Far in the distance, where the sun was beginning to set, loomed the towering shapes of Highstones.

"I wonder if Nightpelt is there yet," Fireheart murmured. In a tunnel below Highstones lay the sacred Moonstone, where the leaders of each Clan shared dreams with StarClan.

"Well, we don't want to find him down there!" Graystripe flicked his tail at the wide expanse of Twoleg land. "It'll be hard enough dodging Twolegs, rats, and dogs, without meeting the new ShadowClan leader as well!"

Fireheart nodded. He thought back to their last journey across this land, with Bluestar and Tigerclaw. They had almost been killed by an attack of rats, and only the arrival of Barley, the loner, had saved them. Even so, Bluestar had lost one of her lives; the memory of it stung Fireheart like a wood ant.

"Do you think we'll find any trace of Ravenpaw down there?" Graystripe meowed, turning his broad face toward Fireheart.

"I hope so," Fireheart replied solemnly. The last he had seen of Ravenpaw had been the white tip of his tail disappearing into the storm on the uplands. Had the ThunderClan apprentice made it safely to Barley's territory?

The two warriors started down the slope, carefully sniffing

each clump of grass to make sure they stayed on the Wind-
Clan trail.

"It doesn't look as if they were heading for Highstones,"
Graystripe remarked. The trail took them sideways into a wide
grassy field. They skirted the edge, staying near the hedgerow
as WindClan had done. The scent led them out of the field
and onto a Twoleg path through a small copse of trees.

"Look!" Graystripe meowed. Sun-bleached piles of prey
bones lay scattered in the undergrowth. Mossy bedding had
been gathered beneath the thickest patches of brambles.

"WindClan must have tried to settle here," Fireheart
meowed in surprise.

"I wonder what made them leave?" asked Graystripe, sniffing the air. "The scent is old."

Fireheart shrugged and the two cats followed the trail
onward to a thick hedge. With a bit of a struggle, they wriggled through onto a grass verge. Beyond a narrow ditch lay a
wide earth track.

Graystripe leaped nimbly over the ditch and onto the hard
red track. Fireheart looked around, stiffening as he recognized a hard-edged silhouette in the distance. "Graystripe!
Stop!" he hissed.

"What's up?"

Fireheart pointed with his nose. "Look at that Twolegplace over there! We must be near Barley's territory."

Graystripe's ears twitched nervously. "That's where those
dogs live! But WindClan definitely came this way. We'll have
to hurry. We need to get past the Twoleg nest before sunset."

Fireheart remembered Barley telling them that the Two-legs let the dogs loose at night, and the sun was already sinking toward the craggy tops of Highstones. He nodded. "Perhaps the dogs chased WindClan out of the woods." With an anxious twinge, he thought of Ravenpaw. "Do you think he found Barley?" he asked.

"Who? Ravenpaw? Why not? We made it this far!" meowed Graystripe. "Don't underestimate him. Remember the time Tigerclaw sent him to Snakerocks? He came back with an adder!"

Fireheart purred at the memory as Graystripe leaped across the track and through the hedge on the far side. Fireheart chased after him, quickening his pace to match his friend step for step.

A dog barked furiously from the Twoleg nest, but its vicious snarling soon faded into the distance. The temperature plunged as the sun set, and frost began to form on the grass.

"Should we keep going?" asked Graystripe. "What if the trail takes us to Highstones after all? Nightpelt will definitely be there by now."

Fireheart lifted his nose and sniffed the browning fronds of some ferns. The smell of WindClan, sour with fear, pricked at him. "We'd better keep going," he meowed. "We'll stop when we have to."

The cold breeze carried another odor to Fireheart's nose—there was a Thunderpath nearby. Graystripe screwed up his face. He'd smelled it too. The warriors exchanged a look of dismay, but pushed on. The stench grew stronger and stronger until they could hear the roar of Thunderpath monsters in the distance. By the time they reached the hedge that ran alongside the wide gray path, it was hard to make out the WindClan trail at all.

Graystripe stopped and looked around, uncertainty showing in his eyes. But Fireheart could just make out the fear-scent. He crept through the shadows beside the hedge until he reached a place where the hedge was less thick. "They sheltered here," Fireheart meowed, imagining the terrified WindClan cats staring through the hedge at the Thunderpath.

"This was probably the first time most of them had seen the Thunderpath," Graystripe remarked as he joined Fireheart by the hedge.

Fireheart looked at his friend in surprise. He had never met a WindClan cat—they had been driven out of their territory almost as soon as he had become an apprentice. "Didn't they patrol their borders?" he asked, puzzled.

"You've seen their territory—it's pretty wild and barren, and the prey's not easy to catch. I guess they never thought any of the other Clans would bother hunting there. After all, RiverClan has their river, and, in a good year, our forests are filled with prey, so no cat needs their skinny rabbits."

A monster roared past on the other side of the hedge, its night eyes glaring. Fireheart and Graystripe flinched as the wind buffeted their fur even through the wall of leaves. When the noise had faded away, they sat up cautiously and sniffed around the roots of the hedge.

"The trail seems to lead under here." Fireheart squeezed onto the grass verge that lay along the Thunderpath. Graystripe scrabbled through behind him.

But on the other side of the hedge the scent trail stopped abruptly.

"They must have either doubled back or crossed the Thunderpath," Fireheart meowed. "You look around here, and I'll check out the other side." He fought to keep his voice calm, but exhaustion was making him desperate. Surely they couldn't have lost the trail now, after coming so far?

CHAPTER 5

♣

Fireheart waited until the only sound he could hear was the pounding of blood in his ears. Then he padded to the edge of the Thunderpath. It stretched ahead of him, wide and foul-smelling, but silent. Fireheart darted out. The ground beneath his paws felt cold and smooth. He didn't stop until he reached the grass on the other side.

The air here was tainted by the acrid smell of the Thunderpath and its monsters, so Fireheart headed toward the hedge. Still, there was no trace of the WindClan cats. His heart sank.

Suddenly a monster tore past, making Fireheart leap into the air with terror. He scrambled underneath the hedge and crouched, trembling, frantically wondering what to do next.

Then he smelled it: the faintest trace carried on the wind that the monster had stirred up. WindClan had been here!

Fireheart called as loudly as he could to Graystripe. There was a pause, then the sound of paws pounding across the Thunderpath to join him.

"Have you found it?" puffed his friend.

"Not sure. I got a whiff, but I can't pinpoint it." Fireheart pushed his way through the hedge, Graystripe right behind him. He lifted his nose toward the open field ahead of them. "Have you any idea what's over there?"

"No," replied Graystripe. "I shouldn't think any Clan cat has ever been this far before."

"Except WindClan," muttered Fireheart darkly. Away from the confusing fumes of the Thunderpath, the trail was suddenly clear. WindClan had definitely come this way. The two cats struck out through the long grass, straight across the field.

"Fireheart!" Graystripe sounded alarmed.

"What is it?"

"Look!"

Fireheart stopped and lifted his head. He saw a Thunderpath ahead of them arching high into the air on massive stone legs, illuminated by the eyes of the monsters that moved along it. Another Thunderpath ran below, veering off into the darkness.

Graystripe nodded toward a tall thistle. "And smell this!"

Fireheart inhaled the scent. It was a fresh WindClan marker!

"They must have settled somewhere near here!" Graystripe murmured in disbelief.

A pang of excitement twisted Fireheart's stomach. Both cats looked silently at each other for a moment. Then, without a word, they moved on toward the stinking Thunderpaths.

Graystripe spoke at last. "Why would WindClan come to a place like this?"

"I guess not even Brokenstar would want to follow them

here," Fireheart answered grimly. He stopped. A thought was nagging at him.

Graystripe paused beside him. "What is it?"

"If WindClan is hiding so near the Thunderpaths," Fireheart meowed slowly, "they must be fairly desperate not to be found. They're more likely to trust us if we arrive in daylight than if we creep up on them in darkness."

"Does that mean we can rest?" asked Graystripe, sitting down heavily.

"Just until it's light," meowed Fireheart. "We'll find somewhere to hide and see if we can get some sleep. Are you hungry?" Graystripe shook his head. "Me neither," Fireheart agreed. "I don't know if it's those herbs or because the stench from the Thunderpath is making me feel sick."

"Where shall we sleep?" Graystripe looked around.

Fireheart had already noticed a dark shadow in the ground up ahead. "What's that?"

"A burrow?" Graystripe sounded puzzled. "It's too big for a rabbit. Surely there can't be a badger set here!"

"Let's take a look," Fireheart suggested.

The hole was larger than a badger set, smooth and lined with stone. Fireheart sniffed it, then put his front paws on its rim and peered cautiously inside. A stone tunnel sloped away, down into the ground. "I can feel air flowing through it," he meowed, his voice echoing away into the shadows. "It must come up somewhere over there." He ducked back out and pointed his nose toward the tangle of Thunderpaths.

"Is it empty?" Graystripe asked.

"Smells like it."

"Come on then." Graystripe led the way into the tunnel. After a few fox-lengths, the slope leveled out.

Fireheart halted and sniffed the damp air. He could smell nothing but the fumes of the Thunderpath. A roaring noise rumbled overhead. Fireheart's paws trembled as the stone floor vibrated. Was the Thunderpath *above* them? He fluffed out his coat against the relentless draft and felt Graystripe's fur brush against him—his friend was circling, preparing to settle down to sleep. Fireheart crouched down and huddled beside his friend. He closed his stinging eyes and thought of the gentle forest breezes and the rustling of the leaves. Exhaustion fought briefly with a pang of longing to be at home in his den, before he gave in to the blackness that swam into his mind.

When Fireheart opened his eyes again, gray light was glowing at the end of the tunnel. Dawn must be near. Fireheart's bones ached from the cold hard ground. He nudged Graystripe, who grunted. "Morning already?"

"Almost," Fireheart answered, getting to his paws. Graystripe stretched and stood up too.

"I think we should head that way," Fireheart meowed, craning his neck away from the light. "I think this tunnel leads right under a Thunderpath. It might take us nearer to the . . ." His voice trailed off; he had no words to describe the tangle of Thunderpaths they had seen last night. Beside him Graystripe nodded, and together they began to pad wordlessly into the darkness.

Before long Fireheart spotted light ahead of them. They quickened their pace until they were racing up a short, steep slope that led them into a world filled with gray dawn light.

They had come up near the edge of a patch of barren, dirty grass. Thunderpaths enclosed it on two sides, and another arched overhead. A fire burned in the middle of the grass. A few Twolegs lay around it. One of them stretched and rolled over, and another grunted angrily in its sleep, but the noise and stench from the Thunderpaths didn't seem to wake them.

Fireheart watched them warily, then froze as something else caught his eye: dark outlines that flitted back and forth in front of the flames. Cats! Could it be WindClan? Fireheart looked at the fire and the cats, and his mind flooded with the memory of his dream—the noise of the Thunderpath, the sight of the flames and the cats, and Spottedleaf's voice murmuring, "Fire will save the Clan."

A surge of emotion made Fireheart's legs feel weak. Did this mean that ThunderClan's fate was bound up with the fate of WindClan?

"Fireheart? Fireheart!"

Graystripe's voice jolted Fireheart back to reality. He breathed deeply to calm himself.

"We must find Tallstar and speak with him," he meowed.

"Then you think it *is* WindClan?" asked Graystripe.

"You smelled their marker—who else could it be?" Fireheart replied.

Graystripe looked at him, his eyes shining with triumph. "We found them!"

Fireheart nodded. He didn't point out that finding Wind-Clan was only half their mission. They still had to convince them that it was safe to return home.

Graystripe braced himself, ready to leap forward. "Let's go!"

"Hang on," Fireheart warned. "We don't want to startle them."

Just then, one of the Twolegs sat up with a jolt and began shouting at the ragged cats around the fire. The noise roused the other Twolegs, who joined in with rough, angry voices.

The WindClan cats scattered. All caution forgotten, Fireheart and Graystripe raced after them. Fireheart could feel his fur prickle with fear as he and Graystripe ran straight toward the fire and the Twolegs. Every instinct told him to keep away, but he dared not lose sight of the fleeing Wind-Clan cats.

One of the Twolegs staggered to its feet, looming up in front of him. Fireheart skidded, sending up a spray of dust. Something exploded beside him, pelting him with hard-edged splinters, but nothing pierced his thick coat. He glanced backward, checking for Graystripe. He was relieved to see his friend right behind him, his eyes wide with alarm and his fur standing on end.

They charged into the safety of the shadows beneath the soaring Thunderpath. Ahead, Fireheart watched the Wind-Clan cats stop close to one of the Thunderpath's great stone legs. And then, one by one, the cats disappeared into the ground.

"Where did they go?" meowed Graystripe in amazement.

"Another tunnel?" Fireheart suggested. "Come on, let's find out."

Cautiously, the two friends approached the spot where the WindClan cats had vanished. As they neared, they saw a hole in the earth. Like their resting place on the previous night, the entrance was round and lined with stone, sloping away into utter blackness.

Fireheart led the way, all his senses alert for a WindClan patrol. The floor beneath his paws felt wet and slimy, and the sound of trickling water echoed around them. As the tunnel leveled out, Fireheart pricked his ears and opened his mouth. The damp air smelled rank and bitter—worse than the tunnel they had slept in. Here the Thunderpath fumes mingled with the fear-scent of WindClan cats.

It was too dark to see anything, but after a few paces Fireheart's whiskers sensed a turning in the tunnel. Fireheart flicked his tail, touching Graystripe lightly with its tip. He couldn't see his friend in the blackness, but Graystripe must have felt the signal, because he stopped beside Fireheart and together they peered around the corner.

Ahead of them, the tunnel was lit by a narrow hole in the ceiling that led to the wasteland above. Fireheart could see many cats huddled together in the gray light—warriors and elders, queens and kits, all pitifully thin. A cold breeze blew relentlessly through the hole in the roof, stirring the thin fur on the skinny bodies. Fireheart shuddered, for the breeze carried to him the stench of sickness and crow-food.

Suddenly the tunnel shook as a monster roared overhead.

Graystripe and Fireheart, already tense, jumped, but the WindClan cats didn't react. They simply huddled with half-closed eyes, numb to their surroundings.

The noise died away. Fireheart took a deep breath and stepped around the corner, out into the thin light.

A gray WindClan tom spun around, his fur standing on end as he yowled an alarm to the rest of the Clan. In one smooth movement, the WindClan warriors formed a line across the tunnel in front of the queens and elders, their backs arched, hissing fiercely.

With a feeling of dread, Fireheart saw the glint of unsheathed claws and thorn-sharp fangs. These half-starved cats were about to attack.

CHAPTER 6

Fireheart pressed his body warningly against Graystripe, who had padded out to join him. They had to show no threat if they were to survive.

The WindClan warriors stood their ground without moving a muscle. *They're waiting for a signal from their leader!* Fireheart realized. *They still follow the warrior code, even though they have to live like this.*

From behind the line of warriors, a black-and-white tom weaved his way to the front. With a jolt, Fireheart recognized the long-tailed cat from his dream. This must be Tallstar, leader of WindClan.

Tallstar sniffed the air, but Fireheart and Graystripe were downwind, their scents carried away by the steady breeze. As the black-and-white cat walked toward them, Fireheart breathed in the rank odor of crow-food that hung on his coat. Like Graystripe, he remained perfectly still, his eyes down, as Tallstar circled them, sniffing their fur closely.

Finally Tallstar returned to his warriors. Fireheart heard him murmur, "ThunderClan." The warriors flattened their fur, but remained in a defensive line, shielding the rest of the cats.

Tallstar turned to face his visitors and sat down, curling his tail carefully around his paws. "I was expecting Shadow-Clan," he growled. His eyes burned with hostility. "Why are you here?"

"We came to find you," Fireheart meowed, feeling his voice crack with tension. "Bluestar and the other Clan leaders want you to return to your home."

The WindClan leader's voice was still wary. "That land is not safe for my Clan anymore," he meowed. There was a hunted look in Tallstar's eye that sent a pang of sorrow through Fireheart.

"ShadowClan has driven out Brokenstar," he meowed. "He is no longer a threat."

The warriors behind Tallstar turned and looked at one another. Murmurs of surprise rippled back through the Clan.

"You must return as soon as possible," Fireheart urged. "ShadowClan and RiverClan are starting to hunt in the uplands. We saw a RiverClan hunting patrol near the old badger set while we were on our way here."

Tallstar bristled angrily.

"But they are poor rabbit hunters," Graystripe added. "I think they went home with empty bellies."

Tallstar and his warriors purred with satisfaction. Their good spirits encouraged Fireheart, but he could see how weak they were. This Clan would find the journey back to the uplands long and hard. "May we travel with you?" he suggested respectfully.

Tallstar's eyes flashed. He knew the question was a tactful offer of help. He looked steadily at Fireheart. "Yes," he replied at last. "Thank you."

Fireheart realized he hadn't introduced himself. "This is Graystripe," he meowed, dipping his head. "And I am Fireheart. We are warriors of ThunderClan."

"Fireheart," repeated Tallstar thoughtfully. Sunlight was flooding through the gap in the roof now, making Fireheart's orange pelt glow in the dim tunnel. "The name suits you."

Another monster roared overhead. Fireheart and Graystripe flinched. Tallstar watched them with amusement and flicked his tail. It must have been a signal, for the line of warriors behind him split up. "We shall leave at once," he announced, standing up.

"Are we all fit for the journey?" Tallstar asked as the warriors began to move among the queens and elders.

"All except Morningflower's kit," replied a mottled brown warrior. "He is too young."

"Then we must take turns carrying him," answered Tallstar.

The WindClan cats shuffled forward, their eyes dull with pain and exhaustion. A tortoiseshell queen was holding a tiny kit gently by the scruff of its neck. The little creature's eyes were hardly open.

"Ready?" called Tallstar.

A black tom with a misshapen paw looked around the Clan

and answered for them. "Ready," he meowed.

Fireheart and Graystripe turned and made their way back to the tunnel entrance and waited while the WindClan cats emerged blinking into the daylight. Some of the elders blinked so long, their faces screwed up against the weak sun, that Fireheart guessed they had not been outside the tunnel for some time. Tallstar padded out of the tunnel last of all and walked to the head of his Clan.

"Shall we take you back the way we came?" Fireheart asked him. "I believe it's a shortcut."

"Is it safe?" asked Tallstar. Fireheart saw the hunted look once more in the leader's eyes.

"We met no trouble coming here," Graystripe meowed.

Tallstar flicked his tail decisively, as though he were brushing away any doubt. "Good," he declared. "You come with me, Graystripe. Show me the way. Fireheart, travel beside the Clan. Tell my deputy if you see trouble."

"Which one is he?" asked Fireheart.

Tallstar nodded toward the black tom. "Deadfoot," he meowed. The warrior turned at the sound of his name and pricked his ears.

Fireheart dipped his head in greeting. He left Graystripe with Tallstar and joined the other cats.

As the Clan made its way under the Thunderpath arch, Fireheart could still smell the fire, but when they padded out onto the patch of wasteland, the Twolegs were nowhere to be seen. Graystripe headed straight for the tunnel where he and Fireheart had spent the night. Tallstar entered first, while Fireheart waited at the back until all the Clan had disappeared inside. Only Deadfoot remained.

"Are you sure it leads to daylight?" the black tom meowed warily.

"It just leads under the Thunderpath. Have you never used this tunnel?" Fireheart asked, surprised.

"When our warriors cross the Thunderpath, they prefer to see where they're heading," growled Deadfoot. Fireheart nodded, and the deputy added, "You go first."

Fireheart padded down into the dark hole. He emerged to find the WindClan cats staring across the field that led to the final Thunderpath. Fireheart saw Tallstar consult briefly with Graystripe before they set off into the long, frost-crisp grass. Fireheart walked with the rest of the Clan, flanking one side while Deadfoot limped steadily on the other.

Before they were halfway across the field, it was clear that many of the cats were having trouble keeping up the pace. "Tallstar!" yowled Deadfoot. "We need to travel more slowly!"

Fireheart looked over his shoulder and saw some of the cats falling farther and farther behind. Morningflower was among them, the kit swinging from her mouth. Fireheart bounded over to her. She was panting heavily. It couldn't have been long since her kitting.

"Let me carry him," Fireheart offered. "Just until you have caught your breath."

Morningflower glanced warily at Fireheart, but her eyes softened when they met his. She put her kit down, and Fireheart took it gently and walked next to her so that she didn't lose sight of her precious bundle.

Tallstar slowed the pace, but only a little. In spite of his obvious exhaustion, and the fact that every rib showed under his fur, he burned with a fierce energy that lent swiftness to his paws.

Fireheart could understand part of the reason for his urgency. The sun was steadily climbing above the horizon. Some of the WindClan cats were sick, some old, and all of them were weak from hunger. If they were going to cross the Thunderpath without losing any cats, they would have to do it quickly, before the monsters came in their swarms.

By the time Fireheart and Morningflower arrived at the hedge, WindClan was gathered around its leader.

"We cross the Thunderpath here," Tallstar announced above the noise of a monster racing past. The WindClan leader squeezed under the hedge. Deadfoot, Graystripe, and a younger warrior followed him.

Morningflower leaned toward Fireheart and took hold of her kit. She had stopped panting now, and as she took the kit from Fireheart she brushed her cheek gratefully against his. He dipped his head to the tortoiseshell queen and followed Graystripe under the hedge.

Tallstar and Deadfoot sat staring wordlessly at the wide gray path. Graystripe stood beside them. He flicked his tail toward the younger warrior. "This is Onewhisker," he told Fireheart.

A monster sped past, almost drowning out Graystripe's words and whipping up stinging dust.

Through streaming eyes, Fireheart mewed a greeting to Onewhisker and turned his attention to the Thunderpath. "We should try to get the Clan over in small groups," he meowed. "Graystripe and I will stay with any that need help." He looked at the Clan leader. "If you agree, Tallstar," he added.

Tallstar nodded. "The strongest group will go first," he meowed.

The other WindClan cats began to appear through the hedge. Before long the whole Clan was clustered beside them, pressed against the sharp twigs, as far back from the Thunderpath as possible.

Fireheart and Graystripe moved to the edge, watching for a break in the line of monsters. The Thunderpath was much busier than it had been when they'd crossed last night.

Onewhisker led the first group forward.

"Do you want us to cross with you?" Fireheart offered. He could smell the young tom's fear. The mottled brown tabby shook his head. The cats beside him peered along the Thunderpath first one way, then the other. All was quiet, and the group dashed safely over to the other side.

Two warriors came next, accompanied by a pair of skinny elders. "Now!" Fireheart ordered as a monster flashed safely past.

The four WindClan cats stepped out onto the empty Thunderpath. The elders winced as they padded across on paws raw from the damp tunnel. Fireheart willed them on breathlessly as they neared the other side. A monster was zooming toward them.

"Look out!" Graystripe yowled, and even the two elders bounded forward, fur bristling, and hurled themselves onto the other side a heartbeat before the monster raced past.

Two larger groups crossed, leaving just one more. Only once they were safely over would Tallstar and Deadfoot cross. Morningflower and her kit stepped up to Fireheart's side. Behind her trembled three very elderly cats.

"We'll cross with you," Fireheart meowed. He looked at Graystripe, who nodded. "Tell us when it's safe to go, Graystripe." Fireheart leaned forward to take Morningflower's kit, but she pulled back, her ears flat. Fireheart looked deep into her frightened amber eyes and understood. She and her kit would live or die together.

"Now!" At Graystripe's yowl, Fireheart and Morningflower stepped out onto the Thunderpath. The elders crept out behind them with Graystripe beside them. Time seemed to stand still as the elders hobbled slowly forward on stiff, battle-scarred legs. *If a monster comes now, we're all fresh-kill*, Fireheart thought. The other side was still several rabbit leaps away.

"Come on," urged Graystripe. The elders tried to hurry, but one stumbled, and Graystripe had to nose him back onto his paws.

Fireheart heard the distant roar of a monster. "Go on ahead!" he hissed to Morningflower. "We'll bring the elders."

Morningflower stumbled forward. Her kit squealed as it

bumped against the hard ground. Fireheart and Graystripe pressed themselves against the elders' scrawny bodies, nudging them forward. The noise of the approaching monster grew louder and louder.

Fireheart grabbed the nearest elder by the scruff of the neck and dragged him forward, before turning to haul the second closer to the verge. The monster raced closer. Fireheart closed his eyes and braced himself.

There was a screech and an acrid smell that stung his throat, then a fading roar as the monster sped away. Fireheart opened his eyes and looked around. Graystripe was crouching in the middle of the Thunderpath, unscathed, but staring with eyes as wide as full moons. One elder cowered between them; the other two trembled near the verge. The monster was hurtling away from them, swerving across the Thunderpath. *Thank StarClan!* It had missed them all.

Fireheart took a shuddering breath. "Come on," he meowed to the last elder. "Almost there."

Tallstar bounded across with Deadfoot and gathered his trembling Clan around him on the verge.

Onewhisker touched Fireheart's nose with his own. "You would have died for us," he murmured. "WindClan will never forget that."

Tallstar's voice sounded behind them. "Onewhisker is right; we shall honor you both in our stories. We must keep going," he continued. "We have a long journey ahead of us."

As the cats prepared to move off, Fireheart padded over to Morningflower. She was busy licking her kit.

"Is he all right?" Fireheart asked.

"Oh, yes," answered Morningflower.

"What about you?" asked Fireheart.

Morningflower didn't answer.

Fireheart turned to a gray queen, who answered his unspoken question. "Don't worry," she meowed. "I'll take the kit next."

The Clan followed the hedgerow along the Thunderpath before turning away to join the track through the woods. The scents here seemed to soothe the WindClan cats, but the journey had taken its toll; they were traveling slower than ever. And when they reached the fence at the far side, it took all Fireheart's strength to help the weakest cats over.

The sun had passed its highest point by the time Fireheart spotted the Twolegplace in the distance. He sniffed the air hopefully but there was still no scent of Ravenpaw. Fireheart felt a stab of grief, and tried to ignore the nagging thought that he should never have sent his friend here alone.

Clouds billowed up over Highstones, growing blacker as they covered the sinking sun. A cold wind ruffled the cats' fur, bringing the first drops of rain.

Fireheart looked at the WindClan cats. There was no way they could travel through a long, wet night. He was tired too, and, for the first time since he'd eaten Yellowfang's herbs, he was feeling the effects of hunger. A glance at Graystripe told him that his friend felt the same way. The big gray warrior's tail drooped, and his ears were flattened against the spattering rain.

"Tallstar," Fireheart called. "Perhaps we should stop soon and shelter for the night."

The WindClan leader stopped and waited while Fireheart caught up with him. "I agree," he meowed. "There's a ditch here; we can shelter in that until sunrise."

Graystripe and Fireheart exchanged glances. "We might be better sheltering in the hedgerow," Fireheart suggested. "There are rats in these ditches."

Tallstar nodded. "Very well." He turned to his Clan and announced that they would be spending the night here. The queens and elders flopped down at once, despite the rain, while the warriors and apprentices gathered to discuss hunting patrols.

Fireheart and Graystripe joined them. "I don't know how good the hunting will be here," Fireheart meowed. "There are too many Twolegs."

Graystripe's stomach growled as if in agreement. The other warriors turned to him with amused but sympathetic eyes. Then they froze as the grass behind them rustled. The WindClan warriors bristled and arched their backs, unsheathing sharp claws, but Fireheart and Graystripe turned their heads joyfully. The wind carried a scent as familiar as their own den.

"Ravenpaw!" Fireheart gasped as a sleek black cat emerged from the long grass.

Fireheart raced over to his old friend and nuzzled him. "Thank StarClan you're safe!" he purred. He stepped back and studied Ravenpaw in surprise. What had happened to the skinny, scared black apprentice? This cat was plump and sleek, and his fur, usually so dull before, now shed the rain like a holly leaf.

"Firepaw!" Ravenpaw meowed in delight.

"Fire*heart*," Graystripe corrected him. He stepped forward and touched noses with the black cat. "We're warriors now! I'm Graystripe."

"Do you know this cat?" snarled Deadfoot.

The hostility in his voice made Fireheart flinch. He looked at the bristling WindClan cats and silently cursed himself for calling Ravenpaw's name out loud. He just hoped Tallstar's warriors had been too distracted to hear it. If WindClan mentioned it at a Gathering, it would spread through the Clans like a forest fire. Ravenpaw was supposed to be dead!

"Is he a loner?" asked Onewhisker.

"He can help us find food," Fireheart meowed quickly, glancing at Ravenpaw.

The black cat nodded. "I know all the best places to hunt around here!" he meowed. His fur didn't even bristle beneath so many hostile gazes. *How much he has changed!* Fireheart thought.

"Why would a loner help us?" demanded Deadfoot.

"Loners have helped us before," Graystripe told him. "Another loner once saved us from a rat attack near here."

Ravenpaw stepped forward and bent his head respectfully as he addressed the WindClan warriors. "Let me help you! I owe my life to Fireheart and Graystripe, and if they're traveling with you, then you must be friends." He lifted his eyes and let his gaze rest on the WindClan cats. They returned his stare, more weary now than hostile. The rain was falling harder and, with their fur bedraggled, they looked skinnier than ever.

"I'll go and find Barley," Ravenpaw meowed. "He will help, too." He turned and disappeared through the long grass.

Tallstar's eyes burned with curiosity, but all he asked Fireheart was, "Can we trust him?"

Fireheart met Tallstar's gaze. "Completely."

Tallstar nodded to his warriors. They let the fur lie flat on their shoulders, and settled down to wait.

Fireheart was almost wet through to his skin when Ravenpaw appeared again. This time Barley was with him. Fireheart greeted the black-and-white loner with a friendly mew. It was good to see him again.

Barley took one look at the dripping cats and meowed, "We need to find you some proper shelter. Follow me!"

Fireheart leaped forward at once, glad to move his stiffening legs. Graystripe was right behind him, but the WindClan cats hung back, fear and suspicion showing in their eyes.

Tallstar blinked at his Clan. "We have to trust him," he growled, before turning to follow the loner. One by one, the WindClan cats fell in step behind their leader.

Barley and Ravenpaw led them through the hedge into another field. In an overgrown corner, among the brambles and nettles, stood an abandoned Twoleg nest. The walls were full of holes where stones had fallen out, and only half the roof was left.

The WindClan cats stared fearfully at it. "You won't get

me in there!" muttered one of the elders.

"Twolegs never come here now," Barley reassured them.

"It'll give us some shelter from the rain," urged Fireheart.

One of the apprentices whispered loudly, "I'm not surprised he wants to hide in a Twoleg nest—once a kittypet, always a kittypet."

Fireheart bristled. He hadn't heard that insult for several moons. But the story that a kittypet had joined a Clan must have made rich gossip at any Gathering. Of course WindClan would know. He whipped around and glared at the apprentice. "You've spent two moons living in a Twoleg tunnel. Does that make you a rat?"

The WindClan apprentice drew himself up, ruffling out his fur, but Graystripe stepped between them. "Come on; we're just getting wetter the longer we stand out here."

Tallstar meowed, "We've faced worse than a Twoleg shelter these past moons. One night here will do us no harm."

The WindClan cats murmured nervously among themselves, clearly reluctant, but with a glance at Fireheart, Morningflower picked up her kit and padded into the Twoleg shelter. The gray queen followed after her, nudging her own kit forward out of the rain. The other cats gradually followed until every cat was inside.

Fireheart looked around the gloomy shelter. The ground was bare except for patches where weeds had burrowed their way under the stone walls. The wind and rain found their way through the gaps in the walls and roof, but it was drier and more sheltered than anywhere outside. He watched the

WindClan cats sniffing cautiously around. As they began to settle themselves away from the dripping holes and drafty cracks, he glanced at Graystripe, relieved. Only Tallstar and Deadfoot remained on their paws.

"What about food?" asked Deadfoot.

Barley spoke. "You should all be resting," he meowed. "Raven—"

Fireheart interrupted him before Barley could finish saying Ravenpaw's name out loud. "Why don't you two show me and Graystripe the best places to hunt around here?"

"Deadfoot and Onewhisker will go with you," meowed Tallstar. Fireheart couldn't decide if the WindClan leader still didn't trust these two strangers, or if he was determined to show that his Clan could look after itself.

The six cats ventured back out into the rain. Hunting would be hard, but Fireheart was starving. Hunger always made him a better hunter. Tonight the voles and mice wouldn't stand a chance. "Just show me where they are!" he meowed to Barley and Ravenpaw.

The two cats led them into a small patch of woodland. Fireheart breathed in a lungful of the familiar scent. Then he dropped into a hunting crouch and began to stalk into the ferns.

When the hunting party returned, each cat carried a mouthful of fresh-kill. The WindClan cats shared a feast with their new allies that night. Every cat from the eldest to the youngest ate their fill, then curled up together to share tongues in mutual grooming, while outside the wind and rain lashed at the walls of the shelter.

As darkness settled in, Barley got to his paws. "I'm off. Rats to catch!" he meowed.

Fireheart stood and touched the loner's nose with his own. "Thank you again," he purred. "This is the second time you've helped us."

"Thanks for sending Ravenpaw to me," replied Barley. "He's turning into a fine ratter. And it's good to share a meal with a fellow cat from time to time."

"Is he happy here?" asked Fireheart.

"Ask him yourself," meowed Barley, and with that he turned and disappeared into the night.

Fireheart padded over to Tallstar, who was washing his paws. Fireheart couldn't help noticing how swollen and painful they looked. "We'll take it in turns to keep watch tonight, if you like," he offered, flicking his head toward Graystripe and Ravenpaw.

Tallstar looked up at him gratefully, exhaustion clouding his eyes. "Thank you," he meowed. Fireheart blinked respectfully at the WindClan leader and went to tell Ravenpaw and Graystripe.

His offer to Tallstar had been genuine, but it also meant he could be alone with his two friends. He was desperate to get Ravenpaw out of earshot of the WindClan cats and ask him what he had been up to. Graystripe and Ravenpaw bounded over to his side as soon as he called them.

Fireheart led them to a corner of the Twoleg nest, close

enough to the entrance for them to keep watch, but far enough away from the other cats that they could talk in private. "So what happened after we left you?" he asked Ravenpaw as soon as the three friends had settled down.

"I headed straight across the WindClan territory, like you suggested."

"What about the Twolegs' dogs?" Graystripe put in. "Were they loose?"

"Yes, but it was easy to avoid them," Ravenpaw told him.

Fireheart was surprised by how casually his friend dismissed the dogs. "Easy?" he echoed.

"I could smell them from a long way off. I just waited until dawn, and once the dogs were tied up again, I tracked down Barley. He's been great. I think he likes having me around." Ravenpaw's expression suddenly clouded. "Which is more than Tigerclaw ever did," he meowed bitterly. "What did you tell him?"

Fireheart recognized the hunted look in Ravenpaw's eyes as he spoke about his old mentor. "We said you'd been killed by a ShadowClan patrol," he answered quietly. Two WindClan apprentices were wandering toward them. Fireheart twitched his ears to warn his friends they had an audience.

"Oh, yes," meowed Ravenpaw, raising his voice. "We loners eat Clan apprentices whenever we can catch one."

The WindClan apprentices shot him a scornful look. "You don't scare us," they mewed.

"Really?" purred Ravenpaw. "Well, I guess your meat would be tough and stringy, anyway."

"How come you're such good friends with a loner?" one apprentice asked Fireheart.

"A wise warrior makes friends wherever he can," Fireheart replied. "If it weren't for this loner, we'd still be cold and hungry instead of dry and well fed!" He narrowed his eyes in warning and the apprentices slunk away.

"So ThunderClan thinks I'm dead," meowed Ravenpaw when they had gone. He gazed down at his paws. "Well, it's probably for the best." He lifted his eyes and looked at Fireheart and Graystripe. "I'm glad I've seen you again," he meowed warmly. Fireheart purred, and Graystripe prodded his friend affectionately with a hind paw. "But you look tired," Ravenpaw continued. "You should get some sleep. I'll keep watch tonight. I can rest tomorrow." He stood up and gently licked each of his old friends on the head. Then he padded to the entrance of the shelter, sat down, and stared out into the rain.

Fireheart looked at Graystripe. "Are you tired?"

"Exhausted," admitted Graystripe. The gray warrior rested his head on his paws and closed his eyes.

Fireheart took a final look at Ravenpaw sitting alone in the entrance. He knew now that he had made the right decision in helping Ravenpaw to leave ThunderClan. Perhaps Bluestar had been right when she'd said Ravenpaw would be better off without the Clan. *Each cat has his own destiny*, he thought. Ravenpaw was happy, and that was all that mattered.

When Fireheart woke, Ravenpaw was gone. It was past dawn. The gray rain clouds had begun to drift away. Tinged by the rosy glow of the rising sun, they looked like blossoms floating across a pond. Fireheart stared through a gap in the roof and watched them as the WindClan cats stirred and helped themselves to the leftovers of last night's catch.

A short-tailed brown tom joined Fireheart and gazed up at the clouds with him. Fireheart jumped as a curious yowl suddenly escaped the brown tom's throat. The noise brought the other WindClan cats crowding around them, murmuring and anxious.

"What is it, Barkface?" prompted Morningflower. "Has StarClan spoken to you?" Fireheart realized that this tom must be WindClan's medicine cat. He tensed instinctively at the sight of Barkface's bristling fur.

"The clouds are stained with blood!" rasped Barkface, his eyes wide and glazed. "It is a sign from our ancestors. There is trouble ahead. This day shall bring an unnecessary death."

CHAPTER 7

For a moment, none of the cats moved or spoke. Then Deadfoot growled, "Any of the Clans could see those clouds. We can't be sure that the message is for us."

Hopeful mews spread through WindClan. Tallstar surveyed his Clan, then meowed calmly, "Whatever StarClan has planned for us, today we return to our home. I can smell more rain in the air. It's time we set off." Fireheart felt relieved at the leader's practical tone. The last thing they needed was hysteria at an ominous prophecy.

Tallstar led the way out into the chilly morning air. Fireheart and Graystripe followed. The WindClan leader was right: the wind carried the promise of more rain, and soon.

"Shall we scout ahead?" Fireheart offered.

"Yes, please," replied Tallstar. "Let me know if you see dogs, Twolegs, or rats. My Clan is stronger this morning, but we had trouble with dogs on the way out. We must stay alert." Fireheart could see from the worried look in the leader's eyes that Barkface's warning had disturbed him more than his confident words suggested. His Clan might be stronger, but it was in no state to fight off attackers.

Fireheart raced away with Graystripe at his heels. They took turns going back to the Clan, telling Tallstar that the way ahead was clear, or warning him to stay back while a Twoleg passed by with a dog. The WindClan cats wordlessly obeyed their leader, plodding on heavy paws in spite of their night's rest.

By sunhigh dark clouds had gathered once more, and the first drops of rain were beginning to fall. The ground began to slope upward, and when Fireheart pushed his way through a hedge, he recognized the red dirt track that led away from Twoleg territory and into WindClan's hunting grounds. His spirits soared, and he met Graystripe's gaze with a look of triumph. *Nearly there!*

The muffled tramp of pawsteps sounded behind the hedge. Fireheart spun around and darted back into the field. The WindClan cats had caught up with them. Deadfoot was at the head of the group. He looked startled by Fireheart's sudden appearance.

"This way," Fireheart meowed, showing him the gap through the dripping leaves. He was eager to see WindClan's reaction when they glimpsed the uplands on the other side. With Deadfoot leading, the cats began to file slowly through.

Fireheart followed close behind the last cat, but Deadfoot and two warriors had already leaped the ditch and crossed the track, and were pushing into the hedgerow on the other side. Their pace had quickened—they clearly knew where they were. Fireheart had to sprint to catch up. He followed them through the hedge and kept up with them as they bounded toward the long slope that led to the uplands, and their home.

At the foot of the slope, Deadfoot and his warriors paused to wait for the rest of the Clan. They closed their eyes against the rain but held their heads high. Fireheart could see their chests rising and falling as they breathed in the familiar scents sweeping from the uplands.

Fireheart ran back to the rest of the Clan, looking for Morningflower. He spotted her walking beside a tabby warrior who held her kit in his mouth. Every few steps the tortoiseshell queen stretched her head to sniff the wet little bundle. It would not be long now before she could settle her kit into the WindClan nursery.

Fireheart fell into step beside Graystripe at the rear. They glanced happily at each other but didn't speak, too caught up in WindClan's excitement at coming home. Even the elders were moving swiftly now, keeping their bodies low and their eyes narrowed against the rain. As the Clan joined Deadfoot at the foot of the slope, the deputy got to his paws and Tallstar took the lead. Without pausing, Tallstar began to follow a narrow sheep trail through the rough grass and heather.

As the Clan neared the top, some of the warriors raced ahead again. At the brow of the hill, they made proud silhouettes against the stormy sky, while the wind sent ripples through their fur. Ahead stretched their old hunting grounds. Suddenly two apprentices charged past Fireheart and bounded away into the familiar heather.

Tallstar stiffened. "Wait!" he yowled. "There might be hunting parties from the other Clans here!"

As soon as they heard him, the apprentices skidded to a halt and pelted back to join the Clan, their eyes still bright with exhilaration.

From a rock-strewn ridge Fireheart saw the dip in the ground that concealed WindClan's camp. With a purr of delight Morningflower took her kit from the mouth of the tabby warrior and hurried toward the hollow. Tallstar flicked his tail and three warriors raced forward to escort her as she disappeared over the edge and down into the camp.

The WindClan leader paused while the rest of his Clan rushed into the sheltering bushes below. He turned to Fireheart and Graystripe, his eyes shining. "My Clan is grateful for your help," he meowed. "You have both proved you are warriors worthy of StarClan. WindClan has come home, and it is time for you to return to yours."

Fireheart felt a pang of disappointment. He'd wanted to see Morningflower settled in the nursery with her kit. But Tallstar was right: there was no need for them to stay here any longer.

Tallstar spoke again. "There may be hostile hunting parties around. Onewhisker and Deadfoot will escort you to Fourtrees."

Fireheart bowed his head. "Thank you, Tallstar."

Tallstar called to his warriors and gave them their orders. Then he turned his tired eyes once more to Fireheart. "You have served WindClan well. Tell Bluestar that WindClan will not forget it was ThunderClan who brought them home."

Deadfoot padded away in the direction of Fourtrees. Fireheart and Graystripe walked after him with Onewhisker at their side. They stayed close together as they followed a narrow path through a solid mass of gorse that provided good shelter against the rain.

Suddenly Onewhisker stopped and sniffed the air. "Rabbit!" he called out joyfully before charging away into the gorse. Deadfoot stopped and waited. Fireheart could see a glint in the deputy's tired eyes. There was a rush of pawsteps in the distance and the rustle of gorse, then silence.

A moment later Onewhisker returned with a large rabbit dangling from his jaws.

Graystripe leaned toward Fireheart. "A little better than the RiverClan warriors, eh?"

Fireheart purred in agreement.

Onewhisker dropped the fresh-kill on the ground. "Anyone hungry?"

They ate the rabbit gratefully. When he'd eaten his share, Fireheart sat up and licked his lips. He felt refreshed by the meal, but a weary coldness was beginning to nag at his bones, and his paws felt sore. If he and Graystripe followed the route they'd come, past Fourtrees, they still had a long way to go. What if they took a shortcut through RiverClan's hunting grounds? After all, they were on a mission that had been agreed to, at the Gathering at least, by all the Clans. Could RiverClan really object if they passed through their territory? It wasn't as if they were going to steal prey.

Fireheart looked around at his companions and meowed tentatively, "You know, it'd be quicker if we followed the river."

Graystripe looked up from washing his paw. "But that would mean crossing into RiverClan territory."

"We could follow the gorge," Fireheart explained. "River-Clan doesn't hunt there; it's too steep for them to get down to the river."

Graystripe gently rested a damp paw on the ground. "Even my claws ache," he murmured. "I wouldn't mind taking a shorter route." He turned his yellow eyes hopefully to the WindClan deputy.

Deadfoot looked thoughtful. "Tallstar ordered us to travel with you to Fourtrees," he meowed.

"If you don't want to come with us, we'll understand," Fireheart answered quickly. "We'll only be in RiverClan territory for a blink. I can't see us meeting any trouble."

Graystripe nodded, but Deadfoot shook his head. "We couldn't let you go into RiverClan territory alone," he meowed. "You're exhausted. If you did meet trouble, you're in no state to deal with it."

"We won't meet anyone!" Fireheart had convinced himself and was determined to convince Deadfoot too.

Deadfoot gazed at him with wise old eyes. "If we did go that way," he mused, "it would let RiverClan know that WindClan is back."

Fireheart pricked his ears in understanding. "And once they've smelled fresh WindClan scent, they might not be so keen to come rabbit hunting in your territory again.'"

Onewhisker licked the last traces of fresh-kill from his lips and remarked, "It'll mean we'll be home before moonrise!"

"You just want to make sure you get a good nest in your den!" Deadfoot retorted. His voice was stern but there was a good-natured gleam in his eye.

"Then we're going through RiverClan territory?" Fireheart asked.

"Yes," decided Deadfoot. He changed direction and led the cats along an old badger trail that took them away from the barren uplands. Soon they were in RiverClan's territory. Even through the wind and the rain, Fireheart could hear the roaring of the river as it crashed and thundered somewhere up ahead.

The cats followed the trail toward the noise. The path shrank until it was little more than a narrow strip of grass on the very edge of a deep gorge. On one side the land stretched upward, steep and rocky; on the other it plunged straight down. Fireheart could see the far side of the gorge only a few fox-lengths away. The space looked tantalizingly narrow, and Fireheart wondered if he could leap the gap. Perhaps if he weren't so tired and hungry . . . His paws prickled with fear at the thought of falling, but he couldn't resist peering over the side.

Beneath his paws, the ground dropped away in a sheer cliff. Ferns clung to tiny ledges, their leaves glistening, not from rain, but from the spray of the swollen torrent that foamed at the bottom of the gorge.

Fireheart pulled back from the edge, the fur along his spine bristling with fear. Ahead of him Deadfoot, Onewhisker, and Graystripe plodded steadily on, heads down. They would have to follow this path until they could cut away from it, through the small strip of forest that stood between them and ThunderClan territory.

Fireheart stumbled as he hurried to catch up. Deadfoot's ears were pricked and his tail flattened so that it almost dragged along the ground. Onewhisker was clearly nervous too; he kept looking sharply up the slope beside them as if he could hear something. Fireheart could hear nothing but the roaring of the river. He glanced anxiously over his shoulder, his eyes darting from side to side. The WindClan cats' wariness was making him uneasy.

The steep slope began to flatten out until they could move farther away from the cliff edge. The rain was still driving into their faces, and the darkening sky told Fireheart that the sun was setting, but it would not be long now before they reached the forest. There would be more shelter there. The thought of food and a dry nest cheered Fireheart.

Suddenly a warning yowl rumbled in Deadfoot's throat. Fireheart stiffened and tasted the air. A RiverClan patrol! A screech sounded from behind them, and the cats spun around to see six RiverClan warriors charging toward them. Fireheart's fur stood on end with horror. The deep gorge with its raging waters was still dangerously close.

A dark brown RiverClan cat landed on top of him. Fireheart rolled away from the gorge, kicking furiously with his back legs. He felt teeth bite into his shoulders and struggled under the weight of the hissing warrior. He scrabbled desperately on the sodden ground, trying to free himself. The RiverClan warrior raked his side with sharp claws. Fireheart twisted and bit into the fur of his attacker. He clamped his jaws tight and heard the warrior yowl, but the other cat's claws only raked him more fiercely. "This will be the last time you set foot in RiverClan territory," hissed the brown tom.

Around him Fireheart was aware of his companions struggling fiercely. He knew they were as exhausted as he was from the long trek. He could hear Graystripe yowling violently. Onewhisker hissed with pain and rage. Then, from the forest behind them, another sound reached Fireheart's ears. It was full of fury—yet it filled Fireheart with a surge of hope. Tigerclaw's war cry! Fireheart smelled the fast-approaching battle-scent of a ThunderClan patrol—Tigerclaw, Willowpelt, Whitestorm, and Sandpaw.

Yowling and spitting, the ThunderClan cats leaped into the fray. The brown tom released Fireheart and he quickly struggled to his paws. He watched as Tigerclaw pinned a gray tabby tom to the ground, giving a warning bite to the tom's hind leg. The tom ran screeching away into the bushes. Tigerclaw whipped around and fixed his pale eyes on Leopardfur. The mottled RiverClan deputy was wrestling with Deadfoot. The lame warrior was no match for the ferocious RiverClan she-cat. Fireheart prepared to leap to the rescue, but Tigerclaw was ahead of him. The dark warrior dived forward and grasped Leopardfur's wide shoulders. With a mighty yowl, he hauled her off the scrawny WindClan deputy.

Fireheart heard a vicious squeal behind him. He spun around to see Sandpaw locked in battle with another River-Clan she-cat. Twisting and tussling, the pair rolled over and over on the wet grass, spitting and clawing each other fiercely. Fireheart gasped. They were rolling toward the rocky edge of the gorge! One more roll and they would be over the side.

Fireheart sprang. With a mighty swipe he bundled the RiverClan warrior off Sandpaw and away from the edge. Sandpaw skidded away, closer to the drop. Fireheart lunged forward and grabbed her by the scruff of her neck with his teeth. She squealed with rage as he dragged her away from the gorge, her paws scrabbling on the muddy ground. She sprang to her paws as soon as he stopped and hissed at Fireheart, her eyes burning with fury, "I can win my own battles without your help!"

Fireheart opened his mouth to explain but a terrible howl made them both turn their heads. Graystripe was leaning perilously over the side of the gorge, his hind legs straining. Beside him, Fireheart glimpsed a white paw clutching at the edge. Graystripe leaned down with his mouth open, trying to get a grip on the paw, but it disappeared out of sight in a terrifying rush. Graystripe cried out after it, his wail echoing along the gorge.

All the cats stopped fighting at the sound of Graystripe's agonized call. Fireheart froze, panting with shock and exhaustion. The RiverClan cats scrambled to the edge of the gorge. Slowly Fireheart followed them and looked over the side. Far below, through the deafening spray, he saw the dark head of a RiverClan warrior sink beneath the foaming water.

With a cold feeling of horror, Fireheart recalled the words of the WindClan medicine cat: "This day shall bring an unnecessary death."

CHAPTER 8

🍀

Leopardfur lifted her head and yowled into the wind, "Whiteclaw! No!"

Graystripe scrambled backward until all four paws were on safe ground. His wet fur was bristling and his eyes were wide with shock. "I tried to grab him . . . he just lost his footing . . . I didn't mean to . . ." The words tumbled out breathlessly. Fireheart bounded across to his friend and pressed his nose into his flank for comfort, but Graystripe backed blindly away.

One by one, the other cats turned away from the edge and looked at Graystripe. The RiverClan cats' eyes were narrowed with fury, their shoulders tense. Willowpelt and Whitestorm moved instinctively toward Graystripe, taking up defensive positions on either side of him.

Leopardfur growled deep in her throat, but it was a warning to her own cats. They were to stay back. The RiverClan deputy stared Tigerclaw straight in the eye. "This has gone beyond a border fight," she murmured. "We shall return to our Clan. It has become a matter to settle at another time and in a different way."

Tigerclaw defiantly returned Leopardfur's stare. He

showed no fear, but merely gave the smallest of nods. Leopardfur flicked the tip of her tail, then turned and padded
away. The RiverClan cats followed her, and the whole patrol
disappeared into the bushes.

Leopardfur's menacing words made Fireheart shiver. A
sense of foreboding settled over his heart like a cold shadow
as he realized that this battle might have started a war.

"We should leave," meowed Deadfoot, limping forward.
"Your two young warriors served us well, and my Clan thanks
you." But the formal words of gratitude sounded hollow after
the tragedy they had just witnessed. Tigerclaw nodded, and
the two WindClan warriors began to head back toward their
own territory. Fireheart meowed a quiet farewell to Onewhisker as he passed. Onewhisker glanced briefly at him, and
walked on.

Fireheart noticed that Sandpaw was standing at the edge
of the gorge, staring down at the torrent below. Her paws
seemed frozen to the ground, and her eyes remained fixed on
the steep drop. Fireheart guessed she had realized how close
she had come to sharing Whiteclaw's fate.

Fireheart started toward her but Tigerclaw growled, "Follow me!"

The tabby warrior charged away through the trees, and the
rest of his patrol followed after him, but Fireheart hesitated
beside Graystripe. "Come on," he urged. "We should keep
up!" Graystripe shrugged, his eyes dull and clouded with pain,
and began to pad after the others, dragging his paws as if they
were made from stone.

Soon the cats ahead of them were out of sight, but Fireheart was able to track them by their scent. Tigerclaw was leading them back toward ThunderClan territory, straight through RiverClan's strip of forest. Fireheart guessed there was no need to worry about RiverClan patrols right now. The damage had been done. It would be pointless to take the long way around by Fourtrees.

Tigerclaw had halted the patrol and was waiting for Fireheart and Graystripe at the border of ThunderClan's territory.

"I thought I told you to follow me," he growled.

"Graystripe was—" Fireheart began.

"The sooner Graystripe gets back to camp, the better," interrupted Tigerclaw.

Graystripe said nothing, but Fireheart bristled at the deputy's harsh tone. "Whiteclaw's death wasn't his fault!"

Tigerclaw turned away. "I know," he meowed. "But it's done. Come on, and this time keep up!" He leaped away, crossing the scent markers that bounded ThunderClan territory.

Fireheart had been looking forward to this moment since leaving WindClan's den among the Thunderpaths. Now he hardly noticed as he pounded past the markers, keeping one eye on Graystripe.

The rain eased as they followed the familiar trail to the camp. When the patrol emerged from the gorse tunnel, some of the other Clan cats bounded out of their dens, their tails held high in greeting.

"Did you find WindClan? Are they safe?" Mousefur

called. Fireheart nodded absently, but felt too hollow to reply. Mousefur's tail dropped. The other cats hung back at the edge of the clearing. The expressions on the faces of the returning cats told them that something serious had happened.

"Come with me," Tigerclaw ordered Fireheart and Graystripe, leading them toward Bluestar's den. Fireheart kept close to Graystripe so that his fur brushed against his friend. Graystripe just padded onward, neither drawing closer to Fireheart nor moving away.

A warm mew welcomed them from the shadows beyond the lichen. The three cats pushed their way into the snug cave.

"Welcome!" Bluestar leaped up, purring. "Did you find WindClan? Did you bring them back?"

"Yes, Bluestar," Fireheart replied quietly. "They are safe in their camp. Tallstar told me to thank you."

"Good, good," meowed Bluestar. Her eyes darkened as she noticed Tigerclaw's grim expression. "What has happened?"

"Fireheart decided to return home through RiverClan territory," growled Tigerclaw.

Graystripe looked up for the first time. "It wasn't just Fireheart who decided—" he began.

Tigerclaw interrupted him. "They were found by a RiverClan patrol. If my patrol hadn't heard their yelps in time, they wouldn't have made it home at all."

"So you rescued them," meowed Bluestar, relaxing. "Thank you, Tigerclaw."

"It's not that simple." Tigerclaw snorted. "They were

fighting beside the gorge. A RiverClan warrior who was battling Graystripe fell over the edge." Fireheart noticed Graystripe flinch at Tigerclaw's words.

Bluestar's eyes widened. "Dead?" she asked, looking horrified.

Fireheart meowed quickly, "It was an accident! Graystripe would never kill a cat over a border fight!"

"I doubt Leopardfur sees it that way." Tigerclaw turned on Fireheart, his tail lashing from side to side. "What were you thinking? Traveling through RiverClan territory! And with WindClan cats. You've sent a message that we are their allies, which will only drive RiverClan and ShadowClan closer together."

"WindClan was with you in RiverClan territory?" Bluestar looked even more alarmed.

"Just two warriors. Tallstar gave us an escort home; we were tired. . . ." Fireheart murmured.

"You should not have been in RiverClan territory," Tigerclaw snarled. "Especially with WindClan cats."

"It wasn't an alliance. They were escorting us back home!" Fireheart protested.

"Does RiverClan know that?" spat Tigerclaw.

"RiverClan knew we were going to find WindClan and bring them back. They agreed to it at the Gathering. They shouldn't have attacked us—it was a special mission, like the journey to Highstones."

"They didn't agree to let you travel through their territory!"

spat Tigerclaw. "You *still* don't understand Clan ways, do you?"

Bluestar stood up. Her eyes flashed as she looked around at the three cats, but her voice was calm. "You should not have entered RiverClan's hunting grounds. It was a dangerous thing to do." She looked sternly from Fireheart to Graystripe. Fireheart searched her eyes for a harsher reproach, but could find none. He felt torn between gratitude and guilt. He had caused a rift with RiverClan that might threaten the safety of his Clan for many moons.

Bluestar went on, flicking her tail uneasily. "At the same time, you did well to find WindClan and bring it back. But we will need to prepare ourselves for an attack from River-Clan. We need to start training more warriors. Fireheart and Graystripe, Frostfur tells me two of her kits are almost ready to begin their training. I want each of you to take a kit as your apprentice."

Fireheart felt stunned. What an honor! He couldn't believe Bluestar had suggested it—especially now. He glanced furtively at Tigerclaw. The deputy sat rigid as a rock.

Graystripe raised his head. "But none of Frostfur's kits are six moons yet!"

"It won't be long before they are. The divisions at the last Gathering troubled me, and today . . ." Bluestar's voice trailed off, and Fireheart noticed Graystripe look down at his paws once more.

Tigerclaw was staring at Bluestar, his amber eyes hard. "Wouldn't it be better to ask more experienced warriors like

Longtail or Darkstripe to take on another apprentice?" he asked. "These two are hardly more than apprentices themselves!"

"I did consider that," replied Bluestar. "But Longtail will be busy enough with Swiftpaw, and Darkstripe is getting Dustpaw ready to become a full warrior."

"What about Runningwind?" Tigerclaw asked.

"Runningwind is a fine hunter and a loyal warrior," Bluestar answered. "But I don't think he has the patience for mentoring. ThunderClan has better use for his skills."

"And you think these two have got what it takes to train ThunderClan warriors?" Tigerclaw meowed scornfully.

Fireheart flinched. Tigerclaw was eyeing him alone as he spoke. *Does he think a kittypet is not fit to train Clanborn cats?* he wondered angrily.

Bluestar stared back at her deputy. "We shall find out. Don't forget, they brought WindClan home. And of course, Tigerclaw," she added, "I am relying on you to oversee the training." Tigerclaw nodded, and Bluestar turned back to Fireheart and Graystripe. "Get something to eat," she ordered. "Then rest. We'll have the naming ceremony for the kits at moonhigh."

Fireheart led Graystripe out of the den, leaving Tigerclaw behind with Bluestar. The rain had eased to a fine drizzle.

"I'm starving," meowed Fireheart. He could smell the warm scent of fresh-kill in the clearing. "Are you coming to get something to eat?"

Graystripe stood behind him, his eyes distant and sad. He slowly shook his head. "I just want to sleep," he muttered.

Once his stomach was full, Fireheart pushed his way into the warriors' den. Graystripe was curled up in a ball, his head tucked beneath his paws. Fireheart's eyes felt heavy, but his fur was still soaked, and he forced himself to wash thoroughly before settling into his warm nest.

Willowpelt woke Fireheart with a gentle prod. "Time for the ceremony," she whispered.

Fireheart lifted his head and blinked. "Thanks, Willowpelt," he meowed as she ducked out of the den.

He nudged Graystripe. "Ceremony," he hissed, then stood and stretched up on his toes until his legs quivered. He was about to become a mentor! Excitement tingled in his paws.

Graystripe stirred and uncurled slowly, like an old cat. Suddenly Fireheart's paws seemed to remember their long journey and began to ache again.

At least the rain had stopped. In silence, Fireheart and Graystripe padded into the clearing. The moon shone above the trees, turning the wet branches silver.

"Well done for bringing WindClan home!" The cheery voice made Fireheart jump. He turned to see Halftail settling down beside him. "You must come and share the story with the elders one night."

Fireheart nodded absently, then looked back into the clearing. Frostfur was already sitting below the Highrock. A kit sat on either side of her, one smudgy gray and one ginger. The white queen twisted her head and licked behind their ears. The little gray she-kit shook her head impatiently as her mother fussed over her.

Once more, excitement made Fireheart's fur tingle.

Beside him Graystripe sat staring at the ground. "Aren't you excited?" Fireheart asked.

Graystripe shrugged.

"Graystripe"—Fireheart lowered his voice—"Whiteclaw's death wasn't your fault. It was the worst place for an attack, and the RiverClan cats would have known that. Sandpaw nearly fell over the edge too," he added.

He glanced at Sandpaw sitting nearby. Beside her, Dustpaw stared at Fireheart with raw jealousy in his eyes. Fireheart couldn't blame him. He was about to become a mentor when Dustpaw hadn't even been given his warrior name. But he flinched when Dustpaw leaned toward Sandpaw and whispered, loud enough for Fireheart to hear, "I feel sorry for Fireheart's apprentice. Imagine a Clan cat being trained by a kittypet!"

But for once Sandpaw didn't react. She just shot an uncomfortable glance at Fireheart.

Fireheart turned back to Graystripe. "Bluestar doesn't blame you," he insisted. "She knows you're a good warrior. She's giving you your own apprentice."

Graystripe lifted his eyes and replied bitterly, "She's just doing it because ThunderClan needs more apprentices. And why do we need them? Because I've given RiverClan an excuse to hate us!"

Fireheart was shocked by the harshness in Graystripe's tone. Bluestar's meow summoned them before he could say anything more. Fireheart padded toward his Clan leader, Graystripe trailing after him.

When they reached the center of the clearing, Bluestar gazed around at the assembly of cats. "This moonhigh, we gather together to name two new apprentices. Come forward, you two."

The gray kit darted from her mother's side into the clearing, her fluffy tail held high and her blue eyes wide. The ginger kit came forward more slowly. His ears were pricked, and he frowned with seriousness as he walked to the foot of the Highrock.

Fireheart's heart began to pound in his chest—which one of these kits would he be given? He couldn't help feeling that the solemn-faced ginger kit would be easier to train, but there was something about the gray kit's clumsy enthusiasm that reminded him of himself when he had first joined the Clan.

"From this day forward," Bluestar meowed, gazing down at the little gray kit, "until she has earned her warrior name, this apprentice will be called Cinderpaw."

"Cinderpaw!" The gray kit couldn't help mewing her new name out loud. A quietening hiss came from Frostfur, and Cinderpaw ducked her head apologetically.

"Fireheart," meowed Bluestar, "you are ready for your first apprentice. You will begin Cinderpaw's training." Pride swelled in Fireheart's chest. "You are fortunate, Fireheart, to have had more than one mentor. I expect you to pass on everything I taught you to this young apprentice"—Fireheart suddenly began to feel a bit overwhelmed. Bluestar's words carried a weight of responsibility he wasn't sure he was ready for—"and share with her the skills you learned from Tigerclaw and Lionheart."

At the mention of Lionheart, Fireheart pictured the golden warrior looking down on him from Silverpelt with warm, encouraging eyes. He lifted his head and returned Bluestar's gaze as steadily as he could.

"And this apprentice"—Bluestar turned her gaze toward the ginger kit—"will be known as Brackenpaw." Brackenpaw didn't move or make a sound.

"Graystripe, you will train Brackenpaw. Our lost friend Lionheart was your mentor. I hope that his skill and wisdom will pass through you to your new apprentice."

Graystripe lifted his head high at Bluestar's words, and for a moment a gleam of pride showed in his eyes. He stepped forward and touched his new apprentice's nose with his own. Brackenpaw returned the touch politely. Only his eyes, which shone like stars, gave away the fact that this young cat was as excited as his sister.

As soon as Fireheart saw the pair touch noses, he realized he should have done the same. He stepped forward quickly. Cinderpaw jerked her head up and their noses collided painfully. Cinderpaw touched his nose again, this time less awkwardly, but Fireheart's eyes were beginning to water. He could see that Cinderpaw was trying to stop her whiskers from twitching with amusement, and a flush of embarrassment washed over him. *I'm a mentor,* he reminded himself.

Fireheart looked around at the rest of the Clan. Every

cat seemed to be nodding approvingly. Then his eyes found Tigerclaw. From the edge of the clearing, the deputy's amber gaze seemed to mock him.

Fireheart looked hastily down at Cinderpaw, who was staring at him with undisguised pride. Fireheart's fur suddenly began to prickle. He wanted to be a great warrior and a good mentor more than anything else, but it seemed painfully clear that Tigerclaw was just waiting for him to fail.

CHAPTER 9

Fireheart woke to find Graystripe sitting beside him, hunched on his belly like a rabbit, his shoulders stiff and his fur fluffed out. "Graystripe?" he meowed quietly.

Graystripe jumped.

"Are you okay?"

Graystripe sat up straight. "I'm fine." Fireheart suspected that his friend's cheery mew wasn't heartfelt, but at least he was trying to be more positive.

"It looks cold," Fireheart meowed. Graystripe's words had billowed out in clouds. Fireheart was still snuggled down among the warm bodies of the other warriors.

"It is!" Graystripe bent to lick his chest.

Fireheart sat up and shook his head. The air tasted of frost. "What are you going to do with Brackenpaw today?" he asked.

"Show him the forest," answered Graystripe.

"I could bring Cinderpaw, and we could travel together."

"It might be better if we travel alone today," answered Graystripe.

Fireheart felt a bit hurt. They had been shown Thunder-Clan's hunting grounds together as apprentices. He would have liked to do it together again as mentors. But if Graystripe wanted to be by himself, then Fireheart could hardly blame him. "Fine," he mewed. "I'll see you later. We can share a mouse and compare apprentices."

"That'd be good," Graystripe meowed.

Fireheart crept out of the den. The air outside was even colder. His breath swirled from his muzzle like smoke. He shivered, ruffling out his fur, and stretched one leg at a time. The ground under his paws felt like stone as he trotted over to the apprentices' den. Cinderpaw was fast asleep inside, a fluffy gray heap that rose and fell as she breathed.

"Cinderpaw," Fireheart called quietly, and the little gray cat lifted her head at once. Fireheart backed out, and in a moment Cinderpaw bounded from the den, wide-awake and enthusiastic.

"What are we doing today?" she mewed, looking up at him with her ears pricked.

"I thought I'd take you on a tour of ThunderClan territory."

"Will we see the Thunderpath?" asked Cinderpaw eagerly.

"Er, yes, we will," Fireheart replied. He couldn't help thinking Cinderpaw would be disappointed when she saw what a dirty, stinking place it was. "Are you hungry?" he asked, wondering if he should tell her to eat first.

"No!" Cinderpaw shook her head.

"Oh, okay. We'll eat later," Fireheart meowed. "Well, follow me."

"Yes, Fireheart." The young cat looked up at him, her eyes

sparkling. The pang of sadness that had been lingering in Fireheart's stomach since talking with Graystripe was swept away by a warm feeling of pride. He turned and padded toward the camp entrance.

Cinderpaw raced past him and charged through the gorse tunnel. Fireheart had to break into a run to catch up. "I thought I said follow me!" he called as she scrambled up the side of the ravine.

"But I want to see the view from the top," Cinderpaw protested.

Fireheart leaped after her. He overtook her easily, climbed to the top, and sat washing a forepaw, keeping an eye on her as she scrambled from rock to rock. By the time she reached the top of the camp ravine she was panting, but no less enthusiastic. "Look at the trees! They look like they're made from moonstone," she mewed breathlessly.

She was right. The trees below them sparkled white in the sunshine. Fireheart took a deep breath of cold air. "You should try to save your energy," he warned. "We have a long way to go today."

"Oh, yes. Okay. Which way now?" She kneaded the ground with impatient paws, ready to dart away into the woods.

"Follow me," meowed Fireheart. He narrowed his eyes playfully. "And this time I do mean *follow*!" He led the way to a trail along the edge of the ravine, into the sandy hollow where he had learned to hunt and fight.

"This is where most of our training sessions will be held," he explained. During greenleaf, the trees that circled the clearing filtered the sunshine into a warm dappled light. Now cold daylight streamed down onto the frozen red earth.

"A river ran here many moons ago. A stream still flows beyond that rise there," meowed Fireheart, pointing with his muzzle. "It's dry most of the summer. That's where I caught my first prey."

"What did you catch?" Cinderpaw didn't wait for an answer. "Will the stream be frozen? Let's look and see if there's ice!" She charged down into the hollow and headed toward the rise.

"You'll see it another time!" Fireheart called. But Cinderpaw kept running, and Fireheart had to race after her. He stopped beside her at the top of the rise and together they looked down at the stream. Ice had formed at the edges, but the speed of the water as it slid over its sandy bed had stopped it from freezing over completely.

"You wouldn't catch much there now," mewed Cinderpaw. "Except fish maybe."

The sight of the spot where he had caught his first prey filled Fireheart with happy memories. He watched Cinderpaw stand at the edge of the stream and crane her neck to peer into the black water. "If I were you, I'd leave fishing to RiverClan," Fireheart warned her. "If they like getting their fur wet, then let them. I prefer dry paws."

Cinderpaw padded restlessly around in a circle. "What now?"

Her excitement, and his own apprentice memories, filled Fireheart with energy. He bounded away, calling over his shoulder, "The Owl Tree!" Cinderpaw charged after him, her short fluffy tail sticking out behind her.

They crossed the stream over a fallen tree Fireheart had used many times before. "There are stepping-stones farther down, but this is a quicker route. Be careful though!" The pale white trunk was stripped of its bark. "It gets slippery when it's wet or icy."

He let Cinderpaw cross first, keeping close behind in case she lost her pawhold. The stream wasn't particularly deep, but it would be cold as ice, and Cinderpaw was still too small to cope with a soaking.

She crossed the log easily, and Fireheart felt a glow of pride as he watched his apprentice jump down onto the forest floor at the far end. "Well done," he purred.

Cinderpaw's eyes shone. "Thanks," she mewed. "Now, where's this Owl Tree?"

"This way!" Fireheart bounded away through the undergrowth. The ferns had turned brown since greenleaf. By the end of leaf-fall, they would be flattened by rain and wind, but now they still stood tall and crisp. Fireheart and Cinderpaw wove their way beneath the arching fronds.

Ahead, a massive oak towered above the surrounding trees. Cinderpaw tipped her head back, looking for the top. "Does an owl really live here?" she mewed.

"Yes," replied Fireheart. "Can you see the hole in the trunk up there?"

Cinderpaw narrowed her eyes to peer through the branches. "How do you know it's not a squirrel hole?"

"Smell!" Fireheart told her.

Cinderpaw sniffed loudly but shook her head, her eyes curious as she looked up at Fireheart.

"I'll show you what squirrels smell like another time," Fireheart meowed. "You won't smell any around here. No squirrel would dare make its nest so near an owl hole. Look at the ground; what do you see?"

Cinderpaw looked down, puzzled. "Leaves?"

"Try burrowing under the leaves."

The forest floor was carpeted with brown oak leaves, crisp with frost. Cinderpaw began snuffling among them and then shoved her nose in right up to her ears. When she sat up there was something the size and shape of a pinecone in her mouth. "Yuck, smells like crow-food!" she spat. Fireheart purred with amusement.

"You knew it was there, didn't you?"

"Bluestar played the same trick on me when I was an apprentice. You'll never forget the stench."

"What is it?"

"An owl pod," Fireheart explained. He remembered what Bluestar had told him. "Owls eat the same prey as us, but they can't digest the bones and fur, so their bellies roll the leftovers into pods and they spit them out. If you find one of those under a tree, it means you've found an owl."

"Why would you want to find an owl?" squeaked Cinderpaw in alarm. Fireheart's whiskers twitched as he looked into her wide eyes, as blue as her mother's. Frostfur must have told her the elders' tale of how owls carried off young kits who strayed from their mother's side.

"Owls get a better view of the forest than we do. On windy nights, when scents are hard to follow, you can look out for owls and follow where they hunt." Cinderpaw's eyes were still wide, but the fear had left them, and she nodded. *She does listen sometimes!* Fireheart thought with relief.

"Where next?" mewed Cinderpaw.

"The Great Sycamore," Fireheart decided. They traveled through the woods as the sun rose into the pale blue sky, crossing a Twoleg path and another tiny stream. Eventually they arrived at the sycamore tree.

"It's huge!" Cinderpaw gasped.

"Smallear says he climbed to the top branch when he was an apprentice," Fireheart meowed.

"No way!" mewed Cinderpaw.

"Mind you, when Smallear was an apprentice, this tree was probably only a sapling!" Fireheart joked. He was still gazing up when a rustling sound behind him told him Cinderpaw had dashed off again. He sighed and chased after her through the bracken. His nose detected a familiar scent that made him nervous. Cinderpaw was heading toward Snakerocks. *Adders!* Fireheart picked up his pace.

He emerged from the trees and looked around anxiously. Cinderpaw was standing on a boulder at the bottom of the steep, rocky slope. "Come on; I'll race you to the top!" she mewed.

Fireheart froze, horror-struck, as she crouched, ready to spring onto the next boulder. "Cinderpaw! Get down from there!" he yowled.

He held his breath as Cinderpaw turned and scrambled down again. She stood trembling, her fur on end, as Fireheart rushed over to her. "This place is called Snakerocks," he puffed.

Cinderpaw looked up at him, her eyes huge. "Snakerocks?"

"Adders live up there. A bite from one of those would kill a cat as small as you!" Fireheart gave Cinderpaw a quick lick on top of her head. "Come on. Let's have a look at the Thunderpath."

Cinderpaw stopped shaking at once. "The Thunderpath?"

"Yep," meowed Fireheart. "Follow me!" He led Cinderpaw through the ferns, along a trail that skirted Snakerocks and took them to the part of the forest where the Thunderpath cut through like a hard, gray river of stone.

Fireheart kept one eye on Cinderpaw as they peered out from the edge of the forest. He could see from her twitching tail that Cinderpaw was desperate to creep forward and sniff the Thunderpath ahead of them. A familiar roar was beginning to ruffle his ear fur, and he could feel the ground trembling beneath his paws. "Stay where you are!" he warned. "There's a monster coming."

Cinderpaw opened her mouth a little. "Yuck!" she mewed, screwing up her nose and flattening her ears. The rumbling noise was coming closer, and a shape appeared on the horizon. "Is that a monster?" she mewed. Fireheart nodded.

Cinderpaw unsheathed her claws to grip the earth as the monster roared closer. She shut her eyes tight as it charged past, stirring the air around them into a storm of wind and thunder. She kept her eyes shut until the noise had faded into the distance.

Fireheart shook his head to clear his scent glands. "Sniff the air," he meowed. "Can you smell anything apart from the Thunderpath stench?" He waited while Cinderpaw lifted her head and took several deep breaths.

After a few moments she mewed, "I remember that scent from when Brokenstar attacked our camp. And it was on the kits he took, when you brought them home. It's ShadowClan! Is that their territory, beyond the Thunderpath?"

"Yes," Fireheart answered, feeling his fur tingle at the thought of being so close to hostile Clan territory. "We'd better get out of here."

He decided to take Cinderpaw the long way home past Twolegplace, so she could see Tallpines and the Treecut place.

As they padded beneath the thin pine trees, the scents of Twolegplace made Fireheart uneasy, even though he'd lived in a place not far from there as a kit. "Stay alert," he warned Cinderpaw as she crept along behind him. "Twolegs sometimes walk here with dogs."

The two cats crouched under the trees to look at the fences that bordered the Twoleg territory. The crisp air carried a scent to Fireheart's nose that stirred an odd feeling of warmth inside him, although he didn't know why.

"Look!" Cinderpaw pointed with her nose at a she-cat padding across the forest floor. The light brown tabby had a distinctive white chest and white front paws. Her belly was swollen, heavy with unborn kits.

"Kittypet!" sneered Cinderpaw, her fur fluffed out. "Let's chase her out!"

Fireheart expected to feel the familiar rush of aggression at the sight of a stranger on ThunderClan territory, but his hackles stayed flat. For some reason he couldn't understand, he knew this cat wasn't a threat. Before Cinderpaw could attack, Fireheart deliberately brushed against a stalk of crunchy bracken.

The she-cat looked up, disturbed by the crackling noise. Her eyes widened with alarm; then she whipped around and set off at a lumbering pace, out of the trees. Within moments she was heaving herself over one of the Twoleg fences.

"Rats!" complained Cinderpaw. "I wanted to chase her! I bet Brackenpaw will have chased hundreds of things today."

"Yeah, but he probably didn't nearly get bitten by an adder," replied Fireheart, twitching his tail at her. "Now come on; I'm getting hungry."

Cinderpaw followed him through Tallpines, grumbling about the pine needles pricking her paws. Fireheart warned her to keep quiet, since there was no undergrowth here to hide in and he felt every Clan cat's discomfort at being in the open. They followed one of the stinking tracks gouged out by the Treecut monster and stopped at the edge of the Treecut place. It was silent, as Fireheart knew it would be until next greenleaf. Until then, only the track marks—deep and wide and frozen into the soil—would remind ThunderClan of the monster that lived in their forest.

By the time they arrived back at camp, Fireheart was exhausted; his muscles were still weary from the long journey with WindClan. Cinderpaw looked tired too. She stifled a yawn and padded away to find Brackenpaw.

Fireheart spotted Graystripe beckoning to him from beside the nettle clump.

"Here, I've got you some fresh-kill," Graystripe meowed. He hooked a dead mouse with his claw and flung it toward Fireheart.

Fireheart caught it in his teeth and lay down next to Graystripe. "Good day?" he mumbled with his mouth full.

"Better than yesterday," answered Graystripe. Fireheart glanced up at him, worried, but Graystripe went on: "I enjoyed it, actually. Brackenpaw's keen to learn, that's for sure!"

"So is Cinderpaw." Fireheart went back to chewing.

"Mind you," Graystripe went on with a sparkle in his eye, "I kept forgetting I was the mentor and not the apprentice!"

"Me too," Fireheart admitted.

They shared tongues until the moon rose and the coldness of the night drove them into their den. Graystripe was snoring within moments, but Fireheart felt strangely awake. The image of the pregnant she-cat kept returning to his mind, and even though he was surrounded by the familiar smells of ThunderClan, her soft kittypet scent lingered in his nostrils.

He fell asleep at last, but his dreams all carried the same scent, until finally he dreamed of his days as a kit. He remembered lying beside his mother's belly, curled in a bed softer than any forest moss with his brothers and sisters. And still the scent of the she-cat lingered.

Fireheart opened his eyes, suddenly jolted out of his sleep. Of course! The she-cat he had seen in the woods . . . was his sister!

CHAPTER 10

Fireheart woke at dawn with the image of his sister still clear in his mind. He pushed his way out of the den, hoping the routine of the day would distract him. It was another cold, frosty morning. Whitestorm and Longtail were waiting near the camp entrance, preparing to leave on patrol. Mousefur padded past on her way to join them and greeted Fireheart with a cheery mew. Whitestorm called for Sandpaw, who came racing out of her den just in time to follow the patrol as it pounded out of the camp. It was a scene Fireheart had watched many times, but for once he didn't yearn to join them as they thundered away into the morning-fresh forest.

He padded across the clearing, wondering if Cinderpaw was awake yet. Brindleface was just squeezing out of the narrow nursery entrance. A speckled kit followed her, then one more. A third kit, pale gray with darker flecks like the other, tumbled out and fell onto the ground.

Brindleface picked it up by its scruff and placed it gently back on its paws. The tenderness of Brindleface's action brought Fireheart's dream flooding back. His mother had probably done the same for him. He knew that Brindleface's fourth kit had died soon after it was born, and she seemed to love the remaining kits even more fiercely now.

Fireheart was overwhelmed by a pang of envy at the thought that the other cats here all shared something he did not—*they were all Clanborn*. Fireheart had always been proud of his loyalty to the Clan that had taken him in and given him a life he would never have known as a kittypet. He still felt that loyalty—he would die to protect ThunderClan—but no one in the Clan understood or even respected his kittypet roots. Fireheart felt certain the she-cat he had seen yesterday would. With an ache in his heart, he wondered what memories they might share.

Fireheart heard Graystripe's heavy pawsteps behind him. He turned to greet his friend, stretching his head to touch Graystripe's nose, and asked, "Could you take Cinderpaw for the day?"

Graystripe looked curiously at Fireheart. "Why?"

"Oh, it's nothing important," replied Fireheart as casually as he could. "I just wanted to check out something I saw yesterday. Watch out for Cinderpaw, though; she doesn't listen to orders very well. Don't take your eyes off her or she'll be charging off in every direction."

Graystripe's whiskers twitched with amusement. "She sounds like a pawful! Still, it'll be good for Brackenpaw. He never charges off anywhere without thinking about it carefully first."

"Thanks, Graystripe!" Fireheart bounded away toward the camp entrance before his friend could remember to ask him where he was going.

As the Twolegplace came into view through the trees, Fireheart dropped into a crouch. He opened his mouth and breathed in the cold morning air. No sign of a ThunderClan patrol, and no Twoleg scents either. He relaxed a little.

Slowly he approached the Twoleg fence where he had seen the she-cat disappear. He hesitated at the bottom and looked around, sniffing the air once more. Then he leaped, landing on a fence post in one easy jump. No Twolegs to be seen—just an empty garden with its strongly scented plants.

Fireheart felt exposed on the post. The branch of a tree hung low overhead. Its leaves had gone, but it would be easier to hide there. Silently he pulled himself up and lay down to wait, flattening himself against the rough bark.

Fireheart could see a swinging flap in the entrance to the Twolegplace. He had used one just like it as a kit. He fixed his gaze on the flap, hoping his sister's face would appear at any moment. The sun rose slowly into the morning sky, but Fireheart started to feel cold. The damp branch was drawing the heat from his body. Perhaps the Twolegs were keeping his sister shut in. After all, her kitting would be soon. Fireheart licked a paw and wondered if he should go back to the camp.

Suddenly he heard a loud clatter. Fireheart looked up and saw his sister pop out through the swinging flap. The fur along his spine rippled with anticipation, and Fireheart fought to stop himself from leaping down into her garden straightaway. He knew he would frighten her, as he had done yesterday. He smelled like a forest cat now, not a friendly kittypet.

Fireheart waited until his sister had reached the end of the grass; then he crept to the tip of the branch and slipped down onto the fence. Quietly he jumped into the bushes below. The she-cat's scent brought his dream flooding back to him.

How could he get her attention without frightening her? Desperately he searched his mind, trying to think of the name his sister had been given. He could remember only his own kittypet name. Fireheart called softly from the bushes, "It's me, Rusty!"

The she-cat stopped dead and looked around. Fireheart took a deep breath and crept out from the bushes.

The cat's eyes widened with terror. Fireheart knew how he must appear to her—lean and wild, with the sharp forest scents on his pelt. The she-cat raised her hackles and hissed ferociously. Fireheart couldn't help feeling impressed by her courage.

In a flash he remembered his sister's name. "Princess! It's me, Rusty, your brother! Do you remember me?"

Princess remained tense. Fireheart guessed she was wondering how this strange cat could know these names. He dropped into a submissive crouch, hope soaring in his chest as he watched his sister's expression slowly change from fear to curiosity.

"Rusty?" Princess sniffed the air, wide-eyed and wary. Fireheart took a careful step forward. Princess did not move, so Fireheart edged closer. Still, his sister held her ground until Fireheart was standing only a mouse-length away.

"You don't smell like Rusty," she mewed.

"I don't live with Twolegs anymore. I've been living in the

forest with ThunderClan. I carry their scent now." *She's probably never heard of the Clans*, Fireheart realized, remembering his own innocence before he'd met Graystripe in the woods.

Princess stretched her nose forward and rubbed her muzzle cautiously along his cheek. "But our mother's smell is still there," she murmured, half to herself. Her words filled Fireheart with happiness, until her eyes narrowed and she took a step backward, her ears flat with distrust. "Why are you here?" she asked.

"I saw you yesterday, in the woods," Fireheart explained. "I had to come back to speak with you."

"Why?"

Fireheart looked at her in surprise. "Because you're my sister." Surely she must feel something for him?

Princess studied him for a moment. To Fireheart's relief, her guarded expression lifted. "You're very thin," she mewed critically.

"Thinner than a kittypet, maybe, but not thin for a Clan— a forest—cat," Fireheart replied. "Your scent was in my dreams last night. I dreamed of you and our brothers and sister and . . ." Fireheart paused. "Where is our mother?"

"She's still with her housefolk," answered Princess.

"What about . . . ?"

Princess guessed what he was going to ask. ". . . our brothers and sisters? Most of them live near here. I see them in their gardens from time to time."

They sat silently for a moment; then Fireheart asked, "Do you remember the soft bedding of our mother's basket?" He felt a flicker of guilt about longing for such kittypet softness, but Princess purred, "Oh, yes. I wish I could have it for my own kitting."

Fireheart's discomfort faded. It felt good to be able to talk of such a tender memory without shame. "Will this litter be your first?"

Princess nodded, uncertainty showing in her eyes. Fireheart felt a wave of sympathy. Even though they were the same age, she seemed to him very young and naive. "You'll be fine," he mewed, remembering Brindleface's kitting. "You look as if your Twolegs treat you well. I'm sure your kits will be healthy and safe."

Princess moved closer to him, pressing her fur against his flank. Fireheart felt his heart swell with emotion. For the first time since he was a kit, he caught a glimpse of what the Clan cats must take for granted: the closeness of kinship, a common bond determined by birth and heritage.

Suddenly Fireheart wanted his sister to know about the life he led now. "Do you know about the Clans?"

Princess gazed at him, mystified. "You mentioned a ThunderClan."

Fireheart nodded. "There are four Clans altogether." He went on, the words tumbling out. "In the Clan, we take care of each other. Younger cats hunt for elders; warriors protect the hunting grounds from other Clans. I trained all greenleaf to become a warrior. Now I have an apprentice of my own." Fireheart could see by her bemused expression that his sister couldn't understand everything he was telling her, yet her eyes brightened with pleasure as he spoke.

"It sounds as if you enjoy your life," she mewed in awe.

A Twoleg voice called from the house. Fireheart instantly darted under the nearest bush.

"I should go," Princess mewed. "They'll be worried if I don't go back, and I have many tiny mouths to feed. I can feel them moving inside me." She glanced at her swollen belly, her eyes soft.

Fireheart looked out from beneath the bush. "Go, then. I have to return to my Clan anyway. But I'll come back and see you."

"Yes, I'd like that!" Princess called over her shoulder. She was already trotting back toward her Twoleg nest. "Goodbye!"

"See you soon," Fireheart called. His sister disappeared from view, and he heard the swinging flap slap shut behind her.

Once the garden was silent, Fireheart crept through the bushes to the fence. He jumped over it and ran into the forest. Memories of kithood scents crowded his mind, suddenly more real than the scents of the forest around him.

Fireheart paused at the top of the ravine and looked down at the ThunderClan camp. He didn't feel ready to go back yet. He was worried that it would all seem strange to him. *I'll go and hunt*, he thought. Cinderpaw would be safe with Graystripe for a while longer, and the Clan would welcome any extra freshkill. He turned away and headed back into the forest.

When he finally returned to camp, he carried a vole and

a wood pigeon in his mouth. The sun was setting, and the Clan cats were gathering for their evening meal. Graystripe sat alone beside the nettle clump, a fat chaffinch at his paws. Fireheart nodded to him as he padded across the clearing to the pile of fresh-kill that had already been collected.

Tigerclaw was sitting below the Highrock, his amber eyes narrow. "I noticed that Cinderpaw spent the day with Graystripe," he meowed as Fireheart dropped his catch onto the pile. "Where were you?"

Fireheart returned Tigerclaw's gaze. "It seemed a good day for hunting—too good to waste," he replied, his heart thudding in his chest. "The Clan needs all the fresh-kill it can get at the moment."

Tigerclaw nodded, suspicion darkening his eyes. "Yes, but we also need warriors. Cinderpaw's training is your responsibility."

"I understand, Tigerclaw," Fireheart meowed. He dipped his head respectfully. "I'll take her out tomorrow."

"Good." The deputy turned his head and looked around the camp. Fireheart picked up a mouse and carried it over to eat next to Graystripe.

"Find what you were looking for?" asked Graystripe absently.

"Yes." Fireheart felt a pang of sorrow for the pain in his friend's eyes. "Are you thinking about that RiverClan warrior?"

"I do try not to," answered Graystripe quietly. "It's just when I'm alone I can't help remembering Barkface's prediction of an unnecessary death and trouble ahead—"

"Here," Fireheart interrupted, and pushed his mouse toward Graystripe. "That chaffinch looks like it'll be half feathers, and I'm not that hungry. Want to swap?" Graystripe shot him a grateful glance, and the two friends exchanged prey and began to eat.

As he crunched on the chaffinch, Fireheart scanned the clearing. He could see Sandpaw and Dustpaw outside the apprentices' den. Dustpaw was busy ripping apart a rabbit. Fireheart caught Sandpaw's eye but she looked away.

Cinderpaw lay beside the old tree stump where he'd shared many meals as an apprentice. She was chatting enthusiastically to Brackenpaw, who nodded from time to time while plucking the feathers from a sparrow. Seeing the two young cats—brother and sister—lying together, so at ease, reminded Fireheart once more of Princess, and for the first time the familiar sights of his clan made Fireheart feel uneasy. He had been careful to lick his sister's smell from his fur before returning to camp, but it was her scent that lingered in his nostrils as the sun disappeared over the distant horizon. He had found the closeness he had missed, but it had given shape to a sense of loneliness that, until now, had lain vague and nameless in his heart. *Were the deep-rooted memories he shared with Princess stronger than his loyalty to the Clan?*

CHAPTER 11

☘

"Another day of sunshine!" Fireheart purred to Graystripe, feeling his flame-colored pelt glow in the weak morning sun. Thanks to the fine weather, he had visited Princess nearly every day recently, slipping away to see her between patrols, hunting, and training sessions. Now he walked with his friend along the short trail to the sandy hollow where Cinderpaw and Brackenpaw would be waiting.

"Let's hope it stays clear for the rest of leaf-bare," Graystripe meowed. Fireheart knew how much his thick-coated friend hated rain—when Graystripe's fur got wet, it clung to him and stayed damp long after Fireheart's shorter fur had dried off.

The two warriors arrived at the edge of the hollow just as Cinderpaw pounced on a pile of frosty leaves, sending them flying in all directions. She leaped and twisted to catch one as it fluttered back to the ground.

Fireheart and Graystripe glanced at each other, amused.

"At least Cinderpaw will be warmed up and ready for today's assignment," Graystripe observed.

Brackenpaw jumped to his paws and looked up at his

mentor, his eyes wide. "Good morning, Graystripe," he meowed. "What *is* today's assignment?"

"A hunting mission," Graystripe told him. He padded down into the hollow, followed by Fireheart.

"Where?" mewed Cinderpaw, dashing toward them. "What are we going to catch?"

"We're going to Sunningrocks," Fireheart replied, suddenly sharing her enthusiasm. "And we'll catch whatever we can."

"I'd like to catch a vole," declared Cinderpaw. "I've never tasted vole."

"I'm afraid everything we catch today goes straight back to the elders," Graystripe warned. "But I'm sure if you asked one of them nicely, they'd be happy to share."

"Okay," mewed Cinderpaw. "Which way is Sunningrocks?" She bounded up one side of the hollow and peered into the forest, her tail sticking straight up.

"This way!" meowed Fireheart, leaping up the opposite side.

"Okay." Cinderpaw raced down the slope, across the hollow, and up to Fireheart's side, sending fallen leaves flying everywhere.

Graystripe leaped up and caught one as it drifted past his nose. He pinned it to the ground with a purr of satisfaction and saw Brackenpaw staring at him. "Er, never miss a chance to practice your hunting skills," Graystripe told him quickly.

The four cats made their way along the familiar scent trails to Sunningrocks. The sun was above the trees by the time they emerged into open territory. Ahead of them, a slope of rock rose out of the soft earth, its smooth surface lined with cracks. The cats had to narrow their eyes as they looked at it. After the shade of the woods, the flat rock face reflected the sun with dazzling glare.

"This is Sunningrocks," Fireheart announced, blinking. "Come on!"

"Mrrrrr! It feels nice!" mewed Cinderpaw as she raced up the stone slope behind him. Fireheart realized she was right. The stone felt comfortingly warm and smooth after the ice-cold forest floor.

They rested at the top, where the far side fell away steeply to the forest. Fireheart listened for the gentle bubbling of the river that followed the RiverClan border, flowing down from the uplands. It touched the Sunningrocks before turning to run deeper into RiverClan territory. He could barely hear it—perhaps the water was low after the dry weather.

Fireheart stretched out, enjoying the warmth of the rock beneath him and the soft heat of the sun on his pelt. He closed his eyes, feeling proud to be lying here, a place where generations of ThunderClan cats had come to warm themselves, and which they had battled hard to keep.

Graystripe joined him. "Come on," he meowed to the two apprentices. "Make the most of the sun while it's here. There are enough cold, damp days ahead of us." The two apprentices lay down beside their mentors and purred as the warmth seeped into their fur.

"Is this where Redtail died?" asked Brackenpaw.

"Yes," Fireheart answered cautiously.

"And where Tigerclaw avenged his death by killing Oak-heart?" Cinderpaw piped up.

Fireheart's fur prickled as he remembered Ravenpaw's account of the fight—that *Redtail* had been responsible for Oakheart's death and then Tigerclaw had killed Redtail, the deputy of his own Clan. Fireheart pushed away the disturbing thoughts and replied simply, "This is the place." The two apprentices fell silent and looked down the slope in awe.

Suddenly Fireheart heard a noise. He pricked his ears. "Hush," he hissed. "What can you hear?"

The two apprentices strained their ears forward.

"I think I can hear some scrabbling," Brackenpaw whispered.

"It might be a vole," murmured Graystripe. "Can you tell where it's coming from?"

"Over there!" mewed Cinderpaw, leaping to her paws. The scrabbling noise became more furious and then disappeared.

"I think it heard you," Fireheart remarked. Cinderpaw looked crestfallen. Brackenpaw purred with amusement at his sister's clumsiness.

"Never mind," meowed Graystripe. "Now you know that it's better to creep up slowly, especially on voles. They're fast!"

"Sit still and listen," Fireheart advised. "Next time we hear something, work out where it is and then begin to move toward it very slowly. A mouse could probably hear even the rustling of your fur, so let him think it's just the wind blowing across the rock."

The cats remained where they were, no one daring to move

until they heard the scrabbling sound again. His ears pricked, Fireheart rose and crept forward, placing each paw noiselessly in front of the other until he reached the edge of a small crack that ran across the rock face. He paused. The scrabbling noise continued. Fireheart lunged forward and reached down into the crack with a forepaw. He scooped out a fat vole that had been hiding in the shadows and flung it onto the bright stone. It squealed as it landed, but the hard ground stunned it and Fireheart finished it off quickly.

"Wow!" mewed Cinderpaw. "I want to do that!"

"Don't worry; you'll have plenty of chances. For now, let's get back to the forest," meowed Graystripe.

"Aren't we going to catch anything else?" Cinderpaw protested.

"Did you hear that vole squeal?" meowed Fireheart. Cinderpaw nodded. "Well, so did every other creature around here. The prey will be hiding for a while. I should have caught it and killed it before it could make a sound."

Graystripe's whiskers twitched with amusement. "I wasn't going to say a word," he purred.

Fireheart picked up the dead vole in his mouth, and together the cats headed down the slope and began to trek onward through the forest. After the open warmth of Sunningrocks, the woods seemed chilly, even though sunhigh was approaching. Fireheart smelled fresh markers at the River-Clan border. Beyond them the ground sloped down to meet the river.

A leaf fluttered down toward Brackenpaw. The young cat

immediately leaped up and caught it between his paws. He landed, looking pleased with himself.

"Well done!" called Graystripe. "You'll have no trouble with voles!" Brackenpaw looked doubly pleased.

"Nice catch, Brackenpaw!" Cinderpaw mewed. She nudged her brother's shoulder with her nose before turning to stare down the wooded slope.

"The river's quiet today," Fireheart mumbled through his mouthful of vole.

"That's because it's frozen," mewed Cinderpaw excitedly. "I can see it through the trees!"

Fireheart dropped the vole. "Frozen? Completely?" He stared down the wooded slope. The river glittered at the bottom, frosty and still. Could Cinderpaw be right? Fireheart's paws tingled with excitement. He had never seen the river frozen over.

"Can we have a look?" asked Cinderpaw. Without waiting for an answer, she bounded past the scent markers. Fireheart's excitement turned to panic as he saw the small gray cat disappear into RiverClan territory. He couldn't call after her—he didn't want to alert any RiverClan patrols that might be in the area. But he had to get her back. He left the vole where he'd dropped it and tore after her, Graystripe and Brackenpaw close behind him.

They caught up with Cinderpaw at the edge of the river. It was almost totally frozen, apart from a narrow channel of dark water that flowed swiftly between two wide fringes of ice. Fireheart remembered Whiteclaw with a shudder. He was about to suggest they leave when he noticed Graystripe's ears were pricked.

"Water vole," the gray warrior hissed. Sure enough, a small vole was scampering along the ice, near the bank.

Fireheart glanced at Cinderpaw and Brackenpaw, afraid that they might try to catch this tiny piece of prey. But neither apprentice moved. Fireheart felt relieved for a moment, and then his heart lurched as Graystripe dashed out onto the ice at hunting speed.

"Come back!" Fireheart hissed.

It was too late. The ice beneath Graystripe's paws gave a terrifying crack and broke. With a startled yowl, Graystripe fell into the water. He paddled madly for a moment before disappearing into the cold, dark depths of the river.

Brackenpaw stared in horror and Cinderpaw gave a desperate mew. Fireheart didn't quiet her. He was rigid with fear, staring into the water after his friend. Was Graystripe trapped underneath the ice? Fireheart stepped onto the ice. It felt cold and slippery beneath his paws, impossible to run on. He jumped back onto the bank. Panic gripped him, then a blaze of relief as a drenched gray head appeared in the water farther along.

But relief turned to alarm as Fireheart saw that Graystripe was being carried downriver, turning and bobbing in the freezing waters. His paws thrashed helplessly, all his instincts to swim thwarted by the fierce current. Fireheart bounded along the bank, forcing his way through the bracken, but Graystripe was swept farther and farther away.

Suddenly Fireheart heard a yowl from the opposite bank and stopped. A slender silver tabby had leaped onto the ice farther downstream. She padded lightly over the frozen sheet and slid into the river ahead of Graystripe. Amazed, Fireheart watched the she-cat swim strongly against the current, holding her position in the icy water with confident churning paws. As Graystripe was swept past, the tabby grabbed a mouthful of his fur between her teeth.

But to Fireheart's horror, Graystripe's weight pulled both cats under. He started running again, his eyes fixed on the river. Where were they? Then a silver-striped head appeared amid the rolling waters, pushing through the waves. The tabby was swimming against the current, dragging Graystripe with her. Fireheart could hardly believe that such a slender cat could swim with such a weight. The tabby grabbed the ice on Fireheart's side of the river with her forepaws, her neck craning awkwardly as she held Graystripe between her teeth. Slipping and sliding, she hauled herself out of the river. Graystripe hung limply in the water, twisting and turning as the current dragged at his fur, but the tabby kept a firm grip.

Fireheart slid down the bank, raced across the ice, and skidded to a halt beside her. Without a word he reached forward and took hold of Graystripe in his teeth. Together the two cats heaved his soaking body out of the water and dragged him to the safety of the riverbank.

Fireheart bent over his friend to see if he was breathing. He felt dizzy with relief as he saw Graystripe's slick gray flank rising and falling. Graystripe coughed and spluttered and spat out a mouthful of river water. Then he lay still.

"Graystripe!" Fireheart meowed urgently.

"I'm okay," wheezed Graystripe. His mew was breathless, but reassuring.

Fireheart sighed and sat down. He looked closely at the silver tabby. She carried the scent of RiverClan on her. After seeing her swim, Fireheart wasn't surprised. The tabby returned his gaze coldly, shook herself, and sat down, her sides heaving as she got her breath back. Water streamed from her glossy fur as if her pelt were made from duck feathers.

Graystripe turned his head and looked at his rescuer. "Thanks," he croaked.

"You idiot!" she spat, flattening her ears. "What are you doing in my territory?"

"Drowning?" replied Graystripe.

The silver tabby flicked her ears, and Fireheart saw a glimmer of amusement in her eyes. "Can't you drown yourself in your own territory?"

Graystripe's whiskers twitched. "Ah, but who would rescue me there?" he rasped.

There was a tiny mew behind Fireheart. He turned to see Cinderpaw crouching by a clump of grass farther up the bank. "Where's Brackenpaw?" he asked.

"Just coming," answered Cinderpaw, pointing with her nose. Her brother was creeping nervously along the bank toward them.

Fireheart sighed and turned to his friend. "Look, Graystripe, we've got to get out of here."

"I know." Graystripe pushed himself to his paws and turned to the silver tabby. "Thanks again."

She dipped her head graciously, but hissed, "Hurry, go now!" She looked over her shoulder. "If my father knew that I'd rescued a ThunderClan intruder he'd shred me for kit bedding!"

"Why'd you save me then?" teased Graystripe.

The tabby looked away. "Instinct. I couldn't watch any cat drown. Now go away!"

Fireheart stood up. "Thanks. I'd have missed this furball if he'd drowned." He nudged Graystripe. His friend hadn't even shaken the icy water from his fur and he was soaked to the skin. "Come on, let's get back to camp. You're freezing!"

"Okay, I'm coming!" Graystripe meowed. But before he followed Fireheart up the slope, he turned back to the silver she-cat. "What's your name? Mine's Graystripe."

"Silverstream," she replied, and bounded away, back onto the ice and over the channel of water to the far side.

Fireheart and Graystripe led their apprentices through the bracken, toward the border. Fireheart couldn't help noticing that Graystripe looked back over his shoulder more than once.

Cinderpaw noticed too. The little gray cat glanced up, mischief dancing in her eyes. "What a pretty RiverClan cat she was!"

Graystripe gave her a playful cuff around the ear and she ran on ahead.

"Stay with us," Fireheart warned in a loud hiss. They were still in RiverClan territory. He flashed Cinderpaw an angry look as she stopped and waited for them. If it weren't for her, they wouldn't be here at all, and Graystripe wouldn't have nearly drowned. He looked at his wet friend. Even though the gray warrior had shaken as much of the water from his fur as he could, his coat was still dripping and ice was beginning to form on the ends of his whiskers.

Fireheart quickened the pace. "Are you okay?" he asked Graystripe.

"F-f-fine!" replied Graystripe, through chattering teeth.

"Sorry," mewed Cinderpaw softly as she fell into step behind Fireheart.

He sighed. "It's not your fault." He felt weighed down with worry. How were they going to explain this to the Clan? No fresh-kill for the elders—there wasn't time to go back for the vole now—and a soaked Graystripe. Fireheart shuddered as he thought how close he had come to losing his closest friend. Thank StarClan that Silverstream had been there to save him.

"The stream near the training hollow is still running with water," Brackenpaw meowed thoughtfully from the back.

"What?" asked Fireheart, puzzled out of his gloomy thoughts.

"The Clan will probably assume that Graystripe fell in there," continued the young apprentice.

"We could say he was showing us how to catch fish," Cinderpaw added.

"I'm not sure any cat would believe Graystripe would get his paws wet on purpose in this weather," Fireheart pointed out.

"Well, I don't want the rest of the Clan to know I had to be rescued by a RiverClan cat!" meowed Graystripe with a flash of his old spirit. "And we can't let them know we were in RiverClan's territory again."

Fireheart nodded. "Come on," he meowed. "Let's run the rest of the way; it'll help Graystripe warm up."

The cats raced across the RiverClan border and past Sunningrocks. As the sun began to dip behind the treetops, they arrived back outside the camp.

Graystripe's fur had dried a little, but frozen droplets hung on his whiskers and tail.

Fireheart led the way through the gorse entrance. His heart sank when he saw Tigerclaw sitting in the clearing watching them.

The deputy fixed his sharp eyes on Fireheart. "No fresh-kill?" he growled. "I thought you were meant to be teaching these two how to hunt today. You look half-drowned, Graystripe. You must have fallen into a river to get that wet." His nostrils flared and he drew himself up to his full height. "Don't tell me you've been into RiverClan territory again!"

CHAPTER 12

❧

Fireheart lifted his head, about to speak, but Cinderpaw beat him to it.

"It's my fault, Tigerclaw." She stared boldly up at the great tabby. "We were hunting on the frozen stream by the training hollow, on the bend by the deep pool. Even that bit was frozen. I slipped and Graystripe came to help me, but the ice wasn't thick enough for him and it cracked and he fell into the water." Tigerclaw looked into her clear, bright eyes as she added, "It really is deep there. Fireheart had to pull him out."

Fireheart cringed, remembering how he had stood motionless with terror at the sight of Graystripe disappearing into the river.

Tigerclaw nodded and looked at Graystripe. "You'd better get yourself to Yellowfang before you freeze to death." The ThunderClan deputy stood up and stalked away, and Fireheart breathed a sigh of relief.

Graystripe didn't hesitate. The long run home hadn't stopped his teeth from chattering. He bounded away to Yellowfang's den. Brackenpaw glanced at Cinderpaw and padded off to his nest, his tail drooping with exhaustion.

Fireheart looked at Cinderpaw. "Aren't you even a bit frightened by Tigerclaw?" he asked curiously.

"Why should I be?" replied Cinderpaw. "He's a great warrior. I admire him."

Of course, why shouldn't she? Fireheart thought. "You lie very well," he growled sternly, trying his best to act like a mentor.

"Well, I try not to," mewed Cinderpaw. "I just thought the truth wouldn't be very helpful here."

Fireheart had to admit she had a point. He shook his head slowly. "Go and get warm."

"Yes, Fireheart!" Cinderpaw dipped her head and charged after Brackenpaw.

Fireheart padded over to the warriors' den. He was worried at how easily the story about Graystripe's soaking had tumbled from Cinderpaw's mouth. But he also believed she was a well-meaning and honest cat. He thought of Ravenpaw, another good cat. Had the story he'd told about Tigerclaw killing Redtail simply been just that—a story that tumbled from his mouth in the heat of the moment? Fireheart shook the thought away. Ravenpaw had been terrified when he spoke to Fireheart. He obviously believed his own story. Why else would he have been frightened enough to leave the Clan?

Fireheart chose a few pieces of fresh-kill and carried them over to the nettle clump. He settled himself beside it and began to gnaw thoughtfully on a mouse. The admiration in Cinderpaw's voice when she had spoken of Tigerclaw worried him. It seemed as though he alone suspected there was more to the ThunderClan deputy than met the eye. Bluestar's attitude toward Tigerclaw certainly hadn't changed. She had been treating him with the same trust and respect that she had always shown him. With a flash of frustration, Fireheart ripped another mouthful from his meal.

A loud sneeze made him look up. Graystripe was heading toward him.

"How are you?" Fireheart asked as Graystripe arrived, smelling of one of Yellowfang's herb concoctions.

Graystripe sat down heavily and coughed.

"I've saved you some food," Fireheart meowed, pushing a plump thrush and a vole toward his friend.

"Yellowfang says I have to stay in camp. She says I have a chill," Graystripe meowed thickly.

"I'm not surprised. What did she dose you with?"

"Feverfew and lavender." Graystripe lay down and began to nibble at the thrush. "This'll be enough for me," he mumbled. "I'm not very hungry."

Fireheart looked at his friend in amazement. That wasn't something he had ever thought he'd hear Graystripe say. "You sure?" he asked. "There's plenty here."

Graystripe stared down at the thrush and didn't reply.

"Are you sure?" Fireheart repeated.

"What?" Graystripe turned his faraway gaze on Fireheart. "Uh, yeah," he meowed.

He must have a fever, Fireheart decided, shaking his head. Oh, well, at least he was still here, thanks to that RiverClan cat.

* * *

A few days later Fireheart woke to find the first fog of leaf-bare filling the den. When he crept outside, he could barely see the other side of the clearing. He heard pawsteps hurrying toward him, and Mousefur appeared out of the gloom.

"Tigerclaw wants to see you," she meowed.

"Right, thanks," answered Fireheart. Alarm shot through him. He'd slipped away to visit Princess yesterday. Had Tigerclaw noticed?

"What was that?" Graystripe's voice wheezed behind him. He sat down beside Fireheart, sneezed, and yawned.

"Tigerclaw wants to see me." Fireheart looked at his friend. "You should be asleep." He was beginning to worry about Graystripe. He ought to have recovered by now. "Did you rest up yesterday?" he asked.

"As much as I could between coughing and sneezing," complained Graystripe.

"Then why weren't you in your nest when I got back from"— Fireheart hesitated, remembering he'd spent the afternoon talking with Princess—"training?"

"Do you think I get any peace and quiet in there?" Graystripe flicked his head back at the den. "Warriors trooping in and out all day! I found somewhere quieter, that's all."

Fireheart was about to ask where, but Graystripe spoke first. "I wonder what Tigerclaw wants?"

Fireheart's paws prickled. "I'd better go and find out."

He could just see the shapes of Tigerclaw and Whitestorm through the mist, sitting below the Highrock. As Fireheart padded over to them, they stopped talking and Tigerclaw turned to him. "It's time Cinderpaw and Brackenpaw were assessed," he growled.

"Already?" Fireheart meowed in surprise. The apprentices had not been training long.

"Bluestar wants to see how their training is progressing. Especially with Graystripe being too ill to train Brackenpaw. If Brackenpaw is falling behind, she needs to know so she can appoint another mentor for him."

Fireheart's tail twitched with annoyance. Surely Graystripe would recover soon. It would be unfair to entrust his first apprentice to someone else. "I've been taking Brackenpaw out with me and Cinderpaw every day," he meowed quickly.

Tigerclaw glanced at Whitestorm and nodded. "Yes, but this is your first time as a mentor. It's a lot for you to take on, and ThunderClan needs well-trained warriors."

I know, and I'm just a kittypet, not a Clanborn warrior, Fireheart thought bitterly. He looked down at his paws, stinging with resentment. No one had asked him to take on Brackenpaw, and he'd been putting in a lot of effort with both apprentices.

Tigerclaw went on. "Send Brackenpaw and Cinderpaw on a hunting mission through Tallpines, as far as Twolegplace. Keep an eye on them, watch them hunt, and report to me. I'll be interested to see how much fresh-kill they add to the pile."

Whitestorm added, "If Cinderpaw's skills match her enthusiasm, there should be plenty to eat tonight. I hear she is a keen apprentice."

"Yes, she is," Fireheart agreed, though he was barely listening. Tigerclaw's words had set his heart racing. *Why was*

Tigerclaw sending him to Twolegplace again? His own hunting assessment had been held over exactly the same route, and Tigerclaw had seen him sharing words with an old kittypet friend; he'd reported it to Bluestar and she had questioned Fireheart's loyalty to the Clan. Fireheart felt the fur along his spine begin to prickle. Was this Tigerclaw's way of warning him that he had been spotted talking to Princess?

Fireheart twisted his head and gave his back a quick lick, brushing his bristling hairs flat with his tongue. He sat up straight again and calmly suggested, "The Sunningrocks would be an equally good place to test their skills. The sun there might have burned away some of this mist, too."

"No," growled Tigerclaw. "The dawn patrol reported scenting RiverClan at Sunningrocks. They may have started hunting there again." Anger flared in his eyes, and his lip curled to reveal sharp teeth. "They will need to be warned off before we do any more training there. For now, Tallpines would be much safer for the assessment."

Whitestorm nodded in agreement while Fireheart's ears twitched uncomfortably at this news. RiverClan at Sunningrocks! It was lucky they hadn't been spotted by enemy patrols when Graystripe fell into the river.

"As for the fog," Tigerclaw continued smoothly, "hunting in difficult conditions will make the test more interesting."

"Yes, Tigerclaw," meowed Fireheart, ducking his head respectfully to the two warriors. "I'll tell Cinderpaw and Brackenpaw. We'll get started right away."

* * *

When Fireheart explained the assessment to the apprentices, Cinderpaw flicked up her tail and ran in an excited circle. "An assessment! Do you think we're ready?"

"Of course," Fireheart meowed, hiding his doubts. "You've been working hard and learning quickly."

"But won't the fog make hunting difficult?" asked Brackenpaw.

Fireheart replied, "There are advantages to the stillness of the air."

Brackenpaw looked thoughtful, then his eyes began to shine and he mewed, "It'll be harder to sniff out prey, but it'll also make it harder for the prey to smell us."

"Exactly," Fireheart agreed.

"Shall we go now?" Cinderpaw asked.

"As soon as you like," answered Fireheart. "But take your time; it's not a race. . . ." His words were wasted on Cinderpaw, who was already charging toward the camp entrance. "You've got till sunset," he called after her. Brackenpaw glanced at Fireheart and turned to follow his sister with a small sigh.

Fireheart tracked the two apprentices through the Tallpines. The springy layer of pine needles underpaw felt strangely soft after the frozen ground in the rest of the forest. He followed Cinderpaw's trail until he could see her stalking eagerly through the forest. Then he picked up Brackenpaw's scent and followed that. The trails crossed here and there. Fireheart could smell where the apprentices had run fast, where they had sat down, even where they had lingered together at one point.

Before long Fireheart found a spot where Cinderpaw had made a kill. She had taken it with her—as he followed her trail, he could smell the scent of her catch mingling with her own. Then he discovered where Brackenpaw had caught a thrush. The feathers were scattered everywhere. The apprentices were hunting well. Fireheart knew this for sure when he detected a scent thick with fresh-kill. He dug down among the needles at the roots of a pine. There was a stash of prey hidden underneath it, left by Cinderpaw to pick up later. Fireheart felt a small glow of pride at her work. She had caught plenty, and now she was heading for the oak woods behind the Twolegplace.

Fireheart followed. Just beyond the edge of the pine forest, he picked up Brackenpaw's scent. It was strong, which meant the apprentice was nearby. Fireheart crept forward and peered around a young oak. The apprentice was crouching beneath a tangle of brambles, well disguised among its shadows. Fireheart could just see his tail moving as it twitched from side to side.

Brackenpaw had his eyes fixed on a wood mouse that was scrambling around the roots of a tree. Brackenpaw was taking his time. *Good*, thought Fireheart. He watched Brackenpaw draw himself forward, one step at a time. The leaves beneath his paws hardly made a sound. He was as quiet as the mouse itself, which continued to hunt for food, suspecting nothing. Fireheart watched breathlessly, remembering his first hunting mission.

Brackenpaw closed in. The soft rustle of his paws on leaves

melted into the background sounds of the forest. Fireheart found himself willing the apprentice on. Brackenpaw was only a rabbit-length away from the mouse now, his body pressed flat against the forest floor. The mouse scampered onto a root and looked around. It froze. Something was wrong.

Now! thought Fireheart. Brackenpaw sprang and landed on the mouse, grasping it in his front paws. The mouse didn't have time to struggle. It was over in a single bite.

Brackenpaw raised his head. Fireheart saw the satisfied expression on the young cat's face as he breathed the scent of his fresh-kill. Then Brackenpaw darted away between the trees. Fireheart realized he was looking forward to reporting back to Tigerclaw about his apprentices.

"Hi!" The small voice behind him made Fireheart jump into the air. He spun around.

"How are we doing?" asked Cinderpaw, looking up at him with her head to one side.

"You're not meant to ask that!" Fireheart spat, and licked his ruffled fur. "You're not supposed to speak to me at all. I'm assessing you, remember?"

"Oh!" mewed Cinderpaw. "Sorry."

Fireheart sighed. He would never have dared to approach Tigerclaw during his own assessment. He didn't want to scare Cinderpaw into obedience, as Tigerclaw had done with Ravenpaw, but he wouldn't mind a little respect every now and then. Sometimes he didn't feel like Cinderpaw's mentor at all.

Cinderpaw looked at the ground for a moment, then glanced up at him, a puzzled expression on her face. "Were you really born over there, in Twolegplace?"

The question caught Fireheart off guard. He glanced nervously in the direction of the Twoleg fence, praying that the strange scents of Cinderpaw and Brackenpaw would keep Princess inside her own garden today. "Why d'you ask?" he mewed, stalling.

"Tigerclaw mentioned it, that's all," answered Cinderpaw. She seemed genuinely curious, but Fireheart felt a dark quiver of menace at the mention of Tigerclaw's name. What else had Tigerclaw been telling Cinderpaw about him?

"I was born a kittypet," Fireheart meowed firmly. "But I'm a warrior now. My life is with the Clan. My old life wasn't bad, but it's over, and I'm glad."

"Oh, okay," mewed Cinderpaw, sounding unconcerned. "See you later!" She spun around and charged off into the trees.

Fireheart stood alone in the woods, his heart thudding as he stared at the Twoleg fence. A moon ago, his words to Cinderpaw about being glad his old life was over would have been utterly true. Now he was not so sure. His fur tingled with the knowledge that some of his happiest moments recently had been spent sharing memories with his gentle kittypet sister.

CHAPTER 13

❦

As the sun sank into the forest, Fireheart waited beside the pine tree where Cinderpaw had buried her first lot of fresh-kill. He heard pawsteps and turned to see Cinderpaw and Brackenpaw padding toward him. Prey dangled from their mouths. Brackenpaw could barely hold his catch, it was so big. Fireheart felt a surge of relief. Even Tigerclaw couldn't criticize the apprentices' efforts.

"I'll help carry this lot back," Fireheart offered, flicking away the covering of pine needles from Cinderpaw's stash. He dug it up, grasped the fresh-kill between his teeth, and set off back to the camp.

When they arrived in the camp clearing, some of the Clan cats were already taking their share of fresh-kill from the pile. Tigerclaw must have been looking out for their return, because he padded over to them as they dropped their catch near the rest.

"They caught all this themselves?" he asked, nudging the pile with a massive paw.

"Oh, yes," Fireheart replied.

"Good," meowed Tigerclaw. "Come and join me and

Bluestar. Bring some fresh-kill for yourself; we're already eating."

Cinderpaw and Brackenpaw looked at Fireheart with admiring stares—it was a privilege to eat with the Clan leader and deputy. Fireheart didn't share their excitement. He'd hoped that he would report to Bluestar alone. The last cat he wanted to share his meal with was Tigerclaw.

"By the way, have you seen Graystripe?" asked Tigerclaw. Fireheart felt a pang of concern as Tigerclaw continued: "He's supposed to stay in camp while he has this cold, but I haven't seen him since sunhigh."

Fireheart shifted his paws. Had Graystripe gone off looking for peace and quiet again? "No," he admitted. "Perhaps he's with Yellowfang?"

"Perhaps," echoed Tigerclaw, and padded away to where Bluestar was gnawing a fat pigeon.

Fireheart followed, trying to push away his growing worry about Graystripe's disappearances. He selected a small chaffinch from the pile of fresh-kill as he passed, then wished he'd chosen a vole. How was he going to give his report with a mouthful of feathers?

"Welcome, Fireheart," meowed Bluestar as Fireheart sat down in front of her. He placed the chaffinch on the ground, but decided not to start eating.

"Tigerclaw tells me your apprentices caught plenty of prey." Bluestar's gaze was friendly. Tigerclaw, sitting up beside her, glared at him more critically, making Fireheart's tail twitch.

"Yes. They've never hunted in the mist before, but it didn't seem to put either of them off," Fireheart meowed. "I watched Brackenpaw catch a wood mouse. His stalking was excellent."

"And what about Cinderpaw?" asked Bluestar.

Fireheart noticed a steely glint appear in her eyes. Was she worried about Cinderpaw's abilities? Fireheart replied, "Her hunting skills are developing well. She has lots of enthusiasm, that's for sure, and she doesn't seem to be scared of anything."

"Aren't you worried that might make her reckless?" asked Bluestar.

"She's quick and inquisitive, which makes her a good learner. I think that will make up for her"—Fireheart searched anxiously for the right word—"eagerness."

Bluestar flicked her tail. "Her *eagerness*, as you say, worries me," she meowed, flashing a glance at Tigerclaw. "She will need careful guidance in her training." Fireheart's spirits plummeted. Was Bluestar unhappy with his mentoring?

Bluestar's eyes softened. "She was always going to be a challenge. But she is clearly turning into a fine hunter. You have done good work with her, Fireheart. With both of them, in fact." Fireheart brightened immediately, and Bluestar went on. "I've noticed how you've taken over Brackenpaw's training without being asked, and I want you to carry on mentoring them both for the time being."

Tigerclaw turned his gaze away, but Fireheart didn't miss the anger that flashed in his eyes. "Thank you, Bluestar," he meowed.

"I see your missing friend has returned," Tigerclaw growled without turning his head.

Fireheart spun around to see Graystripe appearing from behind the nursery. "He was probably just getting some peace and quiet," he suggested. "He's still feverish, and it can't be easy being stuck in the camp all day."

"Easy or not, he should be concentrating on getting better," meowed Tigerclaw. "Leaf-bare is no time for sickness in the camp. Mousefur was coughing on patrol this morning. I just hope StarClan protects us from greencough this season. We lost five kits to it last year."

Bluestar nodded her gray head solemnly. "Let's pray this leaf-bare isn't as long or as hard. It's never an easy time for the Clans." She looked wistful for a moment, then told Fireheart, "Take that chaffinch and share it with Graystripe. He'll want to know how his apprentice did in the assessment."

"Yes, Bluestar. Thanks," meowed Fireheart. He picked up the chaffinch and bounded over to the nettle clump where Graystripe had settled himself with a large wood mouse. Graystripe had eaten half of it by the time Fireheart arrived. Perhaps his cold was on the mend.

As Fireheart dropped the chaffinch beside his friend, Graystripe sneezed.

"Cold no better?" asked Fireheart sympathetically.

"Nope," replied Graystripe with his mouth full. "I guess I'll have to stay in camp awhile longer."

Fireheart thought his friend sounded a lot more cheerful than he had before, but he didn't want to betray his growing suspicion that Graystripe was up to something.

"Brackenpaw did really well in his assessment today," he meowed.

"Really?" Graystripe took another bite of mouse. "That's good."

"Yeah, he's a great hunter." Fireheart started to eat his chaffinch. "Graystripe," he meowed after a long silence, "have you been out of the camp the past few days?"

Graystripe stopped chewing. "Why do you ask?"

Fireheart's tail twitched uncomfortably. "Well, you weren't here when I got in from last night's patrol, and Tigerclaw said he hadn't seen you since sunhigh today."

"Tigerclaw?" Graystripe sounded worried.

"I told him you were probably out looking for peace and quiet, or that you might be with Yellowfang," Fireheart meowed. He took another bite of chaffinch. "Were you?" he asked through the feathers, suddenly desperate for Graystripe to say yes, to stop the suspicion that Graystripe might be keeping a secret from him.

But Graystripe ignored Fireheart's query. "Well, thanks for covering for me." He carried on chewing.

Fireheart didn't ask any more questions, even though he was burning with curiosity. When Graystripe got to his paws and announced he was going to the den, Fireheart was still no wiser about what was on Graystripe's mind.

"Okay," he meowed. "I think I'll stay here a bit longer." Graystripe gave him a brief nod and padded away. Fireheart rolled onto his back for a long stretch, scratching the ground above his head with his claws. He lay on his back for a while, thinking. From the smell of him, Graystripe had given himself a good wash very recently. Was he trying to hide some scent? Fireheart realized that Graystripe had pretty much admitted he had left the camp. But where could he have gone that he couldn't, or wouldn't, tell Fireheart? Suddenly his paws prickled—what about his own visits to Princess, in Twoleg territory, of all places! He'd washed himself thoroughly before returning to camp too, and never mentioned the meetings to Graystripe.

Fireheart flipped over and sat up. There was something caught under one of his claws. He lifted his paw and tugged out the piece of dirt with his teeth. It was a catkin, old and shriveled, but definitely a catkin. What was this doing here? Willow trees didn't grow in ThunderClan's part of the forest—in fact, the only willows Fireheart had ever seen grew close to the river, in RiverClan territory. Fireheart held his breath as his heart began to pound. Had this come from Graystripe's coat?

He crept into the warriors' den. Graystripe was already asleep. Fireheart lay awake beside him and wondered if Graystripe had really been foolish enough to return to RiverClan territory. The look in Leopardfur's eyes after Whiteclaw's death had shown that there was a score to be settled. Fireheart shuddered as he resolved to find out exactly where Graystripe was going and why.

When Fireheart awoke the den felt damp and chilled. One sniff of the air told him rain was on the way. He pushed his way outside, yawning. He hadn't slept well, worrying about Graystripe. Even now, the thought of his friend alone in River-Clan territory sent a shiver through him.

"Chilly, eh?" Runningwind's voice startled Fireheart. Fireheart looked over his shoulder, his tail twitching. The lean tabby warrior was padding out of the den.

"Er, yeah," Fireheart agreed.

"Are you okay?" asked Runningwind. "Not caught your friend's cold, have you? Mousefur's streaming with it this morning, and Longtail said Swiftpaw sneezed all through training yesterday."

Fireheart shook his head. "I'm fine. Just tired after yesterday's assessment."

"Ah. Bluestar thought you might be. That's why she asked me to help you with Cinderpaw's and Brackenpaw's training today. Is that okay with you?"

"Yeah, thanks," Fireheart meowed.

"Right, then," Runningwind decided. "I'll meet you in the hollow after I've eaten. If Swiftpaw's coming down with a cold, we should have the place to ourselves. Are you hungry?" Fireheart shook his head, and Runningwind trotted away to pick through the leftovers from last night's fresh-kill.

Fireheart went straight to the training hollow and waited for the others to arrive. His mind was not on training; he was still thinking about Graystripe. He felt sure his friend would slip out of camp again today.

A rain-laden wind was beginning to sway the leafless branches above the hollow when Cinderpaw and Brackenpaw arrived, followed by Runningwind.

"What are we doing today?" asked Cinderpaw, scampering down into the hollow. Fireheart stared at her blankly. He hadn't thought about it at all.

"Hunting?" Brackenpaw mewed hopefully as he trotted after Cinderpaw.

Runningwind padded across the hollow and joined them. "How about practicing some stalking techniques?" he suggested.

"Good idea," Fireheart agreed quickly.

"Not the old 'rabbit hears you, mouse feels you' lesson again!" Cinderpaw moaned.

Runningwind silenced her with a look and turned to Fireheart.

Fireheart realized with a jump that Runningwind was waiting for him to start. "Er, I'll start by showing you the best way to stalk rabbit," he stammered. He dropped into a crouch and began to move forward, fast and light, until he reached the end of the hollow. He stood and turned to find the other three cats staring at him quizzically.

"Are you sure that'd fool a rabbit?" mewed Cinderpaw, her whiskers twitching.

Fireheart felt confused for a moment until he realized he'd just demonstrated his best bird-stalking technique. A rabbit would have heard the swish of his fur through the undergrowth three fox-lengths away.

Fireheart looked at Runningwind, embarrassed. The tabby warrior frowned. "How about I show you two how to creep up on a shrew?" Cinderpaw turned her bright gaze from Fireheart to Runningwind. Fireheart sighed and padded over to watch.

By sunhigh, Fireheart was still finding it difficult to concentrate on the training session. He kept imagining Graystripe sneaking out of the camp, and longed to follow him. Eventually his restlessness overwhelmed him. He went over to Runningwind and spoke quietly into his ear. "I have a bellyache," he meowed. "Can you take over the training for the rest of the day? I want to see if Yellowfang has anything for it."

"I thought you seemed a little distracted," Runningwind replied. "You go back to camp. I'll take this pair out hunting."

"Thanks, Runningwind," meowed Fireheart, feeling a pang of shame that Runningwind had believed him so easily.

He limped across the hollow, trying to look as if he were in pain. As soon as he was safely among the trees, he broke into a run and raced back to the camp. When Graystripe had returned yesterday, he'd appeared from behind the nursery. Fireheart knew from experience that this was the best place to slip through the camp boundary without being noticed— it was where Yellowfang had escaped from the camp when the Clan had suspected the old medicine cat of Spottedleaf's murder.

Fireheart padded around the outside of the camp and sniffed at the wall of bracken. His heart sank as he picked up Graystripe's scent. Graystripe had definitely been sneaking out of the camp this way, and often, by the smell of it. At least the scent was stale, which meant he hadn't been this way today.

Fireheart crouched behind a nearby tree and settled down to wait. The wood was growing darker as rain clouds began to push across the sky. The shadows hid him perfectly, and he made sure he was downwind so Graystripe wouldn't detect him. His belly really was aching now, tense with guilt and apprehension. He half hoped Graystripe wouldn't come, half hoped he would just lead him to some quiet spot within ThunderClan's borders.

Fireheart's heart lurched as he heard a rustling in the bracken wall. A gray nose was pushing its way through the fronds. Fireheart ducked his head as Graystripe looked around cautiously. After a few moments, the warrior leaped out and set off at a trot toward the training hollow.

Hope flared in Fireheart's chest. Perhaps Graystripe's cold was better and he'd decided to join the training session. He set off after him, keeping a safe distance behind, relying on scent rather than sight to track his friend.

But when the trail veered away from the path that led to the training hollow, Fireheart knew that his hope had been in vain. With an ominous sense of dread, he saw the distinctive gray rock loom ahead through the trees: Sunningrocks. Fireheart pricked his ears and opened his mouth, testing the breeze for the smell of enemy cats. At the edge of the trees, he caught a glimpse of a broad-shouldered gray cat slipping past the rocks, toward the RiverClan border. There was no doubt now where Graystripe was heading.

As soon as his friend was out of sight, Fireheart padded forward and peered down the slope to the river. By the swaying of the undergrowth, Fireheart could guess where Graystripe was. He just hoped there weren't any RiverClan warriors watching too.

Fireheart made his way down through the fronds. The river wasn't frozen anymore—he could hear the water lapping at the bank and splashing over the boulders. He slowed his pace as he reached the edge of the bracken and peered out at the open shore.

Graystripe was sitting on the pebbles. The gray warrior was looking around, his ears pricked, but Fireheart could tell from the relaxed slope of his shoulders that he wasn't listening for prey.

A strange cat's call sounded in the distance. A RiverClan patrol? Fireheart's fur prickled and his muscles instinctively tensed, but Graystripe didn't move. Then Fireheart heard a rustle in the bracken beyond the river. Still Graystripe stayed where he was. Fireheart held his breath as a face appeared on the far riverbank. With barely a sound, the silver she-cat emerged from the undergrowth and slipped into the river. Fireheart felt his heart miss a beat. It was Silverstream, the she-cat who had rescued his friend!

She swam easily across the river. Graystripe stood up and mewed with delight, kneading the pebbles with his paws in anticipation. Holding his tail high, he padded to the edge of the water as she climbed onto the shore.

Silverstream shook the drops from her fur, and the two

gray cats touched noses gently. Graystripe rubbed his muzzle along her jaw and she lifted her chin happily. Then Silverstream stood on tiptoe and wound her slender body around his. For once Graystripe didn't seem to mind getting wet at all, because he purred loud enough for Fireheart to hear as Silverstream pressed her damp fur against him.

CHAPTER 14

❧

Fireheart's hackles bristled with horror. How could Graystripe be so stupid? He was breaking every part of the warrior code by meeting this cat from another Clan.

"Graystripe!" Fireheart hissed as he sprang from the bushes.

The two cats spun around to face him. Silverstream's ears flattened angrily. Graystripe just stared at him, startled. "You followed me!"

Fireheart ignored his stunned meow. "What are you doing? Don't you know how dangerous this is?"

Silverstream spoke up. "It's okay. There won't be a patrol here till after sunset."

"You can be sure of that, can you? As if you know all your Clan's movements!" Fireheart growled.

Silverstream lifted her chin. "Actually, I do. My father is Crookedstar, the leader of RiverClan."

Fireheart froze. "What are you playing at?" he spat at Graystripe. "Could you have chosen worse?"

Graystripe met Fireheart's eyes for an instant, then turned to Silverstream. "I'd better go," he mewed.

Silverstream blinked slowly and stretched her head forward

to touch his cheek. They closed their eyes and remained still
for a moment. Fireheart watched, his paws prickling with
alarm. Silverstream whispered something into Graystripe's
ear and the two cats stepped apart. The RiverClan she-cat
raised her head and stared challengingly into Fireheart's eyes
before slipping back into the river.

Graystripe bounded over to Fireheart's side. The two
friends didn't speak as they raced out of RiverClan territory
and back past Sunningrocks. As they approached the camp,
Graystripe slowed his pace.

Fireheart slowed too. "You must stop seeing her," he
panted. His panic had lessened now they were well away from
the RiverClan border, but he was still angry.

"I can't," replied Graystripe hoarsely. He coughed, his sides
heaving.

"I don't understand," Fireheart meowed. "RiverClan is
completely hostile to ThunderClan at the moment. You heard
Leopardfur after Whiteclaw died." Fireheart winced, knowing that the reminder would be painful for his friend, but he
couldn't stop now. "How do you even know you can trust this
RiverClan cat?"

"You don't know Silverstream," Graystripe spat back. He
stopped and sat down. His eyes glazed with pain. "And there's
no need to remind me about Whiteclaw. Do you think it's easy
knowing I'm responsible for the death of one of Silverstream's
Clan mates?" Fireheart snorted impatiently—Whiteclaw was
an enemy warrior, not a *Clanmate*! But Graystripe went on.
"Silverstream understands it was an accident. The gorge was

no place for a battle. Any cat could have fallen there!"

Fireheart paced around him as Graystripe began to lick the scent of Silverstream from his fur. "It doesn't matter what Silverstream thinks! What about your loyalty to ThunderClan?" he demanded. "You're breaking the Clan code by seeing her!"

Graystripe stopped washing. "You think I don't know that?" he hissed. "Do you doubt my loyalty to ThunderClan?"

"What else can I think? You can't see her without lying to the Clan. And what if we have a battle with RiverClan? Have you thought about that?"

"You worry too much," Graystripe snapped. "It won't come to that. Now that Brokenstar's gone and WindClan is back, the Clans will be at peace."

"RiverClan doesn't seem to be acting very peacefully," Fireheart pointed out. "You know they've been hunting on Sunningrocks, in our territory."

"They've been hunting on Sunningrocks since before I was kitted," scoffed Graystripe, twisting to wash the base of his tail.

Fireheart carried on pacing. Graystripe just didn't seem to understand what he was doing. "Okay. What if a RiverClan patrol catches you?"

"Silverstream won't let that happen," answered Graystripe between long licks along his bushy tail.

"For StarClan's sake, aren't you even a bit worried?" Fireheart burst out, exasperated.

Graystripe stopped washing and looked up at his friend. "You don't get it, do you? StarClan must have planned this.

Look, Silverstream wants to see me—*even after what happened to Whiteclaw.* We share the same thoughts; it's as if we were born into the same Clan."

Fireheart realized it was pointless to argue anymore. "Come on," he meowed heavily. "We'd better get back before you're missed again."

Graystripe got to his paws. Side by side, he and Fireheart walked to the top of the ravine and looked down at the camp. Over and over, one thought echoed in Fireheart's mind—how could Graystripe love Crookedstar's daughter, but remain loyal to ThunderClan?

He glanced at Graystripe, and they began to climb down the steep slope home. They crept back into the camp the same way Graystripe had left it. Fireheart held his breath as he squeezed through the boundary wall, angry with Graystripe for making him sneak around like this. His heart sank as they rounded the nursery to find Whitestorm approaching them.

"Graystripe, you should be resting, not hanging around here. That cough of yours has already begun to spread. We don't want it getting into the nursery!" warned the warrior. Graystripe nodded and padded back toward the warriors' den. "And you"—Fireheart's ears flicked nervously as Whitestorm turned to him—"shouldn't you be training your apprentices?"

"I came back to get something from Yellowfang for a bellyache," Fireheart mumbled.

"Well, go and get it then," replied Whitestorm. "And once you have, you can make yourself useful and find some fresh-kill. It's leaf-bare—we can't have young warriors hanging around the camp doing nothing!"

"Yes, Whitestorm," meowed Fireheart. He turned away, relieved to escape any more questions, and ran toward Yellowfang's den.

Yellowfang was busy mixing herbs. There were several heaps of leaves gathered in front of her. Fireheart stood and watched her for a moment without speaking. He felt sad, drained after the row with Graystripe. He couldn't help wishing it were Spottedleaf here mixing herbs instead of Yellowfang.

Yellowfang glanced up at him. "My supplies are running low. I might need help to restock."

Fireheart didn't reply. He was just wondering if he should confide his worries about Graystripe when she interrupted his thoughts.

"It looks like there's whitecough in the camp," she growled, prodding impatiently at a dried leaf. "Two cases this morning."

"Swiftpaw?" asked Fireheart.

The old medicine cat shook her head. "Swiftpaw's just got a cold. It's Speckletail's kit. And Patchpelt. Not serious at the moment, but we need to concentrate on getting the Clan strong. Leaf-bare always brings the threat of greencough." Fireheart understood her concern. Greencough was a killer. Yellowfang looked up again. "What do you want?"

"Oh, nothing, just a bellyache, but it doesn't matter if you're busy."

"Bad?" she meowed.

"No," Fireheart admitted, unable to meet her gaze.

"Then come back when it is." The medicine cat went back to her mixing. Fireheart turned to leave, but Yellowfang called him back. "Make sure Graystripe stays in his den, will you? He's a strong young warrior. If he were resting, his cough would be better by now."

Fireheart's tail twitched nervously. Had she guessed that Graystripe had been slipping out of the camp? He waited, his heart thudding, in case she was going to say more, but Yellowfang was frowning at the herbs again, so he padded quietly away.

It was getting dark, and Fireheart knew he had only a short time left for hunting. He quickly caught a shrew, a chaffinch, and a mouse, but hesitated before returning to camp. His fears for Graystripe felt more important than anything Whitestorm might say if he didn't add something to the fresh-kill pile in time. Fireheart came to a decision—if Graystripe wouldn't listen to reason, maybe Silverstream would.

He stashed his catch beneath a tree root and covered it with leaves. For the second time that day, he turned toward Sunningrocks. The rain that had been threatening all day finally began to fall. It was drumming steadily on the bracken by the time Fireheart crept down the shadowy slope toward the river.

Even in the rain, Silverstream's scent was easy to find. Fireheart followed the trail to the place where he had found Graystripe and Silverstream together. Hyper-alert, he padded onto the shore. The dark water rushed past relentlessly, sending a shiver down Fireheart's spine. He had no desire to swim across. His fur did not have the oily protection from the water that that of the RiverClan cats had, and leaf-bare was no season to get a soaking.

Suddenly Fireheart froze. He smelled RiverClan warriors!

He dropped to a crouch and looked across the river to see Silverstream pushing her way through the trailing branches of a willow. Behind her came two of her Clan, one of them a warrior with massive shoulders and battle-torn ears. The warrior sniffed the air suspiciously and peered around.

Fireheart heard the blood roaring in his ears. Had the warrior picked up his scent?

CHAPTER 15

❧

Very, very quietly, Fireheart backed into the bracken. The RiverClan warrior had stopped smelling the air, but he was still looking around.

Fireheart turned, still crouching, and began to creep away. He heard a small splash behind him. A cat had slipped into the river. Fireheart glanced over his shoulder, his heart pounding. Through the bracken he could see a silver head bobbing toward him. Silverstream! But where were the two other cats? He circled cautiously, tasting the air with an open mouth. No scent of them nearby. They must have moved on. He looked back at Silverstream, swimming determinedly across the river. For a moment Fireheart wondered if this was a trap, wondered if he should run, but his concern about Graystripe made him stay.

The silver tabby climbed onto the bank and hissed quietly, "Fireheart, I know you're there. I can smell you! It's okay, Stonefur and Shadepaw have gone."

Fireheart didn't move.

"Fireheart, I wouldn't let anything happen to Graystripe's

closest friend!" She sounded impatient. "Believe me, for StarClan's sake!"

Fireheart crept slowly from his hiding place.

Silverstream stared at him, her tail twitching. "What are you doing here?"

"I was looking for you," he whispered, painfully aware he was in enemy territory.

Silverstream flicked her ears in alarm. "Is Graystripe okay? Has his cough gotten worse?"

Fireheart was irritated by her concern. He didn't want to know how much this she-cat cared for his best friend. "He's fine!" he growled, his caution swept away by anger. "But he won't be if he carries on meeting you!"

Silverstream bristled. "I won't let anything bad happen to Graystripe!"

"Oh, really?" Fireheart snorted. "And what could you do to protect him?"

"I am a Clan leader's daughter," meowed Silverstream.

"Does that give you the power to control your father's warriors? You're hardly more than an apprentice!"

"Like you!" she hissed indignantly.

"Yes, that's true," Fireheart admitted. "And that's why I'm not sure I could protect Graystripe from the anger of his own Clan—or yours—if they find out you're seeing each other."

Silverstream tried to glare at him, but her eyes were clouded with emotion. "I can't stop seeing him," she meowed. Her voice softened to a whisper. "I love him."

"But the tension between our Clans is bad enough already!" Fireheart was too angry to feel any sympathy. "We know RiverClan is hunting in our territory. . . ."

The defiant gleam returned to Silverstream's eyes. "If ThunderClan understood why, it wouldn't begrudge what we catch there!"

"Why?" Fireheart flashed back at her.

"My Clan is hungry. Our kits cry because their mothers have no milk. The elders are dying for lack of decent prey."

Fireheart stared, taken aback. "But you've got the river!" he protested. Every cat knew that RiverClan enjoyed the best hunting of all—fish from the river, as well as woodland prey in the fields beyond.

"It's not enough. Twolegs have taken over our territory downstream. They built a camp there all greenleaf and stayed as long as the fish were plentiful. By the time they went, the fishing was scarce. And the damage they've done to the forest means that even woodland prey is harder to find."

Fireheart felt a pang of pity in spite of his anger. He could guess how serious this must be for RiverClan. They were used to their rich diet of fish, and grew fat on it every greenleaf so that they could endure the harsh moons of leaf-bare. He stared at the she-cat with new eyes. She wasn't slim, he realized—she was skinny. As her wet coat clung to her, he could see her ribs. Suddenly he understood Crookedstar's hostility to Bluestar's plan at the Gathering. "That's why you didn't want WindClan to come home!"

"Rabbits run on the moorlands all year round," Silverstream

explained. "They were our only hope of making it through leaf-bare without losing kits." She shook her head slowly before lifting her gaze back to Fireheart.

"Does Graystripe know all this?" he asked.

Silverstream nodded. Fireheart looked at her, perplexed for a moment. But he couldn't let these feelings get in the way of the warrior code—and neither could his friend. "Whatever problems your Clan has, you still have to stop seeing Graystripe."

"No," answered Silverstream, lifting her chin. Her eyes flashed. "How can our love do any harm?"

Fireheart returned her stare. Another shiver ran down his back as the cold rain seeped through his thick pelt.

Suddenly Silverstream hissed, making Fireheart jump. "You must leave, the patrol's coming."

Fireheart heard a faint rustle on the other side of the river. It would be pointless—and dangerous—to stay any longer. The rustling noise was growing closer. Without saying good-bye, he bounded back into the wet bracken and headed home.

He raced back toward the stash of fresh-kill he'd left beneath the oak tree. Halfway home, the scent of a fresh Two-leg trail stopped him in his tracks, reminding him of Princess. He wondered whether there was time to follow the trail back to Twolegplace. He wanted to know if she had kitted yet. But Princess would probably be safely tucked up in her Twoleg nest by now, and the Clan needed fresh-kill. With an uneasy twinge, Fireheart realized that Graystripe wasn't the only one with divided loyalties.

Rain began to drip from the ends of his whiskers. He shook the drops away and bounded on toward his hoard of fresh-kill.

The camp was silent by the time he arrived, the cats sheltering in their dens. Fireheart crossed the muddy clearing and dropped his catch on the pile. Taking a piece for himself, he trotted toward the warriors' den. There was no way he was eating outside tonight.

He pushed his head inside the den. Graystripe was dozing, to Fireheart's relief. He might actually get better if he wasn't charging through the forest, looking for Silverstream.

"Yellowfang hasn't taken any fresh-kill yet." Whitestorm's meow sounded from the shadows. "She's been too busy. I think she would appreciate that mouse you're carrying."

Fireheart nodded and backed out again. If Yellowfang was too busy to fetch food, it must mean the sickness in the camp was getting worse. Fireheart raced across the clearing, stopping only to pick up another mouse before hurrying through the fern tunnel.

A tabby kit lay in a nest of moss in the bracken at the edge of the clearing. Yellowfang crouched beside it, trying to persuade it to eat some herbs. The kit snuffled pitifully, blinking up at her with streaming eyes and nose. Fireheart realized this must be the kit with whitecough.

Yellowfang turned when she heard Fireheart arrive. "Is that for me?" she meowed, looking at the mice hanging from Fireheart's mouth. He nodded and dropped them on the ground. "Thanks. Now that you're here, why don't you see if you can persuade this kit to take his medicine?" She padded over to the mice, moving stiffly from her old shoulder injury, and began to gnaw on one hungrily.

Fireheart approached the kit. It looked up at him, opening its tiny mouth in a rasping, painful cough. Fireheart gently pushed a small green herb toward it. "If you want to be a warrior, you'll have to get used to swallowing these horrible things," he mewed. "When you make your trip to the Moonstone, you have to eat herbs far worse than this."

The kit looked wonderingly at him through half-closed eyes.

"Think of it as practice," Fireheart urged. "Practice for when you become a warrior."

The kit reached forward and took a tentative mouthful.

Fireheart gave it an encouraging purr.

Yellowfang appeared at his side. "Well done," she meowed. She gestured with her nose, and Fireheart understood she wanted to talk to him. He followed her to the shelter of the tall rock where she slept. The rain was still falling, and Yellowfang's matted gray fur was soaked, her sodden tail dragging in the dirt.

"Bluestar has whitecough," she meowed gravely.

"But whitecough isn't that serious, right?"

Yellowfang shook her head. "It came on very quickly," she meowed, "and it's affected her badly." Fireheart's stomach tightened as he remembered the dwindling number of lives left to the Clan leader. "I warned her to stay away from the other sick cats, but she wanted to see them," Yellowfang went on. "She's sleeping in her den at the moment. Frostfur is with her."

The fear in Yellowfang's eyes made Fireheart wonder if she knew the truth about Bluestar's lives. Fireheart had assumed he was the only cat in the camp whom Bluestar had shared her secret with. The rest of the Clan thought she had four lives left, but perhaps a medicine cat could sense these things instinctively.

The truth was, if Bluestar lost this life, she would have only one more left.

CHAPTER 16

❦

The rain continued through the night and into the next morning. But by sunhigh, the clouds began to clear. A somber air hung over the clearing as the Clan waited for news of their leader.

Fireheart crept out from the patch of brambles by the boundary wall, where he'd sheltered since dawn. He padded over to Bluestar's den in the side of Highrock. There was no sound from inside. As he turned away, he ran into Willowpelt carrying food to the nursery. She tipped her head questioningly to one side.

Fireheart knew she was hoping for news of Bluestar. "Nothing to report, I'm afraid." He shrugged.

Fireheart had given Cinderpaw and Brackenpaw a day's rest from training. He could see them now, lounging outside their den, looking bored. Fireheart knew he had let them down, but he wanted to stay in camp while Bluestar was sick. At least Tigerclaw wasn't here to criticize his decision. The great deputy had taken out the dawn patrol.

Suddenly the lichen at Bluestar's den twitched and Frostfur burst through. She raced across the clearing to Yellowfang's den and reappeared within moments with the medicine cat behind her.

Fireheart bounded over to Bluestar's den just as Frost-fur and Yellowfang pushed through the hanging lichen. He stopped outside and sat down, his heart racing. Frostfur peered out.

"What's wrong?" Fireheart asked, his voice trembling.

Frostfur closed her eyes. "She has greencough," she told him bleakly. "Stand watch and make sure no one comes inside." She ducked back inside.

Fireheart sat motionless as shock flooded through him. Greencough! Bluestar really was in danger of losing another life.

A sharp yowl outside the camp made him turn and look toward the gorse tunnel. Dustpaw exploded into the clearing and skidded to a halt beside Fireheart. "I've come from Tiger-claw," he panted. "I have a message for Bluestar."

"She's sick," Fireheart replied. "You can't go in."

Dustpaw flicked his tail impatiently. "Tigerclaw needs to see her at the Thunderpath. It's very urgent."

"What's wrong?"

Dustpaw glared at him. "Tigerclaw asked for Bluestar," he sneered. "Not some kittypet pretending to be a warrior!"

Fury shot through Fireheart and he unsheathed his claws. "Bluestar can't leave the camp," he growled. He flattened his ears and moved so that he blocked the entrance to his leader's den.

"Fireheart is right." Yellowfang's rough meow sounded behind him. She had come out of Bluestar's den.

Dustpaw looked at the medicine cat, shrinking beneath her orange gaze. "Tigerclaw has found evidence of ShadowClan warriors in our territory," he meowed. "They've invaded our hunting grounds!"

In spite of his fear for Bluestar, Fireheart felt his lip curl in anger. How dared they? After what ThunderClan had done for them!

But Yellowfang wasn't interested in Dustpaw's report. She turned to Fireheart, her eyes filled with urgency. "Fireheart," she meowed. "Tell me, do you know whether there is any catnip in the Twolegplace?"

"Catnip?" Fireheart echoed.

"I need it for Bluestar," Yellowfang explained. "It's an herb I haven't used for moons, but I think it will help her." The medicine cat had Fireheart's full attention now. She continued, "It has soft leaves and an irresistible scent. . . ."

Fireheart interrupted her. "Yes, I know where to find some!" He had never seen it in the woods, but as a kit he had rolled in a patch in his Twoleg home.

"Good," replied Yellowfang. "I need as much as you can carry, and fast."

"What about Tigerclaw?" demanded Dustpaw.

"Tigerclaw will have to deal with it on his own for the moment!" Yellowfang snapped.

Cinderpaw had been watching them from the tree stump. She bounded up. "Deal with what himself?" she mewed excitedly. Fireheart signaled her to be quiet with an urgent flick of his tail.

Dustpaw ignored the apprentice. "ShadowClan could be in our territory by now!" he hissed.

Cinderpaw's eyes widened but she held her tongue.

Yellowfang paused to think. "Where's Whitestorm?" she asked.

"Patrolling Sunningrocks with Sandpaw and Mousefur," Dustpaw answered.

Yellowfang nodded. "With Bluestar sick and Fireheart fetching catnip, we can't risk sending any more warriors out of the camp. If ShadowClan *is* in our territory, it might attack here. They've done it before," she reminded him grimly.

"If I'm quick getting the catnip," Fireheart put in, "I could meet Tigerclaw afterward and bring back his message for Bluestar."

Dustpaw's eyes flashed. "But he wants Bluestar to see the evidence for herself. ShadowClan has left the remains of fresh-kill on our side of the Thunderpath!"

Yellowfang silenced him with a growl. "Bluestar doesn't need to see the evidence," she rasped. "The word of her deputy ought to be enough."

"Tigerclaw just needs to be told that Bluestar can't come," meowed Fireheart. "I'll take the message to him after I've fetched the catnip. Where is he?"

"I'll go!" Dustpaw spat. "Do you think you're a better messenger than me because you're a warrior and I'm just an apprentice?" He threw Fireheart a look of pure hatred.

But Yellowfang had no time for quarrels. "The Clan will need protecting while Fireheart is gone!" she hissed at

Dustpaw, flattening her ears. "Isn't that duty important enough for you? Now, where is Tigerclaw?"

"Beside the burned ash tree that overhangs the Thunderpath," Dustpaw replied sulkily.

"Right," Yellowfang growled. "Go now, Fireheart! Quickly!"

As Fireheart sped away across the clearing, he heard small pawsteps sprinting after him. "Fireheart, wait!"

"Go back to your den, Cinderpaw," he meowed over his shoulder without slowing down.

"But I could go and give Tigerclaw the message while you get the catnip!"

Fireheart stopped in his tracks and turned to face his young apprentice. "Cinderpaw, if there are any ShadowClan warriors around, you need to stay in camp." Cinderpaw looked crushed, but Fireheart didn't have time to worry about her feelings. "Go back to your den," he growled. Without waiting to see her reaction, he turned and charged out of the camp.

He raced through Tallpines and wove quickly through the undergrowth that backed onto Twolegplace. As he scrambled onto the fence that bordered his old home, the familiar smell of the garden filled his nostrils. Memories flooded his mind, making him dizzy for a moment. He thought of sunny afternoons playing in the garden with the toys his Twolegs held for him. He almost expected to hear them rattling his dinner and calling his kittypet name. Then he thought of Bluestar, fighting against greencough.

Fireheart leaped down into the garden and bounded across

the lawn to the place where he remembered the catnip had grown. He inhaled deeply, his mouth open, and breathed out with relief. The enticing scent was still here somewhere.

Fireheart padded along the row of plants, sniffing the air. He couldn't see the catnip, and all the time he was getting nearer and nearer to his old Twoleg nest. Fireheart's steps grew slower. Scents of his kithood mingled with the catnip now, confusing him.

Fireheart shook his head to clear it, and concentrated on the catnip scent. He pushed his way under a large bush, still dripping from the overnight rain, and found a large patch of the soft, fragrant herb. The recent frost had killed some of the leaves, but the sheltering bush had protected enough for Yellowfang to use. Fireheart bit off as many leaves as he could carry. Their flavor seeped deliciously into his mouth, but he was careful not to chew, much as he wanted to. Bluestar would need every drop of their precious juice.

With his jaws full, he turned and raced back up the garden. He leaped over the fence and pelted back through the forest, ignoring the brambles that dragged at his coat. He felt as if his lungs would burst—with his jaws closed to hold the herbs, he could breathe only through his nose.

Yellowfang was waiting for him in the gorse tunnel. Fireheart dropped the catnip at her paws and took a long gulp of air, his sides heaving. With a grateful look, Yellowfang picked up the leaves and rushed away toward Bluestar's den.

As he sat gasping for air, Fireheart realized he could smell Cinderpaw's excited scent in the gorse tunnel. He sniffed the ground around him. Had Cinderpaw left the camp even after he'd warned her about the ShadowClan warriors?

Fireheart dashed to the apprentices' den and stuck his head inside. Brackenpaw was alone, sleeping.

"Where's Cinderpaw?" Fireheart meowed.

Brackenpaw lifted his head sleepily. "Uh, what?"

"Cinderpaw! Where is she?"

"Don't know," answered Brackenpaw, confused.

Fireheart withdrew his head and looked around the clearing. Frostfur was pacing outside Bluestar's den, her coat ruffled with agitation.

Fireheart wondered what to do. He didn't have time to find Cinderpaw himself, and he didn't want to tell the other warriors that she was missing. *Graystripe!* he thought suddenly. Graystripe could look for her while he went to find Tigerclaw. Fireheart hurried to the warriors' den and slipped inside.

Graystripe's nest was empty. A flash of anger shot through Fireheart. Where was his friend when he needed him? As if he couldn't guess! Fireheart snorted crossly. Cinderpaw would have to fend for herself until he had found Tigerclaw and told him Bluestar was sick.

Fireheart raced back through the gorse tunnel and began the journey to the Thunderpath. As he followed the trail up the side of the ravine and into the woods, he was aware that Cinderpaw's scent hung in the air. She must have come this way. Of course! She had gone to meet Tigerclaw herself! The fur on Fireheart's spine prickled with worry and frustration. How could she be so foolish?

As he skirted Snakerocks, Fireheart began to smell the Thunderpath and hear the roar of its monsters.

Suddenly a shrill, high-pitched squeal sounded from the edge of the trees. Fireheart felt the blood run cold in his veins. It was the same cry he had heard in his dream.

He raced out of the trees and skidded to a halt on the grass border beside the Thunderpath. He looked desperately up and down the verge and spotted an ash tree, charred by lightning. That must be the place where Dustpaw had said Tigerclaw wanted to meet Bluestar. But the deputy was still some way in the distance, padding calmly toward the ash.

Fireheart broke into a run. The verge was very narrow here, with scarcely room for a rabbit, but Fireheart kept going. He called out to Tigerclaw as he ran.

"Did you hear that cry?" But the roar of an approaching monster drowned out his words.

Fireheart shuddered as it passed, waiting for the noise to die away so he could call out again to Tigerclaw. Then he noticed something beside the ash, a dark shape on the thin strip of grass. With a sickening jolt, he recognized the small body lying motionless beside the Thunderpath. It was Cinderpaw.

CHAPTER 17

Fireheart stared in horror. Ahead of him, Tigerclaw had reached the limp body and stood looking down at it, his massive shoulders rigid with shock. Fireheart forced himself nearer. Tentatively he stretched his head forward and sniffed Cinderpaw's flank. She smelled of Thunderpath. One of her hind legs was twisted and glistening with blood. Fireheart was trembling so much he could hardly stand. Then he saw her side moving. She was still breathing! Speechless with relief, he looked up at Tigerclaw.

"She's alive," the deputy growled. He fixed his amber stare on Fireheart. "What was she doing here?"

"She came to find you," Fireheart whispered.

"You mean you sent her here?"

Fireheart's eyes widened with surprise. Did Tigerclaw think he would be so stupid? "I told her to stay in camp!" he protested. "She came by herself." *Because I couldn't make her listen to me!* he realized with dismay.

Tigerclaw snorted. "We must get her home." He bent down with his mouth open, reaching for the small, crumpled body, but Fireheart dipped his head and picked up the apprentice by the scruff of her neck before Tigerclaw could touch her. He began to drag Cinderpaw into the woods as gently as he could, her body hanging limply between his front paws.

Darkstripe came bounding up to them. "I've checked Snakerocks again, Tigerclaw. There's no sign of Shadow—" He broke off when he saw Cinderpaw dangling from Fireheart's mouth. "What's happened?"

Fireheart didn't wait to hear Tigerclaw's answer. He stumbled away through the trees with his precious burden. He could have prevented this accident! If only he'd made Cinderpaw listen to him; if only he'd been a better mentor. Now her body was damaged and bleeding and she made no sound as she dangled from his jaws. Her hind paws scored a shallow trail through the leaves as, carefully, Fireheart carried her home.

Yellowfang was not in her clearing. The two kits with whitecough were curled together in their shelter, fast asleep. Fireheart laid Cinderpaw on the cold ground, then made a nest for her in the bracken by circling around and around. When he had finished, he grasped Cinderpaw's scruff and gently pulled her inside.

"Fireheart?" Yellowfang meowed from the clearing. Tigerclaw must have told her about Cinderpaw. Fireheart hopped out of the nest. "She's in here," he croaked, feeling weak with relief at seeing the medicine cat.

"Let me look," Yellowfang ordered. She brushed past Fireheart and climbed into the bracken to examine Cinderpaw. Fireheart sat down and waited.

At last Yellowfang jumped out. "She's hurt very badly," she meowed, her eyes dark with concern. "But I think I might be able to save her."

It was a tiny hope, like a single sparkling dewdrop clinging to his pelt. Fireheart felt it glisten for a moment before Yellowfang went on: "I can't promise anything." She looked deep into Fireheart's eyes and murmured, "Bluestar is very sick and I can do no more for her. StarClan must decide her fate now."

Fireheart felt his eyes cloud with emotion; he could hardly see Yellowfang's face, but he heard her speak to him again, her voice gentle. "Go and sit with Bluestar," she meowed. "She was asking for you earlier. I will take care of Cinderpaw."

Fireheart nodded blindly and turned away. Bluestar had been his mentor, and more than that, there had been a bond between them since their first meeting. But he felt torn. He should be with Cinderpaw, too.

A shadow loomed at the far end of the fern tunnel. Tigerclaw was sitting at the entrance to Yellowfang's den, his head held high as usual. Fireheart's shoulders stiffened with anger. Why couldn't the great warrior show some sign of sorrow? After all, Cinderpaw had come looking for him. And for what? There hadn't been any evidence of ShadowClan fresh-kill that Fireheart had noticed! He walked past Tigerclaw without a word, and headed across the clearing toward Blue-star's den.

Longtail was sitting on guard outside. He glanced sideways but didn't try to stop Fireheart as the young warrior pushed through the lichen.

Goldenflower, one of the queens, was inside. Fireheart could see her eyes shining in the gloom, and the pale fur of Bluestar lying curled in her nest. Goldenflower leaned forward and gently licked Bluestar's head to cool it, like a mother nursing her kit. Fireheart's heart ached as he thought of Cinderpaw. Would Frostfur be at her daughter's side by now?

"Yellowfang has given her catnip and feverfew," Goldenflower murmured to Fireheart. "We can only watch and wait now." She got to her paws and touched Fireheart's nose with her muzzle. "Will you be okay to sit with her?" she asked gently. Fireheart nodded and Goldenflower padded softly out of the den.

Fireheart lowered himself onto his belly, stretching his forepaws in front of him so that they just touched his leader's face. He lay very still, his eyes fixed on Bluestar's limp body. She didn't even have the strength to cough now. Fireheart could hear her breathing in the darkness, shallow and rasping, and he listened to the faltering rhythm as the night slowly passed.

Her breathing stopped just before dawn. Fireheart had almost dozed off when he realized the cave was silent. There was no noise from the camp outside either, just a deathly hush, as if the whole Clan were holding its breath.

Bluestar was completely still. Fireheart knew she was with StarClan, preparing for her remaining life. He had watched Bluestar lose a life before. He felt his fur prickle at the eerie peace that seemed to enfold her body, but there was nothing he could do, so he waited.

Suddenly Bluestar gasped. "Fireheart, is that you?" she meowed in a croaky voice.

"Yes, Bluestar," Fireheart murmured. "I'm here."

"I have lost another life." Bluestar's voice was weak, but the relief made Fireheart want to reach forward and lick her between the ears, as Goldenflower had done. "When I lose this one, I will not be able to return."

Fireheart swallowed hard. The thought of the Clan losing its great leader pained him, but the thought of losing his mentor and friend hurt even more. "How do you feel? Shall I fetch Yellowfang?"

Bluestar shook her head slowly. "The fever has gone. I am well enough. I just need to rest."

"Very well," meowed Fireheart. Light was beginning to filter through the lichen, and his head swam from his wakeful night.

"You must be tired," meowed Bluestar. "Go and get some sleep."

"Yes." Fireheart heaved himself up. His legs felt stiff from lying so long. "Is there anything you need?"

"No. Just tell Yellowfang what has happened," answered Bluestar. "Thank you for sitting with me."

Fireheart tried to purr but it caught in his throat. There would be time for more words later. He pushed his way out through the lichen.

Outside a harsh brightness made him blink. It had snowed in the night. Fireheart stared in amazement. He had never seen snow before—his Twoleg owners had kept him shut inside when he was a very young kit whenever it was cold. But he'd heard the Clan elders talk of it. He nodded to Darkstripe, who had replaced Longtail guarding Bluestar's den, and stepped into the strange powder. It felt wet and cold, crunching loudly under his paws.

Tigerclaw was standing in the clearing. It was still snowing and the flakes settled on the tabby's thick fur without melting. Fireheart could hear him giving orders for the nursery wall to be padded with leaves to keep out the cold. "Then I want a hole to be scraped out where we can store prey," the ThunderClan deputy instructed. "Use snow to line it, and cover it with more snow once it has been filled. We may as well make use of the snow while it's here."

Warriors raced around Tigerclaw, following his orders. "Mousefur, Longtail! Organize some hunting parties. We need as much fresh-kill as we can get before the prey takes to their burrows for good!" Tigerclaw spotted Fireheart padding across the clearing. "Fireheart, wait," he called. "Oh, I suppose you'll have to rest. I can't imagine you'll be any use on a hunting party this morning."

Fireheart stared at the dark warrior, hostility rising like bile in his throat. "I'm going to see how Cinderpaw is first," he growled.

Tigerclaw held his gaze for a moment. "How's Bluestar?"

Mistrust ruffled Fireheart's fur like a cold breeze. He'd heard Bluestar lie to Tigerclaw once before about how many lives she had left. "I'm no medicine cat," he answered. "I can't say."

Tigerclaw snorted impatiently, then turned away and went back to giving orders. Fireheart walked over to Yellowfang's den, relieved to escape the frenetic bustle of the camp. His heart began to pound as he wondered what state he would find Cinderpaw in. "Yellowfang," he called.

"Hush!" Yellowfang sprang from Cinderpaw's bracken nest. "She's sleeping at last. She's had a hard night. I couldn't give her poppy seeds to ease the pain until she'd recovered from the shock."

"But she's going to live?" Fireheart's legs felt wobbly with relief.

"I can't be for sure for a few days. She's hurt inside, and one of her hind legs is badly broken."

"But it'll mend, won't it?" Fireheart pleaded desperately. "She'll be training again by newleaf?"

Yellowfang shook her head, her yellow eyes sympathetic. "Fireheart, whatever happens, Cinderpaw will never be a warrior now."

Fireheart's head spun. He was dizzy with lack of sleep, and this devastating news sapped the last of his energy. Cinderpaw had been entrusted to him for her warrior training. Memories of the naming ceremony pricked like cruel thorns—Cinderpaw's excitement, Frostfur's motherly pride . . . "Does Frostfur know?" he meowed, feeling hollow.

"Yes, she was here till dawn. She's back in the nursery now; there are other kits to tend to. I'll ask one of the elders to sit with Cinderpaw. She needs to be kept warm."

"I can do that." Fireheart padded over to the nest where

Cinderpaw was sleeping and looked inside. She squirmed, and her blood-smeared sides heaved, as though she were fighting a battle as she slept.

Yellowfang gently nudged Fireheart with her nose. "You need to get some sleep," she rasped. "Leave Cinderpaw to me."

Fireheart stayed where he was. "Bluestar lost another life," he burst out. Yellowfang blinked for a moment, then lifted her head to StarClan. She didn't utter a word, but Fireheart could see the anguish in her orange eyes. "You know, don't you?" he murmured.

Yellowfang lowered her chin and gazed into his eyes. "That this is Bluestar's final life? Yes, I know. A medicine cat can tell these things."

"Will the rest of the Clan be able to tell as well?" Fireheart asked, thinking of Tigerclaw.

Yellowfang narrowed her eyes. "No. She will be no weaker in this life than she was in any of her others."

Fireheart blinked gratefully at her.

"Now," Yellowfang ordered, "do you want some poppy seeds to help you sleep?"

Fireheart shook his head. Part of him longed for the deep, easy sleep they would bring. But if Tigerclaw was right and ShadowClan really was about to attack ThunderClan's borders, he did not want to dull his senses. He might be needed to defend the camp.

Graystripe was back in the warriors' den. Fireheart did not speak to him; his rage at finding him missing the night before lingered like a dull bruise. He padded silently to his nest, circled once, and settled down to wash.

Graystripe looked up. "You're back, then." He sounded edgy, as if he wanted to say more.

Fireheart stopped licking his forepaw and stared at Graystripe.

"You tried to warn Silverstream off," Graystripe hissed furiously. Willowpelt, who was dozing on the other side of the den, opened one eye, then closed it again.

Graystripe lowered his voice. "Stay out of it, will you?" he spat. "I'm going to keep on seeing her, whatever you do or say."

Fireheart snorted and flashed a resentful glance at his friend. His talk with Silverstream seemed so long ago, he'd almost forgotten it. But he hadn't forgotten that Graystripe had been missing when he'd needed help finding Cinderpaw. He laid his head angrily on his muddy forepaws and closed his eyes. Cinderpaw was battling against her injuries and Bluestar was on her ninth life. As far as Fireheart was concerned, Graystripe could do what he liked.

CHAPTER 18

Graystripe had already left his nest when Fireheart awoke the next day. He could tell it was sunhigh by the light that glowed through the branches. He rose, his body still weary with grief, and pushed his head out of the den. Snow must have been falling all morning, for it lay thick on the ground and had drifted against the den. Fireheart found himself gazing out over a white wall that was as high as his shoulder.

The usual bustle of the camp seemed muted. Fireheart could see Willowpelt and Halftail whispering on the far side of the clearing. Mousefur was picking her way laboriously toward the store of fresh-kill, a rabbit dangling from her jaws. She stopped and sneezed, then carried on.

Fireheart lifted one paw and rested it on top of the snow. It felt hard at first, but when he pressed down, the thin covering of ice cracked and he gasped as his leg plunged into the drift. Fireheart snorted as he found himself up to his muzzle in snow. Shaking his head and lifting his chin, he leaped forward, only to sink into more deep snow. He struggled on, alarm rising in his chest. He felt as if he were drowning in snow! Then, all of a sudden, there was solid ground under his paws. He had reached the edge of the clearing. The snow here was only a mouse-length deep, and Fireheart sat down with a soft crunch, relieved.

He tensed when he saw Graystripe plowing through the snow toward him. The gray warrior seemed unbothered by it, protected from its damp chill by his thick pelt. His face was shadowed with sorrow. "Have you heard about Bluestar?" he asked as he neared. "She lost a life to greencough."

Fireheart flicked his ears impatiently. He could have told his friend that last night. "I know," he snapped. "I was with her."

"Why didn't you tell me?" mewed Graystripe, shocked.

"You weren't exactly in a friendly mood last night, if you remember. Anyway, if you weren't always off breaking the warrior code, you might know what was going on in your own Clan," he snarled.

Graystripe's ears twitched uncomfortably. "I've just seen Cinderpaw," he meowed. "I'm sorry she's so sick."

"How is she?"

"She looked bad, but Yellowfang said she's pulling through," replied Graystripe.

Fireheart stared anxiously across the clearing and stood up. He wanted to see his apprentice for himself.

Graystripe meowed, "She's asleep now. Frostfur's with her, and Yellowfang doesn't want anyone else disturbing her."

Fireheart flinched involuntarily. How was he going to tell Frostfur that it was his fault that Cinderpaw went to the Thunderpath? Instinctively, Fireheart turned to Graystripe, seeking reassurance. But Graystripe was trudging across the snowy clearing toward the nursery. *Off to see Silverstream*, Fireheart guessed resentfully, sheathing and unsheathing his claws as he watched his friend disappear from sight.

Fireheart noticed Speckletail, the oldest queen from the nursery and the mother of the kit with whitecough, only when she stopped right in front of him. "Is Tigerclaw inside?" she asked, pointing with her nose to the warriors' den.

Fireheart shook his head.

Speckletail mewed, "There's greencough in the nursery. Two of Brindleface's kits are sick."

"Greencough!" Fireheart gasped, shaken from his anger. "Will they die?"

"They might. But leaf-bare always brings greencough," Speckletail pointed out gently.

"Surely there's something we can do!" Fireheart protested.

"Yellowfang will do what she can," answered Speckletail. "But in the end, it's up to StarClan."

A new flash of fury flared in Fireheart's belly as Speckletail turned away and padded back to the nursery. How could the Clan tolerate these tragedies? He felt overwhelmed by the need to leave the camp, to escape the gloomy air that the rest of the Clan seemed content to breathe.

He jumped up and raced blindly across the snowy clearing, through the gorse tunnel and out into the forest. He was startled to find himself heading instinctively for the training hollow. The thought that he should be there, teaching Cinderpaw, was more than he could bear. As he veered to avoid it, he heard the voices of Whitestorm and Brackenpaw. The white-furred warrior must have taken Brackenpaw for training while Fireheart had been sleeping. Had no cat stopped to grieve for Bluestar's lost life? Fireheart's throat tightened as he fought back his rage and ran on, desperate to put as much distance as possible between himself and the camp.

He finally stopped beneath Tallpines, his sides heaving with the effort of running through the snow. There was stillness here that calmed him. Even the birds had stopped singing. Fireheart felt as if he were the only creature in the world.

He didn't know where he was going; he just padded on, letting the woods soothe him. As he walked, his mind cleared. He could do nothing for Cinderpaw, and Graystripe was out of reach, but he might be able to help Yellowfang fight the greencough. He would fetch some more catnip.

Fireheart turned his steps toward his old kittypet home, weaving through the brambles in the oak woods that backed onto Twolegplace. He leaped to the top of the fence at the end of his old home, nudging a ridge of snow into the garden below. It fell with a soft clump. Fireheart peered down into the garden. He could see tracks, smaller than a cat's. A squirrel had been out hunting for its store of nuts.

It didn't take Fireheart long to pluck a generous mouthful of leaves from the catnip bush. He wanted to take as much as he could. Its soft leaves might not survive this weather; this could be his last chance to gather it.

With his mouth crammed, Fireheart stared toward the swinging flap he had used as a kit. He wondered if his Twoleg housefolk still lived there. They'd been kind to him. He had spent his first leaf-bare cosseted in their nest, warm and safe from the cruelties of Thunderpaths and greencough.

The scent of this catnip must be going to my head, he thought sharply. He bounded up the garden and onto the fence with a single leap. He was unnerved by how much the thought of his Two-leg home had stirred him. Did he really want the safety and predictability of a kittypet's life? *Of course not!* Fireheart shook the thought away. But the idea of returning to camp didn't appeal to him yet.

Suddenly he thought of Princess.

Fireheart raced along the edge of the woods to the part of Twolegplace where his sister's garden lay. When her fence was in sight, he dug down through the snow and buried the catnip beneath a layer of dead leaves to protect it from the cold. He was still panting from his run when he leaped onto the fence and called out to Princess. Then he scrambled back down into the woods to wait for her.

The snow made his paws ache with cold as he paced restlessly under an oak tree. *Perhaps she is kitting*, he told himself, *or shut inside*. He had just persuaded himself he wasn't going to see her today when he heard her familiar mew. He looked up to see her standing on top of her fence. Fireheart felt a shiver of anticipation. Her belly was no longer swollen. Princess must have kitted.

He breathed in her scent as she approached and felt it warm him. "You've kitted!" he meowed.

Princess gently touched his nose with hers. "Yes," she mewed softly.

"Did it go okay? Are the kits all right?"

Princess purred. "It was fine. I have five healthy kits," she meowed, her eyes glowing with pleasure. Fireheart licked her head and she mewed, "I didn't expect to see you out in this weather."

"I came to find some catnip," Fireheart told her. "There's greencough in the camp."

Princess's eyes clouded with worry. "Are many of your Clan ill?"

"Three so far." Fireheart hesitated for a moment, then meowed sadly, "Our leader lost another life last night."

"Another life?" echoed Princess. "What do you mean? I thought it was only an old she-cat's tale that cats have nine lives."

"Bluestar was granted nine lives by StarClan because she's leader of our Clan," Fireheart explained.

Princess looked at him in awe. "Then it's true!"

"Only for Clan leaders. The rest of us have only one life, like you, and like Cinderpaw. . . ." Fireheart's voice trailed away.

"Cinderpaw?" Princess must have detected the grief in his voice.

Fireheart gazed into her eyes, and the thoughts that had been troubling him began to tumble out. "My apprentice," he meowed. "She was hit on the Thunderpath last night." His voice cracked as he remembered finding her broken, bleeding body. "She's badly hurt. She might still die. And even if she survives, she'll never become a warrior."

Princess moved closer and nuzzled him. "You spoke so fondly of her last time you were here," she mewed. "She sounded full of fun and energy."

"The accident shouldn't have happened," Fireheart growled. "I was supposed to meet Tigerclaw. He'd asked for Bluestar, but Bluestar was ill, so I offered to go instead. I had to fetch catnip first, and Cinderpaw went in my place." Princess looked alarmed and Fireheart added quickly, "I told her not to. But perhaps if I'd been a better mentor she'd have listened to me."

"I'm sure you're a good mentor." Princess tried to soothe him, but Fireheart hardly heard her.

"I don't know why Tigerclaw wanted Bluestar to meet him in such a dangerous place!" he spat. "He said there was evidence that ShadowClan had invaded our territory, but when I arrived there was no scent of them at all!"

"Was it a trap?" Princess suggested.

Fireheart looked into his sister's questioning eyes and suddenly began to wonder. "Why would Tigerclaw want to hurt Cinderpaw?"

"It was Bluestar he asked for," Princess pointed out.

Fireheart's fur bristled. Could his sister be right? Tigerclaw *had* summoned Bluestar to the narrowest part of the Thunderpath verge. Surely even Tigerclaw wouldn't deliberately put his Clan leader in danger? Fireheart shook the thought away. "I d-don't know," he stammered. "Everything's so confusing at the moment. Even Graystripe's hardly speaking to me."

"Why?"

Fireheart shrugged. "It's too complicated to explain." Princess nestled next to him in the snow, pressing her soft fur against his. "I just feel like such an outsider at the moment," Fireheart went on gloomily. "It's not easy being different."

"Different?" Princess looked puzzled.

"Being born a kittypet, when the other cats are all Clanborn."

"You seem like a Clanborn cat to me," mewed Princess. Fireheart blinked gratefully at her. She went on, "But if you're not happy in the Clan, you can always come home with me. My housefolk would look after you, I'm sure."

Fireheart pictured himself living his old kittypet life, warm, cozy, and safe. But he couldn't forget how he'd watched the woods from his Twoleg garden and dreamed of being out in the forest. A breeze stirred his thick fur and carried the scent of a mouse to his nose. Fireheart shook his head firmly. "Thank you, Princess," he meowed. "But I belong with my Clan now. I could never be happy in a Twoleg nest. I would miss the scents of the forest, and sleeping beneath Silverpelt, hunting my own food and sharing it with my Clan."

His sister's eyes gleamed. "It sounds like a good life," she purred. She looked down shyly at her paws. "Sometimes even I stare into the forest and wonder what it feels like to live out there."

Fireheart purred and stood up. "Then you understand?"

Princess nodded. "Are you going back now?"

"Yes. I must take the catnip to Yellowfang while it's fresh."

Princess stretched her head forward to press her muzzle into his side. "Perhaps my kits will be strong enough to meet you next time you come," she mewed.

Excitement tingled in Fireheart's belly. "I hope so!" he meowed.

As he turned to leave, Princess called, "Take care, brother. I don't want to lose you again."

"You won't," Fireheart promised.

"Good thinking, Fireheart," purred Whitestorm. He had seen Fireheart pad back into camp with his jaws crammed with catnip.

Fireheart's mouth had been watering all the way home, although he was beginning to think he'd be happy never to see another catnip bush again. But he was happier than when he'd left the camp. His sister had safely kitted and his head felt clearer.

He was heading toward Yellowfang's den when Tigerclaw appeared at his side.

"More catnip?" observed the great tabby, his eyes suspicious. "I wondered where you'd gone. Brackenpaw can take that to Yellowfang."

Brackenpaw was helping to clear away snow nearby.

"Come and take this catnip to Yellowfang," Tigerclaw ordered the apprentice.

Brackenpaw nodded and bounded over at once.

Fireheart dropped the bunch of leaves onto the ground. "I wanted to visit Cinderpaw," he meowed to Tigerclaw.

"Later," growled the deputy. He waited while Brackenpaw picked up the catnip and carried it off to Yellowfang's den. Then he turned back to Fireheart. "I want to know where Graystripe has been going."

Fireheart felt the heat rising under his fur. "I don't know," he replied, holding Tigerclaw's gaze.

Tigerclaw stared back at him, his eyes cold and hostile. "When you see him," he hissed, "you can tell him he's confined to the fallen oak."

"Yellowfang's old den?" Fireheart glanced at the tangled branches where the medicine cat had lived when she first came into the ThunderClan camp, when she was still considered a ShadowClan outcast. Swiftpaw was there, lying beside Speckletail's dark tabby kit.

"Cats with whitecough are confined there until they are well again."

"But Graystripe only has a cold," Fireheart protested.

"A cold is bad enough. He'll stay at the fallen oak!" Tigerclaw repeated. "Cats with greencough are to nest with Yellowfang. We must stop this sickness from spreading." The deputy's eyes flashed unsympathetically. Fireheart wondered if he thought of illness as a sign of weakness. "It is for the good of the Clan," Tigerclaw added.

"Yes, Tigerclaw. I'll tell Graystripe."

"And keep away from Bluestar," the deputy warned.

"But the greencough has left her," Fireheart objected.

"I am aware of that, but her den still reeks of the sickness. I can't afford to have any of my warriors falling ill. Whitestorm tells me that RiverClan warriors have been scented even closer to the camp. He also told me he had to train Brackenpaw today. I expect you to take charge of Brackenpaw's training tomorrow."

Fireheart nodded. "May I go and see Cinderpaw now?"

Tigerclaw looked at him.

"I doubt if Yellowfang has put her anywhere near the cats with greencough," Fireheart added with a flash of irritation. "I won't get infected."

"Very well," Tigerclaw agreed, and stalked away.

Fireheart met Brackenpaw in the middle of the clearing. "Yellowfang was very grateful for the catnip," Brackenpaw mewed.

"Good," answered Fireheart. "By the way, I'm teaching you how to catch birds tomorrow. I hope you're ready for a bit of tree climbing."

Brackenpaw's whiskers twitched excitedly. "Definitely. I'll meet you at the training hollow."

Fireheart nodded and carried on to Yellowfang's den. He spotted Brindleface's poor kits straightaway. They lay quietly in a bracken nest, coughing, their noses and eyes streaming.

Yellowfang greeted him. "Thanks for the catnip; we're going to need it. Patchpelt has greencough now." She gestured with her nose toward another nest in the bracken. Inside, Fireheart could see the old tom's matted black-and-white fur.

"How's Cinderpaw?" he asked, looking back at the medicine cat.

Yellowfang sighed. "She was awake earlier, but not for long. She has an infection in her leg. StarClan knows, I've tried everything, but she must fight this one herself."

Fireheart peered into Cinderpaw's nest. The little gray cat was twitching in her sleep, her injured leg twisted awkwardly to one side. Fireheart shuddered, suddenly afraid she might yet lose this struggle. He turned back to Yellowfang, looking for words of encouragement, but the medicine cat sat with her head low. She looked exhausted.

"Do you think Spottedleaf would have been able to save these cats?" she meowed unexpectedly, raising her head to meet his gaze.

Fireheart shivered. He could still sense Spottedleaf's presence here in the clearing. He remembered how efficiently she'd tended to Ravenpaw's shoulder wound after the battle with RiverClan, and how carefully she'd advised him about caring for Yellowfang when the old she-cat had first come to the ThunderClan camp. Then he looked at Yellowfang, her shoulders weighed down with experience. "I'm sure there's nothing Spottedleaf would have done differently," he told her.

One of the kits cried out and Yellowfang sprang up. As she passed, Fireheart leaned forward and gently stroked the old cat's side with his muzzle. She twitched her shoulder gratefully at him. Then, filled with sadness, he turned and padded toward the fern tunnel.

The white pelt of Frostfur appeared at the other end. She

must be coming to see Cinderpaw. As he approached the queen, Fireheart lifted his head and looked into her blue eyes. The sorrow in them made his heart twist with pain. "Frostfur?" he began.

The queen stopped.

"I . . . I'm sorry." Fireheart trembled as he spoke.

Frostfur looked confused. "What for?"

"I should have been able to stop Cinderpaw from going to the Thunderpath."

Frostfur gazed at him, but her expression gave away nothing except her sadness. "I don't blame you, Fireheart," she murmured. Then she lowered her head and carried on toward her kit.

Graystripe was back, munching a vole beside the nettle clump.

Fireheart padded over to him. "Tigerclaw says you've got to move to the fallen oak, with the whitecough cats," he meowed. With a prickle of resentment, he remembered how the deputy had questioned him about his friend.

"That won't be necessary," replied Graystripe cheerfully. "I'm better now. Yellowfang gave me the all-clear this morning."

Fireheart looked closely at Graystripe. His eyes were certainly bright again, and his runny nose had dried to an unappealing crust. At any other time Fireheart would have teased him about how much he looked like Runningnose, the ShadowClan medicine cat. Now he spat crossly, "Tigerclaw has noticed your disappearances. You should be more careful. Why can't you stay away from Silverstream, at least for now?"

Graystripe stopped chewing and stared angrily back at Fireheart. "And why can't you mind your own business?"

Fireheart closed his eyes and snorted with frustration. Would he ever get through to his friend? Then he wondered if he even cared anymore. After all, Graystripe hadn't asked about Cinderpaw.

Fireheart's stomach growled to tell him he was hungry. He might as well eat. He took a sparrow from the pile of fresh-kill and carried it away to a deserted corner of the camp to eat alone. As he settled down, he thought of Princess, far away in Twolegplace, with her newborn kits. Lonely and anxious, Fireheart stared across the camp and longed to see her again.

CHAPTER 19

In the following days, Fireheart struggled against the urge to visit his sister. His yearning to be with his kittypet kin was beginning to make him feel uncomfortable. He kept himself busy hunting in the snowy forests, replenishing the camp store.

He had had a successful hunt this afternoon, returning to camp with two mice and a chaffinch as the sun dipped behind the trees. He buried the mice in the snow store and took the chaffinch for his own supper.

As he finished his meal, he noticed Whitestorm padding toward him. "I want you to take Sandpaw out on the dawn patrol," the great white warrior meowed. "ShadowClan has been scented as close as the Owl Tree."

"ShadowClan?" Fireheart echoed in alarm. Perhaps Tigerclaw really had found evidence of an invasion after all. "I was planning to take Brackenpaw out again tomorrow."

"Isn't Graystripe better now?" asked Whitestorm. "He can take Brackenpaw."

Of course! thought Fireheart. And perhaps training his apprentice would keep Graystripe away from Silverstream for once. But that meant he would have to go on patrol with

Sandpaw. And Fireheart couldn't help thinking of the furious look Sandpaw had given him when he'd interrupted her fight with the RiverClan warrior beside the gorge. "Just me and Sandpaw?" he asked.

Whitestorm looked at him in surprise. "Sandpaw's almost a warrior, and you can take care of yourself," he replied.

Whitestorm had misunderstood Fireheart's concern. He wasn't afraid of being attacked by enemy cats; he was afraid Sandpaw hated him as much as Dustpaw did. But Fireheart didn't correct him. "Does Sandpaw know?"

"You can tell her," meowed Whitestorm.

Fireheart's ear twitched. He didn't think Sandpaw would be too thrilled by the idea of patrolling with him, but he didn't argue.

Whitestorm nodded briefly and bounded away toward the warriors' den. Fireheart sighed and padded over to where Sandpaw was sitting with the other apprentices.

"Sandpaw." Fireheart shifted uneasily. "Whitestorm wants you to patrol with me at dawn tomorrow."

He waited for a resentful hiss, but Sandpaw merely looked up at him and meowed, "Fine." Even Dustpaw looked surprised.

"O-okay," echoed Fireheart, taken aback. "Meet you at sunrise then."

"Sunrise," agreed Sandpaw.

Fireheart decided to share the good news about Sandpaw's lack of hostility with Graystripe. It might be a chance for them to start talking to each other again. Graystripe was sharing tongues with Runningwind by the clump of nettles.

"Hi, Fireheart," Runningwind meowed as Fireheart approached.

"Hi." Fireheart looked expectantly at Graystripe. But Graystripe had turned his head away and was staring at the boundary wall. Fireheart's heart sank. He dropped his head and turned back toward his nest. He couldn't wait to be out on patrol tomorrow and away from the camp.

The sky glowed palest pink above Fireheart's head as he pushed his way out of the den the next morning.

Sandpaw was waiting for him outside the gorse tunnel.

"Er, hi," Fireheart meowed, feeling a bit awkward.

"Hi," Sandpaw answered quietly.

Fireheart sat down. "Let's wait for the night patrol to get back," he suggested.

They sat in silence until they heard the familiar rustle of bushes heralding the return of Whitestorm, Longtail, and Mousefur.

"Any sign of ShadowClan?" Fireheart asked.

"We definitely picked up some ShadowClan scents," answered Whitestorm grimly.

"It's strange," meowed Mousefur, frowning. "It's always the same group of scents. ShadowClan must be sending the same warriors each time."

"You two had better check out the RiverClan border," suggested Whitestorm. "We didn't get a chance to patrol there. Be careful, and remember, you don't want to start a fight.

You're just looking for signs they've been hunting on our land again."

"Yes, Whitestorm," meowed Fireheart. Sandpaw nodded respectfully.

Fireheart led the way. "We'll start at Fourtrees and work our way along the border to Tallpines," he meowed as they climbed out of the camp ravine.

"Sounds good," replied Sandpaw. "I've never seen Fourtrees in the snow." Fireheart listened for sarcasm in her voice, but she seemed to be sincere.

They reached the top of the ravine. "Which way now?" Fireheart decided to test her.

"Do you think I don't know the way to Fourtrees?" Sandpaw protested. Fireheart began to regret acting like a mentor until he noticed a good-humored gleam in her eyes. She charged away through the woods without another word, and Fireheart pelted after her.

It felt good to be running through the woods with another cat again. He had to admit Sandpaw was fast. She was still two fox-lengths ahead when she leaped over the trunk of a fallen tree and disappeared.

Fireheart followed, taking the tree in a single bound. As he landed on the other side, something hit him from behind. He skidded in the snow, rolled over, and sprang to his paws.

Sandpaw faced him, her whiskers twitching. "Surprise!"

Fireheart hissed playfully and leaped on top of her. He was impressed by Sandpaw's strength, but he had the advantage of size. When he finally held her down in the snow, she protested, "Get off, you great lump!"

"Okay, okay," meowed Fireheart, letting go of her. "But you asked for it!"

Sandpaw sat up, her orange coat dusted with snow. "You look like you've been caught in a snowstorm!" she mewed.

"So do you." They both shook the flakes from their fur. "Come on," Fireheart meowed. "We'd better get a move on."

They raced side by side, as far as Fourtrees. By the time they reached the top of the slope that overlooked the valley, the sky was milky blue. Pale sunlight lit up the snowy hollow. The four bare oaks stood below them, glittering with frost.

Sandpaw stared down, her eyes wide. Fireheart waited, touched by her enthusiasm, until she turned to leave.

"I didn't know the snow would make everything look so different," she mewed as they began to follow the RiverClan border toward the river. Fireheart nodded in agreement.

Their pace was slower as they traveled in silence along the line of scent markers, alert for any fresh smells of RiverClan this side of the border. Fireheart paused every few trees to leave a new ThunderClan scent mark.

Suddenly Sandpaw stopped dead. "Fancy a little fresh-kill?" she whispered. Fireheart nodded. The apprentice dropped into a hunting crouch and pulled herself forward through the snow, one slow pawstep after another. Fireheart followed her gaze and saw a young rabbit hopping underneath some brambles. With a quick hiss, Sandpaw pounced, diving into the brambles and pinning the rabbit down with a strong forepaw. In one smooth movement she pulled it toward her to finish it off.

Fireheart bounded over. "Great catch, Sandpaw!"

Sandpaw looked pleased. She dropped the warm fresh-kill to the ground. "Share?"

"Thanks!"

"That's one of the best things about patrols," remarked Sandpaw between mouthfuls.

"What?" Fireheart asked.

"You can eat what you catch instead of having to take it back to the Clan," Sandpaw replied. "I don't know how many hunting missions I've nearly starved on!"

Fireheart purred with amusement.

They set off once more, skirting Sunningrocks to follow the trail into the woods again, close to the RiverClan border. As they reached the top of the bracken-covered slope above the river, Fireheart sent a silent prayer to StarClan that they wouldn't find Graystripe here.

"Look!" meowed Sandpaw suddenly. Her body stiffened with excitement. "The river—it's frozen."

Fireheart's heart lurched as he remembered Cinderpaw saying the same words before Graystripe's accident. "We're not going down to look!" he meowed firmly.

"We don't have to. You can see from here. Let's get back and tell the Clan."

"Why?" Fireheart couldn't understand Sandpaw's excitement.

"A patrol of our warriors could cross the river now!" Sand-paw meowed. "We can invade RiverClan's territory and steal back some of the prey they've taken from us."

Fireheart felt a cold chill ripple the fur on his spine. What would Graystripe think about that? And could Fireheart bring himself to go into battle against the starving RiverClan?

Sandpaw circled him impatiently. "Are you coming?"

"Yes," replied Fireheart heavily. He leaped after Sandpaw as she raced off into the woods, back to camp.

Sandpaw tore through the gorse tunnel just ahead of Fire-heart. Tigerclaw glanced up as they skidded to a halt in the clearing.

Fireheart heard a noise behind him. Graystripe was pad-ding through the camp entrance with Brackenpaw.

A call sounded from below the Highrock. "Fireheart, Sandpaw, how was your patrol?"

Fireheart felt a flood of relief when he saw Bluestar look-ing like her normal self, sitting with her chin high and her tail tucked over her front paws.

Sandpaw bounded over to the Highrock. "The river's fro-zen," she burst out. "We could cross it easily right now!"

Bluestar gazed thoughtfully at the apprentice. Fireheart flinched when he saw the ThunderClan leader's eyes gleam. "Thank you, Sandpaw," she meowed.

Fireheart leaned over and murmured into Sandpaw's ear, "Come on, let's tell the others." He guessed that Bluestar would want to discuss the frozen river with her senior warriors.

Sandpaw glanced at him, understanding, and followed him back to the center of the clearing. "This has been such a great day!" she meowed. Fireheart just nodded and glanced anxiously at Graystripe.

"You two look like you had fun!" Dustpaw had emerged from the apprentices' den. "Drowned another RiverClan cat?" he sneered at Fireheart.

Dustpaw looked at Sandpaw expectantly. Fireheart guessed he was waiting for her to agree with him, like she used to, but Sandpaw wasn't listening. Fireheart felt a small prickle of satisfaction at the irritated look on Dustpaw's face as she meowed breathlessly, "We found out that the river's frozen. I think Bluestar's planning a raid on RiverClan!"

At that moment their leader's call sounded from the High-rock, and the Clan began to gather in the clearing. The sun had reached its high point, which in leaf-bare meant that it was barely above the treetops.

"Sandpaw and Fireheart have brought good news. The river is frozen over," Bluestar announced. "We will take this opportunity to make a raid on RiverClan's hunting grounds, to send the message that they must stop stealing our prey. Our warriors will track down one of their patrols and give them a warning that they'll remember for a long time!"

Fireheart winced as he remembered what Silverstream had told him about her starving Clan. Around him, the other cats raised their voices in eager yowls. Fireheart had not heard the Clan this excited for many moons.

"Tigerclaw!" Bluestar called above the din. "Are our warriors fit enough for a raid on RiverClan?"

Tigerclaw nodded.

"Excellent." Bluestar lifted her tail. "Then we shall leave at sunset." The Clan yowled with delight. Fireheart's paws prickled. Was Bluestar going too? Surely she wouldn't risk her last life on a border raid?

Fireheart looked over his shoulder at Graystripe. He was staring up at the Highrock, the tip of his tail twitching nervously. As the yowls died away, Graystripe called out, "It feels warmer today. A thaw would make the ice too dangerous to cross."

Fireheart held his breath as the other cats turned to look curiously at Graystripe.

Tigerclaw stared down at Graystripe, his amber eyes puzzled. "You're not usually reluctant to fight," the dark warrior meowed slowly.

Darkstripe craned his neck and added, "Yes, Graystripe— you're not afraid of those RiverClan fleabags, are you?"

Graystripe fidgeted uncomfortably as the Clan waited for an answer.

"Looks like he's scared!" hissed Dustpaw from Sandpaw's side.

Fireheart's tail flicked angrily, but he managed to keep his voice light as he called, "Yes, of getting his paws wet!

Graystripe's fallen through the ice once this leaf-bare; he's not keen to do it again."

The tension in the Clan dissolved into amused purrs. Graystripe looked down at the ground, his ears flat. Only Tigerclaw kept his suspicious frown.

Bluestar waited until the murmurings had died away. "I must discuss the raid with my senior warriors." She leaped down from the Highrock, landing so lightly that it was hard to believe that she had been fighting for her lives just days ago. Tigerclaw, Whitestorm, and Willowpelt followed her to her den, and the rest of the Clan broke away into groups to discuss the proposed attack.

"I suppose you expect me to thank you for embarrassing me!" Fireheart heard Graystripe's angry hiss in his ear.

"Not at all," he snapped. "But you could at least be grateful I'm still covering up for you!" He bounded away to the edge of the clearing, his fur bristling with fury.

Sandpaw ran over to join him. "It's about time we showed those RiverClan cats that they can't hunt in our territory whenever they like," she meowed, her eyes shining.

"Yes, I suppose so," Fireheart answered absently. He couldn't take his eyes off Graystripe. Was he imagining it, or was the gray warrior edging farther and farther toward the nursery? Was Graystripe planning on slipping away to warn Silverstream?

Fireheart got slowly to his paws and began to pad toward the nursery. Graystripe glared at Fireheart as he approached, but before either warrior could speak, Bluestar's call sounded once more from the Highrock. Fireheart stopped where he was but didn't take his eyes off Graystripe.

"Willowpelt agrees with young Graystripe," Bluestar declared. "A thaw is on the way." Graystripe lifted his chin and flashed a defiant look at Fireheart, but Fireheart didn't care. Bluestar was going to call off the raid! Now Graystripe wouldn't have to choose between his Clan and Silverstream, and Fireheart wouldn't have to join a raiding party against a Clan he knew was already suffering.

But Bluestar hadn't finished. "So we will attack at once!"

Fireheart glanced sideways—Graystripe's look of triumph had turned to one of sheer horror.

Bluestar continued, "We will leave a patrol of warriors here to guard the camp. We have to remember the possible threat from ShadowClan. Five warriors will make the raid. I will remain here."

Good, thought Fireheart. She wasn't planning to risk her final life after all. "Tigerclaw will lead the raiding party. Darkstripe, Willowpelt, and Longtail will go with him. That leaves one more place."

"Can I go?" Fireheart burst out. Even though his heart felt heavy at the thought of attacking hungry RiverClan cats, it meant that Graystripe wouldn't have to make a choice.

"Thank you, Fireheart. You may join the patrol." Bluestar was clearly pleased by her former apprentice's eagerness. Tigerclaw didn't look so happy. He narrowed his eyes at Fireheart, gazing at him with undisguised suspicion. "There's no time to lose," Bluestar yowled. "I can smell the warm winds myself. Tigerclaw will brief you as you travel. Go now!"

Darkstripe, Longtail, and Willowpelt sped after Tigerclaw. Fireheart followed them as they thundered through the gorse tunnel and headed up the ravine, toward RiverClan territory.

They charged past Sunningrocks and reached the enemy border as the low leaf-bare sun began to dip toward the forest. Fireheart sniffed the air—Graystripe and Willowpelt had been right; he could smell warmer winds, and rain clouds were already pushing in over the treetops.

As they raced down the slope toward the river, Fireheart felt a deep sense of disquiet. Silverstream's desperate story rang in his ears, and he fought to push away his feelings of sympathy.

The ThunderClan warriors emerged from the bracken and skidded to a stop at the edge of the river. The sight that greeted them made Fireheart weak with relief. The shining sheet of ice that Fireheart had seen earlier with Sandpaw had broken up into a rushing flow of cold, black water.

CHAPTER 20

❧

Tigerclaw turned to his warriors, his pale eyes flashing with frustration. "We'll have to wait," he snarled.

The patrol turned and began to trudge home. Fireheart sent up a wordless prayer of thanks to StarClan, but there was a bitter taste in his throat. Now he would never know if he could have gone through with the raid. It wasn't only Graystripe he didn't trust; he didn't even trust himself.

Fireheart kept silent all the way home. Every now and then he saw Tigerclaw flash a glance at him over his massive brown shoulder. It was a slow journey. The light of the short leaf-bare day was fading when they finally reached the top of the ravine. Fireheart waited for the other warriors to pick their way down first. By the time he padded through the gorse tunnel, Tigerclaw was already explaining to the disappointed Clan that the river had thawed.

Fireheart skirted the edge of the clearing, looking for Graystripe. He needed to know if his friend had slipped out of the camp. Instinctively he headed for the nursery. As he approached the tangled mass of brambles, he heard a familiar meow. "Fireheart!"

Fireheart felt a glimmer of hope. Perhaps Graystripe was actually grateful he had offered to take the final place in the raiding party? He followed his friend's voice into the shadows behind the nursery.

Fireheart mewed quietly into the gloom, but he couldn't see Graystripe anywhere. Suddenly something crashed into his side with a mighty thump. Fireheart spun around, all his senses alert. He saw Graystripe with his hackles raised, silhouetted in the dimness.

Graystripe lunged again. Fireheart ducked just in time as Graystripe swung a wide gray paw at his ear.

"What are you doing?" Fireheart spluttered.

Graystripe flattened his ears and hissed, "You didn't trust me! You thought I would betray ThunderClan!" He aimed another swipe. This one caught the tip of Fireheart's ear.

Pain and fury shot through him. "I just wanted to save you from having to make a choice!" he spat. "Although it's true that I'm not sure where your loyalties lie right now."

Graystripe flew at him and knocked him backward. The two cats tussled, claws unsheathed. "I make my own choices," Graystripe snarled.

Fireheart struggled free and leaped onto Graystripe's back. "I was trying to protect you."

"I don't need protecting!"

Blinded by anger, Fireheart dug his claws into Graystripe's pelt, but Graystripe flipped Fireheart over and together they rolled out from behind the nursery.

The cats in the clearing sprang out of the way as the two

young warriors bundled into them. Fireheart yowled with rage as Graystripe bit his foreleg. He thrust upward with a claw and raked Graystripe above his eye. Graystripe retaliated by lunging downward and sinking his teeth into Fireheart's hind leg.

"Stop this at once!" Bluestar's stern yowl made Fireheart and Graystripe freeze. Fireheart released his grip on Graystripe and shuffled painfully sideways. Graystripe backed away, his fur bristling. Out of the corner of his eye, Fireheart saw Tigerclaw sneering with barely suppressed delight, curling his lip back to reveal his teeth.

"Fireheart, I want to see you in my den—now!" Bluestar growled, her blue eyes flashing fire. "Graystripe, go to your nest and stay there!"

The rest of the Clan melted away into the shadows. Fireheart limped after Bluestar to her den. He kept his eyes fixed on the ground, feeling worn out and confused.

Bluestar sat down on the sandy floor and stared at Fireheart in disbelief for a moment. Then she meowed angrily, "What was that all about?"

Fireheart shook his head. As furious as he was, he could not reveal his friend's secret.

Bluestar closed her eyes and took a deep breath. "I realize feelings are running high in the camp right now, but I never expected to see you and Graystripe fighting. Are you hurt?"

Fireheart could feel his ear and hind leg stinging, but he shrugged and murmured, "No."

"Are you going to tell me what this is about?"

Fireheart met her gaze as steadily as she could. "Bluestar, I'm sorry. I can't explain." *At least that much is true*, he thought.

"Very well," meowed Bluestar at last. "You two can sort it out on your own. The Clan is facing a difficult time, and I won't tolerate this sort of infighting. Do you understand?"

"Yes, Bluestar," Fireheart answered. "May I go?"

Bluestar nodded and Fireheart turned and slunk out of her den. He knew he had let his old mentor down. But there was no way he could confide in her. Last time he'd done that, about Ravenpaw's accusation against Tigerclaw, she hadn't believed him. And if she believed him this time, he would be betraying his best friend.

Feeling sick with worry, Fireheart crept across the clearing and slipped inside the warriors' den. He settled into his nest beside Graystripe and curled himself into a tight ball. He lay there, unmoving, aware of Graystripe's tense body beside his, until sleep finally overcame him.

Fireheart awoke early the next morning. The sun hadn't risen yet and the clearing was empty as he padded across to Yellowfang's den. He wanted to see Cinderpaw.

Yellowfang was asleep, curled up beside Brindleface's sick kits. They squirmed quietly in their nest, their eyes closed. Yellowfang was snoring loudly. Fireheart didn't want to wake her, so he crept over to Cinderpaw's nest and peered in.

The little gray cat was asleep too. The blood had been washed from her fur. Fireheart wondered whether she had cleaned it herself or whether Yellowfang had washed it off.

Fireheart crouched beside Cinderpaw and watched her breathe. There was something calming about the way her sides rose and fell. She seemed much more peaceful than when he last visited.

He stayed with her until the dawn light filtered through the ferns and he heard the Clan begin to stir. Fireheart got to his paws. He leaned into Cinderpaw's nest and touched her side softly with his nose.

As he turned to leave, Yellowfang stretched and opened her eyes. "Fireheart?"

"I came to see Cinderpaw," he whispered.

"She's doing well," meowed Yellowfang, pushing herself up.

Fireheart's eyes clouded with relief. "Thank you, Yellowfang."

When he reached the clearing, Tigerclaw was addressing a group of warriors and apprentices. He spotted Fireheart straightaway. "Nice of you to show up," he growled. "Graystripe's just joined us, too. He's been having a word with Bluestar." Fireheart glanced at his friend, but Graystripe was staring at the ground. The other warriors watched in silence as Fireheart hurried over and sat down beside Sandpaw.

"During this thaw, the woods will be alive with prey," Tigerclaw meowed. "They'll be hungry after sheltering in their burrows. This will be a good chance to catch as much as we can."

"But there's still fresh-kill in the snow store," Dustpaw mewed.

"It'll be crow-food soon," Tigerclaw told him. "We need

to take every opportunity to hunt. As leaf-bare goes on, the prey will start to disappear, and what stays around will be too thin." The warriors nodded in agreement.

"Longtail"—Tigerclaw turned his eyes on the pale tabby warrior—"I want you to organize the hunting parties." Longtail nodded, and Tigerclaw got up and padded toward Bluestar's den. As Fireheart watched him disappear through the lichen, he couldn't help wondering if the leader and deputy would discuss his fight with Graystripe.

Longtail's voice summoned him away from his thoughts. "Fireheart! You and Sandpaw can join Mousefur. Graystripe can hunt with Whitestorm and Brackenpaw. It's probably best if I don't put you two in the same group."

Amused purrs rippled through the group, but Fireheart narrowed his eyes angrily. He comforted himself by studying the nick he had left in the pale tabby's ear when Longtail had taunted him on his first day in the camp.

"Good fight last night," Mousefur rasped beside him, her eyes gleaming with mischief. "It almost made up for missing out on a battle."

Fireheart scowled as Dustpaw added, "Yeah! Nice moves, Fireheart—for a kittypet." Fireheart gritted his teeth and looked at the ground, sheathing and unsheathing his claws.

The two groups left the camp together. As the hunters filed up the trail out of the ravine, Fireheart looked at the sky. The rain clouds he had seen rolling in last night had covered the sun, and the snow underpaw was turning to slush.

Mousefur led Sandpaw and Fireheart through Tallpines.

"I'll take Sandpaw with me," the brown warrior told Fireheart. "You can hunt alone. Meet us back at camp at sunhigh."

Fireheart couldn't help feeling relieved at the thought of being alone. He stalked away through the trees, still hardly able to believe that he and Graystripe had fought so bitterly. Fireheart felt lost and alone without his old friend, though he barely recognized him anymore. He wondered if they could ever be friends again.

It wasn't until he felt the softness of leaves beneath his paws that Fireheart realized he'd wandered all the way to the oak woods that backed onto the Twolegplace. Instantly he thought of Princess, and wondered if his paws had carried him to her Twoleg nest for a reason.

Fireheart made straight for her fence and called softly down into the garden. Then he jumped back into the woods and waited in the undergrowth for his sister to come looking.

He didn't have to wait long before there was a scrabbling noise on the fence and he smelled her distinctive scent. Fireheart was about to leap out to meet her when he smelled a second, unfamiliar scent.

The bracken rustled, and Princess appeared. In her mouth she carried a tiny white kit. As Fireheart pushed his way out to meet her, she mewed a warm greeting through the bundle of fur in her teeth.

The kit was very small; Fireheart guessed it would not be weaned for another moon. Princess cleared away some slush with her paw and laid it gently down on the leaves. Then she sat down and wrapped her thick tail around it.

Fireheart was overwhelmed with emotion. This was his own kin, kittypet born like he had been! He walked quietly over to Princess, nuzzled a greeting, then bent down and sniffed the kit. It smelled of warmth and milk—strange but somehow familiar. Fireheart gave it a tender lick on the head and it mewled, opening its pink mouth to reveal tiny white teeth.

Princess looked at Fireheart, her eyes shining. "I have brought him for you, Fireheart," she meowed softly. "I want you to take him back with you to your Clan so that he can be your new apprentice."

CHAPTER 21

Fireheart stared at the tiny kit. "I never expected . . ." he began. He dragged his gaze away and stared wordlessly at his sister.

"My housefolk will choose where the rest will live," Princess went on. "But this is my firstborn and *I* want to decide his future." She raised her chin. "Make him a hero, please. Like you!"

The unsettling sense of loneliness that had been dragging at Fireheart for so long began to ebb away. He pictured the white kit among the Clan, as he showed him the ways of the forest and hunted by his side through the thick ferns. At last, there would be another cat in ThunderClan who shared Fireheart's kittypet roots.

Princess tilted her head. "I know how upset you were about your apprentice. I thought if you had a new apprentice— one who's your own kin—you wouldn't feel so lonely." She stretched her neck and rested her nose against Fireheart's side. "I don't understand all your Clan ways, but seeing you, and hearing you talk about your life, I know I would be honored if my son was brought up as a Clan cat."

As the first flare of happiness settled inside him, Fireheart thought of the rest of his Clan, and how desperately they needed fighting cats. Cinderpaw would never be a warrior now. And what if the greencough took more lives than just Bluestar's? ThunderClan might need this kit.

He was suddenly aware of the rain clinging to his fur. The kit needed shelter, and soon. It looked strong, but it was still too small to withstand the cold and wet for long.

"I'll take him," he meowed. "This is a great gift you've given to ThunderClan. And I'll train him to be the finest warrior the Clan has ever seen!" He dipped his head and scooped up the kit by his scruff.

Princess's eyes shone with gratitude and pride. "Thank you, Fireheart," she purred. "Who knows, maybe he'll even become a leader and be given nine lives!"

Fireheart gazed fondly at her trusting, hopeful face. Did his sister really believe this might happen? Then a twinge of doubt pricked him. He was taking this tiny kit back to a camp infected by greencough. What if he didn't even make it to newleaf? But the cozy scent of the kit under his muzzle soothed him. The kit would survive. It was strong, and it shared his blood. Fireheart took a deep breath. He must be quick—the kit was getting cold already. He blinked a farewell at Princess and raced away into the bushes.

The kit was heavier than he'd expected. It dangled from his mouth, bumping against his forelegs with faint protesting squeaks. By the time Fireheart reached the top of the ravine, his neck was aching. He made his way down to the camp, putting one paw carefully in front of the other, wary of slipping on the fast-melting snow.

At the entrance, Fireheart hesitated. For the first time he wondered how he would explain this kit to the Clan—he was going to have to admit to visiting his kittypet sister. But it was too late now. He could feel the kit shivering. Fireheart squared his shoulders and padded through the gorse tunnel. The kit let out a deafening wail as a thorn tugged at its fur. Several pairs of eyes turned to look in amazement as Fireheart emerged into the clearing.

Both hunting parties had returned. Mousefur, Whitestorm, Sandpaw, and Brackenpaw were all in the clearing. Only Graystripe was missing. One by one the rest of the Clan were drawn out of their dens by the noise and the unfamiliar scent. None of the cats made a sound. They stared at Fireheart with hostile, puzzled eyes as though he were a stranger.

Fireheart turned slowly in the center of the clearing, the kit still dangling from his mouth, and looked at the ring of questioning eyes. His mouth began to feel dry. Why had he assumed the Clan would accept a kit that wasn't even forest-born?

He felt a rush of relief when Bluestar emerged from Yellowfang's den. But her eyes widened in surprise as she saw him. "What is this?" she demanded.

A tremor of foreboding ran along Fireheart's spine. He placed the kit between his front paws and wrapped his tail over it to keep it warm. "It's my sister's firstborn," he replied.

"Your *sister*!" Tigerclaw glared at him accusingly.

"You have a sister?" called Speckletail. "Where?"

"The same place as Fireheart was born, of course," Longtail hissed with disgust. "Twolegplace!"

"Is that true?" Bluestar asked, her eyes widening further.

"Yes," Fireheart admitted. "My sister gave it to me to bring to the Clan."

"And why would she do that?" Bluestar asked with menacing calm.

Fireheart stammered nervously. "I told her about Clan life—how great it was. . . ." His voice trailed away under Bluestar's incredulous gaze.

"How long have you been visiting Twolegplace?"

"Not long, just since leaf-bare began. But only to see my sister. My loyalty still lies with ThunderClan."

"Loyalty?" Darkstripe's yowl rang out across the clearing. "And yet you bring a kittypet here?"

"Isn't having one kittypet in the Clan enough?" croaked one of the elders.

"Trust a kittypet to find another kittypet!" snarled Dustpaw, ruffling his fur indignantly. He turned to Sandpaw and nudged her with his nose. Sandpaw glanced uncomfortably at Fireheart and then looked down at her paws.

"Why have you brought it here?" Tigerclaw growled.

"We need warriors. . . ." The tiny kit squirmed beneath his belly as he spoke, and Fireheart realized how ridiculous he must sound. He bowed his head as yowls of scorn met his words.

When the insults had died away, Runningwind spoke up. "The Clan has enough to worry about already without this."

"It'll be nothing but a burden," Mousefur agreed. "It'll be at least five moons before it's ready to begin training."

Whitestorm nodded his head in agreement. "You shouldn't have brought this kittypet here, Fireheart," he meowed. "It'll be too soft for Clan life."

Fireheart bristled. "I was born a kittypet. Am I soft?" He thought that he'd begun to challenge the Clan's prejudice against kittypets, but he was wrong. He couldn't see one friendly face in the crowd.

A voice sounded from behind Whitestorm. "If it carries Fireheart's blood, it'll make a good Clan cat."

Fireheart felt relief surge through his body. It was Graystripe! A brief flame of hope flared in Fireheart's chest as Whitestorm stood aside and the other cats turned to look at the gray warrior. Graystripe stared around the circle of cats, meeting their gazes one by one with wide, steady eyes.

"Makes a change to see you speak up for your friend, Graystripe. Last night you wanted to shred him!" sneered Longtail.

Graystripe glared at the pale tabby, then whipped around as Darkstripe challenged him. "Yeah, Graystripe! How do you know Fireheart has blood worthy of ThunderClan? Did you taste it last night when you tried to take a chunk out of his leg?"

Bluestar stepped forward, her blue eyes clouded with worry. "Fireheart, I believe that you meant no disloyalty to the Clan by visiting your sister, but why did you agree to bring her kit here? It is not your place to make decisions like this. What you have done affects the whole Clan."

Fireheart looked at Graystripe, hoping for more support, but Graystripe wouldn't meet his eyes. Fireheart craned his head around, and every cat turned their gaze away from him. Fireheart began to panic. Had he endangered his own position in the Clan by bringing Princess's kit here?

Bluestar spoke again. "Tigerclaw, what do you think?"

"What do I think?" meowed Tigerclaw. Fireheart felt his heart sink at the note of arrogant satisfaction in the deputy's voice. "I think he should get rid of it at once."

"Goldenflower?"

"It certainly looks too small to survive until newleaf," the ginger queen remarked.

"It'll have greencough by sunrise!" added Mousefur.

"Or it'll eat our fresh-kill until next snowfall and then die of cold!" spat Runningwind.

Bluestar dipped her head. "That's enough. I must think about this." She padded to her den and disappeared inside. The rest of the Clan slipped away, muttering darkly.

Fireheart picked up the bedraggled kit and carried him to the warriors' den. The kit was shivering and mewling pathetically. Fireheart curled his body around the little scrap and closed his eyes, but hostile faces of the Clan swam around his mind, filling his heart with dread. He thought he had been lonely before, but now it seemed as if the entire Clan had disowned him.

Graystripe pushed his way into the den and settled down into his nest. Fireheart glanced nervously at him. Graystripe had been the only cat to speak in his defense, and Fireheart wanted to thank him. After an uncomfortable pause, in which the kit cried and cried, Fireheart mumbled, "Thanks for sticking up for me."

Graystripe shrugged. "Yeah, well," he meowed, "no one else was going to do it." He twisted his head around and began to wash his tail.

The kit carried on mewling, his cries growing louder. Some of the other warriors padded into the den to escape the rain outside. Willowpelt glanced briefly at Fireheart and the kit, but she didn't speak.

"Can't you shut that thing up?" complained Darkstripe as he prodded the moss in his nest.

Fireheart licked the kit desperately. It must be very hungry by now. A rustle in the den wall made him lift his head. It was Frostfur. She crept over to Fireheart's nest and looked down at the miserable kit. Suddenly she dipped her head and sniffed the kit's soft fur. "He'd be better off in the nursery," she murmured. "Brindleface has milk to spare. I could ask her to feed it."

Fireheart stared at the queen in surprise.

Frostfur gazed back at him, her eyes warm. "I haven't forgotten that you rescued my kits from ShadowClan."

Fireheart picked up the kit yet again and followed Frostfur out of the warriors' den. The rain was even heavier now. Together they padded quickly to the nursery. Frostfur disappeared through its narrow entrance, and Fireheart squeezed in after her. He paused inside the thicket of brambles, blinking until his eyes got used to the dim light.

Inside the dry, dark cocoon, Brindleface was curled around her two healthy kits. She looked suspiciously at Fireheart, then at the kit that dangled from his jaws.

Frostfur whispered to Fireheart, "One of Brindleface's kits died last night." Fireheart remembered the sick kits squirming beside Yellowfang and wondered, with a pang, which one had gone. He put Princess's kit down and turned to Brindleface. "I'm sorry," he murmured.

The queen blinked at him, her grief raw in her eyes.

"Brindleface," Frostfur began, "I can only guess at how much pain you feel. But this kit is starving, and you have milk. Will you feed him?"

Brindleface shook her head and shut her eyes tight as if to deny Fireheart's presence in her den.

Frostfur stretched her head forward and pressed her muzzle gently against Brindleface's cheek. "I know he won't replace your son," she whispered. "But he needs your warmth and care."

Fireheart waited anxiously. The kit's cries grew louder. It could smell Brindleface's milk and began to squirm blindly toward her soft belly. It nuzzled its way between Brindleface's other two kits. Brindleface looked down as it wriggled forward, following her milk-scent. She watched, without resisting, as he latched onto her belly and began to suckle. Fireheart ached with relief and gratitude as he saw Brindleface's eyes soften and the white kittypet began to purr, kneading her swollen stomach with tiny paws.

Frostfur nodded. "Thank you, Brindleface. Can I tell

Bluestar that you will care for the kit?"

"Yes," replied Brindleface quietly, not taking her eyes off the white kit. She nudged him closer to her belly with one hind paw.

Fireheart purred and bent his head to nose her shoulder. "Thank you. I promise I'll bring you extra fresh-kill every day."

"I'll go and tell Bluestar," meowed Frostfur.

Fireheart looked up at the white queen, stirred by her kindness. "Thank you," he mewed.

"No kit deserves to starve, Clanborn or not." Frostfur turned and pushed her way out of the brambles.

"You can go now," Brindleface murmured to Fireheart. "Your kit will be safe with me."

Fireheart nodded and followed Frostfur out into the rain. He thought about returning to his den, but until he'd heard Bluestar's decision about the kit, he knew he could not settle.

As he paced around the clearing, his fur matting into wet clumps, he saw Frostfur slip out of Bluestar's den and hurry back to the nursery.

Willowpelt was preparing to lead evening patrol out of the camp when Bluestar finally came out of her den. Fireheart stopped, his heart pounding so fast he thought his legs would give way under him. Bluestar leaped onto the Highrock and began the familiar summons. "Let all cats old enough to catch their own prey gather below the Highrock."

The patrol turned away from the camp entrance and padded after Willowpelt, back toward the Highrock. The rest of the Clan began to leave their dry nests, grumbling about the rain. Tigerclaw leaped onto the rock beside Bluestar, his face grim.

They're going to make me take him back, thought Fireheart. His breath began to come in shallow gasps. Darker thoughts pushed their way into Fireheart's mind. *What if Bluestar asks Tigerclaw to abandon him in the forest? He'll never survive. Oh, StarClan, what am I going to say to Princess?*

When all the cats were settled, Bluestar spoke. "Cats of ThunderClan, no cat can deny that we need warriors. We have lost one cat to greencough already, and there are many moons until newleaf. Cinderpaw has been gravely injured, and she will never be a warrior. As Graystripe rightly pointed out . . ."

Fireheart heard Dustpaw whispering nearby, "Graystripe's turning into a kittypet himself these days!" He turned his head sharply, but a warning hiss from one of the elders silenced Dustpaw before Fireheart could say anything.

"As Graystripe pointed out," Bluestar repeated, "this kittypet carries Fireheart's blood. There is every chance the kit will make a fine warrior." Some of the Clan glanced at Fireheart, who had barely heard Bluestar's compliment. Hope was surging in his chest, making him dizzy.

Bluestar paused for a moment to survey the cats in front of her. "I have decided we will take this kit into the Clan," she declared.

No cat made a sound. Fireheart wanted to yowl his thanks to StarClan, but he held his tongue. He took his first deep breath since sunhigh. His own kin was going to be part of ThunderClan!

"Brindleface has offered to nurse it," Bluestar went on, "so Fireheart will take on the duty of providing for her." The Clan leader met Fireheart's eyes, but he couldn't read her expression. "Finally, the kit should have a name. It shall be known as Cloudkit."

"Will there be a naming ceremony?" Mousefur called from the crowd.

Fireheart looked eagerly up at the Highrock. Would his sister's kit be granted this privilege, as he had been when the Clan had formally accepted him?

Bluestar looked down at Mousefur, her eyes cold. "No," she answered.

CHAPTER 22

❧

The days leading up to the next full moon dragged by slowly for Fireheart. It already seemed ages since the last Gathering. Rain clouds had kept the moon covered the last time, and the Clans had stayed away from Fourtrees. Meanwhile patrol after patrol reported scenting RiverClan warriors at Sunningrocks, and ShadowClan scent had been discovered again by the Owl Tree.

When he wasn't hunting or patrolling, Fireheart divided his time between Cloudkit, Cinderpaw, and Brackenpaw. Even though Graystripe had resumed his role as Brackenpaw's mentor, Fireheart soon began to notice the young apprentice at loose ends from time to time, his mentor nowhere in sight. "Hunting," was all Brackenpaw would say when Fireheart asked where Graystripe had gone.

"Why didn't you go with him?" meowed Fireheart.

"He said I could go tomorrow."

Fireheart felt the usual prickle of anger at Graystripe's stubbornness, but he shrugged it away. He'd given up trying to make Graystripe see sense—they'd hardly spoken since Fireheart had brought Cloudkit into the camp—but he made an effort to take Brackenpaw out whenever Graystripe went missing, just to keep the apprentice out of sight. Fireheart knew that Tigerclaw wouldn't accept Brackenpaw's answers so easily.

Finally the full moon appeared in a cloudless sky. Fireheart came back from hunting early. He passed the fallen oak, deserted now that Swiftpaw and Speckletail's kit had recovered. He dropped his catch on the pile and headed toward Yellowfang's den to visit Cinderpaw. Even the threat of greencough had left the camp, for now. Only Cinderpaw remained with the medicine cat.

As Fireheart padded through the tunnel he could see the small gray she-cat in the clearing ahead. She was helping Yellowfang prepare some herbs. Fireheart winced as he watched Cinderpaw limp heavily toward the split rock with a mouthful of dried leaves.

"Fireheart!" Cinderpaw spat out the herbs and turned to greet him as he emerged from the tunnel. "I could only just scent you through these disgusting things!"

"Those disgusting things helped cure your leg!" growled Yellowfang.

"Well, you should have used more," retorted Cinderpaw, but Fireheart was relieved to see she had a mischievous glint in her eye. "Look at this!" She twitched her twisted hind leg. "I can hardly reach my claws to wash them."

"Perhaps I should give you a few more exercises to loosen it up," meowed Yellowfang.

"No, thanks!" mewed Cinderpaw quickly. "They hurt!"

"They're meant to hurt! It shows they're working." The old medicine cat turned to Fireheart. "Perhaps you'll have more luck persuading her to do them. I'm going into the forest to dig up some comfrey roots."

"I'll try," Fireheart promised as Yellowfang padded past him.

"You'll know if she's doing them right," the medicine cat called over her shoulder, "because she'll complain!"

Cinderpaw limped over to Fireheart and touched her nose to his. "Thanks for coming to see me." She sat down and grimaced as she tucked her bad leg under her.

"I like coming to see you," Fireheart purred. "I miss our training sessions." He regretted his words as soon as he'd uttered them.

A wistful look clouded Cinderpaw's eyes. "Me too," she meowed. "When do you think I'll be able to start again?"

Fireheart stared at her, his heart sinking. Clearly Yellowfang hadn't told her yet that she would never be a warrior. "Perhaps if we try some of your exercises, it'll help," he meowed evasively.

"Okay," mewed Cinderpaw. "But just a few."

She lay on her side and stretched out her leg till her face was twisted with pain. Slowly, her teeth clenched, she began to move it backward and forward.

"You're doing really well," Fireheart meowed, hiding the sorrow that lay like a rock in his stomach.

Cinderpaw let her leg drop and lay still for a moment; then she pushed herself up. Fireheart watched her quietly as she shook her head. "I'm never going to be a warrior, am I?"

Fireheart couldn't lie to her. "No," he whispered. "I'm so sorry." He stretched his muzzle toward her and licked her head. After a few moments, she gave a long sigh and lay down again.

"I knew it really," she mewed. "It's just that sometimes I dream about being in the forest, hunting with Brackenpaw, and then I wake up and the pain in my leg reminds me I'll never hunt again. It feels too much to bear. I have to pretend that maybe, one day, I'll be able to hunt."

Fireheart couldn't bear to see her in such low spirits. "I'll take you out into the forest again," he promised. "We'll find the oldest, slowest mouse in the woods. It won't stand a chance against you."

Cinderpaw looked at him and purred gratefully.

Fireheart purred back at her, but there was a question that had been nagging at him since the accident. "Cinderpaw," he began, "can you remember what happened when the monster hit you? Was Tigerclaw there?"

Cinderpaw's eyes clouded with confusion. "I d-don't know," she stammered. Fireheart felt a pang of guilt as he saw her flinch away from the memory. "I went straight to the burned ash where Dustpaw said Tigerclaw would be, and then there was the monster and . . . I don't really remember."

"You wouldn't have realized how thin the verge was there." Fireheart shook his head slowly. "You must have run straight onto the Thunderpath." *Why wasn't Tigerclaw where he said he'd be?* he thought with a flash of rage. *He could have stopped her from running out!* Princess's words rang ominously in his head. *Was it a trap?* He pictured Tigerclaw, crouching downwind, hidden among the trees, staring out at the verge, waiting—

"How's Cloudkit?" Cinderpaw's mew cut short his thoughts. She clearly wanted to change the subject.

Fireheart was happy to oblige, especially if it meant talking about Princess's son. "Getting bigger every day," he meowed proudly.

"I'm dying to meet him. When are you going to bring him to visit me?"

"As soon as Brindleface lets me," Fireheart answered. "She won't let him out of her sight at the moment."

"She likes him, then?"

"She treats him just like her other kits," Fireheart meowed, "thank StarClan. To be honest, I wasn't sure if she'd take to him. He looks so different from her other kits." Even Fireheart couldn't deny that Cloudkit's snowy pelt of soft fur looked out of place beside the other kits, with their forest-colored coats of short, mottled fur. "At least he gets on well with his nursery mates. . . ." Fireheart's voice trailed away. He stared at the ground, feeling a twinge of anxiety.

"What's the matter?" Cinderpaw prompted gently.

Fireheart shrugged. "I'm just sick of the way some of the other cats look at him, like he's stupid or worthless."

"Does Cloudkit notice these looks?"

Fireheart shook his head.

"Well, don't worry then," Cinderpaw mewed.

"But Cloudkit doesn't even know he was born a kittypet. I

think he just assumes he's from a different Clan. But if they keep giving him these dirty looks, he's going to realize there's something wrong with him." Fireheart looked at his paws fretfully.

"Something wrong with him?" echoed Cinderpaw in wonder. "*You* were born a kittypet and there's nothing wrong with you! Look, by the time Cloudkit works out where he comes from, he'll be able to start proving that a kittypet can be as good as any Clanborn warrior. Just like you've done."

"What if someone tells him before he's ready?"

"If he's anything like you, he was *born* ready!"

"When did you get so smart?" Fireheart meowed, rather surprised by his apprentice's sharpness.

Cinderpaw rolled onto her back with a dramatic moan. "Suffering can do that to a cat!" Fireheart prodded her stomach with a paw, and Cinderpaw squeaked before scrambling back onto her side. "No, really," she mewed. "Look who I've been hanging out with lately!"

Fireheart tipped his head on one side questioningly.

"Yellowfang, you dope," Cinderpaw scoffed. "She's one sharp old cat. I'm learning a lot." She sat up. "Yellowfang said there's a Gathering tonight. Are you going?"

"I don't know," Fireheart admitted. "I'm going to ask Bluestar later. I'm not exactly popular with the Clan at the moment."

"They'll get over it," Cinderpaw promised. She nudged his shoulder. "Shouldn't you go and find out if you're going, then? They'll be leaving soon."

"You're right," Fireheart replied. "Will you be okay till Yellowfang gets back? Do you want me to fetch you some fresh-kill?"

"I'll be fine," Cinderpaw assured him. "And Yellowfang'll bring me something. She always does. I'm going to be the fattest cat in the Clan by the time she's finished with me."

Fireheart felt a burst of happiness to see his former apprentice recovering her spirit. He was tempted to stay and keep her company, but she was right—he should find out if he could go to the Gathering. "I'll see you tomorrow, then," he meowed. "There should be plenty of news from the Gathering."

"Yeah, and I want to hear it all," Cinderpaw mewed. "Make sure Bluestar lets you go! Quick!"

"I'm going, I'm going," Fireheart retorted, getting to his paws. "'Bye, Cinderpaw."

"'Bye!"

Fireheart stopped at the edge of the clearing and looked around for Bluestar. She was talking with Willowpelt outside her den. Fireheart reached them just as Willowpelt stood up to leave. The slender gray warrior nodded to Fireheart as she padded away.

Bluestar gazed at Fireheart with knowing eyes. "You want to go to the Gathering," she meowed. Fireheart opened his mouth to speak, but Bluestar interrupted him. "All the warriors want to go tonight, but I can't take every cat."

Fireheart felt disappointed. "I wanted to see WindClan again," he explained. "To find out how they've been getting on since Graystripe and I brought them home."

Bluestar narrowed her eyes. "I don't need reminding of what you did for WindClan," she meowed sharply, and Fireheart flinched. "But you're right to be concerned," Bluestar went on. "You and Graystripe may come to the Gathering tonight."

"Thank you, Bluestar," Fireheart meowed.

"It'll be an interesting Gathering," Bluestar warned him. "RiverClan and ShadowClan have much to explain."

Fireheart felt his ears twitch nervously, but he couldn't help feeling a thrill of excitement as well. Bluestar clearly meant to challenge Crookedstar and Nightstar about their invasions into ThunderClan territory. He dipped his head respectfully to Bluestar and padded away.

As he collected two voles for Brindleface from the pile of fresh-kill, Fireheart noticed Yellowfang trudging into the camp. Her paws were muddy and her mouth was crammed with fat, knobbly roots. Her search for comfrey had clearly been successful.

Fireheart carried the fresh-kill over to the nursery. Brindleface was curled up inside feeding Cloudkit. The other kits had recently given up their mother's milk, and soon Cloudkit too would have his first taste of fresh-kill.

Brindleface looked up as he entered, her eyes shadowed with concern. "I've just sent for Yellowfang," she mewed.

Fireheart was instantly alarmed. "Is there something wrong with Cloudkit?"

"He's been a little feverish today." Brindleface leaned down and licked the kit's head as he stopped feeding and began squirming restlessly. "It's probably nothing, but I thought I'd see what Yellowfang thought. I . . . I don't want to take any chances."

Fireheart remembered that the dappled queen had recently lost a kit, and he hoped she was just being overcautious. But Cloudkit did look uncomfortable. "I'll come and see you after the Gathering," he promised.

He ducked out of the nursery and headed back to the pile of fresh-kill to pick out his own food. Brindleface's news had spoiled his appetite, but he knew he should eat something before the journey to Fourtrees tonight.

Longtail and Dustpaw were already standing over the pile. Fireheart sat down and waited for them to leave.

"Haven't seen the Cloudchick today," meowed Longtail. Fireheart felt a familiar ripple of frustration at Longtail's snide comment.

"He's probably realized how silly he looks and decided to hide in the nursery!" mewed Dustpaw.

"I'd like to be there when he tries hunting for the first time. The prey'll spot him coming a tree's length away with all that white fluff," Longtail sneered.

"Unless they mistake him for a puffball mushroom!" Dustpaw's whiskers twitched as he threw a sideways glance at Fireheart.

Fireheart flattened his ears and looked away. He watched Yellowfang hurry into the nursery with a mouthful of feverfew. Unfortunately Longtail and Dustpaw noticed too. "Looks like the kittypet's caught a chill. What a surprise," meowed Longtail. "Goldenflower was right—he won't last through leaf-bare!" The tabby warrior turned and stared at Fireheart, waiting for a reaction, but Fireheart ignored him and walked over to the pile of fresh-kill. He chose a thrush and carried it away to eat, feeling drained by the endless spite.

Graystripe was sharing his meal with Runningwind by the nettle clump. "Hi, did you have a good hunt?" Runningwind called as Fireheart passed.

"Yes, thanks," Fireheart replied.

Graystripe didn't look up.

"Bluestar said you could go to the Gathering," Fireheart told Graystripe. .

"I know," Graystripe answered, still chewing.

"Are you going?" Fireheart turned to Runningwind.

"You bet! I wouldn't miss this one for anything!"

Fireheart padded on and found a quiet spot at the edge of the clearing. Longtail's words echoed in his head. Would the Clan ever accept the little white kit? Fireheart closed his eyes and began to wash himself.

As he turned to lick his side, his whiskers brushed against something. He opened his eyes to find Sandpaw standing beside him. Her orange pelt glowed silver beneath the rising moon. "Thought you might like some company," she mewed. She sat down and began to wash Fireheart's back with long, soothing strokes.

Through half-closed eyes, Fireheart caught a glimpse of Dustpaw staring from outside the apprentices' den, unable to disguise his envy and amazement. Dustpaw wasn't the only one surprised by Sandpaw's gesture—Fireheart hadn't expected such friendliness from the fiery young she-cat, but her warmth was welcome, and he wasn't going to question it. "Are you going to the Gathering?" he asked.

Sandpaw paused. "Yes. You?"

"Yes. I think Bluestar's going to challenge Crookedstar and Nightstar about their hunting." He waited for Sandpaw to reply, but she was staring up at the darkening sky.

"I wish I were going as a *warrior*," she murmured. Fireheart tensed, but for once there was no hint of jealousy or bitterness in her mew.

Fireheart felt awkward. He knew his training had started after Sandpaw's, and he had been a warrior for more than two moons already. "It can't be long till Bluestar gives you your warrior name," he meowed, trying to sound encouraging.

"Why do you think it's taking so long?" Sandpaw asked, turning her pale green eyes on Fireheart.

"I don't know," he admitted. "Bluestar's been ill, and there's RiverClan and ShadowClan causing trouble. I guess she's got other things on her mind."

"You'd think she'd need warriors more than ever!" meowed Sandpaw.

Fireheart felt a stab of sympathy. "I suppose she's just waiting for the . . . the right time." He knew it didn't sound very helpful, but it was all he could think to say.

"Maybe by newleaf." Sandpaw sighed. "When do you think you'll get a new apprentice?"

"Bluestar hasn't said anything yet."

"Perhaps she'll give you Cloudkit when he's old enough."

"I hope so." Fireheart stared across the clearing at the nursery, wondering if Yellowfang had finished treating Cloudkit. "If he makes it that far."

"Of course he'll make it!" Sandpaw meowed confidently.

"But he has a fever." Fireheart let his shoulders sag with worry.

"All kits get fevers!" Sandpaw retorted. "With his thick fur, he'll recover in no time. That coat's going to be handy in leaf-bare, perfect for hunting in the snow. The prey'll never see him coming, and he'll be able to stay out twice as long as thin-pelts like Longtail!"

Fireheart purred and felt himself relax. Sandpaw had lifted his spirits again. He stood up and gave her a brisk lick on the head. "Come on," he meowed. "Bluestar is calling the cats for the Gathering."

They joined the other cats beside the camp entrance, a silent, purposeful group.

Bluestar signaled to them with a flick of her tail, then led them through the gorse tunnel and out of the ravine. The forest glistened in the cold moonlight as they sprinted toward Fourtrees. Clouds of breath billowed from Fireheart's muzzle, and the forest floor felt frozen beneath his paws.

For the first time since Fireheart had joined the Clan, Bluestar didn't hesitate at the ridge above Fourtrees to prepare herself for the meeting. Instead her cats followed their leader wordlessly as she plunged straight down the slope into the clearing.

❦

RiverClan and ShadowClan had not yet arrived, but WindClan was already there. Tallstar greeted Bluestar with a respectful nod.

Fireheart spotted Onewhisker and bounded over to meet him. "Hi!" he meowed. It had been over two moons since he'd last seen the small brown tabby warrior who had battled beside him at the gorge. For the first time in ages, Fireheart recalled Whiteclaw's death and felt the familiar bristle of horror as he pictured the RiverClan warrior disappearing beneath the rushing river.

"Where's Graystripe?" Onewhisker asked. "Is he okay?"

Fireheart could see from the concern in his eyes that the WindClan warrior was thinking about Whiteclaw's death too. "He's fine," Fireheart answered. "He's over there with the others." Fireheart remembered the WindClan queen whose kit he'd helped to carry. "How's Morningflower?"

"Happy to be home," replied Onewhisker. "Her kit is growing quickly now." Fireheart purred with pleasure. "The whole Clan is well," Onewhisker added. He glanced at Fireheart with an amused gleam in his eyes. "It's great to eat rabbit again. I hope I never have to taste another rat as long as I live!"

Fireheart detected a fresh scent on the night air. RiverClan was coming. He could smell ShadowClan, too. He scanned the ridge that ran around the edge of the hollow. Sure enough, RiverClan cats were streaming down one side. On the opposite ridge, Fireheart saw ShadowClan cats poised at the top, their coats gleaming in the moonlight. The lean figure of Nightstar stood at the head of the group.

"At last," growled Onewhisker. He'd spotted them as well. "It's too cold to be hanging around tonight."

Fireheart nodded absently. He was searching the crowd of RiverClan cats as they entered the clearing, looking for Silverstream. He recognized the pale gray she-cat easily. She skidded to a halt at the bottom of the slope, then followed her father as he exchanged reserved greetings with the warriors from the other Clans.

Nervously Fireheart scanned the growing throng of cats for Graystripe. Would he dare speak to Silverstream tonight? The gray warrior had his back to Silverstream while he talked with a WindClan warrior.

Fireheart was watching Graystripe so closely that he didn't hear Deadfoot approach. "Good evening, Fireheart," meowed the WindClan deputy. "How are you?"

Fireheart turned. "Hello," he meowed. "I'm fine, thank you."

Deadfoot nodded. "Good," he meowed, and limped away.

Onewhisker gave Fireheart a friendly nudge. "You're

privileged!" Fireheart felt a small glimmer of pride.

Bluestar's yowl sounded from the Great Rock. Fireheart turned and looked up, surprised. The leaders didn't usually call the meeting so soon. Crookedstar and Nightstar were standing close together on the rock. Bluestar waited beside Tallstar for the cats to gather beneath them. It was the first time Fireheart had seen the WindClan leader at a Gathering, he realized with a jolt.

Fireheart and Onewhisker followed the other cats as they settled themselves beneath the rock. Fireheart looked up expectantly, waiting for Bluestar to welcome Tallstar and WindClan back, but the ThunderClan leader was clearly in no mood to waste time on friendly words.

"RiverClan has been hunting at Sunningrocks," she began angrily. "Our patrols have scented your warriors many times, Crookedstar. Sunningrocks belongs to ThunderClan!"

Crookedstar met Bluestar's gaze steadily. "Have you forgotten how recently one of our warriors was killed defending our territory from ThunderClan?"

"You had no need to *defend your territory*," Bluestar answered. "My warriors were not hunting there. They were returning home after finding WindClan. It was a mission we all agreed on! According to the warrior code, they should not have been attacked."

"You speak of the warrior code?" spat Crookedstar. "What about the ThunderClan warrior who has been spying on our territory since then?"

Bluestar was caught off guard. "Warrior?" she echoed. "Have you seen him?"

"Not yet," Crookedstar hissed. "But we find his scent so often, it won't be long before we do."

Fireheart glanced at Graystripe in alarm. He knew only too well which warrior had been detected in Crookedstar's territory. Would any of the RiverClan warriors recognize his scent tonight?

Graystripe sat motionless, not taking his eyes off the leaders on the Great Rock.

Tigerclaw's deep growl sounded from the crowd. "We have scented ShadowClan in our territory as well as RiverClan this past moon. And not just one warrior, but a whole patrol, always the same cats."

The ShadowClan leader's eyes flashed indignantly. "ShadowClan has not been in your territory. Clearly your warriors can't tell the difference in the scents of cats outside their own Clan. You have been smelling the scent of rogue cats. They have been stealing prey from our territory as well!"

Tigerclaw snorted in disbelief and Nightstar glared down at him. "Do you doubt the word of ShadowClan, Tigerclaw?" The crowd murmured uncomfortably as Tigerclaw stared back at Nightpelt with unconcealed distrust.

For the first time, Tallstar spoke, his tail twitching uncertainly. "My warriors have also found strange scents in WindClan territory. They seem to be ShadowClan."

"I knew it!" Tigerclaw snarled. "RiverClan and Shadow-Clan have united against us!"

"*Us?* What do you mean by *us*!" spat Crookedstar. "I think it's you and WindClan that have formed the alliance! Is that why you were so keen to bring them back? So you can use them to invade the rest of the forest?"

Tallstar's fur bristled. "That's not why we returned, and you know it. We have kept to our own hunting grounds these past moons."

"Then why have we found strange warrior scents in our territory?" Crookedstar growled.

"They don't belong to WindClan!" hissed Tallstar. "They must be rogue cats, as Nightstar says."

"But rogue cats would be a convenient excuse for invading our territories, would they not?" Bluestar murmured. She stared dangerously at the RiverClan and ShadowClan leaders.

Crookedstar raised his hackles and Nightstar arched his back. With a flash of alarm, Fireheart saw Tigerclaw stand up and stalk toward the Great Rock, every muscle tensed. Would the leaders really fight at a Gathering?

At that moment a shadow fell over the valley. The cats fell silent as they were plunged into blackness. Fireheart looked up, trembling. A cloud had covered the full moon, completely blocking out its light.

"StarClan has sent the darkness!" Fireheart recognized the meow of Halftail, a ThunderClan elder.

The ShadowClan medicine cat yowled in agreement,

"StarClan is angry. These meetings are meant to be held in peace."

"Runningnose is right!" It was Yellowfang. "We shouldn't be fighting among ourselves, especially during leaf-bare. We should be worrying about keeping our Clans safe!" Her voice echoed in the frightened silence. "We must listen to StarClan."

CHAPTER 24

❧

Tallstar spoke up, a dim silhouette on top of the Great Rock. "This Gathering is over, by the will of StarClan." The crowd murmured in agreement. The air was thick with the scents of fear and hostility.

"Come, ThunderClan." Fireheart could barely see Bluestar as she leaped down from the Great Rock and headed for the edge of the clearing. He pushed his way through the other cats and hurried after her. He saw the massive outline of Tigerclaw as the deputy fell in step beside his leader, and the pale gray shapes of the other ThunderClan cats as they gathered behind the two great warriors. No cat spoke as they trekked solemnly up the slope toward home. Fireheart glanced over his shoulder. The other Clans were withdrawing too. By the time he reached the top of the slope, Fourtrees was deserted.

The Clan ran silently through the forest, following the familiar scent-lined trail. Fireheart spotted Graystripe at the back and he slowed his pace. Maybe Graystripe would be more prepared to talk about Silverstream, now that it was clear how tense things were between the Clans. His scent had been detected in RiverClan territory! Graystripe was putting himself and the Clan in danger with his secret meetings.

Fireheart searched for the right words but Graystripe hissed first, "I know what you're going to say. And I won't stop seeing her!"

"You're a mouse-brained fool!" Fireheart spat back. "They'll soon work out it's you. Bluestar will guess, or some cat from RiverClan'll recognize your scent. Tigerclaw's probably guessed already!"

Graystripe shot Fireheart an anxious glance. "Do you really think so?"

"I don't know," Fireheart admitted, relieved to hear a note of fear in Graystripe's voice. Graystripe had been acting as if he had no idea what might happen if the Clan found out about his affair. "But once he starts thinking about it . . . "

"Okay, okay!" spat Graystripe. He was silent for a moment. "What if I promise we'll meet only at Fourtrees? That way our scent will be hard to detect, and I won't have to go into RiverClan territory. Will you leave me alone then?"

Fireheart felt his heart sink. Graystripe was not going to give up Silverstream that easily. Then he nodded. This had to be better than creeping into hostile Clan territory to see her.

"Satisfied?" Graystripe's eyes flashed in the gloom, but his voice sounded shaky. Fireheart felt a pang of regret for their lost friendship, and a rush of sympathy for the gray warrior. He stretched his head forward to nuzzle Graystripe's flank, but Graystripe ran on ahead, leaving Fireheart alone at the back of the group.

Even though the cats were tired from the journey, Bluestar

called a meeting as soon as they were home. Most of the Clan was still awake anyway. The Gathering had been shorter than usual, and the sudden cloud cover had alarmed even the cats left in the camp.

While Bluestar and Tigerclaw settled themselves on the Highrock, Fireheart hurried over to the nursery. He wanted to know how Cloudkit was. He poked his head through the entrance. It was pitch black and warm inside.

"Hello, Fireheart," Brindleface whispered, a faint shadow shifting in the gloom. "Cloudkit's much better. Yellowfang gave him feverfew. It was just a chill." The queen sounded relieved. "What happened at the Gathering?"

"StarClan sent clouds to cover the moon. Bluestar's called a meeting. Can you come?"

Fireheart listened to Brindleface sniffing her kits. "Yes, I think I can," she answered finally. "My kits will sleep for a while."

Fireheart withdrew his head, and together they joined the cats gathered in the clearing. Fireheart felt fur brush against him, and Cinderpaw glanced up at him with wide, worried eyes.

Bluestar had already begun. "The greatest threat seems to be from RiverClan and ShadowClan. We must be prepared for the possibility that these two Clans have united against us."

Shocked meows rippled through the Clan.

"Do you really think they've joined together?" Yellowfang rasped. "RiverClan has the best sources of prey, but I can't imagine they'd want to share with ShadowClan." Fireheart remembered Silverstream's words about RiverClan's hunger after the Twoleg invasion, but he held his tongue, fearful that Bluestar would want to know where he'd heard such a story.

"They didn't deny it," Tigerclaw pointed out.

Bluestar nodded. "Whatever the truth, we must be on full alert. From tonight, each patrol will have four cats, at least three of them warriors. The patrols will be more frequent, two each night, and one during the day, as well as the dawn and dusk patrols. We must put a stop to RiverClan's and ShadowClan's raids on our territory, and since they have chosen to ignore our words, we must be prepared to fight."

The Clan yowled their agreement. Fireheart joined in even though he was worried about what this open hostility might mean for Graystripe. He looked around at the other cats. He could see all their eyes shining—except Graystripe's. The gray warrior sat with his head bowed in the shadows at the edge of the clearing.

When the noise died away, Bluestar spoke again. "The first patrol will leave before dawn." She jumped down from the Highrock. Tigerclaw followed, and the rest of the Clan broke up into small groups. Fireheart could hear them murmuring nervously as he padded to the warriors' den.

Fireheart settled into his nest, kneading the moss with his paws to make it comfortable. An owl hooted at the top of the ravine. He knew he would not sleep yet. His mind was racing with the accusations that had flown around the Gathering. He understood RiverClan's anger. They had picked up the scent of ThunderClan cats in their territory, and they were hungry now that their prey had been depleted by the Twoleg invasion.

But what about ShadowClan? It was smaller since ThunderClan had helped them to chase out their tyrannical former leader and his band of followers. Brokenstar had even admitted to killing Raggedstar, his own father, to become Clan leader. But the Clan had been left in peace to recover from Brokenstar's bloody rule. And Fireheart couldn't help thinking that, with fewer mouths to feed, ShadowClan had no need to raid ThunderClan's hunting grounds, or anyone else's.

As he puzzled over these thoughts, Whitestorm and Darkstripe pushed their way into the den. Before Whitestorm went to his nest, he stopped beside Fireheart. "You're to join me with Sandpaw and Mousefur on patrol at sunhigh," he meowed.

"Yes, Whitestorm," Fireheart answered before resting his chin on his paws. He had to get some sleep—his Clan needed him to be fit and ready to fight.

The clouds that had covered the moon had rolled away by the next morning. Fireheart enjoyed the faint warmth of the sun on his back as he washed himself in the clearing. Cloudkit jumped out of the nursery entrance opposite him, looking bright and happy.

Fireheart thanked StarClan that he had recovered so quickly. Sandpaw had been right about the kit's resilience. He looked around to see if Longtail and Dustpaw were there to see it too, but the clearing was empty.

Fireheart crossed over to the nursery. "Hi, Cloudkit," he meowed. "Feeling better?"

"Yep," squeaked Cloudkit. He spun around in a circle, grasping for his tail with his tiny jaws. A small ball of moss that had been sticking to his fur fell off and rolled along the ground. Cloudkit leaped on it and pawed it into the air. It bounced onto the ground beside Fireheart.

Fireheart knocked it back toward the kit, and Cloudkit sprang up to catch it in his teeth.

"Well done!" Fireheart was impressed. With one paw he scooped the moss ball high into the air, sending it flying across the clearing.

Cloudkit raced after the moss and grabbed it. He rolled onto his back, threw the ball up with his forepaws, and kicked it away with his hind legs. It landed next to the nursery. Cloudkit scrambled up and scooted after it. He crouched a rabbit leap away, his hindquarters bunched in the air.

Fireheart watched as the kit prepared to pounce. Suddenly his fur prickled. A long, dark foreleg was reaching toward the moss ball from behind the nursery.

"Cloudkit," Fireheart called, "wait!" Shadowy images of rogue cats were still fresh in his mind.

Cloudkit sat up and looked around at him, puzzled.

Tigerclaw emerged from behind the kitten, holding the moss ball between his teeth. He carried the ball over to the kit and dropped it by Cloudkit's fluffy white paws. "Be careful," he growled. "You wouldn't want to lose such a precious plaything." As he spoke, the dark warrior stared at Fireheart over Cloudkit's head.

Fireheart shivered. What did Tigerclaw mean by that? He seemed to be talking about the moss ball—but did he really mean that *Cloudkit* was a plaything? An image of Cinderpaw flashed into Fireheart's mind, a wounded huddle beside the Thunderpath. Was that another *plaything* he had lost? A cold feeling of dread seeped into his heart as once more he wondered if the ThunderClan deputy was somehow responsible for his apprentice's accident.

CHAPTER 25

❦

"Cloudkit!"

Fireheart heard Brindleface calling from inside the nursery. Tigerclaw turned and padded away. Cloudkit gave the moss ball a final shove and ran over to the nursery entrance. "'Bye, Fireheart," he mewed before he disappeared inside.

Fireheart looked up at the sky. It was almost sunhigh, time to join his patrol. He was hungry, but no fresh-kill had been gathered yet. Perhaps he might find something while they were out. He hurried across the clearing and out through the gorse tunnel, frozen leaves crunching beneath his paws.

Sandpaw and Mousefur were already waiting at the foot of the slope. Fireheart raised his tail in greeting, unexpectedly happy to see Sandpaw.

"Hi," meowed Sandpaw. Mousefur nodded to him.

Whitestorm emerged from the gorse tunnel. "Is the dawn patrol back yet?"

"No sign of them," answered Mousefur. But as she spoke, Fireheart heard the rustle of undergrowth above them. Out of the bushes came Willowpelt, Runningwind, Darkstripe, and Dustpaw.

"We've patrolled the entire RiverClan border," Willowpelt reported. "No sign of any hunting parties so far. Bluestar's patrol will check the area again this afternoon."

"Good," replied Whitestorm. "We'll take the ShadowClan border."

"Hopefully they'll have the same good sense as RiverClan and stay away," meowed Darkstripe. "After last night, they must know we'll be looking out for them."

"I hope so," growled Whitestorm. He turned to his patrol. "Are you ready?" Fireheart nodded. Whitestorm flicked the tip of his tail and leaped away into the bracken.

Fireheart followed Mousefur and Whitestorm. They kept up a fast pace as they climbed out of the ravine. Sandpaw was right behind Fireheart; he could feel her warm breath as she scrambled up the boulders.

They had not even reached Snakerocks when Fireheart picked up a sinister, familiar scent. He opened his mouth to warn the others but Mousefur spoke first. "ShadowClan!"

The four cats stopped to smell the rank stench.

"I can't believe they've come back already!" Sandpaw murmured. Fireheart noticed the fur quiver along her spine.

"The scent is recent." Whitestorm's eyes glittered with fury. "I had hoped Nightstar might bring some honor to his Clan. But I suppose the cold winds beyond the Thunderpath blow over every ShadowClan cat's heart."

Fireheart turned away and began pushing his way into a thick patch of bracken. He rubbed his teeth along the fronds to pick up the scent that hung there. It was ShadowClan all right. The smell was familiar. *Very* familiar. Fireheart paused. The scent belonged to a ShadowClan warrior he had encountered before, but which one?

Fireheart pushed onward, hoping more scent-markings might jog his memory. Now he could smell something else. Fireheart looked down. On the ground, among the bracken stems, lay a pile of rabbit bones. Clan cats normally buried the bones of their prey as a sign of respect for the life they had taken. Suddenly aware of what this might mean, Fireheart picked up a mouthful and wove back through the bracken. He dropped them at Whitestorm's paws.

Whitestorm stared at the bones in fury. "Rabbit bones? The warriors who left these want us to know they've been hunting on our land! Bluestar must know about this immediately."

"Will she send a battle party against ShadowClan?" asked Fireheart. He had never seen Whitestorm so angry.

"She should!" hissed the great white warrior. "And I'll lead it myself if I can. Nightstar has betrayed our trust, and StarClan knows he must be punished."

"Bluestar!" Whitestorm flung the rabbit bones down in the middle of the camp clearing.

"Bluestar has already left on patrol," Tigerclaw told him, stepping out from the shadows.

Halftail and Frostfur came hurrying from their dens to find out what was going on.

Whitestorm stared at Tigerclaw, still furious. "Look at these!" he spat.

Tigerclaw didn't need to be told what they meant; their scent carried the whole story. His eyes began to burn with anger.

Fireheart hung back at the edge of the clearing and watched the two great warriors. The evidence was certainly ominous, but the discovery of the bones had filled his mind with questions, not anger. It was only three moons since ShadowClan had driven out their cruel leader, with the help of ThunderClan. How could that same Clan possibly be ready to risk war with ThunderClan?

Tigerclaw clearly had no such doubts. Already he was calling Darkstripe and Runningwind to him. "Willowpelt and Mousefur will join us too!" he announced. "We'll find a ShadowClan patrol and leave them with some wounds that'll remind them to keep out of our territory in the future."

Whitestorm nodded.

"Can I come?" Sandpaw meowed. She had been pacing excitedly behind the white warrior. Now she stopped and looked at him with glittering eyes.

"Not this time," Whitestorm told her.

Frustration flickered across her face. "But what about Fireheart?" she meowed. "He found the bones."

Tigerclaw narrowed his eyes, his hackles raised. "*Fireheart* can stay here and tell Bluestar when she arrives," he hissed contemptuously.

"You're going to leave before she gets back?" Fireheart asked.

"Of course," Tigerclaw spat. "This needs to be settled

now!" He turned to Whitestorm and flicked his tail. Fireheart watched as the two warriors charged out of the camp, Darkstripe, Willowpelt, Runningwind, and Mousefur close behind. He could hear their paws pounding the frozen earth as they headed for the side of the ravine.

Fireheart was suddenly aware how empty the camp was. As Frostfur and Halftail came forward and began sniffing the rabbit bones, he meowed, "Who went with Bluestar?"

Frostfur looked up. "Graystripe, Longtail, and Swiftpaw."

A cold wind ruffled Fireheart's fur. He hoped that was what made him shiver. He was the only warrior left in camp. "Will you check the apprentices' den to see if Dustpaw's there?" Fireheart asked Sandpaw.

She nodded, bounded across the clearing, and poked her head into the den. "He's there," she called back, ducking out again. "Asleep, with Brackenpaw."

Yellowfang came padding out of her den and lifted her head. Fireheart relaxed a little at the familiar sight of the old medicine cat. He narrowed his eyes, ready to greet her. But as Yellowfang tasted the air, her eyes clouded with fear. With slow, stiff steps, she approached the rabbit bones and carefully sniffed each one.

Fireheart watched her, wondering why she was so interested in the old bones.

At last she looked up and stared into Fireheart's eyes. "Brokenstar!" she rasped, in a voice choked with horror.

"Brokenstar?" Fireheart echoed. Then it hit him. That was why the scent in the bracken had been so familiar. It was

Brokenstar's scent. "Are you sure?" he meowed urgently. "Tiger-claw has already left for ShadowClan territory."

"ShadowClan isn't to blame for this!" cried Yellowfang. "This is Brokenstar and his old warrior friends. I was Shadow-Clan's medicine cat. I was there at their kitting. I know their scents as well as I know my own." She paused. "You must find Tigerclaw and stop him. He will be making a terrible mistake if he attacks them!"

The blood roared in Fireheart's ears, making him dizzy. What should he do? "But I'm the only warrior left!" he meowed breathlessly to Yellowfang. "What if Brokenstar attacks the camp while I'm gone? He's done it before. He might have left the bones as a trap so that our camp was left unguarded."

"You *must* tell Tigerclaw before he—" Yellowfang pleaded, but Fireheart shook his head.

"I can't leave you all alone."

"Then I shall go!" Yellowfang hissed.

"No! I'll go!" meowed Sandpaw.

Fireheart looked from one cat to the other. He couldn't afford to send either—their strength and training were needed here to protect the Clan. But Yellowfang was right; innocent blood couldn't be shed. Brokenstar was the invader here; ThunderClan had no quarrel with ShadowClan. He would have to send another cat. He closed his eyes and thought hard. The answer came in a moment. "Brackenpaw!" Fireheart hissed, opening his eyes wide. He called the appren-tice's name out loud.

The young cat pushed his way out of his den and padded

across the clearing toward Fireheart. "What is it?" he asked, blinking the sleep from his eyes.

"I have an urgent mission for you," Fireheart told him.

Brackenpaw shook himself and stood taller. "Yes, Fireheart," he mewed.

"You must find Tigerclaw. He's taken a raiding party to attack a ShadowClan patrol. Stop him and tell him that it was Brokenstar who has been invading our territory!" Brackenpaw's eyes widened with alarm, but Fireheart went on: "You might have to cross the Thunderpath. I know you haven't been trained. . . ." Images of Cinderpaw's broken body flashed in Fireheart's mind, but he forced them away. He looked deep into Brackenpaw's eyes. "You must find Tigerclaw," he repeated, "or there will be a war between the Clans for no reason!"

Brackenpaw nodded, his eyes calm and filled with purpose. "I'll find him," the tabby apprentice promised.

"May StarClan go with you," Fireheart murmured, reaching forward to touch Brackenpaw's flank with his nose.

Brackenpaw turned and sprinted out through the gorse tunnel. Fireheart watched him go, struggling to keep calm. Cinderpaw . . . the Thunderpath . . . the images kept flashing back. Fireheart shook his head to clear it. There was no time to worry now. If Brokenstar was in ThunderClan territory, the camp had to prepare for an attack.

"What's happening?" Dustpaw had emerged from the apprentices' den. Fireheart glanced at him, ran to the head of the clearing, and scrambled up onto the Highrock. The clearing seemed a long way below his trembling legs. He swallowed hard and began the customary call. "Let all cats old enough to . . ." But the words were taking too long! "The camp is in danger. Come here now!" he yowled urgently.

The elders and queens rushed from their dens, followed by their kits. They looked bewildered when they saw Fireheart on top of the Highrock. Cinderpaw limped out of the fern tunnel and looked up at Fireheart with a strong, bright gaze. When Fireheart saw her, the camp suddenly stopped swaying beneath him.

"What's going on?" demanded One-eye, the oldest ThunderClan cat. "What do you think you're doing up there?"

Fireheart didn't hesitate. "Brokenstar is back. He might be in ThunderClan territory right now. All our other warriors are out of the camp. If Brokenstar attacks, we must be ready. Kits and elders stay in the nursery. The rest of you must be ready to fight—"

A menacing yowl from the camp entrance cut short Fireheart's speech. A lean dark brown tabby with matted fur and torn ears strode into the camp. His bristling tail was bent in the middle like a broken branch.

"Brokenstar!" Fireheart gasped, instinctively unsheathing his claws as every hair on his body stood on end.

Four mangy warriors prowled in behind their leader, their eyes glittering with hatred.

"So you're the only warrior left!" Brokenstar hissed, his lips drawn back in a snarl. "This will be easier than I thought!"

CHAPTER 26

Yellowfang, Dustpaw, and Sandpaw rushed forward in a defensive row, and the queens lined up behind them. Fireheart saw Cinderpaw hobbling to join them, but Dustpaw spat angrily at the small gray cat as she neared, and Cinderpaw scrabbled clumsily away, ears flat, back into Yellowfang's den.

The elders grabbed the kits, bundled them into the nursery, and squeezed inside after them. Brindleface picked up Cloudkit in her jaws and pushed him in last. She tugged at the brambles with her paws, ignoring the thorns, and covered the entrance before turning to join the rest of her Clan in the clearing.

Fireheart leaped down from the Highrock and raced to Yellowfang's side. He arched his back and hissed at Brokenstar, "You lost the last time we fought, and you'll lose again!"

"Never!" Brokenstar spat back. "You might have taken my Clan away from me, but you can't kill me—I have more lives than you!"

"One ThunderClan life is worth ten of yours!" Fireheart growled. He gave a warrior's yowl and the clearing exploded into battle.

Fireheart leaped straight for Brokenstar and grasped the dark brown tabby with his claws. Life as an outlaw had treated the former Clan leader harshly—Fireheart could feel the ribs of the flea-bitten tom beneath his fur. But Brokenstar was still strong. He twisted around and sank his teeth into Fireheart's hind leg. Fireheart yowled and hissed with rage, but kept his grip. Brokenstar struggled forward, scrabbling with his paws on the frozen ground. Fireheart felt his claws raking along Brokenstar's bony flanks as the rogue warrior ripped himself free. Fireheart lunged after him, but other claws were grasping at his hind leg. He looked over his shoulder to see who it was. Clawface crouched there, staring at Fireheart with narrowed, mocking eyes.

Fireheart looked back at him in disbelief. He had never expected to see this cat again. He forgot Brokenstar instantly. It was Clawface who had killed Spottedleaf six moons ago; he had murdered the ThunderClan medicine cat in cold blood so that Brokenstar could steal Frostfur's kits. Rage roared in Fireheart's ears. As he twisted around and threw himself on top of the scrawny brown tom, Fireheart glimpsed a flash of tortoiseshell fur out of the corner of his eye, and the sweet scent of Spottedleaf hit the roof of his mouth. He felt her spirit beside him. She had come to help him avenge her death.

Fireheart hardly noticed the pain in his leg as he tore it free from Clawface's grasp and flew at him. The tom reared up and flailed his wide front paws. Thorn-sharp claws caught Fireheart behind his ear. Pain ripped through him like fire, and he staggered. Clawface was on him in an instant, pinning

Fireheart to the ground and sinking his teeth into the back of his neck.

Fireheart screeched in agony, "Help me, Spottedleaf! I can't do it!"

Suddenly the weight was wrenched off his back. Fireheart sprang to his paws and spun around. Graystripe! The gray warrior stood motionless, his eyes filled with horror. Clawface's body hung limply from his jaws. Graystripe opened his mouth and Clawface fell to the ground, dead.

Fireheart took a step forward. "He killed Spottedleaf, Graystripe!" This was no time for remorse. "Is Bluestar with you?" he went on urgently.

Graystripe shook his head. "She sent me back to fetch Tigerclaw," he replied. "We found bones. Bluestar recognized Brokenstar's stench and guessed he must be leading the rogue cats."

A hiss sounded nearby and two cats crashed into Fireheart. He leaped out of the way. It was Frostfur battling with another of the attacking cats. The queen was fighting with all the power of StarClan. These were the cats who had stolen her kits. Hate shone in her eyes as she struggled. Fireheart held himself back—Frostfur didn't need his help. A moment later the rogue warrior was sent screeching away, through the bracken camp wall.

Frostfur chased after him, but Fireheart called her back. "You have given him enough wounds to remember you!" The queen skidded to a halt by the bracken wall and turned, her sides heaving and her white fur stained with her enemy's blood.

Another rogue warrior screeched past Fireheart and headed for the camp wall. Dustpaw chased after him and managed to give the mottled tabby a fierce bite before he let him scrabble out of the camp. *Only Brokenstar and one warrior left*, Fireheart thought.

Sandpaw had the rogue warrior pinned to the ground. The tom was lying motionless beneath her. *Watch out!* thought Fireheart, remembering his favorite trick of letting an enemy think he had won. But Sandpaw was not deceived. When the tom leaped to his paws, she was ready. She sprang off him, and then lunged, grasping the warrior with her claws to flip him over and rake his belly with her hind legs. Only when he squealed like a kit did she let go of him. The rogue tore out of the camp entrance, still wailing.

There was an eerie moment of stillness. The ThunderClan cats stood in silence and stared at the blood and fur that was scattered around the clearing. In the middle lay Clawface's body.

Where was Brokenstar? Fireheart spun around in alarm, scanning the camp. Could he have broken into the nursery? He was about to spring toward the bramble den when a wretched howl from Yellowfang's den tore the air. Fireheart tore across to the fern tunnel. Cinderpaw! He raced into the den, expecting the worst, but saw instead Brokenstar lying in a heap on the ground. The old medicine cat stood over him.

Brokenstar's eyes were closed and bloody. Fireheart saw his sides heave once, and stop moving. He recognized from the deep stillness in the rogue warrior's body that Brokenstar was losing a life.

Yellowfang's claws were unsheathed and glistened red. Her face was twisted and her eyes glazed.

Suddenly Brokenstar gasped and began to breathe again. Fireheart waited for Yellowfang to lunge at him with another killing bite, but she hesitated. Brokenstar didn't get up.

Fireheart ran to the medicine cat's side. "Is this his last life? Why don't you finish him off?" he urged. "He murdered his father, banished you from your Clan, and tried to kill you."

"It's not his last life," she rasped, "and even if it were, I couldn't kill him."

"Why not? StarClan would honor you for it." Fireheart could not believe her words. The name Brokenstar had always made this old she-cat bristle with rage.

Yellowfang dragged her gaze from Brokenstar and looked at Fireheart. Her eyes clouded with pain and grief as she murmured, "He is my son."

Fireheart felt the ground lurch under his paws. "But medicine cats are forbidden from having kits," he blurted out.

"I know," answered Yellowfang. "I never intended to have kits. But then I fell in love with Raggedstar." Her voice was thick with sorrow. Suddenly Fireheart thought back to the battle when Brokenstar was driven out of the ShadowClan camp. Just before he fled, the cruel leader had told Yellowfang that he had murdered his father. Yellowfang had been devastated, and now Fireheart understood why.

"There were three kits in my litter," Yellowfang went on. "But only Brokenstar survived. I gave him to a ShadowClan queen to bring up as her own. I thought that losing two of my kits was punishment from StarClan for breaking the warrior code. But I was wrong. My punishment wasn't that two of my kits died. It was that *this* one survived!" Yellowfang looked in disgust at Brokenstar's bleeding body. "And now I cannot kill him. I must accept my fate, as StarClan wishes it."

Yellowfang staggered, and Fireheart thought she was going to collapse. He pressed his body against her flank to support her and whispered, "Does he know you're his mother?"

Yellowfang shook her head.

Brokenstar began to wail pitifully. "I can't see!" Fireheart realized with horror that the rogue cat's eyes had been scratched beyond repair.

Fireheart cautiously approached him. Brokenstar lay still. Fireheart poked him with a forepaw and Yellowfang's son moaned again. "Don't kill me," he whined. Fireheart backed away, feeling a shudder of revulsion at the warrior's fear.

Yellowfang took a deep breath. "I will see to him." She walked over to her wounded son, grasped him by the scruff of his neck, and dragged him to the nest that Patchpelt had left.

Fireheart let her go. He wanted to check that Cinderpaw was all right. He caught sight of a dark shape moving inside the split rock where Yellowfang slept. "Cinderpaw?" he called.

Cinderpaw poked her head out.

"Are you okay?" Fireheart asked.

"Have the rogue cats gone?" she whispered.

"Yes, except Brokenstar. He's badly injured. Yellowfang's seeing to him." He waited for Cinderpaw's shocked reaction, but she just shook her head slowly and stared at the ground.

"Are you okay?" Fireheart repeated.

"I should have fought alongside you." Cinderpaw's voice was choked with shame.

"You would have been killed!"

"That's what Dustpaw said. He told me to go and hide with the kits." The small cat's eyes were full of despair. "But I wouldn't have minded being killed. What good am I like this? I'm just a burden on this Clan."

Fireheart felt a thorn-sharp pang of pity. He searched for words to comfort her, but before he could speak, Yellowfang's rasping mew sounded from the bracken.

"Cinderpaw," she called. "Fetch me some cobwebs, quickly!" Cinderpaw turned at once and disappeared inside the rock, returning a moment later with one paw wrapped in a swathe of cobwebs. As quickly as she could, she scrambled awkwardly over to Yellowfang and thrust the cobwebs inside the nest.

"Now get me some of that comfrey root," ordered Yellowfang.

As Cinderpaw limped back to the split rock, Fireheart turned to leave. There was nothing more he could do here. He must find out how the rest of the Clan was.

Hardly any cat had moved in the camp clearing. Fireheart

padded straight to Dustpaw and meowed, "Yellowfang is tending to Brokenstar's wounds. Cinderpaw's helping her." He ignored Dustpaw's gasp of disbelief. "Go and guard him." Dustpaw ran to the tunnel and disappeared inside.

Fireheart went over to Graystripe. The gray warrior was still staring at Clawface's body. "You saved my life," Fireheart murmured. "Thank you."

Graystripe lifted his gaze to Fireheart. "I would give my life for you," he answered simply.

Feeling choked, Fireheart watched his friend turn and walk away. Perhaps their friendship was not over after all.

The sound of paws pounding through the gorse tunnel broke into his thoughts. Bluestar came rushing into the camp, followed by Longtail and Swiftpaw. Fireheart felt his shoulders droop with relief at the sight of his Clan leader. She looked around at the blood-spattered clearing, her eyes wide, until her gaze rested on Clawface's body. "Brokenstar attacked?" she meowed.

Fireheart nodded.

"Is he dead?"

"He's with Yellowfang," Fireheart answered, forcing out the words in spite of his exhaustion. "He's been wounded—his eyes."

"And the other rogue warriors?"

"We chased them off."

"Are any of our Clan badly hurt?" Bluestar demanded, looking once more around the clearing. The cats shook their heads. "Good," she meowed. "Sandpaw, Swiftpaw, take this body out of the camp and bury it. No elders need be present. No rogue deserves to be buried with the honor of StarClan ritual."

Swiftpaw and Sandpaw began to drag Clawface toward the tunnel.

"Are the elders safe?" Bluestar asked.

"They're in the nursery," Fireheart told her. As he spoke a rustling sounded from the bramble den, and Halftail appeared, followed by the other kits and elders. Fireheart saw Cloudkit tumble out and scamper excitedly across the clearing to Brindleface. She greeted him with a brisk lick, and the kit turned to watch Clawface's body as it disappeared away through the tunnel.

"Is he dead?" Cloudkit asked curiously. "Can I go and see?"

"Hush," whispered Brindleface, tucking her tail around him.

"Where's Tigerclaw?" Bluestar asked.

"He's taken a party to attack a ShadowClan patrol," Fireheart explained. "We found bones on our patrol. They smelled of ShadowClan so Tigerclaw decided to attack. I sent Brackenpaw to stop him when Yellowfang realized it was Brokenstar's scent on them."

"Brackenpaw?" meowed Bluestar, narrowing her eyes. "Even though he might have to cross the Thunderpath?"

"I was the only warrior left in camp. There was no one else I could send."

Bluestar nodded, the concern in her eyes giving way

to understanding. "You didn't want to leave the camp unguarded?" she meowed. "You did well, Fireheart. I think Brokenstar hoped to lure all our warriors away from the camp. We found bones, too."

"Graystripe told me." Fireheart looked around for his friend, but Graystripe had disappeared.

"Send Yellowfang to me when she's finished with Brokenstar," Bluestar ordered. She pricked her ears at the noise of more paws in the gorse tunnel. Tigerclaw came racing into the camp, followed by Whitestorm and the rest of the raiding party. Fireheart craned his neck to peer around the warriors until he saw Brackenpaw, right at the back. The young apprentice looked exhausted but unhurt. Fireheart let out a quiet sigh of relief.

"Did Brackenpaw reach you before you found a patrol?" asked Bluestar, walking over to her deputy.

"We hadn't even entered their territory," Tigerclaw answered. "We were just about to cross the Thunderpath." His eyes narrowed. "Was that Clawface they were burying?"

Bluestar nodded.

"Then Brackenpaw was right," meowed the deputy. "Brokenstar was planning to attack the camp. Is he dead too?"

"No. Yellowfang is tending to his wounds."

"Surely not!" Mousefur exclaimed, exchanging a glance with Runningwind beside her.

Tigerclaw's face darkened. "Tending to his wounds?" he snarled. "We should kill him, not waste time making him better!"

"We'll discuss that once I've spoken to Yellowfang," meowed Bluestar calmly.

"You can discuss it with me now, Bluestar." Yellowfang padded into the clearing, her head drooping with exhaustion.

"Have you left Brokenstar alone?" growled Tigerclaw, his amber eyes flashing.

Yellowfang raised her head and looked at the dark warrior. "Dustpaw is guarding him. And I've given him poppy seeds, so he'll sleep for a while. Brokenstar is blind now, Tigerclaw. There's no way he'll try to escape. He'd die of hunger in a week, if a fox or a gang of crows didn't kill him first."

"Well, that makes it easier," Tigerclaw snarled. "We won't have to kill him ourselves. We can let the forest deal with him."

Yellowfang turned to Bluestar. "We cannot let him die," she meowed.

"Why not?"

Fireheart held his breath as he watched the leader's eyes flick from Yellowfang to Tigerclaw and back again. He wondered if Yellowfang was going to tell Bluestar that Brokenstar was her son.

"If we did, we would be no better than he is," replied Yellowfang calmly.

Tigerclaw's tail flicked in anger.

"What do you think, Whitestorm?" Bluestar meowed before Tigerclaw could speak.

"It will be a burden on our Clan to look after him," Whitestorm answered thoughtfully. "But Yellowfang is right—if we send him out into the forest, or kill him in cold blood, StarClan will know we have stooped as low as he."

One-eye stepped forward. "Bluestar," she meowed in her croaky old voice. "In the past we have sometimes kept prisoners for many moons. We could do it again." Fireheart remembered that Yellowfang herself had been a prisoner when she first came to the camp. He waited for the medicine cat to remind Bluestar of this, but she said nothing.

"So you would really consider keeping this rogue inside our camp?" Tigerclaw's eyes blazed with rage as he challenged his leader. With a pang, Fireheart couldn't help agreeing with the dark warrior's words. The thought of killing Brokenstar appalled him—he knew better than any of these cats what that would mean to Yellowfang—but Brokenstar was a fearsome enemy, even without his sight. Keeping him in the camp would be difficult and dangerous for all the members of the Clan.

"Is he really blind?" Bluestar asked Yellowfang.

"Yes, he is."

"Has he other wounds?"

Fireheart replied this time. "I clawed him pretty badly," he admitted. He looked over to Yellowfang and was relieved when the old she-cat dipped her head just enough for him to know she forgave him for wounding her son.

"How long till they heal?" asked Bluestar.

"About a moon," Yellowfang answered.

"Then you may nurse him till then. After that we will discuss his future again. And from now on, he will be known as Brokentail, not Brokenstar. We cannot take away the lives that StarClan gave him, but this cat is no longer a Clan leader." Bluestar looked questioningly at Tigerclaw. His tail twitched, but he didn't speak.

"It is decided," Bluestar meowed. "He stays."

CHAPTER 27

Fireheart limped over to the clump of nettles and began to lick his wounds. He would go and see Yellowfang later, when she had finished tending to the other cats.

The weak rays of the setting sun threw long shadows across the clearing. Dustpaw had been relieved from his guard duty by Longtail. Tigerclaw had taken the rest of his unscathed raiding party out in search of fresh-kill. Fireheart's stomach growled. He looked up at the sound of pawsteps, but it was only Sandpaw and Swiftpaw returning from their burial duty.

The two cats padded over to Bluestar, who was sitting beneath the Highrock with Whitestorm. Fireheart pushed himself to his paws and walked over to join them. With a flick of his tail he beckoned to Dustpaw, who was licking his own scratches beside the tree stump. Dustpaw flashed him a doubtful look but got up wearily and followed him.

"We've buried Clawface," meowed Sandpaw.

"Thank you," Bluestar replied. The ThunderClan leader looked directly at Swiftpaw. "You may go." The black-and-white apprentice dipped his head and headed for his den.

Fireheart signaled to Dustpaw again to come closer. The

tabby apprentice narrowed his eyes and padded forward to stand beside Sandpaw.

"Bluestar," Fireheart began hesitantly, "Sandpaw and Dustpaw fought like warriors when Brokentail attacked. We would have been in much more trouble without their strength and courage." Dustpaw's eyes widened and Sandpaw looked at the ground as Fireheart spoke.

A purr rumbled from Whitestorm's throat. "It's not like you to be shy," he meowed to his apprentice.

Sandpaw's ears twitched uncomfortably. "Fireheart's the one who saved the Clan," she burst out. "He was the one who alerted the camp so that we were ready for Brokentail's attack."

It was Fireheart's turn to feel embarrassed. He was relieved when Tigerclaw and the hunting party trotted into the camp at that moment, carrying plenty of fresh-kill.

Bluestar nodded at Tigerclaw and then turned to face Dustpaw and Sandpaw. "It makes me proud to know that ThunderClan has such fine warriors," she meowed. "It's time you both took your warrior names. We shall have the naming ceremony now, while the sun is setting, and then we can eat."

Sandpaw and Dustpaw looked excitedly at each other. Fireheart lifted his chin and purred. Bluestar called to the Clan, and Fireheart felt even happier when he saw Graystripe appear from the warriors' den. He hadn't left the camp after all.

The Clan gathered around the edge of the clearing. Elders and queens sat with the apprentices and kits on one side;

Fireheart waited with the warriors on the other. He looked at Cloudkit nestled beside Brindleface. The kit's eyes shone with excitement, and Fireheart felt a rush of pride that his kin-kit could see him sitting with the Clan warriors. Bluestar stood in the center with Sandpaw and Dustpaw.

The last arc of sun glowed pink on the horizon. The Clan waited silently as it dipped out of sight, leaving the darkening sky pricked with stars.

Bluestar looked up and fixed her eyes on the brightest star in Silverpelt. "I, Bluestar, leader of ThunderClan, call upon my warrior ancestors to look down on these two apprentices. They have trained hard to understand the ways of your code, and I commend them to you as warriors in their turn." She gazed down at the pair of young cats in front of her. "Sandpaw, Dustpaw, do you promise to uphold the warrior code and to protect and defend this Clan, even at the cost of your life?"

Sandpaw stared back, her eyes gleaming. "I do," she replied.

Dustpaw echoed her words, his voice strong and low. "I do."

"Then by the powers of StarClan I give you your warrior names: Sandpaw, from this moment you will be known as Sandstorm. StarClan honors your courage and your spirit, and we welcome you as a full warrior of ThunderClan." Bluestar stepped forward and rested her muzzle on top of Sandstorm's bowed head.

Sandstorm licked Bluestar's shoulder respectfully before she turned and walked toward Whitestorm. Fireheart saw her eyes flash proudly at her mentor as she settled down beside him in her new place with the warriors.

Bluestar turned her eyes to the dark brown tabby. "Dust-paw, from this moment you will be known as Dustpelt. StarClan honors your bravery and your honesty, and we welcome you as a full warrior of ThunderClan." She touched his head with her muzzle, and he too gave the leader's shoulder a respectful lick before joining the other warriors.

The voices of the Clan rose in tribute, sending clouds of misty breath into the night air. As one they chanted the new warrior names. "Sandstorm! Dustpelt! Sandstorm! Dustpelt!"

"In the tradition of our ancestors," meowed Bluestar, raising her voice, "Sandstorm and Dustpelt must sit in silent vigil until dawn, and guard the camp alone while we sleep. But before they begin their vigil, the Clan will share a meal. It has been a long day and we have reason to be proud of these cats who defended our camp against the rogues. Fireheart, StarClan thanks you for your courage. You are a great warrior, and I'm proud to count you as a member of my Clan."

The cats meowed again. A purr burst from Fireheart's throat as he looked around at his Clan. Only Tigerclaw and Dustpelt eyed him with hostility, but for once he felt untouched by their jealousy. Bluestar had praised him, and that was enough.

One by one the cats stepped forward to take some of the fresh-kill Tigerclaw's party had brought.

Fireheart walked over to Sandstorm. "We can eat together as warriors tonight," he meowed happily. "If that's okay with you?" he added. Sandstorm purred at him and Fireheart felt a prickle of pleasure.

"Choose something for me," she called as Fireheart dashed away to the pile of fresh-kill. "I'm starving!"

Fireheart picked out a mouse for Sandpaw, temptingly plump for so late in leaf-bare. He took a bluetit for himself and turned to carry his catch back to Sandstorm. Then his heart sank—Dustpelt, Whitestorm, and Darkstripe had joined her. He'd been foolish to expect they would share their meal alone. This was a time for the whole Clan to share together in celebration.

The thought reminded Fireheart of Cinderpaw. He looked around and realized that he hadn't seen her at the naming ceremony. She must still be in Yellowfang's clearing. He bounded over to Sandstorm and dropped the fresh-kill beside her. "I'll be back in five rabbit hops," he meowed. "I want to take something to Cinderpaw."

"Sure." Sandstorm shrugged.

Fireheart quickly collected a vole from the fresh-kill pile and carried it across the clearing. He was surprised to see Yellowfang sitting in her den. She'd been at the naming ceremony, so she must have come straight back afterward.

"I hope that's not for me," she growled as Fireheart approached. "I've already had my share."

Fireheart dropped the vole on the ground. "I brought it for Cinderpaw," he answered. "I thought she might want something. She wasn't at the naming ceremony."

"I've given her some mouse meat, but you're welcome to give her that as well."

Fireheart looked around the fern-shaded clearing.

Brokenstar's brown fur was just visible through the stems of Patchpelt's old nest. The warrior was not moving.

"He's still asleep." Yellowfang's tone was brisk, the voice of a medicine cat rather than a mother. Fireheart couldn't help feeling relieved. He wanted to believe Yellowfang's loyalties still lay with ThunderClan. He picked up the vole and carried it to Cinderpaw's nest. "Hey, Cinderpaw," he meowed softly into the bracken.

The gray cat stirred and pushed herself to a sitting position. "Fireheart."

Fireheart stepped through the fronds and sat in the small space beside her. He dropped the vole at her paws. "Here," he meowed. "Yellowfang's not the only one trying to fatten you up!"

"Thanks," Cinderpaw mewed. But she left the vole lying beside her paw and didn't even bend down to sniff it.

"Are you still thinking about the battle?" Fireheart asked gently.

Cinderpaw shrugged. "I *am* just a burden, aren't I?" She looked up at Fireheart with sad, round eyes.

"Who's a burden?" Yellowfang's growl interrupted them as the old gray medicine cat poked her head into the nest. "Are you upsetting my helper?" she meowed at Fireheart. "I don't know how I would have coped today if it hadn't been for this one." She looked warmly at Cinderpaw, her yellow eyes soft. "I even had her mixing herbs this evening!"

Cinderpaw looked down shyly and dipped her head to take a bite of the vole.

"I think I might keep her with me awhile longer," Yellow-fang went on. "She's becoming more useful every day. Besides, I'm getting used to her company."

Cinderpaw glanced up at the old medicine cat, a teasing glint in her eyes. "Only because you're deaf enough to put up with my chattering!" Yellowfang pretended to spit crossly at the young cat, and Cinderpaw added to Fireheart, "Well, that's what she keeps telling me, anyway."

Fireheart was surprised to feel a pang of envy at the close bond these two cats had developed. He'd always thought of himself as Yellowfang's only real friend in the Clan, but now it looked like she had another. But at least Cinderpaw had somewhere to stay—if she couldn't train to be a warrior, she'd feel out of place in the apprentices' den.

Fireheart stood up. It was time he went back to Sandstorm. "Will you be okay here with Brokentail?" he asked.

Yellowfang gave him a disdainful look. "I think we can manage, don't you, Cinderpaw?"

"He wouldn't dare cause trouble," she agreed confidently. "And Longtail's here to help."

Yellowfang ducked her head out of the nest, and Fireheart squeezed out after her. "'Bye, Cinderpaw!" he called.

"'Bye, and thanks for the food."

"No problem," he meowed. He turned to Yellowfang. "Have you got anything for this bite on my neck?"

Yellowfang looked closely at his wound. "Looks like a nasty one," she growled.

"It's from Brokentail," Fireheart confessed.

Yellowfang nodded. "Wait there." She padded quickly to her den and returned with a bundle of herbs wrapped in leaves. "Can you manage them yourself? Just chew them up and rub the juice into the wounds. It'll sting, but nothing a brave warrior can't handle!"

"Thanks, Yellowfang." Fireheart picked up the bundle in his teeth.

Yellowfang led him to the tunnel entrance. "I appreciate your coming," she meowed, glancing at Cinderpaw's nest. "She was feeling pretty low, I think. She felt bad after the battle, and then the naming ceremony."

Fireheart nodded. He understood. He gave a last wary glance at where Brokentail lay. "You sure you'll be safe?" he asked again through the bundle of herbs.

"He's blind," meowed Yellowfang. She sighed, and then added more brightly, "And I'm not *that* old!"

Fireheart woke the following morning to find dazzling white light streaming through the den wall. He guessed it had snowed again. At least his wounds had stopped aching. Yellowfang had been right—the herb juice *had* stung, but he felt much better after a good night's sleep.

Fireheart wondered how Sandstorm and Dustpelt had managed their vigil. It must have been bitterly cold in the snow. He got to his paws and stretched his forelegs, arching his back and curling his tail up over his head. Thunder-Clan's two newest warriors were bundled up, fast asleep on the far edge of the den. Whitestorm must have sent them in when he left on the dawn patrol.

Fireheart padded out into the snow-covered clearing. He could just make out Frostfur's white pelt skirting the nursery as she slipped out to stretch her legs. There were two bare spots in the center of the clearing, where Sandstorm and Dustpelt had spent the night. Fireheart shivered at the thought, but still he envied them as he remembered the thrill of his first night as a warrior. It had filled him with a warmth not even the hardest frost could have chilled.

The sky was thick with snow-heavy clouds. Flakes were still falling, softly and silently. There would be plenty of hunting to do today, Fireheart realized. The Clan would need to stock up if the snow was going to get deeper.

He heard Bluestar call from the Highrock. The Clan cats began to creep from their dens and pick their way through the snow to hear their leader's words. Fireheart settled himself into one of the bare spots. It smelled of Sandstorm. He noticed Graystripe sitting on the other side of the clearing, looking tired. Fireheart wondered if he'd slipped out last night to tell Silverstream about the rogue cats.

Bluestar began to speak. "I wanted to make sure you all know that Brokentail is in the camp." None of the cats uttered a noise. They knew already. The rumor had spread through the camp like a forest fire.

"He is blind, and harmless." A few cats snorted their displeasure, and Bluestar nodded to acknowledge their fears. "I am as concerned as you are for the safety of our Clan. But, StarClan knows, we cannot turn him out to die in the forest.

Yellowfang will nurse him until his wounds heal. Once they have, we'll discuss this again."

Bluestar looked around, listening for voices from the crowd, but no cat spoke, so she leaped down from Highrock. As the cats dispersed Fireheart noticed that the leader was walking toward him.

"Fireheart," she meowed. "One thing concerns me. You still haven't settled things with Graystripe. I've not seen you eat together for days. I told you before, there's no room for fighting within ThunderClan. I want you to hunt together today."

Fireheart nodded. "Yes, Bluestar." That was fine by him. And after yesterday's battle, he felt hopeful that Graystripe would like the idea too. As Bluestar walked away, Fireheart scanned the clearing, hoping that Graystripe hadn't disappeared again. No, there he was, helping to clear the snow from the nursery entrance.

"Hey, Graystripe," Fireheart called. Graystripe carried on with his work. Fireheart bounded over to him. "Do you want to go hunting this morning?"

Graystripe turned to face him, his eyes cold. "Are you making sure I don't disappear again?" he snarled.

Fireheart was startled. "N-no, I just thought . . . after yesterday . . . Clawface . . ."

"I would have done the same for any ThunderClan cat. That's what Clan loyalty is about!" Graystripe's meow was harsh with anger as he went back to pushing snow.

Fireheart's hopes plummeted. Had he lost his friend's

trust forever? He turned away, tail down, and began to trudge through the snow toward the camp entrance. He called over his shoulder, "Bluestar told me to go hunting with you this morning, actually, so you can explain to her why you're not coming."

"Oh, I see, you were just trying to please Bluestar, as usual!" Graystripe hissed. Fireheart stopped and whipped around, ready to throw back a retort, but he paused when he saw that Graystripe was crossing the clearing toward him, shaking snowflakes from his wide shoulders.

"Come on, then," Graystripe growled, leading the way through the gorse tunnel.

It was a slow climb out of the ravine, with the boulders covered in snow. When they reached the top, the icebound forest stretched before them. Graystripe charged away at once, his face set with grim determination. Fireheart followed him. As he tracked a mouse around the roots of an oak tree he saw Graystripe racing after a rabbit that had been foolish enough to stray from its burrow. Graystripe pelted furiously after the creature until he finished it off with a well-aimed pounce. Fireheart sat and watched as Graystripe padded back to him and dropped the rabbit at Fireheart's paws.

"That should feed a kit or two." He grunted.

"You don't have to prove anything to me," Fireheart told him.

"No?" Graystripe answered bitterly. His eyes met Fireheart's, cold and angry. "Maybe you should start acting as if you trusted me, then." He turned away before Fireheart could reply.

By sunhigh Graystripe had caught more than Fireheart, but both cats had done well. They returned to the camp, their jaws heavy with fresh-kill. They padded into the clearing and dropped their prey in the usual place. The spot had been empty so far.

Fireheart wondered if they should go out again. The snow was heavier now, and a cold wind was beginning to blow through the ravine. Fireheart was studying the darkening sky when he heard Brindleface's worried meow near the nursery. He bounded over to see what was wrong. "What's the matter?"

"Have you seen Cloudkit?" she demanded.

Fireheart shook his head. "Is he missing?" His paws prickled as Brindleface's rising panic began to infect him.

"Yes. So are my other kits. I only closed my eyes for a moment. I just woke up and I can't find them anywhere! It's too cold for them to be out. They'll freeze to death!" The queen swayed on her paws.

Alarm shot through Fireheart as he pictured the last time a young cat had disappeared from the camp. It had been Cinderpaw.

CHAPTER 28

❧

"I'll find them," Fireheart promised. *He* automatically looked around for Graystripe. The wind was rising and the snow was growing thicker—he didn't want to search alone. Fireheart rushed to the warriors' den and pushed his way inside, but Graystripe wasn't there.

Sandstorm was just waking up. "What's wrong?" she meowed, seeing Fireheart peering around the den.

"Brindleface's kits are missing."

"Cloudkit too?" Sandstorm scrambled to her paws, instantly awake.

"Yes! I was looking for Graystripe so we could look for them together, but he isn't here," Fireheart meowed, his words tumbling out in a rush. He felt a stab of rage that Graystripe was missing yet again—right after accusing Fireheart of not trusting him!

"I'll come with you," Sandstorm offered.

Fireheart blinked. "Thanks," he meowed gratefully. "Come on. We should tell Bluestar before we leave."

"Dustpelt can tell her. Is it still snowing?"

"Yes, and it's getting heavier. We'd better hurry." Fireheart looked at Dustpelt's sleeping form. "You wake him. I'll tell Brindleface we're going and meet you by the entrance." He bounded away, back to the nursery. Brindleface was still sniffing around in search of scents.

"Any sign?" Fireheart asked.

"No, nothing." Brindleface's voice was trembling. "Frostfur's gone to tell Bluestar!"

"Well, don't worry. I'm going out to look for them," he reassured her. "Sandstorm's coming with me. We'll find them."

Brindleface nodded and carried on searching.

Fireheart and Sandstorm arrived at the gorse tunnel together and hurried out into the woods. Outside the camp, the wind felt even fiercer. Fireheart narrowed his eyes and hunched his shoulders against the blizzard.

"It's going to be hard picking up a scent through the fresh snow," he warned Sandstorm. "Let's start by checking to see if they've climbed up to the forest."

"Okay," meowed Sandstorm.

"You take that side." Fireheart pointed with his nose. "And I'll take the other. Meet you back here. Don't be long."

Sandstorm bounded away, and Fireheart leaped over a fallen tree, heading toward the trail the Clan followed most often. The sides of the ravine were even more thickly coated than they had been that morning, and slippery now where the snow had frozen into ice. Fireheart stopped and lifted his head, his mouth open, but he could find no scent of the kits. He looked in vain for pawsteps—would their trail already be covered by fresh snow?

He trekked along the bottom of the slope but found no sign of any cats, let alone lost kits. The wind blew until Fireheart could hardly feel the tips of his ears. No kits could survive in this weather, and it wouldn't be long before the sun began to set. He had to find them before nightfall.

Fireheart raced back to the camp entrance. Sandstorm was waiting for him, her fur striped with small ridges of snow. She shook them off as she saw him coming.

"Any sign?" Fireheart meowed.

"No, nothing."

"They can't have gotten far," Fireheart pointed out. "Come on, let's try this way." He headed toward the training hollow.

Sandstorm battled after him. The snow was getting deeper, and she sank up to her belly with every step.

The training hollow was empty.

"Do you think Bluestar realizes how bad the weather is out here?" asked Sandstorm, raising her voice against the wind.

"She'll know," Fireheart called back to her.

"We should go back and get help, join up with another search party," meowed Sandstorm.

Fireheart looked at the shivering warrior. It was not just the kits who might freeze out here. Perhaps Sandstorm was right. "I agree," he meowed. "We can't do this by ourselves."

As they turned toward camp, Fireheart thought he heard a tiny squeal through the wind. "Did you hear that?" he called.

Sandstorm stopped and began sniffing the air furiously. Suddenly she lifted her head. "That way!" she meowed, pointing with her nose to a fallen tree.

Fireheart leaped toward it with Sandstorm right behind him. The squealing grew louder until Fireheart could make out several little voices. He scrambled up onto the log and looked down the other side. Huddled in the snow were two small kits. Fireheart felt a rush of relief until he realized Cloudkit was not with them. "Where's Cloudkit?" he yowled.

"Hunting," squeaked one of the kits. Her voice trembled with cold and fear, but there was a note of defiance in it.

Fireheart lifted his head. "Cloudkit!" he called, peering through the snowflakes.

"Fireheart, look!" Sandstorm was on top of the log. Fireheart spun around. A bedraggled white shape was struggling through the snow toward them. Cloudkit! Every step was a massive leap for the tiny kit—the snow was as high as he was. But he kept coming, and in his mouth he carried a small, snow-encrusted vole.

A surge of relief and fury shot through Fireheart. He left Sandstorm with the others and bounded through the snow to scoop up the kit by the scruff of his neck. Cloudkit grunted in protest but refused to drop the vole that dangled from his mouth.

Fireheart turned to see Sandstorm nudging the others toward him. They stumbled ahead of her, sinking up to their ears in the deep snow, but she kept pushing them on.

Cloudkit squirmed in Fireheart's mouth. Fireheart dropped him back into the snow. Cloudkit looked up at him, proudly holding his catch. Fireheart couldn't help feeling impressed.

In spite of the snow and wind, Cloudkit had caught his first prey!

"Wait there," he ordered, and dashed back to help Sandstorm. He picked up a tiny she-kit who was mewling pitifully, and began nosing the other one forward.

The bedraggled group struggled back to the camp. Brindleface was waiting outside the gorse tunnel. Bluestar stood beside her, her eyes narrowed against the driving snow. As soon as they spotted Fireheart's party, they rushed forward to help. Bluestar scooped up Cloudkit and Brindleface grabbed the other kit; then they turned and raced into the shelter of the camp with Fireheart and Sandstorm hurrying behind.

Once in the clearing, the three cats dropped their frozen bundles onto the ground. Fireheart shook the snow from his fur and looked down at Cloudkit, who was still stubbornly clinging to his catch.

Bluestar glared at the three kits. "What did you think you were doing out there? You know it's against the warrior code for kits to hunt!"

Brindleface's two kits shrank under their leader's angry gaze, but Cloudkit looked back at her with round blue eyes. He dropped his vole and mewed, "The Clan needed fresh-kill, so we decided to catch some."

Fireheart flinched at his boldness.

"Whose idea was it?" Bluestar demanded.

"Mine," Cloudkit announced, his head still unbowed.

Bluestar fixed her eyes on the defiant little kit and yowled, "You could have frozen to death out there!"

Cloudkit was startled by the anger in her voice and dropped into a crouch. "We did it for the Clan," he mewed defensively.

Fireheart held his breath as he waited to see what Bluestar would do next. Cloudkit had broken the warrior code. Would Bluestar change her mind about letting him stay?

"Your intention," Bluestar meowed slowly, "was good. But it was a foolish thing to do." Fireheart felt a flicker of hope. Then he cringed as Cloudkit piped up again.

"I *caught* something, though."

"I can see that," replied Bluestar coldly. She gazed at all three kits. "I shall leave it to your mother to decide what to do with you. But I don't want to find you doing anything like this again. Do you understand?"

Fireheart relaxed a little as Cloudkit nodded with the others. "Cloudkit, you may add your catch to the fresh-kill pile," Bluestar added. "Then all three of you go straight to the nursery and get yourselves dry and warm." Fireheart felt surprised. Was that a motherly tone he detected in the ThunderClan leader's voice?

Brindleface's kits stumbled toward the nursery, followed by their mother, while Cloudkit picked up his vole and trotted off toward the pile of fresh-kill. The proud tilt of his head made Fireheart's paws prickle with worry, but as Bluestar watched him go, Fireheart thought he detected a glint of admiration in his leader's eyes.

"Well done, you two," she meowed, turning her attention to Sandstorm and Fireheart. "I'll send Longtail out to retrieve the other search party. You should go to your den and try to warm up too!"

"Yes, Bluestar," Fireheart answered. He turned to leave with Sandstorm but Bluestar called him back. "Fireheart," she meowed, "I want to talk to you." Her tone made Fireheart feel apprehensive. Perhaps he'd relaxed too soon.

"Cloudkit showed some fine hunting skills today," Bluestar began. "But all the skill in the world is worthless if he can't learn to obey the warrior code. It may be for his own safety now, but in the future the safety of the whole Clan will depend on it."

Fireheart stared down at the ground. He knew Bluestar was right, but he couldn't help feeling that she was expecting too much of the young kit. Cloudkit was still very young, and he'd been with the Clan only a short time. Fireheart swallowed a pang of resentment as he thought of how shamelessly Graystripe, a Clanborn cat, was disobeying the warrior code. He looked up at the Clan leader. "Yes, Bluestar," he meowed. "I'll make sure he learns."

"Good." Bluestar sounded satisfied. She turned away and padded to her den.

Fireheart made his way to the warriors' den even though he no longer felt cold. Bluestar's words had made him burn. He pushed his way inside, settled into his nest, and began to wash. He stayed in his nest all afternoon, brooding about Graystripe and Cloudkit. He knew that Bluestar was right. The pride and defiance he'd seen in the white kit's eyes made

Fireheart wonder if he really would be able to adjust to Clan life.

As evening came, hunger drew Fireheart from the den. He picked a thrush from the pile of fresh-kill and settled down by the nettle clump to eat it. It was dark now, and the snow had eased. Once his eyes had adjusted to the night, Fireheart could see the camp entrance clearly.

He spotted Graystripe as soon as he appeared, and watched him walk to the pile of fresh-kill. The gray warrior was carrying prey. Perhaps he'd just been hunting after all.

Graystripe dropped most of his catch onto the pile. He kept a large mouse for himself and took it to a sheltered spot near the camp wall. Fireheart's brief hope faded. The distracted look in Graystripe's eyes told him that his suspicions were right—Graystripe had been with Silverstream.

Fireheart got to his paws and padded into the den. He had no trouble falling into a deep sleep. And as he slept, he dreamed again.

The snowy forest spread out around him, glowing white beneath the cold moon. Fireheart stood on a tall, jagged rock. Beside him stood Cloudkit—a fully grown warrior, his thick white pelt rippling in the wind. Frost sparkled on the stone beneath their paws.

"Watch!" Fireheart hissed to Cloudkit. A wood mouse scuttled around the frozen roots of a tree. Cloudkit followed his gaze and leaped silently from the rock onto the forest floor. Fireheart watched the white tom prowl toward the prey. Suddenly he smelled a scent so warm and familiar, his fur quivered. He felt warm breath on his ear and turned sharply. Spottedleaf was standing beside him.

Her dappled pelt shone in the moonlight as she touched her soft pink nose to his. "Fireheart," she whispered. "I have a warning for you from StarClan." Her tone was somber and her eyes burned into his. "A battle is coming, Fireheart. Beware a warrior you cannot trust."

The squeal of a mouse made Fireheart jump and look around. Cloudkit must have made his kill. He turned back to Spottedleaf but she had disappeared.

Fireheart woke up with a start and turned to the nest beside him. Graystripe was curled up, fast asleep, his nose tucked under his thick tail. Spottedleaf's words echoed in Fireheart's mind: "Beware a warrior you cannot trust!"

He shivered. The bitter cold of the forest seemed to cling to his fur even here, and the sweet fragrance of Spottedleaf lingered in his nostrils. Graystripe stirred beside him, muttering in his sleep, and Fireheart flinched. He knew he wouldn't go back to sleep again, but he stayed in his nest and watched his friend sleeping until the dawn light began to shine through the walls of the den.

CHAPTER 29

❧

As the den grew lighter, Willowpelt woke up. Fireheart watched as she rose and stretched, then pushed her way out of the den. He gave a last glance at Graystripe's sleeping form, and followed her.

"It's stopped snowing," he meowed, desperate to break the ghostly silence that enfolded the snowbound camp. His voice echoed around the clearing, and Willowpelt nodded.

A rustling noise accompanied the scent of Tigerclaw and Runningwind as they emerged from the den. They settled themselves beside Willowpelt to wash. *Ready for the dawn patrol,* Fireheart thought. He wondered if he should offer to join them, since he could do with a run through the woods, but part of him wanted to stay behind and keep an eye on Graystripe. Spottedleaf's words still lay heavy in his heart. He couldn't shake off the idea that Graystripe was the warrior he could not trust. Graystripe insisted his relationship with Silverstream didn't change his loyalty to the Clan, but how could it not? He was breaking the warrior code just by seeing her!

Suddenly Tigerclaw lifted his head as though he had smelled something. Fireheart tensed. His ears twitched—he could hear paws crunching through the snow in the distance, moving fast. The breeze carried the scent of WindClan. The pawsteps grew louder. As one, the warriors stiffened—a cat was rushing toward them through the gorse tunnel. Tiger-claw arched his back and hissed as Onewhisker burst into the clearing.

The WindClan warrior skidded to a halt in front of them, his eyes filled with dread. "ShadowClan and RiverClan!" he gasped. "They're attacking our camp! We're outnumbered and fighting for our lives. Tallstar refuses to be driven off this time. You must help or my Clan will be wiped out!"

Bluestar bounded out of her den. All eyes turned from Onewhisker to her. "I heard," she meowed. Without mounting the Highrock, the ThunderClan leader gave the yowl she used to call the Clan together. Onewhisker's fear-scent filled the clearing as he watched the cats emerge into the morning light.

As soon as the Clan had gathered, Bluestar began. "There's no time to waste. It's as we feared—ShadowClan and RiverClan have joined together, and now they're attacking the WindClan camp. We must help them." She paused and looked around at the faces staring back at her in dismay. Onewhisker stood beside her, listening silently with wide, hopeful eyes.

Fireheart was appalled. After the rogue cats had been discovered, he'd thought Nightstar could be trusted. Now it seemed the ShadowClan leader had broken the warrior code after all by uniting with RiverClan to drive WindClan from their home yet again.

"But we are leaf-bare—weak!" protested Patchpelt. "We've taken a risk for WindClan once before. Let them take care of themselves this time." A few murmurs of agreement rose from the elders and queens.

It was Tigerclaw who answered him, stepping forward to stand beside Bluestar. "You're right to be cautious, Patchpelt. But if ShadowClan and RiverClan have united, it is only a matter of time before they turn on us. It's better we fight now, with WindClan, than later, alone!"

Bluestar looked at Patchpelt, who closed his eyes and lifted his tail, accepting Tigerclaw's words.

Yellowfang pushed her way forward and spoke quietly to the leader. "I think you should remain behind in camp, Bluestar. The fever from the greencough may have gone, but you'll still be weak." The two cats exchanged a look that Fireheart understood with a jolt. Bluestar was on her ninth and final life. For the sake of the Clan, she could not afford to risk it in battle.

Bluestar nodded briskly. "Tigerclaw, I want you to organize two parties, one to head the attack, one to back it up. We need to get there as fast as we can!"

"Yes, Bluestar." Tigerclaw turned to the warriors. "Whitestorm, you'll head the second party; I'll head the first. I'll take Darkstripe, Mousefur, Longtail, Dustpelt, and Fireheart." Fireheart lifted his head as Tigerclaw called his name, feeling a thrill run through him. He was to join the lead party!

"You!" Tigerclaw called to Onewhisker. "What's your name?" The WindClan warrior looked startled by Tigerclaw's tone.

Fireheart answered for him. "Onewhisker," he meowed.

Tigerclaw nodded, barely pausing to look at Fireheart. "Onewhisker, you'll be in my party. The rest of the Thunder-Clan warriors will join Whitestorm. You too, Brackenpaw."

"Are we all ready?" called Tigerclaw. The warriors raised their heads and let out a battle cry. Tigerclaw charged for the gorse tunnel and they raced after him.

Up the ravine they climbed, into the forest. They were heading for Fourtrees and the uplands beyond. Fireheart glanced over his shoulder as he ran through the trees. Graystripe was near the back, his face grim, his eyes staring blankly ahead. Fireheart wondered if Silverstream would be at the battle. Fireheart felt a pang of sorrow for his friend, but this time he had no doubts about his own readiness to fight. After bringing WindClan home, he couldn't help feeling responsible for them. He would not let any Clan drive them back to those Thunderpath tunnels.

Spottedleaf's fragrance filled his nostrils once more, and Fireheart's fur prickled. "Beware a warrior you cannot trust!" This was going to be a difficult battle in more ways than one. Graystripe would have no choice about proving his loyalty now.

Even though the snow had stopped falling, it was hard work getting through the drifts. An icy crust had formed over the top of the snow, but the warriors were heavy enough to break through and sink into the softer snow underneath.

"Tigerclaw!" Willowpelt's yowl sounded from the rear. The deputy halted and turned.

"We're being followed!" Willowpelt called.

Her words sent a quiver of alarm through Fireheart. Had they run into a trap? Quietly the patrol retraced its pawsteps, alert and suspicious. A snow-laden branch creaked above, making Brackenpaw jump.

"Wait," hissed Tigerclaw.

The cats crouched in the deep snow. Fireheart could hear the noise of pawsteps heading toward them. They sounded light, like small paws stepping delicately over the top of the ice crust. With a sinking heart, Fireheart guessed who it was a heartbeat before Cloudkit and Brindleface's two kits appeared from behind a log.

Tigerclaw reared up at them and the kits squealed in fright. The warrior recognized them instantly and dropped down onto all four paws. "What are you doing here!" he spat.

"We wanted to join the battle," mewed Cloudkit. Fireheart winced.

"Fireheart!" called Tigerclaw. Fireheart hurried forward, and the dark warrior spat impatiently, "You brought this kit into the Clan; you deal with it."

Fireheart looked into Tigerclaw's blazing eyes. He knew that the deputy was trying to force him to choose: Fireheart could either join the battle party and fight for the Clan or take care of his kittypet kin. The whole patrol waited in silence for Fireheart to speak.

Fireheart knew he would choose to fight for the Clan, but he couldn't sacrifice his sister's kit. Cloudkit and the others must be taken home safely by another cat. But which warrior could the raiding party do without?

"Brackenpaw," Fireheart called to Graystripe's apprentice. "Please take these kits home!" Fireheart waited for Graystripe to object, but the gray warrior remained silent as Fireheart ordered his apprentice back to camp.

Brackenpaw's tail drooped and Fireheart felt a stab of guilt. "There'll be plenty more battles for you to fight," he promised.

"But, Fireheart, you said one day we'd fight side by side!" Cloudkit's protest rang through the trees. Tigerclaw shot Fireheart a mocking look. Fireheart felt his fur prickle uncomfortably as amusement rippled through the patrol at the tiny kit's words. But he refused to show his embarrassment. "One day we will," he meowed. "But not today!"

The white kit's shoulders sagged and Fireheart let out a sigh of relief as he watched Cloudkit reluctantly join the other kits following Brackenpaw back to the camp.

"I'm surprised by your choice, Fireheart," Tigerclaw sneered. "I didn't expect you to be so keen to fight *this* battle."

Fireheart stared at Tigerclaw and felt the blood pulse through him, so that his whole body throbbed with rage. "If only you were keen too!" he retorted. "You'd give the battle cry instead of keeping us here while WindClan warriors die!"

Tigerclaw flashed him a look of loathing, threw back his head, and yowled to the sky before charging on toward the WindClan camp. Fireheart and the others raced after him, past Fourtrees to the steep slope that led to the uplands. They bounded up, their paws made noiseless by the snow.

When they reached the top, Fireheart was battered by a

howling wind that turned his ears inside out. The WindClan hunting grounds looked more barren than ever, the gorse hidden by a layer of snow.

"Fireheart! You know the way to the WindClan camp!" yowled Tigerclaw above the wind. "Lead us there." He slowed to let Fireheart pass. Fireheart wondered if the deputy didn't trust Onewhisker enough to let the WindClan warrior guide them. He looked back at Graystripe, hoping for some help, but the gray warrior had his head bowed low and his shoulders hunched miserably as the wind buffeted his thick fur. There would be little help there. Fireheart turned his eyes to StarClan and sent up a prayer for guidance.

He was surprised to find that he recognized the shape of the land even beneath the snow. There was the badger set and the rock Graystripe had climbed to get a better view. He followed the contours he remembered from his journey with Graystripe until he reached the dip in the land that marked the WindClan camp.

Fireheart paused at the rim of the hollow. "Down there!" he yowled. For a heartbeat the wind dropped, and from below they heard the sounds of battle—screams and howls as cat furiously fought with cat.

CHAPTER 30

❧

Tigerclaw addressed the warriors in a fierce hiss that carried through the blizzard. "Whitestorm, wait until you hear my battle cry! Onewhisker, you lead us through the camp entrance; we'll take care of the rest."

Onewhisker began to race down the slope toward the snow-covered bushes. Tigerclaw thundered after him, Darkstripe at his heels. Fireheart charged behind the sleek gray tabby, through the narrow tunnel that led into the WindClan camp. The gorse was as dense and sharp as he remembered. Graystripe and the other warriors stayed at the top of the slope, a fresh wave of attack ready to strike after the initial barrage.

Fireheart skidded to a halt, reeling at the sight that greeted him in the camp clearing. Last time he'd been here, in search of the scent trail that would lead them to the missing Clan, the place had been deserted and silent. Now the clearing swarmed with writhing, screeching, fighting cats. Onewhisker had been right—the WindClan cats were hopelessly outnumbered. A fresh party of ShadowClan and RiverClan warriors waited at the edge of the clearing, but WindClan could spare no backup group. The whole Clan was fighting, apprentices and elders, warriors and queens.

Fireheart spotted Morningflower wrestling with a ShadowClan warrior. The WindClan queen looked exhausted and
frightened, her fur standing in ragged clumps. Still, she nimbly turned and scratched her attacker, but he was much bigger
and knocked her easily to the ground with a heavy blow.

With a howl, Fireheart leaped and landed squarely on the
shoulders of the ShadowClan tom. He clung on while the
surprised warrior spun and tried to shake him loose. Morningflower raked the tom with her claws as Fireheart dragged
him to the ground. The ShadowClan warrior screeched and
ripped himself free. He ran into the prickly camp wall and
pushed his way through. Morningflower shot a grateful glance
at Fireheart and turned back to the battle.

Fireheart looked around, shaking drops of blood from his
nose. The fresh patrols of ShadowClan and RiverClan cats
had joined the fight now. ThunderClan's arrival had evened
the numbers for a while, but now the second party was needed.
Fireheart heard Tigerclaw's battle cry ring out, and a moment
later Whitestorm exploded into the clearing, followed by
Graystripe, Runningwind, and the rest of the ThunderClan
warriors.

Fireheart grabbed a RiverClan warrior, tripping him with
one paw and holding him down with another. He rolled the
tom over and thrashed at his belly with his hind claws. The
RiverClan cat leaped away and crashed into a WindClan
warrior. The warrior turned in surprise. Fireheart recognized Onewhisker straightaway and watched as he reared and

attacked the RiverClan tom without a moment's pause. Fire-heart could see the fire in Onewhisker's eyes. He could leave him to finish this fight.

A familiar hiss caught Fireheart's attention. Graystripe was battling with a gray ShadowClan cat. It was Wetfoot, a warrior who had helped them fight to rid ShadowClan of Brokenstar. The two warriors were well matched. Graystripe thrust Wetfoot away with his back legs and spun around, looking for another cat to attack. Fireheart could see a River-Clan cat right behind Graystripe. Above the din of battle, he heard the blood roar in his ears. Would Graystripe attack one of Silverstream's fellow warriors?

Graystripe leaped, and Fireheart held his breath. But instead of jumping onto the RiverClan cat, Graystripe sailed over him and landed instead on the back of another Shadow-Clan warrior.

Fireheart heard Tigerclaw call his name. He twisted his head and saw the warrior at the other end of the clearing. The fighting was thick up there, with cats from all Clans battling together.

As he charged through to the ThunderClan deputy, Fire-heart felt Leopardfur grasp his hind leg, pulling him down.

"You!" hissed the RiverClan deputy. They had last met at the gorge, where Whiteclaw had died.

Fireheart threw her off and flipped over onto his back. Too late, he realized that he'd exposed his soft belly. Leopardfur didn't waste a moment. She reared up and came down on Fireheart with all her might. Fireheart felt the wind knocked out of him before the thorn-sharp claws dug into his belly. He screamed in agony. As his eyes rolled he saw Tigerclaw at the side of the clearing, watching him with cold, expressionless eyes.

"Tigerclaw," Fireheart howled. "Help me!"

But Tigerclaw didn't move. He just stared as Leopardfur clawed Fireheart again and again.

Sheer rage gave Fireheart the strength he needed. He fought through the pain, drew back his hind legs, and pushed up against Leopardfur's belly as hard as he could. Fireheart saw a look of shock on the deputy's face as his kick lifted the warrior and flung her halfway across the clearing. Fireheart struggled to his paws and glared at Tigerclaw, burning with pain and rage. Tigerclaw met his gaze with a look of undisguised hatred, and leaped away into the thick of the battle.

A blow on the back of his head knocked Fireheart off balance. He staggered and turned to see Stonefur. The RiverClan warrior was preparing to aim another swipe. Fireheart ducked out of the way and shoved Stonefur straight into Whitestorm. The ThunderClan cat whipped around and grasped Stonefur by the scruff of his neck. Fireheart tried to dart forward and help the white-furred warrior, but claws held him back, digging into his haunches. He twisted to see who it was and glimpsed gray fur. It was Silverstream.

The she-cat's face was twisted with battle rage as she reared up at him. Blood was dripping into her eyes, and Fireheart could tell that she hadn't recognized him. She drew back a paw and he saw her long claws flash as she prepared to swipe him. As Fireheart screwed up his eyes, bracing himself for the blow, he heard an achingly familiar yowl. "Silverstream! No!"

Graystripe, thought Fireheart.

Silverstream hesitated, shook her head, and recognized Fireheart with a muted gasp. She dropped back down to all four paws, her eyes wide with shock.

Fireheart reacted instinctively, his blood aflame with battle. Without thinking, he leaped onto the back of the RiverClan she-cat and pinned her to the ground. She didn't struggle as he drew back his head and prepared to give her a vicious bite on her shoulder. But as Fireheart raised his head he felt Graystripe's eyes boring into him. The gray warrior was watching in horror from the edge of the battle.

The look of pain and disbelief in his friend's eyes brought Fireheart to his senses. He stopped, sheathed his claws, and loosened his grip on Silverstream. The she-cat slipped away from him and disappeared into the surrounding gorse. Fireheart stared, still in shock, as Graystripe raced after her.

Fireheart felt as if he were still being watched. He looked around and his eyes met Darkstripe's on the other side of the clearing. Fireheart flinched. Graystripe's affair had forced him into disloyalty to ThunderClan after all—he had let an enemy warrior go! How much had Darkstripe seen? Just then Fireheart heard Runningwind yowl for help. The tabby warrior was grappling desperately with Nightstar, ShadowClan's treacherous leader. Fireheart darted through the throng to Runningwind's side.

Without pausing to think, Fireheart leaped, grabbing

Nightstar from behind. The black warrior howled in rage as Fireheart pulled him backward and sank his claws deep into Nightstar's fur. He had fought side by side with this warrior only a few moons ago to help him drive out Brokenstar. Now he sank his teeth into Nightstar's shoulder with the same ferocity he had used against the former ShadowClan leader.

Nightstar squealed and twisted in Fireheart's grip. This tom had not been made leader for nothing, thought Fireheart, struggling to hang on. Nightstar scrabbled free, but Running-wind was ready. He pounced, and together the two warriors rolled across the frozen clearing. Fireheart watched them struggle and twist, timing his moment perfectly so that when he finally leaped, he landed squarely on Nightstar's back. He grasped him more firmly this time, ready for the warrior to wriggle free. But Runningwind also had a grip. Together they scratched and bit the ShadowClan leader till he screeched out loud. Then they released him, springing backward with their claws still unsheathed.

Nightstar leaped to his paws and spun around, hissing. Fireheart saw the fury in his eyes, but the ShadowClan leader knew he was beaten. He backed away, his eyes darting around the clearing where his warriors were suffering similar treat-ment from the other ThunderClan warriors. He gave the yowl of retreat. Instantly his warriors stopped fighting and, like their leader, backed into the gorse that surrounded the camp. The RiverClan warriors were left alone to fend off ThunderClan and WindClan.

Fireheart paused to catch his breath, blinking blood from

his eyes. Whitestorm was grappling with Leopardfur now, with Mousefur at his side. Sandstorm was battling with a RiverClan warrior almost twice her size. But her opponent was only half her speed. Fireheart watched Sandstorm nip and twist around him until the RiverClan warrior looked overwhelmed.

Dustpelt was fighting a smoky-black tom nearby. Fireheart recognized Blackclaw, the RiverClan warrior he had seen chasing rabbits in the uplands. Dustpelt was stubbornly refusing to be cowed by the blows and bites aimed at him. Each time he was struck, the young warrior turned and gave as good as he got. It looked as if he didn't need any help, and Fireheart guessed Dustpelt would not thank him for interfering in this fight.

Where was Crookedstar? Fireheart searched the clearing for the RiverClan leader. It wasn't hard to find him. Now that ShadowClan had run away, the clearing was less crowded. Fireheart soon spotted the light-colored tabby with the twisted jaw. He was crouching low, face-to-face with Tigerclaw. The two warriors stared at each other, their tails thrashing menacingly. Fireheart's blood pounded through his veins as he waited for one of them to make a move. It was Crookedstar who leaped first, but Tigerclaw jumped nimbly aside and Crookedstar missed. Tigerclaw was more accurate; he turned and lunged at Crookedstar's back. The ThunderClan warrior grasped the RiverClan leader with his long claws, and Crookedstar went limp beneath him. Fireheart watched breathlessly as Tigerclaw bared his teeth, lunged forward, and sank them deep into Crookedstar's neck.

Firehcart gasped. Had Tigerclaw really killed the River-Clan leader? Crookedstar's pained screech told Fireheart that Tigerclaw had missed the spine. But it was a blow to win the battle. Tigerclaw released his opponent and let him race, yowling, toward the camp entrance. As soon as Crookedstar's tail shot out of sight, his warriors struggled free and pelted after him.

In a heartbeat, the WindClan camp fell silent apart from the howling of the wind above the gorse. Fireheart stared around him. The ThunderClan warriors were tired and battered, but the WindClan cats looked far worse. Every one of them was bleeding, while some lay unmoving on the frozen ground. Barkface, their medicine cat, wasted no time in rushing from one cat to another, attending to their injuries.

Tallstar limped toward Tigerclaw, blood dripping from his cheek. As he watched the WindClan leader, Fireheart remembered his dream from moons ago—Tallstar had been silhouetted against a bright fire, like a warrior sent from StarClan to save them. "Fire will save the Clan," according to Spottedleaf's prophecy. But looking at the WindClan cats, exhausted and beaten, Fireheart wondered if his dream had misled him. How could these cats represent the fire that StarClan promised would save his Clan? Surely it was ThunderClan that had just saved WindClan—again?

Tallstar spoke quietly to Tigerclaw. Fireheart couldn't hear the words they shared, but he could guess by Tallstar's bowed head that the WindClan leader was acknowledging the debt he owed to ThunderClan. Tigerclaw sat up straight and accepted the thanks with his chin held high. Fireheart felt a wave of revulsion at the dark warrior's arrogance. He would never forget that Tigerclaw had stood by and watched while Leopardfur had nearly ripped him to shreds.

"Here." Fireheart was shaken from his thoughts by the soft voice of Willowpelt offering him a mouthful of the medicine cat's herbs. Fireheart purred his thanks as Willowpelt began squeezing juice from the herbs into the bite marks on Fireheart's shoulders. The juice stung, but the smell took him straight back to another time, with Spottedleaf. She had given him the same herb to treat Yellowfang so many moons ago. As the odor of the herbs wafted up, Fireheart remembered his dream from the night before. "Beware a warrior . . ." Spottedleaf had warned him. Beware a warrior?

The truth washed over Fireheart like a chill wind—it wasn't Graystripe he should have been wary of, but Tigerclaw! How could he have suspected his friend, when he knew what Tigerclaw was capable of? Suddenly Fireheart was sure Ravenpaw had been telling the truth, whatever Bluestar had said. Seeing the dark warrior's performance today, Fireheart realized that Tigerclaw could easily have killed Redtail and walked away without remorse.

"You fought well, Fireheart!" Runningwind interrupted his thoughts. The brown tabby blinked warmly at Fireheart as he promised, "I'll make sure Bluestar hears about it!"

"Yes," agreed Willowpelt. "You're a fine warrior. StarClan will honor you for this." Fireheart looked at them both, his ears twitching with pleasure. It was a relief to feel part of the Clan again.

Suddenly Fireheart's fur prickled. Darkstripe was stalking across the clearing toward Tigerclaw. He sat down behind Tallstar and waited until the WindClan leader walked away; then he leaned forward and whispered urgently into Tigerclaw's ear. The two warriors kept glancing toward Fireheart.

He saw, thought Fireheart, feeling dizzy with horror. *He saw me let Silverstream go.*

"Are you okay?" asked Willowpelt.

Fireheart realized he'd shivered. "Er, yes, sorry. Just thinking." Tigerclaw was stalking toward him, his eyes shining with spiteful satisfaction.

"Well, if you're sure, I'll go and see to some others," meowed Willowpelt.

"Yes—fine," meowed Fireheart. "Thanks."

Willowpelt picked up her herbs and padded away. Runningwind followed her.

Tigerclaw flattened his ears and drew back his lip in a snarl as he looked down at Fireheart. "Darkstripe says you let a RiverClan she-cat escape!"

Fireheart realized there was nothing he could say. No matter how difficult Graystripe had made things for him, there was no way he was going to betray his friend to this warrior. He longed to yowl back that Tigerclaw had stood and watched while a RiverClan warrior tried to kill him. But who would believe him? Darkstripe padded up to stand beside Tigerclaw. Fireheart longed for the wisdom and fairness of Bluestar, but she was far away, back at the ThunderClan camp.

He took a deep breath, preparing to speak as Tigerclaw stared menacingly down at him. Then it dawned on Fireheart that any disloyalty he had shown on Graystripe's behalf meant nothing to this great warrior. That wasn't the real reason for Tigerclaw's persecution of him. The deputy was still afraid of what Fireheart might have learned from Ravenpaw about Redtail's death all those moons ago. But unlike Ravenpaw, Fireheart wasn't going to give in to fear. His eyes challenged the dark deputy, and he growled, "She escaped, yes, like Crookedstar escaped from you. Why? Did you want me to kill her?"

Tigerclaw's tail lashed the cold ground. "Darkstripe says you didn't even scratch her."

Fireheart shrugged. "Perhaps Darkstripe should chase after the she-cat and ask her if it's true!"

Darkstripe looked ready to spit, but he remained silent as Tigerclaw spoke. "He doesn't need to. Darkstripe tells me your young gray friend chased after her. Perhaps *he'll* be able to tell us how badly she was scratched."

For the first time since they'd entered the battle Fireheart felt the chill of the wind. The gleam in Tigerclaw's eye hinted at a veiled threat. Had the dark warrior guessed about Graystripe's love for Silverstream?

Fireheart was still searching for words when Graystripe appeared, squeezing through the camp entrance.

"Look who's back," sneered Tigerclaw. "Do you want to ask him how the she-cat is? No, wait, I can guess his answer. He'll just tell me he didn't manage to catch up with her." Not bothering to disguise the scorn in his eyes, Tigerclaw stalked away with Darkstripe behind him.

Fireheart looked over at Graystripe. His friend's face was lined with exhaustion and worry. Fireheart padded across the clearing to meet him. Would Graystripe still be resentful of Fireheart's interference? Would he be angry that Fireheart had tried to attack Silverstream, or grateful that he'd let her go?

Graystripe stood silently, his broad head hanging down. Fireheart reached forward with his nose and gently touched his friend's cold, gray flank. He felt Graystripe's rumbling purr and looked up. Graystripe gazed back at him. His eyes were sad, but there was no trace of the anger that Fireheart had seen in them lately.

"Is she okay?" Fireheart asked under his breath.

"Yes," whispered Graystripe. "And thanks for letting her go."

Fireheart blinked at him. "I'm glad she wasn't hurt," he meowed.

Graystripe held his gaze for a moment, then meowed, "Fireheart, you were right. The battle wasn't easy. It felt like I was fighting Silverstream's Clanmates, not enemy warriors." He lowered his eyes, ashamed. "But I still can't give her up."

The gray warrior's words filled Fireheart with foreboding, but he couldn't help sympathizing with his friend. "This is something you have to work out by yourself," he meowed. "It's not my place to judge you." Graystripe looked up as Fireheart went on. "Graystripe, whatever you decide to do, I will always be your friend."

Graystripe stared at him, his eyes clouded with relief and gratitude. Then, without speaking, the two warriors lay down, side to side, in the unfamiliar clearing. For the first time in moons, their fur was pressed together in friendship. Above them, the snow-heavy gorse offered them a brief shelter from the storm that raged over their heads.

ERIN
HUNTER

is inspired by a love of cats and a
fascination with the ferocity of the
natural world. As well as having great
respect for nature in all its forms,
Erin enjoys creating rich mythical
explanations for animal behavior. She
is also the author of the bestselling
Seekers and Survivors series.

Download the free Warriors app
and chat on the Warriors message
boards at www.warriorcats.com!

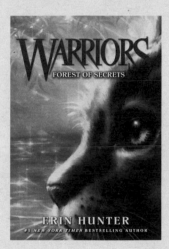

CHAPTER 1

❧

The icy wind whirled snow into Fireheart's face as he struggled down the ravine toward the ThunderClan camp, the mouse he had just killed gripped firmly in his jaws. The flakes were falling so thickly that he could scarcely see where he was going.

His mouth watered as the prey-scent of mouse filled his nostrils. He hadn't eaten since the previous night, a grim sign of how scarce prey was in leaf-bare. Hunger clawed at his belly, but Fireheart would not break the warrior code: The Clan must be fed first.

A glow of pride briefly drove off the chill from the snow that matted his flame-colored coat, as Fireheart remembered the battle that had taken place only three days before. He had joined the other ThunderClan warriors to help support WindClan when the moorland cats were attacked by the other two Clans in the forest. Many cats had been injured in that battle, so it was even more important for those who could still hunt to bring home prey.

As Fireheart pushed his way through the gorse tunnel leading into the camp, he dislodged snow from the spiky branches above, and he flicked his ears as the cold lumps fell on his

3

head. The thorn trees around the camp gave some shelter from the wind, but the clearing in the center of the camp was deserted; all the cats preferred to stay in their dens to keep warm when the snow lay this thick. Broken tree stumps and the branches of a fallen tree poked above the covering of snow. A single line of pawprints crossed from the apprentices' den to the bramble thicket where the kits were cared for. Seeing the trail, Fireheart could not help remembering that he was without an apprentice now, since Cinderpaw had been injured beside the Thunderpath.

Trotting across the snow into the heart of the camp, Fireheart dropped his mouse on the pile of fresh-kill near the bush where the warriors slept. The pile was pitifully small. Such prey as could be found was thin and scrawny, hardly a mouthful for a famished warrior. There would be no more plump mice until newleaf, and that was many moons away.

Fireheart was turning away, ready to go back on hunting duty, when a loud meow sounded behind him. He whirled around.

Shouldering his way out of the warriors' den was the Clan deputy, Tigerclaw. "Fireheart!"

Fireheart padded through the snow toward him, respectfully lowering his head, but conscious that the huge tabby's amber eyes burned into him. All his misgivings about Tigerclaw flooded through him again. The deputy was strong, respected, and an outstanding fighter, but Fireheart knew there was darkness in his heart.

"You don't need to go out hunting again tonight," Tigerclaw

growled as Fireheart approached. "Bluestar has chosen you and Graystripe to go to the Gathering."

Fireheart's ears twitched with excitement. It was an honor to accompany the Clan leader to the Gathering, where all four Clans met in peace at full moon.

"You had better eat now," added the dark-coated deputy. "We leave at moonrise." He began to stalk across the clearing toward the Highrock, where Bluestar, the Clan leader, had her den; then he paused and swiveled his massive head to look back at Fireheart. "Just make sure you remember which Clan you belong to at the Gathering," he hissed.

Fireheart felt his fur bristle as anger flared inside him. "What makes you say that?" he demanded boldly. "Do you think I would be disloyal to my own Clan?"

Tigerclaw turned to face him, and Fireheart tried hard not to flinch at the menace in the cat's tensed shoulders. "I saw you in the last battle." The deputy's voice was a low growl, and his ears were flattened against his head as he spat, "I saw you let that RiverClan warrior escape."

Fireheart winced, his mind flashing back to the battle in the WindClan camp. What Tigerclaw said was true. Fireheart had allowed a RiverClan warrior to flee without a scratch, but not out of cowardice or disloyalty. The warrior had been Silverstream. Unknown to the rest of ThunderClan, Fireheart's best friend, Graystripe, was in love with her, and Fireheart could not bring himself to wound her.

Fireheart had done his best to talk his friend out of visiting Silverstream—their relationship went against the warrior code and put both of them in grave danger. But Fireheart also knew that he would never betray Graystripe.

Besides, Tigerclaw had no right to accuse any cat of disloyalty. He had stood on the edge of the battle, watching while Fireheart fought for his life against another RiverClan warrior, and turned away instead of helping him. And that was not the worst accusation Fireheart could make against the deputy. He suspected Tigerclaw of murdering the former ThunderClan deputy, Redtail, and even planning to get rid of their leader herself.

"If you think I'm disloyal, tell Bluestar," he meowed challengingly.

Tigerclaw drew back his lips in a snarl and dropped into a half crouch, sliding out his long claws. "I don't need to bother Bluestar," he hissed. "I can deal with a kittypet like you."

He stared at Fireheart for a moment longer. Fireheart realized with a jolt that there was a trace of fear as well as distrust in the blazing amber eyes. *Tigerclaw wonders how much I know*, he thought suddenly.

Fireheart's friend Ravenpaw, Tigerclaw's own apprentice, had witnessed the murder of Redtail. Tigerclaw had tried to kill him to keep him quiet, so Fireheart had taken him to live with Barley, a loner who lived near a Twoleg farm on the other side of WindClan's territory. Fireheart had tried to tell Ravenpaw's story to Bluestar, but the Clan leader refused to believe that her brave deputy could be guilty of such a thing. As he glared at Tigerclaw, Fireheart's frustration returned; he felt as if a tree had fallen and pinned him to the ground.

Without another word, Tigerclaw swung around and stalked away. As Fireheart watched him go, there was a rustling from inside the warriors' den, and Graystripe poked his head out through the branches.

"What on earth are you doing?" he meowed. "Picking fights with Tigerclaw like that! He'll turn you into crow-food!"

"No cat has the right to call me disloyal," Fireheart argued.

Graystripe bent his head and gave his chest fur a couple of quick licks. "I'm sorry, Fireheart," he muttered. "I know this is all because of me and Silverstream—"

"No, it isn't," Fireheart interrupted, "and you know it. Tigerclaw's the problem, not you." He shook himself, scattering snow from his coat. "Come on; let's eat."

Graystripe pushed the rest of the way out and bounded toward the pile of fresh-kill. Fireheart followed him, picked out a vole, and carried it back to the warriors' den to eat. Graystripe crouched beside him, near the outer curtain of branches.

Whitestorm and a couple of other senior warriors were curled up asleep in the center of the bush, but otherwise the den was empty. Their sleeping bodies warmed the air, and barely any snow had penetrated the thick canopy of branches.

Fireheart took a mouthful of vole. The meat was tough and stringy, but he was so hungry that it tasted delicious. It was gone far too quickly, but it was better than nothing, and it would give him the strength he needed to travel to the Gathering.

When Graystripe had finished his meal in a few ravenous gulps, the two cats lay close together, grooming each other's

cold fur. It was a relief to Fireheart to share tongues like
this with Graystripe again, after the troubling time when it
seemed that Graystripe's love for Silverstream would destroy
his friendship with Fireheart. Even though Fireheart still
worried about his friend's forbidden affair, since the battle
he and Graystripe had rekindled their friendship so it was as
close as before. They needed to trust each other if they were
to survive the long season of leaf-bare, and even more than
that, Fireheart knew he needed Graystripe's support against
Tigerclaw's growing hostility.

"I wonder what news we'll hear tonight," he murmured in
his friend's gray ear. "I hope RiverClan and ShadowClan have
learned their lesson. WindClan won't be driven out of its territory again."

Graystripe shifted uncomfortably. "The battle wasn't just
greed for territory," he pointed out. "Prey is even scarcer than
usual—RiverClan is starving since the Twolegs moved into
their territory."

"I know." Fireheart flicked his ears in reluctant sympathy, understanding that his friend would want to defend
Silverstream's Clan. "But forcing another Clan out of its territory isn't the answer."

Graystripe muttered agreement, and then fell silent. Fireheart knew how he must've felt. It was only a few moons since
they had crossed the Thunderpath to find WindClan and to
bring them home. Yet Graystripe was bound to sympathize
with RiverClan too, because of his love for Silverstream.
There were no easy answers. The shortage of prey would be

a desperate problem for all four Clans, at least until leaf-bare relaxed its cruel grip on the forest.

Growing drowsy under the steady rasp of Graystripe's tongue, Fireheart jumped at the rustle of branches outside the den. Tigerclaw entered, followed by Darkstripe and Longtail. All three of them glowered at Fireheart as they settled in a huddle closer to the center of the bush. Fireheart watched them through slitted eyes, wishing that he could make out their conversation. It was too easy to imagine they were plotting against him. Fireheart's muscles tensed as he realized that he would never be safe within his own Clan while Tigerclaw's treachery remained a secret.

"What's the matter?" asked Graystripe, lifting his head.

Fireheart stretched, trying to relax again. "I don't trust them," he murmured, flicking his ears in the direction of Tigerclaw and the others.

"I don't blame you," meowed Graystripe. "If Tigerclaw ever found out about Silverstream . . ." He shuddered.

Fireheart pressed closer to his side, comforting him, while his ears still strained to catch what Tigerclaw was saying. He thought he heard his own name, and was tempted to creep a little closer, but just then he caught Longtail's eye.

"What are you staring at, *kittypet*?" hissed the tabby warrior. "ThunderClan only wants *loyal* cats." Deliberately he turned his back on Fireheart.

Fireheart sprang to his paws at once. "And who gave *you* the right to question our loyalty?" he spat.

Longtail ignored him.

"That does it!" Fireheart mewed in a fierce undertone to Graystripe. "It's obvious that Tigerclaw is spreading rumors about me."

"But what can you do?" Graystripe sounded resigned to the deputy's hostility.

"I want to talk to Ravenpaw again," Fireheart meowed. "He might remember something else about the battle, something I could use to convince Bluestar."

"But Ravenpaw lives at the Twoleg farm now. You'd have to go all the way across WindClan territory. How would you explain being out of the camp for so long? It would only make Tigerclaw's lies seem like the truth."

Fireheart knew he was willing to take that risk. He had never asked Ravenpaw for any details about how Redtail had died in the battle against RiverClan all those moons ago. At the time it had seemed more important to get the apprentice out of Tigerclaw's way.

Now he knew that he had to find out exactly what Ravenpaw saw. Because he was becoming more and more certain that his friend *must* know something that could prove just how dangerous Tigerclaw was to the Clan.

"I'll go tonight," Fireheart mewed softly. "After the Gathering, I'm going to slip away. If I bring back fresh-kill, I can say I've been hunting."

"You're taking a big risk," mewed Graystripe, giving Fireheart's ear a quick and affectionate lick. "But Tigerclaw is my problem too. If you're determined to go, then I'm coming with you."

* * *

The snow had stopped and the clouds had cleared away by the time the ThunderClan cats, Fireheart and Graystripe among them, left the camp and headed through the forest toward Fourtrees. The snow-covered ground seemed to glow in the white light of the full moon, and frost glittered on every twig and stone.

A breeze blew toward them, ruffling the surface of the snow and bearing the scent of many cats. Fireheart shivered with excitement. The territories of all four Clans met in the sacred hollow, and at every full moon a truce was declared for the Clans to gather beneath the four great oaks that stood in the center of the steep-sided clearing.

Fireheart fell in behind Bluestar, who had already dropped into a crouch to creep the last few tail-lengths to the top of the slope and peer down into the glade. A rock reared up in the center of the clearing between the oaks, its jagged outline black against the snow. As Fireheart waited for Bluestar's signal to move, he watched the other Clan cats greeting one another below. He could not help noticing the glares and raised hackles as WindClan faced the cats of RiverClan and ShadowClan. Clearly none of them had forgotten the recent battle; if it weren't for the truce, they would be clawing one another's fur.

Fireheart recognized Tallstar, the leader of WindClan, sitting near the Great Rock, with his deputy, Deadfoot, beside him. Not far away, Runningnose and Mudfur, the medicine cats of ShadowClan and RiverClan, sat side by side, gazing at the other cats with eyes that reflected the moon.

Beside Fireheart, Graystripe's muscles were tense, and his yellow eyes glowed with excitement as he stared down into the glade. Following his gaze, Fireheart saw Silverstream emerge from the shadow, her beautiful black-and-silver coat rippling in the moonlight.

Fireheart suppressed a sigh. "If you're going to talk to her, be careful who sees you," he warned his friend.

"Don't worry," Graystripe meowed. His front paws kneaded the hard ground as he waited for the moment when he could be with the RiverClan cat again.

Fireheart glanced at Bluestar, expecting her to give the signal to descend into the clearing, but instead he saw Whitestorm pad up and crouch beside her in the snow. "Bluestar," Fireheart heard the noble white warrior murmur, "what are you going to say about Brokentail? Will you tell the other Clans that we're sheltering him?"

Fireheart waited tensely for Bluestar's answer. Brokentail had once been Brokenstar, leader of ShadowClan. He had murdered his own father, Raggedstar, and stolen kits from ThunderClan. In retaliation, ThunderClan had helped Brokenstar's own Clan to drive him out into the forest. Not long after, Brokenstar had led a band of rogue cats to attack the ThunderClan camp. In the battle, Yellowfang, the ThunderClan medicine cat, had scratched his eyes, and now Brokentail was a prisoner, blind and defeated. Even though the former leader had been stripped of his StarClan-given name, and was kept under close guard, Fireheart knew that the other Clans would expect ThunderClan to have killed him, or driven him out to die in the forest. They wouldn't welcome the news that Brokentail was still alive.

Bluestar kept her gaze fixed on the cats in the clearing below. "I will say nothing," she replied to Whitestorm. "It doesn't concern the other Clans. Brokentail is ThunderClan's responsibility now."

"Brave words," growled Tigerclaw from where he sat on the other side of Bluestar. "Or are we ashamed to admit what we've done?"

"ThunderClan has no need to be ashamed for showing mercy," Bluestar retorted coolly. "But I see no reason to go looking for trouble." Before Tigerclaw could protest, she sprang to her paws and faced the rest of the ThunderClan cats. "Listen," she meowed. "No cat is to talk about the attack by the rogue cats, or mention Brokentail. These are matters for our Clan alone."

She waited until meows of agreement came from the assembled cats. Then she flicked her tail to signal that the ThunderClan cats could join the other Clans below. She raced down through the bushes, with Tigerclaw just behind her, his huge paws scattering snow.

Fireheart bounded after them. As he slid out of the bushes into the clearing he saw that Tigerclaw had stopped close by, and was giving him a suspicious stare. "Graystripe," Fireheart hissed quietly over his shoulder, "I don't think you should go off with Silverstream tonight. Tigerclaw's already—"

Fireheart suddenly realized that Graystripe was no longer

beside him. Looking around, he saw his friend disappearing behind the Great Rock. A heartbeat or two later, Silverstream skirted around a group of ShadowClan cats and followed him.

Fireheart sighed. He glanced at Tigerclaw, wondering if the deputy had seen them go. But Tigerclaw had padded away to join Onewhisker from WindClan, and Fireheart let the fur lie flat on his shoulders again.

Pacing restlessly across the clearing, Fireheart found himself near a group of elders—Patchpelt from ThunderClan, and others he did not know, crouching beneath a glossy-leaved holly bush, where the snow did not lie so thickly. Keeping one eye out for Graystripe, Fireheart settled down to listen to their conversation.

"I remember a leaf-bare even worse than this." It was an old black tom who spoke, his muzzle turned to silver and his flank scarred from many a fight. He had the scent of Wind-Clan on his short, patchy fur. "The river was frozen for more than three moons."

"You're right, Crowfur," a tabby queen agreed. "And prey was scarcer, too, even for RiverClan."

For a heartbeat Fireheart felt surprised that two elders from recently hostile Clans could talk calmly without spitting hatred at each other. But then, they were elders, he reflected. They must have seen many battles in their long lives.

"Young warriors today," the old black cat added with a glance at Fireheart. "They don't know what hardship is."

Fireheart scuffled among the dead leaves under the bush and tried to look respectful. Patchpelt, crouched close to him, gave him a friendly flick with his tail.

"That must have been the season when Bluestar lost her kits," recalled the ThunderClan elder. Fireheart pricked up his ears. He remembered Dappletail saying something once before about Bluestar's kits, which were born just before she became Clan deputy. But he had never learned how many kits she had had, or how old they were when they died.

"And do you remember the thaw that leaf-bare?" Crowfur interrupted Fireheart's thoughts, his eyes unfocused as he lost himself to his memories. "The river in the gorge rose nearly as far as the badger sets."

Patchpelt shivered. "I remember it well. ThunderClan couldn't cross the stream to come here for the Gathering."

"Cats were drowned," the RiverClan queen remembered sadly.

"Prey too," Crowfur added. "The cats who survived nearly starved."

"May StarClan grant it's not so bad this season!" Patchpelt mewed fervently.

Crowfur spat, "These young cats would never cope. We were tougher in those days."

Fireheart could not help protesting. "We have strong warriors now—"

"Who asked your opinion?" growled the cranky old tom. "You're hardly more than a kit!"

"But we—" Fireheart broke off as the air was filled with a shrill yowl and all the cats fell silent. He turned his head to see four cats on top of the Great Rock, silhouettes in the silver moonlight.

"Shh!" hissed Patchpelt. "The meeting's about to start." He twitched his ears at Fireheart and purred softly, "Take no notice of Crowfur. He'd find fault with StarClan."

Fireheart gave Patchpelt a grateful look, tucked his paws under him, and settled down to listen.

Tallstar, the WindClan leader, began by announcing how his cats were recovering after the recent battle against RiverClan and ShadowClan. "One of our elders has died," he meowed, "but all our warriors will live—to fight another day," he added meaningfully.

Nightstar flattened his ears and narrowed his eyes, while Crookedstar let out a threatening growl from deep in his throat.

Fireheart's fur prickled. If the leaders started to fight, their cats would fight too. Had it ever happened at a Gathering? he wondered. Surely not even Nightstar, ShadowClan's bold new leader, would risk the anger of StarClan by breaking the sacred truce!

THE TIME HAS COME
FOR DOGS TO RULE THE WILD

SURVIVORS

BOOK ONE:
THE EMPTY CITY

Lucky is a golden-haired mutt with a nose for survival. Other dogs have Packs, but Lucky stands on his own . . . until the Big Growl strikes. Suddenly the ground splits wide open. The longpaws disappear. And enemies threaten Lucky at every turn. For the first time in his life, Lucky needs to rely on other dogs to survive. But can he ever be a true Pack dog?

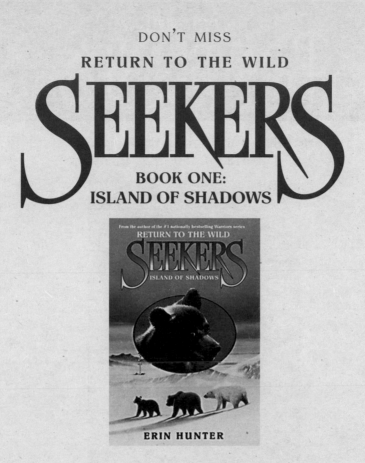
Toklo, Kallik, and Lusa survived the perilous mission that brought them together, and now it's time for them to find their way home. When the group reaches a shadowy island covered in mountains and ice, Kallik is sure they're almost back to the Frozen Sea. But a terrifying accident leads them into a maze of abandoned tunnels, unlike anything they've ever seen before—making them question their path once again.

A NEW WARRIORS ADVENTURE HAS BEGUN

1

2

3

Alderpaw, son of Bramblestar and Squirrelflight,
must embark on a treacherous journey
to save the Clans from a mysterious threat.

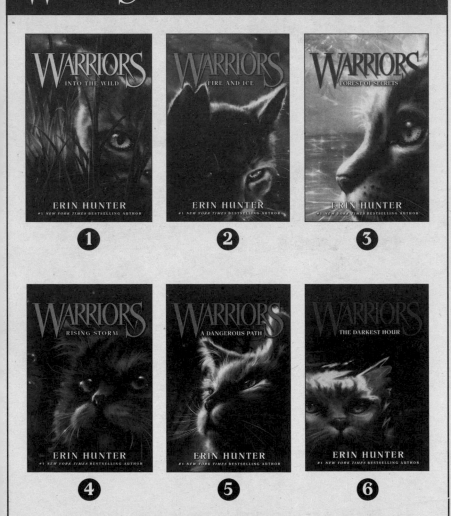

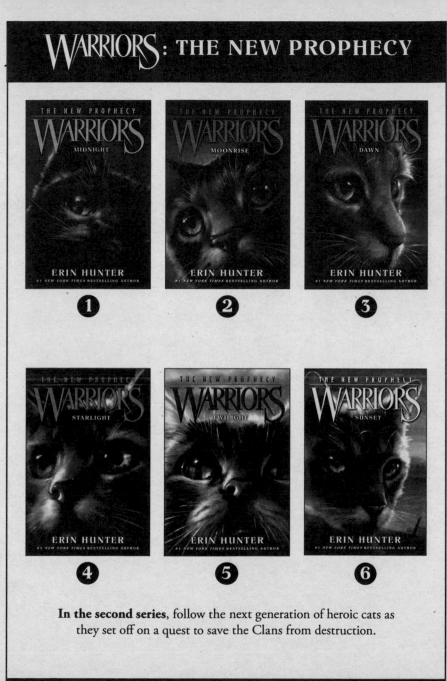

WARRIORS: THE NEW PROPHECY

In the second series, follow the next generation of heroic cats as they set off on a quest to save the Clans from destruction.

HARPER
An Imprint of HarperCollinsPublishers

www.warriorcats.com

WARRIORS: POWER OF THREE

1. POWER OF THREE — WARRIORS — THE SIGHT — ERIN HUNTER — #1 NEW YORK TIMES BESTSELLING AUTHOR
2. POWER OF THREE — WARRIORS — DARK RIVER — ERIN HUNTER — #1 NEW YORK TIMES BESTSELLING AUTHOR
3. POWER OF THREE — WARRIORS — OUTCAST — ERIN HUNTER — #1 NEW YORK TIMES BESTSELLING AUTHOR
4. POWER OF THREE — WARRIORS — ECLIPSE — ERIN HUNTER — #1 NEW YORK TIMES BESTSELLING AUTHOR
5. POWER OF THREE — WARRIORS — LONG SHADOWS — ERIN HUNTER — #1 NEW YORK TIMES BESTSELLING AUTHOR
6. POWER OF THREE — WARRIORS — SUNRISE — ERIN HUNTER — #1 NEW YORK TIMES BESTSELLING AUTHOR

In the third series, Firestar's grandchildren begin their training as warrior cats. Prophecy foretells that they will hold more power than any cats before them.

HARPER
An Imprint of HarperCollinsPublishers

www.warriorcats.com

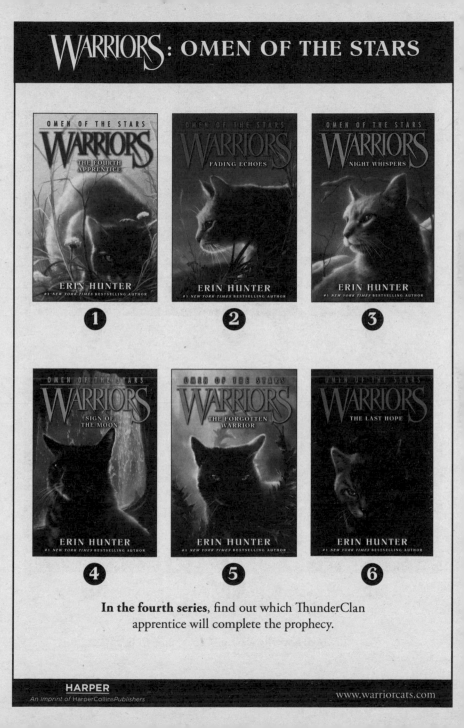

These extra-long, stand-alone adventures will take you deep inside each of the Clans with thrilling tales featuring the most legendary warrior cats.

WARRIORS: FIELD GUIDES

FOR THE ULTIMATE FAN!

Delve deeper into the Clans with these Warriors field guides.

ALSO BY ERIN HUNTER:
SURVIVORS

Survivors: The Original Series

The time has come for dogs to rule the wild.

HARPER
An Imprint of HarperCollinsPublishers

SURVIVORS: THE GATHERING DARKNESS

In the **second series**, tensions are rising within the pack.

SURVIVORS: BONUS STORIES

Download the three separate ebook novellas or
read them in one paperback bind-up!